SEARCHING FOR THE EMINENT: THE COLLAPSE OF REALITY

BOOK THREE OF THE EMINENT TRILOGY

Marvin North

BOOKS IN THE TRILOGY

March of the Meek
Towards the Apocalypse
The Collapse of Reality

Copyright © 2022 Marvin North

All rights reserved. No part of this publication may be reproduced, stored in a retrieval system, or transmitted in any form or by any means, electronic, mechanical, recording or otherwise, without the prior written permission of the author.

The characters and events in this book are fictitious. Any similarity to real persons, living or dead, is coincidental and not intended by the author.

First Edition

ACKNOWLEDGMENTS

March of the Meek was the first book I finished and felt satisfied enough to publish. It had been a long time coming; not just from a writing standpoint, but from how long I mulled over the idea of it since I was a kid. The Eminent trilogy is the first writing project that I feel that I've finished—which is both somber and exciting for me. I want to thank everyone who has supported my writing thus far, and especially anyone who has given me their feedback and comments.

Secondly, I want to thank Melody for collaborating with me to design the covers for each of the three Eminent books. She's gone through a lot of trouble to help me realize my visions.

Lastly, and most importantly, I want to thank my wife, Sarah. She's been my biggest fan, and the first person I go to with any new ideas. Without all her help and support over the years since I began writing March of the Meek, I don't know if I would have made it this far.

I first created Rekco in 2001. It took nearly twenty years of revisiting and revising to fully realize his story. The Collapse of Reality retains many of the ideas that I came up with so many years ago. This world and these characters were once but a dream to me, one that I would only gleefully share to any close friends who cared to listen to my ramblings. It makes me incredibly happy to finally make these ideas a reality.

Thanks again to everyone who has read the Eminent trilogy up until this point. Even though this concludes Rekco's story, know that I have more stories to share. I hope you will look forward to them as much as I do!

-Marvin

Table of Contents

CHAPTER 1: HALF 9

CHAPTER 2: CONSEQUENCE 26

CHAPTER 3: CONCEPT 37

CHAPTER 4: XIMEN JUDD 44

CHAPTER 5: SUNNY DAY 62

CHAPTER 6: LEVEL HEAD 75

CHAPTER 7: BEYOND MEASURE 83

CHAPTER 8: THE OTHER SIDE 98

CHAPTER 9: THE TEN 107

CHAPTER 10: HOU 118

CHAPTER 11: THE WORTH OF A WORLD 136

CHAPTER 12: APOCALYPTIC ACQUAINTANCES ... 157

CHAPTER 13: THE GLASS SWORD 175

CHAPTER 14: RUBY BULLET 183

CHAPTER 15: CLUB TOWER 204

CHAPTER 16: THE DAY AFTER THE STORM 221

CHAPTER 17: COSMIC FLESH 233

CHAPTER 18: KEEPER OF THE HALL 247

CHAPTER 19: BLUE DRESS 258

CHAPTER 20: DO PARASITES PRAY? 273

CHAPTER 21: MEMORIES OF A DREAM 295

CHAPTER 22: A RIVALRY ENDED 314

CHAPTER 23: DEEP END 329

CHAPTER 24: ALL THINGS.. 340

EPILOGUE 376

LAST THESI

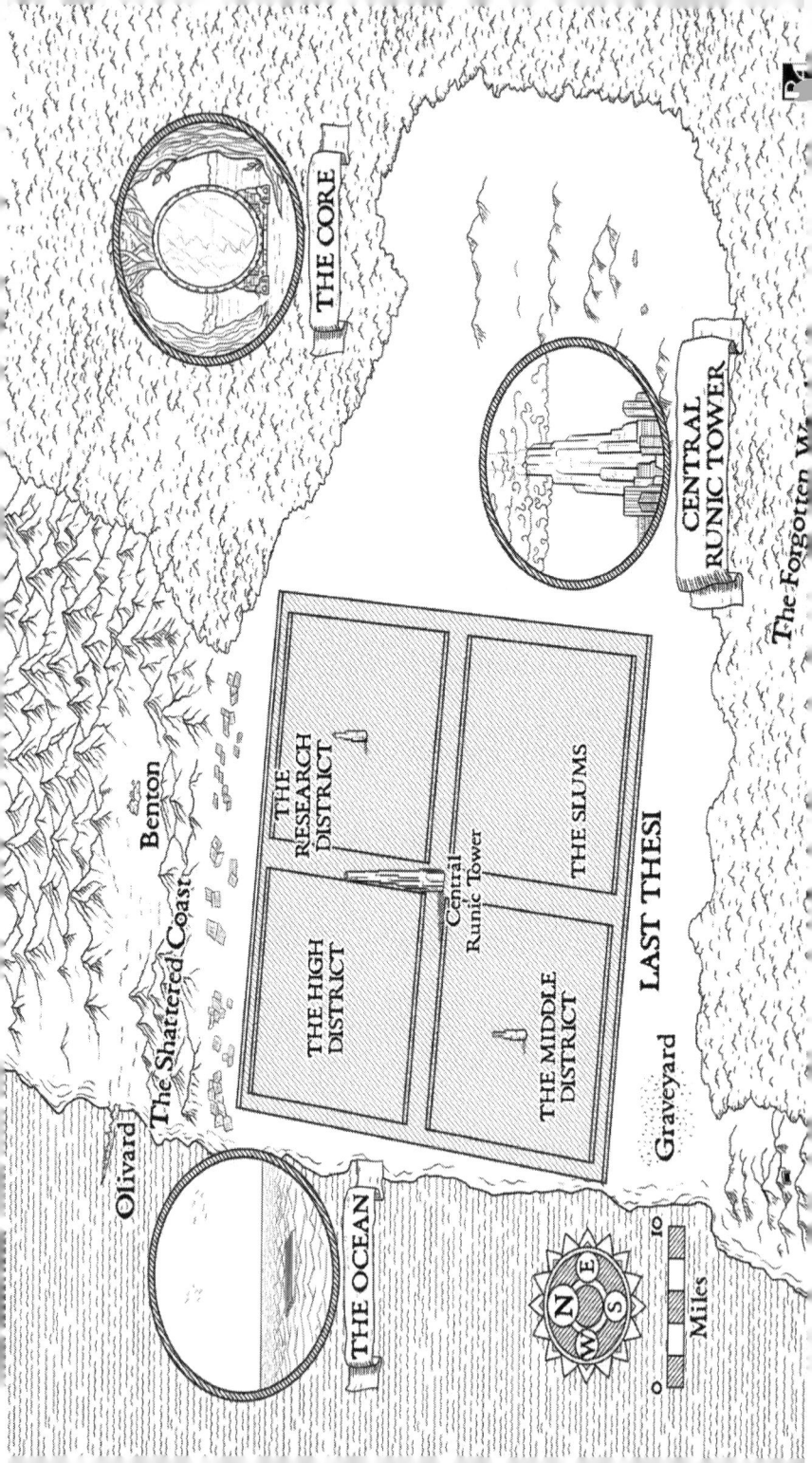

- THE CORE
- CENTRAL RUNIC TOWER
- THE OCEAN
- THE HIGH DISTRICT
- THE RESEARCH DISTRICT
- THE MIDDLE DISTRICT
- THE SLUMS
- Central Runic Tower
- Olivard
- The Shattered Coast
- Benton
- Graveyard
- The Forgotten W...

0 — 10 Miles

Chapter 1: Half

Sara ran a brush through her hair before the mirror in her office. The lights that outlined the mirror accentuated the wrinkles forming at the corners of her eyes and mouth. *Cracked earth,* her colleagues called them. She hated them; the wrinkles, *and* her colleagues. The door opened and an unwelcome guest entered.

"C'mon, Sara. It's time to go. The story isn't going to report itself," The stocky young man, Barnov, said as he barged into her private office, inconsiderate and petulant as ever. His voice was flatulence to her ears. She was embarrassed to be seen in public with him, but his camera work was better than decent.

"*Story?*" she scoffed, turning her eyes from the creases that lined her scowl to aim her glare at him instead. "I won't do it."

"Wait, *what?* Since when?"

"Since now. I'm not going to stoop to reporting on how safe the new checkpoint is between the High District and *middle child*. Just pawn it off to Mindy's crew. I'm sure she'll look *perkier* than me in the light right now anyways."

"Just pawn it? But Sara, if we don't work, we don't get paid. That's not—"

"*You* don't get paid. That's not *my* problem. If you're so desperate to up your balance, then go ahead and roll with Mindy for all I care."

Barnov gave a chuckle and plopped down in a chair in the corner of the room. It groaned beneath his weight. "I'm not *that* desperate." He popped open a bag of some magically engineered snack that filled the room with a nauseating greasy smell. "So, what's the plan then?"

"Plan for what?"

"I just thought if you didn't want to do the checkpoint story that you'd have some lead of your own," Barnov said, crunching away as though this were a lunchroom.

"Well, if I had it my way, I'd rather be investigating why the wall disappeared. Now that's a story!"

"The wall between the slums and the Middle District, right? That is a real mystery, for sure. But you know the Retallors don't want us reporting on that kind of stuff. They say it's too political."

"Screw the Retallors! And screw politics! I'd go there right now if I wasn't so worried about catching a disease from that rotten place. I know there's an even bigger scoop out there; some *real* news!"

Barnov crinkled up the empty bag and threw it in the trash. The unhealthy smell seemed to linger even so. "Hey, you're the boss. Just tell me where to go and I'll go. In the meantime, Mindy is going to keep cleaning up with all the stories she takes on."

"Because Mindy is young and eager, with little self-worth. Nobody cares about the new checkpoint or remodeled RM Mart down the street. They just want to see a pretty face in these dark times. They want a womanly voice to tell them *it's okay* so they can turn their eyes away from the truth. I don't want to be that anymore."

"You don't want to, or you're just getting too old to?" Barnov began to laugh, until the brush flew from Sara's hand and shot towards him. "Hey! I was joking—"

The door burst open again. This time it was Psilen, Sara's wiry sound engineer. The bags under his eyes were as dark as ever, yet he looked desperately alert. "Guys! We just got word that Retallor Tower is under attack!"

"Att—" Barnov began, stifled by Sara's hand over his face.

"Attack?!" Sara cried in excitement. "By who?!"

"I have no clue! The tip came in from some place down the street from there. They said this big fog surrounded the base of the tower and that they heard shots fired. Then—get this—the whole tower just closed up!"

"Huh? *Closed up*, how?"

"Like, these steel plates came down and sealed up all the doors and windows—all at once! That's what I was told, at least."

Sara let her hand off Barnov's face, her eyes burning with passion. "This is it! This is the scoop! We've got to get over there before those hounds at *Letsky* do!"

"You want us to go to Retallor Tower in the middle of an attack? We can't do that!" Barnov said.

"Hey! I'm the boss. Remember? Let's go, Psilen. The van is still set up for us to do the checkpoint story, right?"

"Sure is," Psilen said, following her as she stormed out of the office. Barnov, though apprehensive, followed not a moment later.

The dimly lit newsroom was hectic. Everyone was spouting rumors and speculation about the attack. Sara wasn't interested in that. She wanted the truth. She emerged from the building, having to adjust to the bright light of day. The van was there, parked just outside, beneath the neon red sign that read, "High District's High-Definition News."

Sara hopped in the front seat while Psilen got in the back. Barnov trailed behind, getting into the driver's seat moments later. He was already sweating up a storm as he turned to face her before starting it up.

"Are you sure about this?" Barnov asked. "You know the Retallors own HDHD. They'll have our jobs if we give them bad press."

"Remember what I said? Screw the Retallors! This is my scoop, and I won't let *anything* stand in the way!" Sara reached over and slapped the ignition button. The van's Ather engine roared and Barnov turned his eyes to the road, speeding off without any other objections.

HDHD was clear across town from Retallor Tower, up in the northern corner of the High District. By the time they arrived, the scene appeared far less chaotic than described. The fog had all but dispersed, though the wisps that remained gave the street an eerie vibe.

They parked on the curb in front of the tower and Sara stepped out. She stared up at the enormous skyscraper with a frown on her face. "Where are the metal plates? I'm not seeing any steel over the doors or windows like the tip said."

Barnov stepped out with his camera, looking at the scene through its lens. "Maybe ... it's over?" he said with a boorish sigh of relief.

"Come. We're going in," Sara commanded, not turning back to see whether Barnov and Psilen were behind her.

The ground floor of the tower painted a puzzling picture. Trails of fog still floated about the air, but there was no damage done, nor any sign of struggle. Her heart continued to race as fast as it had the whole drive over.

Sara searched high and low throughout the vast room for someone to question, until, at last, she found a woman hiding behind the fabled, golden bust of Irol Retallor sitting atop a pedestal at the center of the room.

"Ma'am. Are you alright?" Sara asked, donning a professional disposition. She extended her hand to the woman, who appeared to be too lost in fright to notice her. "Ma'am! My name is Sara Stone. I'm a reporter with HDHD News. Can you tell me what happened here?"

The woman opened her eyes, and her curled up body relaxed at the sight of a friendly face. She climbed to her knees, her eyes darting about, before taking Sara's hand. She stood up, still trembling. "D—Doombringers! They attacked the tower! I—I don't know where they went!" The woman became frantic, as if she just remembered something dire. She scrambled towards the desk on the other end of the room. "I have to phone the mayor and make sure he's okay—"

A loud *ding* sounded and all four of their hearts seemed to skip a beat in unison. Sara turned her attention to the elevator as the light above it lit up. She inched backwards, the point of her elevated heel scraping against the tile. All eyes were on the door with silent anticipation as it opened.

A single man stepped out; a boy, it seemed, really. He was dressed in a black leather vest with black cargo pants, the kind of attire Sara had only ever heard was worn by the Shadows. There was a purple bruise on his face and a streak of dried blood stretched from his nose down to his chin. He hobbled over to the reception desk looking dumbfounded and dazed.

"Did you see him?" the boy asked.

Before the woman could answer, Sara stepped in, microphone in hand. "Young man. *See him?* Who do you mean? Is the mayor safe?"

He turned to Sara, then did a double take, as if confused to see two women at the desk. "The guy with green hair. He took out my whole squad, all by himself. I ... was coming down to ..." he stared into the camera and hesitated, the way Sara so often saw before someone told a lie, "... make sure he didn't escape."

"Green hair?" She said, turning her eyes to the pictures on the wall behind the desk. A single black and white picture brought back a host of memories. Such unusual hair colors were not common in Last Thesi. The last time she had seen a person with green hair was ... *him,* she thought. Gazing at the picture upon the wall of a man shaking hands with Irol Retallor, she couldn't help but mutter, "The Eminent?"

"The *who?*" The boy said, slumping over the counter, looking as though he would lose consciousness.

"Oh, sorry. Could you tell me any more details about this green haired man?" As Sara probed the teenager for more information, her mind raced. She still remembered that day like it was yesterday; how those two fabled legends smiled and laughed and crossed blades. She was but a rookie reporter back then, only able to attend the lustrous meeting by chance as an employee of Retallor Tower. She remembered the smear campaigns that all the news outlets ran afterwards. It was an all too convenient way for the Eminent to fade into obscurity. She always thought Irol Retallor's death felt so abrupt and out of place too. She never spoke her mind when it came to what she suspected was collusion. The same thoughts plagued her now as did back then. *Could they have planned it all? Could they both still be out there? It must be true! Who else has green hair in this day and age? But why would he want to attack Retallor Tower? I must find out the truth!*

The woman behind the counter let out a distressed gasp and Barnov turned the camera onto her. "The mayor isn't answering!"

"Woah! He could be in trouble," Barnov said. "Shouldn't we call the Runic Guard—"

"Shush!" Sara hissed off camera, reminding Barnov not to speak while the camera was rolling.

"No, I can't." The woman shook her head. "The mayor forbids it. He said to call the Shadows if there's an emergency. But I can't get through to any of them either—not even the elites. Whoever defeated the trainee squad must still be in the tower!"

"We have to go up!" Sara said, nudging Barnov before stepping back into frame. "Ma'am, please grant us access to the elevator. We will go check on the mayor's wellbeing."

"B—but ... what about the Doombringers?" Barnov whispered. Sara gave him a smack on the shoulder to remind him to keep the camera steady.

"The elites took care of the Doombringers," the trainee said, lifting his head. "That was the last thing I heard from 'em, at least."

"*Really?*" Sara said with a gleam in her eyes. "Maybe the Shadows are engaging with the green-haired man right now then! We must go up to be sure!"

"W—what floor though?" the receptionist asked.

"Seventy would be my guess," said the trainee. "That's where we were told to meet up with the elites and Cecil."

"Seventy it is then," Sara said enthusiastically, trying not to scowl at the grimaces plastered across Barnov and Psilen's faces. *You better wipe those terrified expressions off your faces! I've got a reputation to uphold!*

"Alright. I'll send you up," the receptionist said. "You, trainee, accompany them so they don't get lost." She guided them to the elevator.

Sara glanced at the metal archway before the elevator then turned back to the equipment in her crew's possession. "Ma'am, is that an Ather detector? Our equipment will surely set it off. Is that okay?"

"Unfortunately, no, I cannot allow you to take any Ather up the tower. You'll have to leave your Ather-made belongings with me."

"Not a problem, ma'am. You two, leave the equipment behind. We'll just have to take a *minimalist* approach!" Sara put her microphone down and pulled an electric recorder from her blazer's breast pocket. Barnov set his hefty camera down and drew the compact camera from his vest. *The picture and sound quality may be garbage, but the story is going to be gold!*

"Do I still need to go up with you two?" Psilen whined, having no back up device to replace his portable sound mixer.

"Yes! Now, get in," Sara demanded as she, Barnov, and the trainee entered the elevator. Psilen gave a sigh and complied. Once inside, the metal door closed, and the elevator zoomed up to the seventieth floor faster than they could exchange formalities with the trainee assigned to accompany them.

A *bing* sounded as the door opened, and Sara pushed her crew out of the way to exit. She glanced around, eager to see what the upper reaches of the tower was like. From what she knew, no civilians were permitted beyond the fifty-ninth floor. To her disappointment, there was nothing to be seen. The vast ballroom appeared empty at first glance, save for a pile of scrap metal at the center.

"What is that?" she mumbled as she approached it, waving in Barnov to get it on camera. It was some sort of broken-down machine, one made of a metal unlike any she had ever seen.

"I don't know, ma'am," the trainee said, kneeling down beside it. "I've never seen anything like this in the tower before. Maybe some kind of defense mechanism to protect the upper floors?"

"It seems that it didn't work very well to stop the intruder. Where is everyone else? You said Cecil would be here with the Shadow elites."

The trainee frowned, his whole-body trembling as he looked around. He pointed to a staircase on the far end of the room. "There! Maybe they all went up ... to ... the mayor's office."

"The mayor's office?!" Sara gasped. "The intruder must already be there! We have to hurry!" She made a dash for the stairs, paying little mind to the extravagant wood carvings etched into the handrail.

"Wait!" Barnov huffed as he tried to keep up, his podgy body not accustomed to running. "You can't just ... barge into ... the mayor's office!"

Sara was already crossing the final step to the next floor by the time his words reached her. Psilen and the trainee were close behind, but she needed more than a voice recording for this story to be perfect—she needed a steady shot. "Hurry up!" she called. "You're lucky you don't have to haul the big camera around like this!" Her words were a swift slap to Barnov's behind. He puffed out his chest and trudged up the stairs to meet them.

The stairs led to a narrow hallway. "Which way now?" she asked the trainee.

"The mayor's office is just ahead. It's the only room on this floor. You can't miss it," he said, sounding as if he did not plan to follow.

"Come now. We have to make sure the mayor is okay!" she said, pushing the trainee forward to lead the way.

They followed the apprehensive Shadow down the hall and around a corner. There, Sara saw it—the mayor's office. The wide double doors were open and the security eye above it appeared hollow and unresponsive. A watery gurgling sound could be heard as they approached the door.

Sara gasped when she saw the state of the room. It was the result of utter chaos; broken glass and cracked tile littered the floor, what remained of the furniture was a shredded mess of fluff and debris, and there were small holes all about the walls and protective glass windows. Yet it seemed that the chaos had concluded before they arrived.

"We have to find the mayor!" she urged. "Everyone, split up!" The awful gurgling sound she heard before entering the room grew louder as she searched around piles of broken artifacts and ancient things that were likely worth more than her entire career.

"Here!" she heard Barnov cry out. She whipped around and ran across the room. An intense pain shot through her leg as her pointed heel slipped into a hole in the floor, twisting her ankle. She contained her scream and pushed through the agony until she reached Barnov.

"Mayor Welzig!" Sara shrieked when she saw him on the ground; massive, yet broken. Cecil Retallor was bent over his brother, but he was not himself. The lanky Retallor brother's hands were at Welzig's throat, squeezing without restraint. Sara's trained eyes saw past the deplorable scene and saw the truth in Cecil's eyes: foggy blue and inhumanly cruel. "Cecil Retallor has gone mad! He's going to kill the mayor! Somebody stop him!"

As she turned for help, she heard the song of blade piercing flesh, followed by a hollow gasp. She saw blood trail down from Psilen's mouth, the black sword of the timid trainee protruding from his chest. Psilen fell dead to the ground, revealing a pair of blazing blue eyes behind him. The glazed stare of the maddened trainee sent a chill down her spine. His mouth contorted to form a crazed smirk and he threw himself at her.

Sara closed her eyes and screamed a hopeless scream, having no time to reflect on her life. Her mind was blank, against all expectations of what death was like. There was a loud *thud* and a *crash*, follow by a gentle touch upon her shoulder. She opened her eyes, half-expecting to face the afterlife, but that was not the case. It was Barnov, breathing heavily, his balled-up fist was red and swollen.

"Sara, we have to run! *Now!*" he said as he tried to inch her forward. The slight shift in weight sent an electric pain to her ankle. A yelp escaped the prison where she kept anything she deemed as weakness. Barnov looked at her with softened eyes; eyes she never knew he had. Together, they glanced down at the purple pigment in her ankle. "You're hurt bad."

"Yes ..." she thought for only a moment before making up her mind. "You ... you need to get out of here and make sure the story is told." She held the voice recorder out to him. "Take this and run."

Barnov nodded, but instead of taking the device from her hand, he grabbed her by the wrist and pulled her close, kneeling down as he draped her over his shoulders. "This is *your* story, Sara. If you don't tell it, no one will." The madness-afflicted trainee clambered to his feet, his face bloodied from the fall. "Hold on tight!"

Barnov dodged as the trainee lurched at him, narrowly avoiding being tackled. He bolted out of the mayor's office, not turning another glance at the carnage behind them. Sara held on as tight as she could, though she could feel Barnov's muscles trembling beneath her. Despite that, Barnov didn't stop running until he reached the elevator.

He set her down as they waited for it to arrive. "I ... just need ... a ... moment to ..." he panted.

At the bing, Sara carried herself across the threshold, trying to ignore the excruciating pain. She leaned against the wall inside the elevator, saying as she turned to Barnov who limped in behind her, "Rest a bit longer. We'll be fine once we get back to ground level."

The elevator took off, reaching its destination only a moment later. When the doors opened, the fog within the lobby had all but gone. She limped out with some assistance from Barnov, her eyes frantically searching for the receptionist to tell her the grim happenings taking place on the seventy-first floor.

Sara's eyes grew wide with terror when she found the woman, splayed out on the floor with a bloody gash across her chest. She didn't have more than a split second to question why before she saw them on the other side of the lobby—Shadows elites, their blades drawn against one another, eyes lost within a blue fog. They recklessly wailed away at one another while making ghoulish sounds, not paying any mind to Sara and Barnov across the room.

"Madness? Again?" Sara questioned. "But ... there have never been reports of maddened people attacking others afflicted with madness before."

"Never heard of one using a sword either," Barnov added. "C'mon. I'll carry you back to the van."

Sara hopped onto Barnov's back again. She could not shake the trouble from her mind. *Something's not right here. Something's ...* her thoughts were derailed the moment the automatic glass doors slid open, revealing pandemonium in the streets outside. A mob had gathered on the vehicle-only street. People were fighting one another; punching and clawing, kicking and stomping, and wrestling each other to the ground. It was a chaotic mosh of furious blows. It was animalistic, with no rhyme or reason. It was ... *madness*.

"*Look!* Their eyes!" Barnov shouted. Sara had seen it too. She knew just what he was about to say. "They've gone mad!" His body began to quake again. "We need to hurry to the van and get out of here."

Parking directly in front of Retallor Tower was not permitted, so they had a ways to go to reach safety. Desperate, ululating cries pierced through the crowd of madmen. Sara tried not to imagine the pain of being stomped to death while pinned beneath the merciless weight of a friend or colleague gone mad. She half expected Barnov to drop her to the pavement and bash her skull in any moment—if the mob didn't do it first.

The madmen seemed satisfied with the poor souls they had in their clutches, but for how much longer? The van was on the opposite end of the street as the crowd of mystic-blue-eyed heathens. Barnov heaved as he slogged down the street. The closer they got to the mob, the more

Sara could feel her heart beating into Barnov's back. The abhorrent noises grew louder as they reached the van. Sara couldn't block out the sloppy crunches and blood-filled cries. It made her woozy.

The next thing she knew, Barnov was setting her down in the passenger seat. Her heart sank, eyes glued on him as he made his way around the front of the van, praying that he would make it. When the driver door opened, she turned to face what she expected to be a pair of glazed over blue eyes and a pair of hands aimed at her throat, but it didn't come. Barnov got in, closed the door, and started the engine, then after a moment of reprieve where Sara felt her muscles relax and her body sink into the cushioned seat, the van sped off.

The chaos was not relegated to that street alone; it seemed to revel in all of the High District. People all over, spurned by madness tore into anyone they could get their hands on, rending flesh and muscle from bone with their bare hands. Businessmen and women threw themselves from buildings, becoming blots of red mixed with broken bones and cartilage on impact. The screams, gods, the screams, seemed to fill all the air, turning everything about the warm and sunny day to cold. Sara could hear them still, even when she put her hands over her ears.

She felt a hand grab her wrist and screamed. The van swerved. "Sara! Calm down!" Barnov cried. "We need to get somewhere safe. I don't have enough fuel to drive around all day. Do you have any ideas?"

"I ... don't know," she sobbed, wiping snot and tears mixed with makeup from her face.

Barnov stayed calmer than she. It was the only thing keeping her from going insane and throwing herself from the van. He made a sharp turn down a street she didn't recognize. It must have been somewhere east of Retallor Tower, a place she seldom went, where autonomous factories produced many of the everyday items she took for granted.

Barnov drove through a gate to what appeared to be a rundown factory. It didn't look like a place that belonged in the High District. He stopped the van and huddled over the wheel, panting terribly.

"Where are we?" Sara asked.

"This ... this used to be one of the hip places some friends of mine threw parties at."

"And you're sure it's safe here?"

"Yeah, I think so. Nobody comes around here anymore since *Club Tower* opened."

"Okay ... so, what now?"

"I don't know ... I guess, now, we wait."

"For how long ..." Sara wondered, yet said aloud. She felt hopeless. Was this the end of the world? The apocalypse that everyone feared?

"As long as it takes—" Barnov began but was startled by the beeping of Sara's communicator in her pocket. He looked at her as it continued to beep. "Are you going to get that?"

His words reminded Sara of its existence more than the beeping could at that moment. She drew it from her pocket and hit the green button. "Hello?"

"Hey, Sara! It's Daniel, from HDHD. I just wanted to check if you were safe."

"I ... I am, yes. Why do you ask? Did something happen?"

"Yes ... you could say that. It's actually ... really not good."

"What happened?" she gulped, having an idea already what Daniel was going to say.

"I ... had just gotten back from picking up lunch for the office, ya know ... it was my turn today. But ... when I go back ... they were all ..."

"*Mad?*" Sara wondered, yet said, still unable to keep her thoughts under wraps.

"Yes ... mad. I couldn't tell who was and who wasn't, to be honest. It was ... just out of control. As soon as I saw it ... I ran. I didn't know what else to do ... I ... Sara—" Daniel let out a garbled scream that was cut off by the call ending.

Sara sat in silence for minutes to come, not turning her eyes away from the blue sky above. It was a perfectly calm day to the world above, yet upon the ground was hell. How much time had passed, she did not know. She merely watched the gentle clouds above as they drifted through the air as slow as sap down a tree. She wanted everything to end, for that sight to be the last she saw, until she heard a voice. It was low, forming amidst static. Her eyes shot to the radio in the dash and thrust her hand to the volume dial.

"... today will be forever remembered as the most gruesome one Last Thesi has ever seen."

She twisted the tuning dial to another channel.

"... widespread madness has been observed all throughout Last Thesi."

Again, she twisted.

"... experts estimate that nearly half the population was affected during the ungodly happenstance that befell Last Thesi today."

"*Half*," she muttered, lips trembling as tears rolled down her cheeks. When she swallowed, it felt like a boulder was stuck in her throat. Both she and Barnov hung their heads and she let her hand fall limp from the tuning dial.

"Nobody knows how or why such a horrifying thing would happen. Scientists in the Research District have declined to make any comments at this time, but we expect a formal statement to be given within the next few days. All we can do for now is unite and persevere as a people while we mourn those that were lost today—a day that will go down in history. Right now, gate guards and civilians alike are hard at work to identify the bodies and search for survivors. If you have any information regarding the event and wish to report it, give us a call ..."

The reporter's voice seemed to blend into the radio static and the static that filled Sara's mind after a while. It wasn't until after sundown that Barnov spoke again.

"Sara. Do you want me to take you home?" he asked, seeming concerned for her still.

"Ah, yes, please. I'll ... give you directions."

"There's ... no rush. If you want to wait a bit longer ... just to be sure ... I understand."

"No. It's been long enough. I'm ready now," she assured with a great sigh.

Barnov gave a nod and fired the engine up once more.

The roads were as clear as one would expect after a city-wide genocide, though Sara could still make out the bloodstains baked into the pavement after the hours of sun exposure. When they arrived at her studio apartment, which was not far from the now abandoned HDHD office, Barnov assisted her inside. He set her down on the couch and fetched her some ice for her ankle.

"Are sure you'll be okay? I could hang around for a bit if you want."

"I'll be fine. You can go ... and do whatever it is you would do on any other night."

"Okay ..." he sounded sullen. Sara didn't mean to direct her emotions at him, but she felt unable to bottle them up any longer after what she saw that day.

"*Club Tower,* you said? Is that where you'll go?"

"Probably, yeah," he said. His eyes lit up as if a thought hid the darkness of the world from his mind for a fraction of a second. "I could ... take you with me, if you'd like. Some relaxing would do you some good, I think. It's

... a good way to avoid wrinkles, I hear," he gave the lightest of chuckles, seeming uninspired by his own jest.

"No," Sara scowled. "I wouldn't be caught dead in that cesspool." She nearly exploded, until all the events from that day replayed in her mind in an instant, and tears began to well up behind her eyes.

"I ... understand. I'll get going then," Barnov turned to leave.

"Thanks ..." she said in a low voice, stopping him in his tracks, "... for saving me today."

"Of course," he turned to give a tearful smile.

"Be careful out there, Barnie," Sara said, calling him by the nickname she only ever used whenever he did a more than decent job at anything. "Say hello to the *boys* for me."

Barnov blushed, appearing fully detached from the horrors of the world for the first time since that afternoon. He smirked, saying, "Will do," and left.

After the door closed and Barnov's footsteps disappeared, Sara sat alone in her dark apartment. The complex she lived in was one sought after by anyone who worked in the High District. Finding an available space to rent there was thought to be nigh impossible, yet that night it was quiet, so quiet.

Chapter 2: Consequence

Rekco teetered in and out of a feverish consciousness. Images of the incident at Retallor Tower flashed throughout his intermittent dreams. He saw sedated pregnant women hooked up to nightmarish machines, Shadows with their blades drawn, and Welzig's twisted expression as he fired a barrage of bullets at him. The sound of gunshots that echoed off the walls in his mind played a duet with Tony Pukstein's wretched cries as his body was crushed within the automaton he was forced to pilot.

Rekco felt like he was moving, though he could not tell what was real and what was not. Hues of orange, brown, and red washed away the atrocious visions that plagued his dreams, and a warm sensation filled his body.

He opened his eyes, surprised to find himself in a bed, looking up at the wooden rafters high above him. His whole body was leaden with aches and pain. There was a stale, earthy scent in the air. He wanted to look around, but he couldn't move an inch from where he lay.

Where am I? Am I even awake? Rekco glanced at the oil lamp hanging from the wall. It cast just enough light for him to see himself and the bloodied bandages wrapped all around him. He thought to call out for help but feared the possibility that the Retallors held him captive in a forsaken dungeon.

A loud scraping sound made him flinch, and orange light filled the room. A voice called out, "He's awake!"

Rekco tried to sit up, but all his muscles were useless. His elevated breathing caused his wounds to throb with pain. His eyes darted about—it was all he could do. A person came into view; blurry at first, but Rekco's vision became clearer the longer they stood over him.

"Awake, huh? I'm surprised he's even alive!" the man said. He was older, wearing a hat with a brim as wide as his pearly white smile. Sweaty locks of greying hair poked out from beneath it. "Are you with us, son?"

Rekco opened his mouth, but all that came forth was a husked groan. The man before him did not look familiar, though it was hard to tell, for his vision doubled and crossed every other moment. The man's voice was not malicious. Instead, it was just calming enough to settle his frantic pulse.

"Good enough, I suppose. You were in pretty bad shape when my workers found ya." A host of faint murmurs could be heard through the walls accompanied by the gentle rumble of footsteps against earth. The sounds became louder, and Rekco could hear those murmurs turn into rowdy voices. "Speaking of *workers*— it looks like it's break time. I hope you don't mind sharing space with them for a bit," the man laughed.

The rambunctious workers quieted down as they entered the room and caught sight of him. His vision was still too foggy to see anything more than silhouettes in the crowd, but one of them rushed forward, calling out, "Rekco?!" When the man stepped into the light, Rekco recognized him at once.

"G—Gar—y?" he muttered, staring up at him in confusion.

"That's right! You remember me!"

The old man turned his lazy smile to Gary, his eyes appearing more alert than his expression. "Gary Robinson, right? Do you know this man? Another one of your buddies from The What's-it-called?"

"*The Underground*, Mr. Davis," Gary nodded. "And yes, I know him. Boy do I! This man saved my life!"

Rekco couldn't tell if he was blushing or if he was going to pass out. Mr. Davis looked at him again, now with a fiery glint in his eyes. "Oh! Is that so? I'm glad we got to 'em then, before the grim reaper did."

Gary only now seemed to notice the state Rekco was in. He gasped. "W—what happened to him? Is he going to be all right?"

"Dunno. This is how we found 'em—all pre-wrapped, lookin' like he escaped from a hospital or somethin'. Do you know if he has any family or friends we can send 'em off to? I'm sure if he's got a home, he wouldn't want to stay in a barn."

Barn? Rekco thought. "Wh ... er ..." he tried to speak, but every time he tried to push himself, he felt as if he would faint.

"Hum? Whe ... re? *Where?*" Mr. Davis tried to decipher his words. "Where are we, maybe? The farmland—*my farmland*—that's where!"

Rekco's eyes spoke more than his mouth could. *The farmland! It makes sense now. But ... how could I have gotten here from Retallor Tower? And what happened to ...* Everything in his vision became wavy. He could hold on no longer. *... the women ... and ... the doctors?*

*

This time, Rekco's dream lasted for what felt like no longer than a second. When he awoke again, he was lying on the couch in front of the fireplace at his home in the plains. *But ... how? Was it all a ...* "dream?" he said aloud, his own voice startling him.

He tried to sit up, his body more cooperative than it had been before. Just as his shoulders lifted off the couch, he felt hands upon him and a voice cried, "Rekco! No!" He tilted his head back to see Cathy. She gently pushed him back down to rest his head on the cushions. "No moving!" she said firmly. "The last time you tried to move, you ended up busting your stitches and bleeding all over the place. How did you end up with stitches, anyways?"

"Wha? Cathy? How ... did I get here?" he asked, still trying to recollect what happened after he freed the women and doctors in Retallor Tower.

She sat down on the floor in front of the couch. "You have Zeke to thank for that. Dim and I were with him when he got a call from a *Gary Robinson,* who said he found you at the farm. After that, Zeke was able to get a hold of Bragau to pick you up and bring you here. He said you were a mess—you still are, really. You—"

"Where's Dim?" Rekco blurted out, glancing around to find the scholar, Dim Smithy, was nowhere in sight. A terrible feeling bubbled inside his gut, and he began to feel incredibly warm.

"Dim's fine," Cathy assured. "He just ... had something important come up while we were at *the Coop*. He said he'll meet up with us later on."

Rekco's ability to think critically was impaired enough that he did not pick up on Cathy's hesitation or the grim look on her face. He was content enough in knowing that Dim was okay. "Good," he muttered. His eyelids became leaden with the want for sleep.

Cathy smiled, her face fading as darkness encroached upon his vision. "Get some rest, okay? I'll be here if you need anything ..." her voice got quiet, until it, too, faded.

As Rekco slept, he struggled to stay comfortable. At times, his body ached and became clammy after profuse bouts of sweating. His heart dropped, stricken by a fear that he was falling each time he turned over on the couch. Whenever he stopped fidgeting, it seemed for naught, for the blackness in his mind never remained that way. Colors flitted through his dreams; purples, oranges, yellows, and that accursed Ather-blue, blazing yet foggy, like the eyes of men gone mad.

The sound of static buzzed within his ears until he couldn't take it anymore. He shouted for it to stop, but he knew he wasn't awake, and that his cries would go unheard. After a time, the static transitioned into a garbled mess of incoherent voices and screams—which was no less torturous. He was so warm that he wanted to lie in the grass outside, but he felt paralyzed inside his own dreams.

After an arduous struggle, Rekco broke free from sleep and jolted upright, his clothes and hair moist with sweat. Across the room, he saw into the dining room. There, the radio sat on the kitchen table—at its heart was an azure light behind a layer of thick glass. The way it seemed to look back at him was unsettling. Seeing that blaze of Ather in the radio reminded him of Maven—his mentor, guardian, and friend; the man who raised him in his parent's stead, the man taken by the *madness* before it ever had a name.

Rekco stared into the radio's shimmering core, and all he could see in it were Maven's eyes glazed over by that same color. He remembered it looked as though his master's true eyes were trapped beneath tiny pools of water. It pained his heart to be reminded of it.

A female voice spoke over the radio, reminding him that it was, in fact, still a radio. "We interrupt this program to bring you this breaking news: A hostage situation is underway in the High District. Reports say that the suspect is a blue, human-like creature that was spotted in the streets outside of Retallor Tower, not long after a mysterious fog disappeared from the scene. It is said that the suspect has bound all of the employees and residents that were recently evacuated from the tower and brought them into the street. If you are in the High District today, we implore you to avoid the area at all costs until the situation is diffused."

Rekco's eyes widened at the phrase, *blue creature*. It was the same term he read in an old newspaper article about the death of Irol Retallor. It was said that a blue creature was spotted in the High District the same day that Irol Retallor was supposedly killed by a meteor strike. Rekco's mind raced faster than his heart. *I have to do something. I can't let all those people I rescued from Retallor Tower be killed. I can't!*

Rekco stood up, which was surprising in itself, and looked around the room. Cathy was nowhere in sight. He saw his sword propped up against the wall by the fireplace; the black blade that was given to him when he became employed by the Retallor Corporation to be Dim's bodyguard. He picked it up, noticing that his grip felt strong and steady. *There's no time to waste,* he thought as he stormed out the door—off towards the High District.

He remembered little about the mad dash he made for Retallor Tower. Actually, to him, it felt as though he were transported there by his will. As he walked down the vacant vehicle-only street, he began to notice a crowd up ahead. Their faces became clear and familiar moments later. He saw among them: pregnant women, doctors, aristocrats, Shadow trainees and elites alike, businesspeople, and many more, all bound and gagged, sitting on the pavement.

A lone figure stood within the crowd. It walked forward, each step mirroring Rekco's as he drew closer. It stopped the moment he did, the moment he saw it clearly enough to tell what he was looking at—a blue creature, shaped much like a human, yet much unlike one at the same time. It was a creature far beyond what Rekco's imagination could conjure, standing double his height, with skin the color of the darkest reaches of the ocean.

It spoke, though it had no lips or mouth that Rekco could see. "I didn't think you would show up. Though, you aren't quite what I hoped for." It's voice was feminine, yet distorted, projecting out of what looked like a voice box on their face; a rather flat face on a slab of flesh akin to where a human's head should be, though their pillar-like head was impossible to discern from their neck.

"So, you can speak then, monster? What do you want with these people?" Rekco asked, still trying to study his unearthly foe. He saw two beady, yellow eyes that were close together just above the woven, mesh-like grid where her voice came from. A line of long, thin spines ran down the back of her head to a fleshy cape that protruded from her neck, extending down to her mid back like hair.

She took a single step forward, her massive three-pronged foot cracking the pavement beneath her weight. "First, allow me to introduce myself. My name is Oglis Inima, and to be honest, I am searching for the same thing as you: I am searching for the *Eminent*." Rekco's heart sank at the word. Oglis turned to the crowd of hostages behind her. "Are any among you the *Eminent?*" she taunted. The gagged and bound hostages let out muffled cries in response to their captor's question. She laughed at their misery—if you could even call the devilish sound that came from her voice box a laugh. "*No?* None of you? Are you certain?" She pivoted back to Rekco. "It looks like he's not here after all. What a shame. If that's the case, I guess I don't *want* anything with these people."

Oglis raised her arm to the crowd. Rekco did not know what kind of devious plan she had, but the very notion made his blood boil. He shot forward towards her faster than he knew he could move and swung his sword across her back with such explosive force that it caused a gust of wind to roll through the street. But his sword struck nothing but air; Oglis had vanished.

"You're fast," Rekco heard a voice from behind. He spun around in disbelief and saw her standing where he once was before, her left arm pointing at him now. "But you're not what I'm looking for." It wasn't until then that he noticed her left arm had no hand, and only half a forearm. There was a hole at the tip of her arm, making it look like a cannon. A yellow glow began to emit from the barrel. "If you wish to live, move out of the way."

Rekco had no idea what kind of attack she was preparing, yet he was frozen in place all the same. "Wait! I have a question for you."

The glow faded and Oglis lowered her arm. "A question, you say?"

"Yes. I must know ... were you the one who killed Irol Retallor?"

Oglis' face looked like one incapable of expressing emotions, but there was a subtle shift in the muscles above her beady eyes. Rekco did not know if it meant intrigue or confusion. She raised her arm yet again, saying, "This is your last warning. Let those beneath you die. As is the way of life."

Rekco's stalling had done nothing to help him regain control of his legs. *I have to deflect whatever it is she tries. It's the only way to save these people now.* He gulped, squinting to focus his sights on Oglis' arm. As he watched the yellow glow ignite again, he thought back on his experiences with magic; the teachings Gofun gave him to repel spells using the magic within himself. He tried to remember how it felt when he accidentally deflected Kyoku's lightning—all those years ago.

The yellow glow within Oglis' arm erupted into a geyser of light that shot towards him. Rekco raised his blade to the beam, trying to think of it the way Gofun once taught him to; like falling leaves or flimsy tree branches, to be swept aside by his blade. The laser struck his blade, knocking him to his knees. He gripped his sword with both hands, trying to keep it steady as the yellow energy continuously bounded off it. The wayward beam split off his sword and cut through everything it touched; it seared the pavement, cut through walls, and shattered the glass of nearby buildings.

It's working! But ... What am I supposed to do now? Rekco couldn't see anything other than yellow light before him. The people behind him clamored in a frenzy, just as stuck as he. The beam seemed to know no end. It annihilated the street and reduced the adjacent buildings to nothing but rubble. Dust and debris filled the air, making it hard to see.

The heat from the laser made Rekco sweat. He could feel a burning sensation in his trembling hands and arms. He felt so tired—it reminded him of the first time he experienced magic, when he faced the magical storm outside of Gofun and Kyoku's home; how it drained him like nothing else ever had. He became dizzy, suddenly feeling like a child who stayed up far beyond his bedtime.

"That feeling, as if your muscles are being eaten away, on the cusp of betraying you—that's *fatigue*," Oglis' voice called to Rekco. It sounded so close and soft, as though she were whispering into his ear. "The magic inside of you is about to gutter out. I'll admit, you're strong. But not strong enough—not yet."

Rekco didn't have time to feel fear. His whole body became numb. His vision tremored, becoming constricted by an ever-growing dark circle. "I can't ..." he heard himself say before everything faded away.

He opened his eyes, heart racing, a layer of sweat soaked into his clothes. He was lying flat on his back. He tried to shoot upright but felt hands upon him.

"Rekco! No! You need to stay put!" The hands tried to push him back down, but he resisted with all his might, feeling the weight of his own blood as it poured into the bandages he wore. His eyes bulged as he struggled desperately, heart racing with adrenaline. He growled as the voice called out again, "Rekco!" then he saw her looming over him again. Cathy's eyes were full of fear, as if she were watching him go mad. Her short, pink hair was a tousled mess. Seeing her made his muscles relax.

He lied back down and felt the couch cushions beneath him. His mind was foggy, full of confusion. Cathy rounded the couch and knelt down. He noticed her staring at his eyes. "I'm fine," Rekco assured. "I haven't gone mad." Her tired eyes fell low, looking away uncomfortably. "I just ... how did I get here ... again?"

Cathy looked back up. "*Again?*" she asked. "What do you mean?"

Rekco stammered, feeling abashed, now reminded of his condition by the pain and blood. "I ... heard on the radio, and I had to do something."

"*Oh,*" Cathy said within a deflated breath. "You heard about *it* then?"

"Yes. I'm sorry I put myself in danger by going after it. Please ... tell me ... what happened to the hostages, and the blue creature."

Cathy squeezed her eyebrows together. "Blue ... *creature?* I don't know what you're talking about."

"But I ... it was so ..." Rekco paused. Though frazzled, he noticed the pain on Cathy's face. "What did you think I heard on the radio? Did something else happen?"

Cathy nodded, her eyes wet with the tears she could no longer hold back. "There was ... an outbreak." She got choked up and put her hand over her mouth to stifle her sobs.

"*Outbreak?* Of what—" as he said it, he realized, though he did not realize the extent.

"Madness ... it ... all over the city ... all at once ... half." She inhaled sharply between words, snot and tears flowing from her face to no end.

Rekco's heartbeat began to quicken again. "*Half?* Of what?"

Cathy wiped her face with the sleeve of her pajamas and looked Rekco in the face with an expression of guilt, as though it were somehow her burden to bear. "Half of ... the population. That's what they said on the radio afterwards. They estimated that half of Last Thesi was lost."

Tears rolled down Rekco's cheeks, his mind suddenly blank. He sat silent for a moment. "When?" he heard himself say, though he did not remember speaking it.

"Some time in the afternoon. Either while you were at Retallor Tower, or afterwards. It caused a big commotion at the Coop, where Dim and I were at the time. At least a dozen of the patrons and workers turned. Luckily, Zeke was there to fend most of them off. That's why ... Dim ... didn't come back with me."

Rekco choked on his own breath as his insides roiled. "Don't tell me ... Dim ... he—"

"No. Dim's fine. He might have gotten a scrape or two in the chaos, but he's okay. It's ... Kinnley ... he ... didn't make it."

"I see," Rekco said, dumbstruck, his mind unwilling to process the thought that Kinnley was dead. The grey, old gate guard's face popped into his head; how he smiled and waved his arm high every time he saw Rekco. The image grew faded and dark, until it was gone, just as Kinnley now was. "And ... everyone else? What about Barbier and the others at the Coop?"

Cathy nodded. "Barbier is okay. Farooq was taken though, among others ... many others," she frowned, gnawing at her lip.

"What about Koku? Have you seen or heard from him?"

"*Koku?* No. I thought he was with you."

"He was, but I lost contact with him at some point while I was in Retallor Tower. I wonder what could have happened to him."

Chapter 3: Concept

What happened to the wizard, indeed? Had Kyoku told a soul what happened that day outside of Retallor Tower, not a single one would have believed him.

Using an earpiece of his own creation, Kyoku aided in Rekco's assault on the tower from the safety of a rooftop vantage point adjacent to the gaudy skyscraper. A camera mounted on the device allowed him to cover Rekco's blind spots and alert him of any incoming flanks. All had been going according to plan, up until the moment Rekco fell into a trap devised by Welzig Retallor's personal group of assassins, the Shadows. When Rekco was surrounded by attackers in a pitch-black room, Kyoku was quick to create a tactical flashbang by amplifying the camera's flashlight.

At that moment, Kyoku relied solely on his ears to tell what was going on inside. His long, pointed ears often caused him to receive much unwanted attention, but they also allowed him the luxury of superhuman hearing. His senses were so keen that he could perceive every detail of the scene as Rekco faced off against the disoriented Shadows, taking them down one by one. Yet somehow, he could not sense the presence that lingered behind him, encroaching upon his safety with each passing moment.

Kyoku was waiting patiently for his opportunity to warp into the tower and confront the mayor himself and make him pay for what he did to the people of the Underground—and most of all, for the assassination of his mentor and friend, Mandie, the Queen of The Underground. The thought of causing Mayor Welzig pain made him overflow with excitement. *Just a little while longer until—*

"Bird watching, are you? But I don't see a bird in sight," A hollow female voice called to him like the remnants of an echo.

Kyoku whipped around in haste, jarred by the notion that anyone could sneak up on him, but what he saw did not appear to be a woman—or a human at all, for that matter. The massive blue creature only scarcely resembled the shape of a person. His eyes wanted to take in every detail of the alien, but in his heart he felt threatened. He had no choice but to assume this was another one of the Retallor's creations sent to terminate him.

Kyoku did not question or make to respond to the creature's question. Instead, he flicked his wrist and sent a bolt of electricity hurling towards her. A fraction of a moment passed, within a single blink of the eye, and the monster was gone. Kyoku's heart raced at the thought, *only the Runic Guard can move so fast—*

The next moment, the dark ocean blue of the creature's flesh was all that filled his vision—she was right on top of him. The air was forced from his lungs as his feet left the ground, and a sharp pain was felt in his ribs. His eyes darted about, trying to reorient his perplexed mind. He glanced downward and saw one of the monster's long legs, which were thicker than his midsection, pressing into his abdomen. He followed the leg to a fleshy talon that was gripping him tight, similar to that of the long extinct birds he saw only in books.

Sirens blared in the depths of Kyoku's mind—he was in danger, and he had to act thusly. Without hesitation, he swung his arm like it were a paintbrush across the creature's chest, sending a wave of crimson light through her. She recoiled in pain and gave a grunt, but did not loosen her grip. Kyoku's ultimate spell continued to eat through her flesh, yet it seemed after a moment that it had its fill, and the red destructive energy simply slid off her as though it were water.

A gust of wind blew that sent flecks of ash flying from the wound on the monster's chest. Kyoku watched in both amazement and horror as the scarred crater in her flesh mended itself less than a second after the spell had gone. "How ..." he mouthed, having put his all into the attack.

The blue menace threw back her elongated head and neck and let out a ghastly laugh. Though there was no mouth to be seen, Kyoku felt the vibrations of her laughter emitting from the fleshy grate that ran from the base of her neck up to just below her eyes like a kind of speaker box. Silence filled the air, and she brought her beady yellow eyes upon him. "You truly are as powerful as they say! It seems that the old man was right about you. Unfortunately, your spells are but broken swords against me." She pointed the longest of her three fingers at the point where he had struck her. "My body can regenerate far more quickly than your magic can erode me. It's almost as though I were made to counter you," she said with a chuckle.

Though she spoke in a non-threatening tone, Kyoku felt that the pressure of her talons boring on his chest would soon force his ribs to collapse onto his organs. He knew that as long as she remained in contact with him, he would not be able to warp away without bringing her with him. It seemed a hapless situation to the wizard who had never truly tasted defeat in battle. He gritted his teeth and knew he had no other choice but to acknowledge the creature, "What do you want from me?"

A warm scoff came from her voice box and cascaded over Kyoku's pale face; it smelled of plastic and salt. "Like I said before, I wish to have a word with you."

"Have it then. I'm all ears!" Kyoku sneered in frustration.

"Not here. You'll meet me at the northern corner of the city, just outside the walls, in five minutes. And make no attempt to escape or elude me. Those ears of yours aren't the only thing that make you *stand out*." She brushed her finger against the tip of Kyoku's pointed ear. The leathery texture of her skin sent a terrifying chill through him. Kyoku turned his head and glanced back at Retallor Tower, its windows veiled by thick metal plates. "Don't worry about your little friend. He will be just fine in there. Those who oppose him in that building currently are nothing but flies to him now."

"Okay. Will you put me down now?"

"Gladly." She bent her knee, and with one swift motion, tossed Kyoku from the rooftop.

He let out a harrowing cry in surprise as he fell but was quick to regain his composure. This was not the first time he had fallen from a high place. He stabilized his hands with the intent to create a shift in the wind and propel himself upward, but the magic would not come. *A fluke*, he thought, *a malfunction from the stress I was just put under, it seems.* He instead tried a simpler solution: to warp himself far away from there. Again, his magic disobeyed his will. His heart dropped. He looked down at the pavement rapidly approaching. His thoughts escaped him and his mind felt foggy, as though he were in a helpless dream. He closed his eyes tight—impact was imminent.

Kyoku felt his legs buckle beneath him, and his body went limp. He opened his eyes, surprised to be alive, and saw a great blue foot plant down before him. He was sweating profusely, and his brain felt inflamed with pain. He glanced up at the blue creature standing over him, then looked about himself. He was on the rooftop where he had been moments prior.

He watched as a taloned foot loomed over him; the shadow it cast was cold and dark. Without a word, it came down hard upon his left arm. Kyoku's eyes wavered as he felt his elbow snap and the surrounding bones fracture beneath the weight. He screamed, though the pain had not fully set in beyond what seemed to be an electric shock that coursed through his whole body.

"Let that be a warning to you as to what might happen should you not heed my request," the creature said coldly. She lifted her foot from his broken arm and was gone in an instant.

Kyoku laid there in shock, his mind overwhelmed by the tincture of agony and bewilderment it had taken in. He tried to push himself up with one arm, taking care not to move his shattered left. To his surprise, the pain had all but gone the moment he sat up. He reached to touch his broken arm with hesitation, his hand trembling as he did so. The mind-numbing pain he anticipated did not come. Even the memory of the pain seemed to fade by the moment.

He stood up, clutching his arm, and looked down at the street below as if he were remembering something from a fleeting dream. The northern corner of the wall was visible from where he stood. He was expected to arrive in less than three minutes, a feat he could do easily, should his magic not fail him again. His eyes squinted—with the flick of his wrist, a small pop of air blew the dust at his feet away. He sighed, "Was that part of the dream too?"

There was no other choice for him, it seemed. He gave Retallor Tower a final glance, just noticing that the communicator in his ear was no longer functioning. He pulled it out and glanced at it; the circuits were fried.

A moment later, he would appear outside the walls in the place he was expected.

*

Oglis was standing there at a point where the beach and the farmland converged. The trees around her stood as her peers, accentuating her stature. Reddened leaves littered the ground, concealing her taloned feet. "Good. You came. I knew you were *intelligent*."

Though he had been bested by her mere minutes prior, Kyoku did not cower in her presence. He was fed up with how prolonged this ordeal was becoming. "Yes, I am here, just like you asked. Now, just who are you—*what* are you, and what do you want from me?"

She uncrossed her arms, which brought Kyoku's attention to the fact that her left arm was far shorter, appearing as nothing more than a stub that ended at the elbow. "My name is Oglis Inima. I was once a galactic sentry, commanding my fleet to conquer worlds for thousands of years—"

"So, is that why you're here? To take over this world?" Kyoku interjected in fraught anger, though he rued the thought of another terrible foe entering the already bleak picture.

Oglis' voice remained calm in the face of his hostility, "My days of conquering are long past. I have since been recruited to serve a *higher* purpose."

"Okay," Kyoku said with much relief. "What does that *purpose* have to do with me?"

Oglis seemed to ignore the question. "You see, I am in the business of finding things—important treasures with the power to defy destiny itself." The word *destiny* made Kyoku's ears perk up. It was his most hated concept, something that gave hope to the hopeless, while also staying them from the path of hard work and dedication. "I've come to this world seeking an important piece of the puzzle—two pieces, in fact." Kyoku did not speak a response aloud. His mind merely contemplated Oglis' words as if *they* were the true puzzle. "I have something to show you that will help you understand, a place where we can speak more on the matter and how it pertains to you."

Oglis waved her three-pronged hand, the massive tendril-like fingers aglow with a light as yellow as her eyes. A portal as tall as she opened from thin air where she stood. "Come with me, Kyoku." She said without a stutter in her voice. Hearing his name unaltered made the cogs in his mind cease to spin. It was then that Oglis truly attained his interest. She vanished into the portal, leaving him to decide his fate.

The yellow energy swirled in a mesmerizing pattern before him. He knew not what lay beyond it, but for that moment, he did not think of the risks or calculate any probabilities. He kicked his foot forward and stepped through the light.

Chapter 4: Ximen Judd

Barnov sped through the streets of the High District, spinning the steering wheel of the van hard as he took desperate turns. Sara sat beside him in the passenger seat with eyes unfocused. The sight of those streets unearthed the awful memories of *the halvening;* the kind that often haunted her dreams. The overwhelming mixture of emotions simply resulted with orneriness, something she couldn't help but let out through her tone when she spoke.

"Can't this damn thing go any faster?" She seethed, pounding her fist on the rattling dash. The whole van warbled with uncertainty whenever Barnov maneuvered it in any way.

"No, it can't!" Barnov cried, trying to steady the wheel while the van sputtered through a plight of turbulence. "Be thankful if we can make it there *at all!*" His brow was thick with sweat, a new symptom of stress Sara noticed ever since they both escaped certain death only two weeks ago.

Sara shifted her lips in annoyance, but kept her mouth shut, knowing that fussing would do neither of them any favors. She hung her head out the open window to check on the van. This was not the pristine chariot HDHD once supplied them with. In fact, High District's High Definition News was no more. The vibrating mess of Ather-tempered metal and bolts that they rode instead was all Barnov could afford when HDHD disbanded and repossessed all of its equipment.

Sara sighed. *How we've fallen. From the top of the news world, to the lowest depths of hell on earth,* she thought. But she was not alone. Nearly all of the Retallor-owned businesses had closed their doors since Retallor

Tower's downfall. What remained of the Retallor legacy were the many Ather-driven factories and RM Marts throughout Last Thesi. The factories that produced foodstuffs were autonomous, requiring only a handful of workers to operate. What's more, the Retallors had a monopoly on the food production industry—and Last Thesi needed food, even if only a scarce amount of its people remained.

"I wonder how the silver spoon-fed shareholders are holding up. Probably tucked away in their bunkers with their riches and feasts and servants at their beck and call. I hope they all go mad," Sara muttered to herself.

"What? Who?" Barnov questioned, glancing over at Sara. The split second he took his eyes off the road caused the van to veer left, as if possessed to end its suffering against one of the many abandoned office buildings within the High District. He gasped and twisted the wheel hard to the right to narrowly avoid crashing.

"It's nothing," Sara said with a frown that accentuated the wrinkles at the corners of her mouth; wrinkles that she could no longer hide. Not only had they lost the cameras, the microphones, and the van, but the expensive makeup as well. Because of that, Sara looked much unlike herself; even her voluptuous golden hair that once glistened in the sun now looked flat and unkempt as the black roots rose from her scalp. "How much longer until we arrive?" she asked, her voice cooling down ever so slightly.

"Not long," Barnov assured. "Do you think it's really going to happen?" His voice shrunk down, as though some omnipresence was eavesdropping. "Do you really think the leader of the Runic Guard will be there?"

Sara shrugged. "That's what was broadcasted across every TV and radio station. *The leader of the Runic Guard will host a live press conference outside of the Central Tower today at four P.M.*"

Barnov was grimacing. "And you don't think that ... maybe it's a trap of some sort? What if they're bringing us all out there to execute us?" He shuddered.

"Well, if they are, at least it'll be a public execution, since every news camera in the city will be pointed at that tower."

Barnov inflated his big belly and let out an elongated sigh. The van's engine shut off at the end of his exhale—they had arrived at the gate. Within the shadow of the enormous wall that caged the High District, one might think night was nigh. There were a plethora of other vehicles parked all around the gate; vans with logos and business names painted both professionally and crudely, minimalist cars with only two seats, and even rental motorbikes, to name a few.

Two guards were posted outside, eyeing anyone who came near the gate. One of them approached the driver's side window. "No vehicles are permitted within the Parade Grounds. You'll have to park it here and walk the rest of the way like everyone else."

"I know, I know. Can't you see that I'm already parked?" Barnov pushed open the van's door with a loud metal screech. He shooed the guards away as he aggressively circled around to the back of the van where he had the equipment stashed. Sara joined him as he pulled his camera from the back. It shone in the little bit of sunlight there was, appearing as though it were brand new, completely out of place within the rundown van.

"Is *that* why you can't afford a properly functioning news van?" Sara scoffed, though she found it hard not to fawn at the beautiful piece of equipment.

"Yes, it is. The *van* won't be capturing you in front of Central Tower in high definition, though, will it?" He winked as he hoisted the camera onto his broad shoulder.

Sara gave the beginnings of a smirk before reverting her expression into a scowl. "Well, maybe we can ride the camera home when the van breaks down." She said, shooting the rickety heap of metal a glare before strutting towards the gate.

Much like Barnov, Sara had her own *equipment*, funded by her own pockets. Her purple blazer was immaculate, smelling of flowers, with a perfect crease that lined up with the crease in her matching pants. She psyched herself up as she made her way to the gate. By the time she arrived, she was ready to take on the world—or the end of the world, should it so happen.

"What organization are you two with?" one of the guards asked with a snicker, giving their shoddy van a glance.

Sara ignored the man's belittling tone. "We're independents. Now, open up the gate, *guard*," she said, the final word flying from her tongue like a venomous dart. She knew just how to make any word sound like an insult. The guard's expression soured at her command, but he heeded it all the same. The barred gate rose before her, and she stepped inside while giving a signal with her hand for Barnov to follow. Her scowl warped into a victorious smirk once the gate was closed behind them.

Lights within the tunnel guided them through the twisting innards of the wall. They passed by many closed gates along the way, ones that barred entry to places Sara did not know. For now, she was not interested in such mysteries. Instead, she pushed onward, seeking the sunlit end of the catacomb.

When Sara and Barnov emerged from the tunnel into the Parade Grounds, they were berated by the murmurs of the crowd gathered around Central Tower. The metal fence that normally protected the tower was gone, as well as the motion sensor alarm that signaled the Runic Guard to dispatch any intruders. Sara scanned the crowd, unsurprised to see so many familiar faces. *Every reporter and news crew member that survived the halvening must be here,* she thought. It was a spectacle like she had never witnessed before.

She circled around the tower with Barnov in tow as she tried to listen in on whatever gossip was spreading, all while searching for a door where their scoop would appear from. It was a chore to discern coherent thoughts from the garbled mess of overlapping voices, but it was a skill Sara felt that every good reporter must have. She first heard doubts and concern running rampant through the throngs of people:

"Is it really safe to be here?"

"I don't see any doors or windows on the tower. How can we expect anyone to show up here?"

Those notions began to take a chilling shift as unease and restlessness took hold of the crowd.

"I don't feel so good."

"Whenever I look at the tower my head starts to hurt."

"Is it just me or are the walls moving farther away from us?"

"Knock it off. You're making *me* feel weird now!"

"Don't worry. You're just nervous."

"It's just the heat, I'm sure."

Sara touched the back of her hand to her forehead, starting to feel woozy herself. The air was stiflingly hot in that cramped space around the tower, but that wasn't all; a grim tension filled the air and everyone in the vicinity seemed to feel it.

"Are you okay Sara? You look a bit flush," she heard a voice say. She whipped around to snap at Barnov, only to find that it was not him who spoke.

"*Mindy?*" Sara asked dumbfounded.

"Yeah, it's me." Mindy drew her eyes to the ground in embarrassment. She looked like a shell of her former self. The young woman who once erupted into the news world and swiped the title of HDHD's most famed reporter—the woman Sara vied against ever since, now appeared frumpy, gaunt, and altogether downtrodden. Her dark hair was flat without any shine to it and uncharacteristically wavy in places, with ends that were tired and frayed. Blemishes were scattered all over her brown cheeks and she had deep, dark bags beneath her eyes. Even her prized, perky breasts appeared deflated.

Sara's eyes were drawn away from Mindy's imperfections to the only place on her that remained immaculate: the dark green blazer that she was known for. It was crisp and unsullied, unlike the rest of her. The sight of it made Sara smile weakly, for at the end of the day, Mindy was still a professional, as much as any of them could be during such trying times, at least.

The shock of seeing Mindy in such a state made Sara forget the question she had asked her for a moment. When she came to, at last, she responded, "I'm fine, thanks. But ... you—what happened?" She was unable to restrain the concern in her voice for her rival.

"I know ... I'm a mess," Mindy said abashed. "I just ... Things haven't been the same since ..."

"That day ..." Sara finished, trying not to let her mind be corrupted by the gruesome memories of that traumatic event.

Tears were forming in Mindy's green eyes; eyes that looked like they had been stripped of their youthful fire. "I ... watched my whole crew be killed. They each threw their lives away so that I could escape. But *why?* I was so helpless ... and worthless. Why would they do that for me?" She hung her head low in self-loathing.

"Because you're a woman—as in, you can't contract the madness," Sara said bluntly.

Mindy reeled at Sara's stern response, but it seemed just what she needed to lift her spirits. She wiped the tears from her eyes saying, "I guess that makes more sense. I never thought of it that way. I was so afraid that they thought my life was more valuable than theirs, either because of my status or because I was their superior."

Mindy's fear struck a chord with Sara. She experienced a similar sense of guilt and loathing when Barnov did all he could to save her, despite how easily he could have escaped without her. Sara's eyes were getting rheumy just recalling how she felt at the time. She glanced down for a moment, then brought her eyes back up to meet Mindy's, which were puffy, red, and full of tears. Sara shook her head, saying, "Everyone at HDHD loved you. You were a part of our family—a younger sister to everyone—even me. That's the true reason your crew tried to save you. Try not to mistake their love for adoration."

Mindy smiled weakly, and for a brief moment, she appeared as vibrant as she once was. "Thank you, Sara. That means a lot, especially coming from you. I—"

"Mindy! Look there!" a man cried from behind her. She turned around and Sara saw that it was Ronaldo, Mindy's vigilant cinematographer, who beckoned her.

Sara's glance shot towards the great red tower. There was not much to see beyond the many raised cameras and upturned heads. What she did see was that the crowd was backing away from the tower in unison.

Barnov brandished his pristine camera and began to walk closer to the crowd, "C'mon Sara, get behind me. I'll lead the way through."

Sara followed behind the stocky man. One thing Barnov excelled at was muscling his way through a crowd; whether it was pedestrians at the scene of an accident or other reporters tightly packed together outside of a Runic Tower, he was tough as a bulldozer. Barnov pushed and shoved his way through, all the while making sure his camera went untouched. Not after long, he and Sara broke into the front line of the reporters, where many of them stood with mouths agape, staring at the sight

Searching for The Eminent: The Collapse of Reality 51

before them: a lone man stood behind a podium of white marble.

The man was older, with thick white hair that had an unearthly blue tint to it, the same tint that seemed to lurk beneath his wrinkled pale skin. His grey eyes were sunken, looking tired, yet full of resolve. The clothes he wore looked militant, like something a general out of the days of old would have donned to lead a company of soldiers; a weathered navy blue jacket with long sleeves with pants to match and a dark red scarf that stuck out of his collar and fell upon the white button up shirt he wore beneath it.

The man's gaze alone made the crowd reel with terror as they inched away from the tower, as if to escape his leering eyes. He gripped the podium with his rough hands, elbows bent and head low as he scanned the sea of reporters. After he pushed himself back up and straightened his posture in a militant fashion, he spoke with a sturdy, gravelly voice, full of commanding confidence. "Welcome, citizens of Last Thesi. Thank you all for coming here today after such short notice. My name is Ximen Judd, and I am the leader and founder of the Runic Guard." The crowd was deathly silent. Some reporters looked as though they wanted to turn tail and run, while others held their sickness in and stood their ground uncomfortably. "These are desperate times we live in, and desperation must be met with an iron will—that I know for certain. What else I know for certain, is that this city lacks such a will. This city lacks the military might to protect itself from harm. It's run by politicians and businessmen, those who skirted by on the coattails of the late Irol Retallor's good fortune.

"I founded the Runic Guard to put an end to that, to bring protection to *all* of Last Thesi, regardless of their wealth or status. You must be asking yourselves, *why* or *how?* You see, long ago, I fought in the war for this great city against the treacherous *Nomads*. I fought alongside the Eminent. I saw his power firsthand and recognized it for what it truly was: not some superhuman feat—but Ather, pure and simple. I've since harnessed that power for the sake of the city, giving birth to the Runic Guard—an army of superhumans, ready to do whatever it takes to ensure this city survives."

There was a silence in the Parade Grounds that only that name could cause—*the Eminent*, a title of superstition, even amongst reporters these days. There had been no news about the Eminent since his inconspicuous death years ago. Many of the citizens who did know of the fabled superhuman considered the stories of him to be exaggerated myths more than anything else. Sara, too, found herself a part of that hive mind at one point—but lately, her speculations regarding Rekston Curse rose, and hearing Ximen Judd's mention of him only fueled those thoughts.

Ximen Judd stood before the silent crowd, his iron will and deadly eyes unwavering. He cleared his throat and spoke again. "I think now would be a good time for me to take a few questions from the crowd. I, unlike the late mayor, do not fetishize hearing my own voice, so why don't we have a little back and forth?" The crowd remained silent, terrified even, at the notion, as though Ximen Judd's proposition were some kind of trap. "Who wants to go first? Don't be shy. I will answer any question you may have to the best of my ability." He eyed the crowd, creating a wave of bashfulness as heads shied away from his cold gaze.

Sara stepped forward from the sea of cold footed reporters. Though she felt as nervous as the rest of them, her desire to seek the truth trumped all other instincts. All eyes behind and around her shifted upon her, and in a way, it gave her strength, as if all the other reporters were channeling what little courage they had in their hearts into her. Each camera lens that targeted her seemed to make her grow an inch taller, until she met eye to eye with Ximen Judd.

Sara's mouth was so dry that when she opened her mouth, she feared that nothing would come out but dust, but she didn't care; even if her voice were husked and laced with fear, she would make herself heard. When she spoke, the words seemed to pour out of her soul, exuding the confidence that once made her famous. "Mr. Judd, my name is Sara Stone, an independent reporter based in the High District. It would appear that your knowledge of Ather is second to none, even more than the Retallors who adapted it into nearly every aspect of life in Last Thesi over the years. So, my question to you is in regard to this mysterious resource we call Ather. Could you tell us the origin of Ather, and what implications Ather might have in relation to the madness that has assaulted the population for the last five years?" After the words left her mouth, the spirit that seemed to possess her had all but gone, leaving her feeling small and fragile before Ximen Judd's stoic glare. She wanted to shrink down and recede back into the crowd, but she forced herself to stand tall for the cameras, and for the sake of the city.

Ximen Judd's grey eyes lit up. He clapped his hand on the podium, causing a shockwave of palpitation through the crowd. "Those are magnificent questions, my dear. Let's begin with the first one: *the origins of Ather*. The answer to that is simple: The Eminent is the origin of Ather—he birthed it into our world, excreting it from his body whenever he used his superhuman powers—and it never leaves. Ather will forever rise from the wreckage of old buildings, out from the sewers, and even from the leftover debris of food on our fingertips. It is infinite, which is why it can be recycled from the air and repurposed infinitely. But despite how incredible it is,

Ather is not without faults. It can be tampered with—poisoned, in fact!"

Murmurs began to circulate throughout the crowd, once again emboldening Sara's heart. She grew tall again, tall enough to speak on behalf of the entire city when she asked, "Are you implying that the Retallors were *poisoning* the Ather?"

"Yes!" Ximen Judd cried to the audible gasps that filled the Parade Grounds. He spoke louder now, his words eclipsing the crowd's outrage before it could manifest fully. "That is exactly what I am implying, but not *only* implying! My men have found proof of such foul deeds within the Retallor's vacant tower, amongst many other secrets they had kept from the people of Last Thesi."

Ximen Judd shot a powerful gaze at Sara, both finalizing his answer and commanding her to step back. She let out a deep sigh of relief, as though her life had just been spared. Sara wanted to collapse on the white brick of the Parade Grounds, and she might have if Barnov had not lent her a shoulder to lean on. He gave his silent approval in the form of a thumbs up, his camera still fixed upon Ximen Judd.

"Next question!" Ximen Judd commanded, sounding exhilarated after his first response. His bold voice silenced the murmuring crowd, relegating the other reporters to cower as they desperately scrawled in their notepads. All but one, that is. This time it was Mindy who stepped forward, her dark skin glistening with sweat before the scrutiny of the Runic Guard's leader.

"Yes, Mr. Judd, I have a question. My name is Mindy Chakrabarti, a former representative of HDHD news in the High District, a news effort that was owned by the Retallor Corporation. Could you explain more about what your *men*, who I presume to be the Runic Guard, found within Retallor Tower, and do those findings have any connection to the recent horrific outbreak of madness that erupted throughout all of Last Thesi two weeks ago?"

Sara smiled at the fire she saw in Mindy's eyes, at the young reporter's trembling fist clenching onto a tape recorder beneath her mouth. At that moment, for the first time, Sara saw Mindy as a reflection of herself and was reminded of the true meaning of being a news reporter. She no longer saw her as an obstacle in the path to reclaim success, but instead, as an equal in the pursuit of truth.

Ximen Judd's demeanor remained the same in the face of Mindy's question as it had with Sara's. "Another great question, young lady. I believe that the time for secrets has long passed here in Last Thesi. I will withhold no information—for the sake of our survival. With that said, my men found many things when they scoured Retallor Tower days after it went dark. There were abandoned labs where we discovered research regarding genetic modification using Ather, weapon production, and even machines that ran on human life itself! After seeing what nefarious schemes they had stored in their steel fortress, it became clear that the Retallors did not have the people of Last Thesi's best interest in mind. It is without question, in fact, that the Retallors sought to exterminate the population, save for a select few, and rebuild the city in their image. And thus, the *madness* was born—a disease carefully crafted by their mad scientists, one that they could administer to all the population through the poisoned Ather products they produced! Every crumb of food they serve you, every drop of sweet nectar they tempt you with, all at prices too low to pass up, each bring you one step closer to madness." The crowd went wild with disgust. People spat their drinks and threw their crumbly cakes to the floor, repulsed at the thought that they were ingesting poison. Sara felt her stomach sour, thinking back on the bag of greasy snacks Barnov offered her on the drive down that she was far too famished to pass up.

"But why not women, or children, you ask? Why are they unaffected by the madness? Because the Retallors built the disease that way! If they want to build a new city, they need women to reproduce, and children to mold into hard working laborers, ready to break their backs to raise the Retallor legacy from the ashes of the Irol Age. Still don't believe me? Then ask yourself this: how many cases of the madness have been reported since the day regarded as *the halvening?* Not a one, my sources say. *Why?* Because that massive spread of madness was the Retallors' master stroke! It went into effect the moment their tower sealed itself up. Thank the gods for whatever stopped it and saved the half of Last Thesi that survived that wretched day. This is your awakening, citizens of Last Thesi, and it is a rude one, unfortunately." With that, Ximen Judd pounded the podium with his fist before sweeping his white hair back, saying, "I'll take one more question."

A timid-looking man emerged from the rowdy crowd. His knees were quaking, and he couldn't look Ximen Judd in the eyes when he spoke. "M—Mr. Judd, I—I'm a reporter with S—sunset Press in the Middle District. Steven Pole is my name. I—Well, you mentioned that you founded and led the Runic Guard, which has been a mysterious, and to be frank, fear-inspiring organization since its inception. Not a lot is known about the Runic Guard. In fact, there aren't even any reports on if the *men* within its ranks are men at all. Who are the Runic Guard? *What* are they?"

Ximen Judd did not turn his gaze upon the apprehensive reporter, as if knowing that doing so might cause the poor man to faint. Instead, he spoke his response for all those in attendance. "That might be the best question of all, one I need not answer with words alone. Instead, allow me to *show* you!" Ximen Judd spread his arms at length and raised them up, shouting, "Runic Guard, assemble!" Out of thin air appeared six masses of blue light, three on either side of him. They floated in the air above the heads of all the awestruck reporters, shimmering like brilliant stars. Their bodies resembled the shape of elongated shadows, full of cosmic dust that became blindingly bright when looked at from certain angles. A sword extended from each of their ethereal limbs. It was the iconic sword depicted on the crest of the Runic Guard; blue and radiant, with white wings at the hilt.

Terror filled Sara's heart at the sight of their blades. Were Barnov's fears about to become true? Would they all be executed on the spot? She thought to turn around and try to escape what felt like certain death, but a moment later, the six Runic Guard were gone. Horrified shouts sounded from the edges of the crowd and Sara spun around to see what had happened. The six executioners had moved faster than the eye could track to surround the reporters, blocking them in from every angle.

Sara struggled to breathe, her eyes bulging so much that they threatened to fall from her head. She gripped onto Barnov's denim jacket as the crowd moshed this way and that, attempting to retreat from the Runic Guard. She felt like a ragdoll being pulled and shoved by two quibbling siblings, her mind blanking more by the moment. She stared up helplessly at the Runic Tower; red clay with enigmatic blue patterns etched all over it, its spire thrust deep into the heavens, nowhere in sight.

Amidst all the trepidation that washed over the crowd, Ximen Judd cleared his throat loudly and spoke again. "I think it's time this press conference came to a close." Screams and gasps rang through the crowd, as all of them feared this to be their final moment. "Runic Guard—stand down! Allow our guests safe passage to return from whence they came." At his command, the six guards relaxed their threatening auras and drew away from the crowd and returned to him. "I thank you all for coming and speaking with me today. In place of these kinds of inconvenient gatherings, I have been working on a remedy. Soon, I plan to open up a direct communication line to Central Tower, where any citizen can phone in to speak their concerns to me directly. I hope when that time comes, I can rely on you all to get the *news* out," he said with something resembling a chuckle. "Now, depart, and remember: the Runic Guard serves you, and all of Last Thesi!" With that word, the six guards surrounded him, obscuring him from sight. They vanished with the blink of an eye, and when the curtain of blue sparkling terror was drawn, Ximen Judd and his marble podium were gone too.

No one was quicker to depart than Sara and Barnov. The moment Ximen Judd was gone, Sara pulled Barnov to act as a plow to part the crowd so they could exit the grounds. The rest of the reporters and news crews acted shortly after, following not far behind Sara and Barnov through the gated tunnel that led back to the High District. Sara didn't say a word, her whole body tense with anxiety, feeling the wrinkles on her mouth and brow growing deeper by the moment.

They raced for Barnov's tired jalopy of a news van, hoping to beat the rush of traffic that was soon to depart from the corner of the High District. Sara waited impatiently in the passenger's seat while Barnov carefully packed his camera in the back as if it were a newborn baby. She scowled at him as he entered the van, though her eyes softened when she realized the distress that still lingered on his sweaty face.

"Let's get out of here," Barnov said as he struck the ignition with his finger. The van's engine rattled and sputtered before guttering out. He raised an eyebrow, his cheeks and ears growing flush, then pushed the button again. The engine did the same as before, this time with a loud cough or two sounding out of the van's tailpipe. "Oh no," he said, his voice deflated.

"What's the problem?" Sara asked, looking around at the other vehicles starting to crowd the narrow streets behind their parked van. Such a small area was not meant for any sort of traffic. "Gosh, getting out of here is going to be a nightmare at this rate."

Barnov let out a deep sigh. "Tell me about it. I'm just glad we got out of *there*. Though, now it looks like we're stuck. The engine sounds like it's dead—or dying. Do you have anyone you can call that could help us out?"

Sara frowned, no longer able to keep down all the stress that had built up within her, she exploded. "No! I don't have anyone to call! Almost everyone I know is dead by now! Just looking at the contacts on my phone and imagining what terrible, lonely deaths they all suffered makes me want to vomit! Why don't we call the Runic Guard? Ring up Ximen Judd's direct line." She mockingly held up her thumb and extended pinky to the side of her face. "*Excuse me, Mr. Judd, could you send one of your death-dealing strobe lights to come pick us up and fly me to my apartment across town? You can drop the fat one off at Club Tower along the way. Great! thanks.*"

Sara's chest was rising and falling hard by the time she was finished, and her eyes were seeing red. From the corner of her eye, she saw Barnov dejectedly looking down at his feet, his head slumped against the steering wheel. Her rage passed as quick as it came on, and she felt a fool for how she acted. "I ... I'm sorry. I didn't mean to yell at you. I'm just ..."

"Stressed," Barnov finished. "I know. I am too. It's okay to let it out, ya know? Don't worry. I'll figure something out. Just try to relax while I go check under the hood." He made to exit the van, but the sound of a honking horn made him freeze in place. Both he and Sara looked outside to find a clean, white van parked beside them. Mindy rolled down the passenger window and popped her head out.

"You two need a lift?" she asked with a smile. Sara and Barnov turned to one another without uttering a response. "Go on, leave that bucket of bolts and get in."

Sara's mind was so rattled that she didn't remember exiting Barnov's van or entering Mindy's. The next thing she remembered were Mindy's words to her as they inched at a snail's pace behind the long line of cars.

"I'm glad we waited," Mindy said. "When everyone else was racing to funnel out of the Parade Grounds, I was still busy jotting down notes on the key points from Ximen Judd's responses to all of our questions. I'd love to hear your take on it all, Sara."

"*My take?*" Sara said with contempt. "My take is that I don't trust him any more than I ever trusted the Retallors. Why wait until the Retallors are out of the picture before telling us the *truth* about Ather?"

"Because that way he can create his own narrative, unchallenged, right?" Mindy laughed.

"Exactly." Sara smirked back, her anger dampened by the comradery she felt in finding that she and Mindy were like-minded when it came to Ximen Judd.

"You know, Sara, I believe your story about what happened to you and your crew in Retallor Tower; about Cecil killing Welzig and about the lone man assailing the tower."

Sara reeled, her heart skipping a beat. "Really? You read my report? After all the news stations threw my story in the trash and called me crazy, I thought I was finished. I'm trying to make it on my own, but it's hard to be heard when the world no longer trusts your voice."

"Yeah, I did," Mindy's voice matched the sad look in her eyes. "That was actually the reason I've been trying to talk to you—because I believe you, even though nobody else does. They think the halvening drove you insane—though, maybe it drove us all a *little* insane," she said with a weak chuckle. "I want to help you uncover the truth and make sure all the world hears it and remembers it long after we're all gone. I think there's a story here that could change the world—maybe even save it."

"I—Thank you. It means a lot to hear that somebody is on my side."

"Of course," Mindy smiled. "So, what's the next step then? Do you have any leads?"

Sara looked down, the gears turning in her head, trying to put together the intricate puzzle of a story; each piece felt like it was made of smoke being held together by the wispy cobwebs of long extinct spiders. She looked Mindy in the face with eyes full of determination and stated, "I do. A big lead—so big that I think it could be the key to cracking this story."

"For real?" Mindy asked, a glimmer in her eyes. "What is it?"

"Not *what*," Sara began, "but *who*. If we're going to find the truth, we're going to need to begin our search—for the Eminent!"

Chapter 5: Sunny Day

Cathy wiped the sweat from her brow with a sigh after having toiled away at cleaning all the vacant tables in Barbier's Soup Coop in preparation for the dinner rush. She hung her tired head forward, getting so close to the polished wood that she could smell the disinfectant upon its surface. But it wasn't a thankless job. Barbier was as generous as his wealthy farmer of a father; he made sure all of his workers were paid and fed every day, even if he had to take money from his own pocket.

The music and mirth seemed to rush back to her all at once the moment Cathy lifted her head up. The Coop had been getting more attention as of late as word of Barbier's wondrous recipes spread from the slums all the way to the far end of the Middle District—and they featured more than just soup. Dishes of fish or chicken over stewed greens recently became a permanent addition to the menu, which brought pleasant thoughts and warmth to Cathy's heart. It was the reminder that Ikeh, the little boy she and Kyoku brought back from the Shattered Coast, had truly made an impact on the world—more so than she herself ever hoped to.

Between tending to Rekco's bedside, the busyness of work, and all the other chaos that had spread throughout Last Thesi as of late, Cathy hadn't been able to find the time to visit the farmland and see how Ikeh was doing. She prayed that he was okay and that the halvening had not caused him irreparable trauma, or worse.

She glanced up at a TV mounted in the upper corner of the room. The news station it broadcasted silently played a repeat of Ximen Judd's press conference, so as not to disturb the merry band playing on the stage beside it. She saw the black and white subtitles pass along the bottom of the screen as the Runic Guard's leader spoke, but she couldn't make out the words from so far away. Such technology felt so foreign to her, as did much of the other new clothes and devices that made its way into the slums since the wall segregating it from the Middle District fell.

There were more TVs in the lounge upstairs, all of which only seemed to broadcast news stations. It was no surprise, though, for the news had been good as of late. For the first time in a long time, hope circulated within Last Thesi. There had not been a single report of madness since the halvening. It seemed that Ximen Judd's claims about the mysterious disease were correct, despite how little faith Cathy had in the Runic Guard. Just imagining the thought that the Retallors could have been poisoning the people of Last Thesi made her fume.

She looked around the room at all the unfamiliar faces. Everyone was smiling and laughing with their bowls of food and mugs full of drink. It made her feel like something was wrong with her. *Shouldn't I be happy like the rest of them? I survived the end of the world, but why me over anyone else?* It was known that women and persons under the age of sixteen could not contract the madness, so to her, her survival felt unwarranted. She had not fought harder or planned better than anyone else who did not make it, yet she lived.

The guilt gnawed at her as her eyes were drawn to the shrine dedicated to the patrons and workers alike that were lost on that horrid day. A picture of Farooq sat among the many other faces she had seen during their final maddened moments. A voice called to her, breaking her free from her dejected trance.

"Hey Cathy! I'm glad I caught you before you left for the day. Could you do me a huge favor?"

She turned around, her head still swimming and feeling heavy. "Oh. Hey Latif. What's up?"

The bronze-skinned young man with short black hair before her was the Coop's newest bouncer. Latif stood only a hair or so taller than her, but he made up for it in bulk. He wore a tight white shirt with no sleeves to accentuate his muscles and show off his chiseled biceps. He was the son of a warrior who migrated from The Underground, and it showed. His wiry black mustache flapped as he spoke. "Oh, you know, just getting ready to take on another dinner rush," he said, turning his sharp jawline upward as he grinned. The gleam in his eyes guttered out when he remembered why he beckoned her in the first place. "Wait! I almost forgot! Barbier prepared a care package of food and supplies. Could you take it to," his voice got quiet, "*you know where?*"

Cathy furrowed her eyebrows at Latif. "You know you don't have to be so secretive. They aren't criminals, ya know?" The boisterous young man grew red in the face. Cathy laughed, the plight that had troubled her mind dispersing more with each passing moment. "Lighten up, will ya? I'd love to deliver the package. I was planning to swing by there on my way home."

Latif lit up, acting coy to his own embarrassment. "Great! Let me grab it for you then." He crouched down behind the serving counter and pulled up a hefty burlap sack from a low shelf. "There. Not too heavy, is it?"

"It's a little heavy, but I'll manage," Cathy said with a grin. The sack reminded her of the ones she was forced to wear as a child growing up in the orphanage. She often forgot that the gloomy orphanage she was raised and abused in once stood in the very place Barbier's Coop now shone. She shook the memories of that terrible place from her mind like a bad dream and turned from Latif, waving her hand. "I'll be going now. Be safe, Latif!"

Latif thumped his fist against his puffed out chest in salute, saying, "Will do! And you as well!"

Cathy turned back, tapping the upgraded steam gun hanging from her hip with her finger and gave a wink. "I always am! Later!"

"Later! Oh, and say hi to Bugbear for me!"

To her relief, a crowd had yet to gather outside of the Coop by the time she was leaving. The nearby streets were as quiet as ever, though the slums were much less gloomy overall lately. She glanced up at the sky. The suffocating brown smog that normally blanketed the sky was all but gone, replaced by wispy tendrils of fleeting grime smeared upon the horizon. In the vast distance, floating air purifiers could be seen above the blotches of buildings in the Middle District. She was not yet accustomed to the absence of the enormous brick wall that stood between the slums and the Middle District, but she was glad it was gone all the while.

Cathy had yet to venture beyond the border of the fallen wall. Whether she was still waiting for Rekco to go with her or was held back by the fear of seeing the Last Thesi that was hidden from her all her life, she was not sure. It was a thought not for her already overburdened mind.

She made her way to one of the many abandoned apartment complexes in the slums, along the way passing by the blocked off streets that led to the industrial part of the quadrant. She would have thought nothing of it had she not known the truth—that beyond those barricades was a great big hole that led to the ruined underground city beneath Last Thesi. When the Runic Guard raided The Underground, an explosion was set off that leveled much of the industrial area and shook the whole of the slums. News reports followed that said one of the rundown warehouses collapsed, causing the commotion, and that access to the area would be forbidden until further notice.

Cathy climbed up a flight of uneven metal stairs to the second story, where far down a row of doors loose from their hinges and shattered windows was a fortified steel door. The barred windows to the apartment were blacked out by tarps raised from the inside. She approached the door and banged on it with her fist. A moment later, a quiet voice, barely audible, came from behind it.

"How do you plan to stop the apocaly—"

"Shut up with that! It's me. Cathy," she interrupted. She could hear the overabundance of locks disengaging, then at last, the door creaked open. "Here. I brought supplies from the Coop," she said to the old doorman who took the sack from her and slunk away from his post without another word.

Cathy closed the door and locked it behind her. The tiny, dark room was empty and dingy, and there wasn't anyone around. The sound of faint voices could be heard from beneath the floorboards. She searched around the tired room for a grey rug and lifted it to reveal a trapdoor. When she swung the door open, the voices all stopped, and the air became still.

Cathy proceeded down into the hidden room, which was much less a room than it was an entirely separate apartment. The room was dimly lit and modestly furnished. When she emerged from the stairs into it, a joyous clamor rang.

"Cathy!" A woman's voice called. From the far edge of her sight came a dark-skinned young woman with wild, curly brown hair. She wrapped her arms around Cathy tight, squeezing the air out of her.

"H—hey Mikayla. It's good to see you too," she said with a wince.

"I'm so glad you're okay! You haven't come by since the—*you know*." Mikayla broke away from her and smiled, the medallion dangling from her neck bobbing with each step. It was an unusual thing, made up from a metal Cathy had never seen anywhere else, said to be derived from meteorite. Mikayla was one of the many refugees Rekco, Kyoku, and Zeke saved from The Underground when the Runic Guard attacked. She and Cathy became fast friends when Zeke first introduced them at the Coop—the very same day she and Dim were hiding out while Rekco and Kyoku took on the Retallors. Cathy was happy to meet another woman around her age after all these years of hardly meeting any women at all.

"I know. I've been fine. I was just so busy taking care of Rekco that I took off work for a couple weeks. I'm glad to see you're doing well too." Cathy looked around the room for a certain familiar face—or body, rather. "Where's Zeke?"

"He's in the command room. C'mon, this way." Mikayla led Cathy through a string of rooms where hosts of refugees were gathered, chatting by candle light, playing cards to pass the time, or resting their weary bodies. She was still stunned to see so many women amongst the survivors who escaped the fall of The Underground. It was said that men outnumbered women in Last Thesi ten to one, but within Zeke's hideout, they were fifty-fifty.

"I'm happy to see the numbers haven't dwindled here. Not many were lost during halvening, I take it?" Cathy asked.

"Nope, I don't think we lost any, actually. That lines up pretty well with what that Ximen Judd guy said, since the people of The Underground never ingested any food chock-full of Ather."

"*That guy*," Cathy said in a venomous tone, put off by how popular and well-trusted the Runic Guard had become all of a sudden. "I know I can't prove it, but something about what he said doesn't sit right with me.

It's just ... hard to believe someone who only just went public after all these years, ya know?"

"Oh, I know. I don't think anyone here truly believes everything he said, but like you said, it's hard to prove anything. The fact remains that nobody has gone mad since then, right? And since then, people on the surface seem happier. That is a relief in itself, don't you agree?"

Cathy had to remember that Mikayla was not like many of the other refugees who had never seen the light of day. She originally worked for the Queen of The Underground for a time, as a Doombringer, creating chaos throughout the city in hopes of driving a wedge between the people of Last Thesi and their tyrant overlords, the Retallors and the Runic Guard. Cathy wondered how many people Mikayla had seen gone mad and how many times she had to fight for her life to escape the clutches of the Runic Guard. "What about you? What do *you* believe?"

Mikayla stopped before a large, makeshift wooden gate acting as a door and turned to face Cathy. "To tell you the truth, I don't know *what* to believe or *who* to trust nowadays, other than Bugbear of course, but he's got his own plans—you'll see."

Hearing Zeke called by that name was still something she was not used to. The people of The Underground truly revered him, it seemed. It made her wonder what kind of secret lives anyone else she knew could have been leading.

Mikayla slid the wooden gate aside and she and Cathy entered. The room was vast, with a high ceiling. Hosts of rugged-looking men and women dressed in leather and fur stood around a great big table with a spotlight beaming onto it. Bugg Zeke stood at the helm of the table, dressed in a black shirt with brown slacks that were custom made to fit his mountainous stature. Cathy glanced back and wondered for a moment how someone as massive as Zeke even got into the building.

"Cathy!" Zeke's deep voice boomed with delight. "C'mere!" He beckoned, scooping her up between his giant bicep and forearm when she got close. "Got here just in time. Discussing some plans right now. Grab a seat if you want." He gestured to a chair that looked puny compared to him.

"Oh, I'm fine with standing," Cathy said. Feeling the eyes of stoic warriors upon her made her sweat more than the blistering light that hung overhead.

Zeke's soft expression hardened, and he drew a Zeke-sized sheet of rolled up parchment from his back pocket. He unfurled it on the table, saying, "Look. Here."

Cathy lit up at the sight. "A map?" The map depicted all the continents of the world, in a more detailed fashion than any of the maps she ever saw at the library in the slums. She got close to it, eyeing all the places she had never heard of before, places that were considered long forsaken to the people of Last Thesi. She looked at the picture of the Shattered Coast just north of the city, depicted as a crater. Inside it was the Awakki settlement, Benton, and the port of Olivard to the west of it. Cathy often wondered about what the world was like beyond the Plains of Thesi and the Forgotten Woods that surrounded it, but never sat down to look over a map like this one before.

"Right," Zeke nodded. Cathy shifted her lips with impatience when he didn't say anything more.

"What are you planning to do with a map, Zeke?" When she said the name, all the warriors turned their dagger-like gazes upon her once more. She had no intention of calling him by his underground nickname when all she knew him as was Bugg Zeke.

Zeke placed his normal-sized hand on the map, tracing his finger from Last Thesi eastward to the

Forgotten Woods, then beyond to the *Redlands*, as it was marked on the map. "An escape plan. In case anything were to happen—in case Last Thesi were to fall."

"*Fall?*" Cathy gulped. "Why would you expect that? What do you think is going to happen?" Her chest began to rise and plummet at the thought, and her heart grew heavy with anxiety.

Zeke shrugged. "Never know. The Underground fell too—outta nowhere. Have to plan for anything nowadays."

Cathy felt a mild relief in that there wasn't some kind of secret war being plotted. She gave a sigh and spoke weakly, "I see. So, is this where you would plan to go? The *Redlands?* Why there?"

"'Cause, it's not too far, and people used to live there not long ago. Already buildings, farm-ready land, and most importantly, no Ather. We could survive there. Could expand farther east if we have to without worry."

"Really? That doesn't sound too bad, actually." Cathy wondered if Zeke really came up with that plan by himself. She always knew him to be strong and soft-spoken, but never considered his intelligence.

"Yeah. And Barbier agrees. Said we could take seeds from the farm and chickens. Some of the refugees are working at the farm now, learning."

"But how do you plan to cross the Forgotten Woods? There's monstrous creatures in there—and those aren't just stories—they're real!" She shuddered just mentioning them and being forced to remember Rekco's recounting of the time he and Kyoku ventured into that abysmal place when they were kids.

"We know. We will request safe passage to the Redlands if we encounter creatures but will be prepared to fight if we have to." The warriors around the table all grunted and nodded with confidence, while clutching spears, axes, and other bludgeons.

Cathy felt a glimmer of hope for humanity after hearing Zeke's plan and was glad to know that it didn't involve attempting to overthrow or retake Last Thesi. The idea of leaving the city altogether and starting a new civilization elsewhere was one that never crossed her mind before. The thought of it made her heart leap, wanting to join the cause, but she knew Rekco wouldn't agree—not while he believed his father, the Eminent, still lived somewhere in Last Thesi.

"That sounds like a great plan, Zeke! Please let me know if there's anything I can do to help." Zeke responded with a thumbs up. Cathy turned to Mikayla, who was grinning behind her. "What do you think about leaving and starting new somewhere else?"

"Well, I'm not from Last Thesi, so I don't have any attachment to the place. In truth, I'd be glad to be away from it."

Cathy frowned, trying to imagine what it would be like to have her home town destroyed by the Runic Guard without any warning or reason. She feared that such a fate could happen anywhere in Last Thesi at this point, knowing what kind of power they have. "Even though I am from here, I kinda feel the same way. I wouldn't mind leaving either," she smiled for Mikayla's sake, who continued to beam at the thought. "By the way, I really should get going. I need to make sure Rekco is doing okay."

"Oh, right! You should! You're all he's got now, right?" Mikayla asked.

"Yeah ... I am," Cathy's voice became hollow, thinking of how devastated he would be if she left him to join Zeke's brigade, and how worried she would be about him all the while if she did.

"Well, c'mon then. I'll walk you out." Mikayla led the way out of the room and back the way they came. When they reached the steel door adorned with all its locks, she spoke again, "It was good seeing you again, Cathy. Be safe out there, and make sure to bring Rekco by once he's able. A lot of people here would be happy to see him. Wish him a speedy recovery from all of us."

"I will, for sure. And I'll tell him you said that. I'm sure that'll cheer him up," Cathy said with a smile. "By the way, Barbier is always looking for more workers at the Coop. I think it would be fun to work together."

Mikayla raised an eyebrow at the suggestion. "Eh? I'm not sure about that. I don't think waiting on others is my style anymore. Plus, there's a lot to be done here still. I'm learning to sew right now, ya know, so I can help repair clothes and maybe even make some new ones when we travel."

"Oh, I understand," Cathy said, feeling a little jealous, though she could not express why.

Mikayla seemed to take note of her change in tone. "But, hey, maybe we can still hang out sometime when things calm down a little more?"

"I'd love that! You know, I've been really wanting to check out the Middle District. I've never been there before. Would that be something you'd be interested in doing?"

Mikayla gave a weak snicker. "Maybe. I've been there once before, but it wasn't on the best of terms. I think seeing it as a civilian and not a *Doombringer* could be nice. Go on now, before any riffraff picks up on our voices from outside."

Cathy turned red and gave an abashed grin. "Right. I'll see you later then." The two hugged one last time and Cathy departed.

*

After a long day spent in the slums, the plains outside the city welcomed her. The fresh breeze that wafted the scent of the grass and budding Hope Lilies was still her favorite part of the day. The rolling hills that stood along either side of the dirt path to her home were littered with flowers this time of year, and for once, they seemed to toll with purpose—for there seemed to be hope in this dying world after all.

Cathy stared at the Forgotten Woods from atop a high hill that overlooked the wild grass that grew waist-high near Kyoku's dark abandoned cabin. The place looked as daunting as ever. She imagined herself being a part of Zeke's company as they made to traverse it to the Redlands on the other side, and what it might be like trying to calm the other noncombatants if chaos were to ensue. The thought didn't seem that bad to her.

She wanted to help but was unsure if it was fear or obligation that held her back. It was something she knew she would need to ponder more. Most of all, she wanted to hear what Rekco thought about Zeke's plan.

She carefully plodded down the side of the steep hill and continued her effort towards home. A hot bath sounded good right now. She had instinctively plucked a Hope Lily from the hilltop and tucked it behind her ear, only realizing it was there when she arrived at the last hill between her and a relaxing evening. It was a nervous habit, she knew, but still, she loved those flowers.

Upon reaching the top of the grassy knoll, Cathy let forth a surprised gasp. She saw a man standing outside her and Rekco's cabin. His hair was long and green as the leaves on the dark foreboding trees at the edge of the plains. She could scarcely see him swinging a sword at the air, all by his lonesome. She raced down the hill, almost falling on her face all the while, her mind trying to process what she was seeing.

Rekco had been fast asleep, bandaged and bedridden for the last week, hardly able to move a muscle to take a sip of water, so she knew it couldn't have been him. A faint notion in her troubled mind told her that man had to be *him*—Rekco's long lost father, *the Eminent*, returned after all these years. There was no other explanation perceivable in her mind. She felt her body growing thick with sweat as she anxiously hurried to the man. *I can't let him get away!*

Cathy's lungs ached by the time she reached the cabin. She could hear the swooshing of the blade cutting through the air, as the man faced away from her, still not taking notice of her presence. She gave a heaving sigh, which seemed to startle the man. He whipped around, pointing the bronze blade upon her, and her dire expression became confused.

Chapter 6: Level Head

"Rekco?!" Cathy cried in disbelief.

"Oh, it's only you," Rekco said, his expression softening as he lowered his sword. "Are you okay, Cathy? You look stressed."

"Wha—What are you doing out here?!" she stammered, her cheeks red with strain and laced with sweat, as though she had just run a mile. "How did you get out here? And what about your wounds? Where are your bandages and arm sling?"

"I'm all better now," Rekco said, stretching his arms up high to the setting sun in the orange and purple sky. "I feel like I just had the best sleep of my life!"

Cathy's eyes bulged with concerned rage as she stomped towards him, all the while resisting the urge to shove him. "*NO!* You're not! I saw you just this morning! I had to force water into your mouth because you were so dehydrated and weak that you couldn't do it yourself! And now you're nonchalantly swinging a sword outside? *How?*"

Rekco sheathed his sword in the damp earth, lowering his glance in embarrassment. "I ... don't know, actually. Something strange is happening to me, Cathy, and it's a little concerning." He stayed his eyes from hers, as if trying to come up with the words to express his thoughts, something she knew wasn't his strong suit.

"What do you mean? What exactly happened to you in Retallor Tower? The news never mentioned anything about you *or* Koku."

Rekco turned to face her once again, his eyes blazoned with newfound purpose. He stood straight and proper in a way that was unlike himself. "I want to tell you more than anything, but I'm not sure how to explain it. So instead—let me try to show you."

Cathy gulped, unsettled by how suspicious he was being. "Sh—show me what, exactly?"

"Just ... watch—and tell me what you see." Rekco took a deep inhale, turning his body slightly so it was no longer facing her head on. He stood for a moment, breathing slow and heavy. Cathy stared at him, unsure what to expect. The next moment, he was gone.

Cathy felt the grass rustle by her left foot and let out a sharp yelp as a skidding *thud* sounded just beside her. She nearly jumped out of her skin, leaping to the right while glancing down at what had touched her. There, she saw Rekco, splayed out on the ground, surrounded by an upheaval of grass and mud. He clambered to his feet while Cathy watched on dumbfounded.

"Wha—how did you?" she asked, hardly able to speak.

Rekco patted tufts of grass and dirt from his clothes after he stood up. "What did you see?"

"Nothing! One moment you were standing still, the next you were gone! I didn't see anything between the time you disappeared and reappeared on the ground next to me."

"I see," Rekco said in a deflated tone. "Let's go inside. I have a lot to tell you." He drew the bronze sword from the ground and returned it to the weapon's rack before retreating inside the cabin. Cathy followed behind, still discombobulated, but eager to hear Rekco's explanation.

*

Once inside, settled beside the crackling fireplace, Rekco recounted the tale of his ascent up Retallor Tower. He told Cathy about how, on occasion, the flow of time seemed to slow to a crawl during his battles with the Shadows and Welzig Retallor, allowing him to achieve victory against all odds. It was a phenomena that he had no name for, and could scarcely describe. All he knew for certain was that something inside him was changing—whether for better or worse, he did not know.

Next, he explained the dream he had where he was pitted against a blue creature that could speak the common language. He did his best to describe the monster's features to Cathy, but it didn't seem like she understood fully.

"That was just a dream, though," Cathy assured. "I seldom left your side during the first week you were recovering at home. I would've known if you went off to do battle with some—*alien*." She looked to be reflecting on her own words.

"But it felt so much more real than a dream!" he argued. "Plus, look at this!" He held up the black blade given to him when he was employed by the Retallors. The once straight sword was now warped and bent in the places where Oglis' beam struck it. There were cracks forming all throughout the so-called *unbreakable* metal.

"That ... must have happened at some point when you were in the tower. Maybe when Welzig was shooting at you with that massive gun? A weapon with that much power could've been able to damage the sword like that, right?"

"I don't know," Rekco responded, feeling frustrated with his own memories at that point. In truth, he could hardly remember anything from after he defeated Welzig Retallor, and even the memories from his trek up the tower were muddled.

"What about your injuries? I redressed your bandages just yesterday. The gunshot wounds were healing, sure, but there's no way you should be able to walk around the way you are right now."

Rekco lifted his shirt, having already forgotten about his wounds. He and Cathy glanced together at the places where he was struck amidst the foray of bullets Welzig fired upon him. They both gasped at the sight. There was nary a scar or scratch on him, as though it had never happened at all. Cathy babbled incoherently, as if she had witnessed a perplexing magic trick.

Rekco simply shook his head. "I can't explain that either. I feel fine, though. Trust me—better than ever before, really."

Cathy shifted her lips and clasped her hand to his forehead, her eyes darting upward in thought. "Even your fever is gone," she sighed, removing her hand and sitting back on the wood floor. "I—don't get it. And I don't trust it, either! What if Welzig shot you with some poisoned Ather mind control bullet?" She pinched her eyebrows together, straining with thought. "Well, even if that were the case, he's dead now so he couldn't—"

"Welzig's dead?" Rekco interrupted, shocked by the revelation Cathy so nonchalantly added.

"Oh, yeah. I forgot you've been out the last couple of weeks. Sometime after you left Retallor Tower, when the *halvening* happened and so many people went mad, that's when it happened. Nobody seems to know for sure how, but both Welzig and his brother Cecil Retallor were found dead in the mayor's office."

"*The halvening,* huh? Is that what they're calling it?" Rekco could suddenly feel the severity of how much time had passed him by while he was bedridden. The way Cathy casually mentioned such a catastrophic event made it seem like she had grown numb to death in a way he refused to, and it was no surprise, considering what she must have experienced that horrific day. The next question that came to mind filled him with dread, but he needed to know the truth. "And ... what about everyone else in Retallor Tower? Was there any news about what happened to them all?"

Cathy's lips thinned with reproach, knowing her words would drive a dagger into Rekco's heart. "They all ... died too. Reports say that there were *no* survivors found within Retallor Tower the day Welzig was found dead."

"Even the women and their unborn babies?" Rekco heard himself say in a trembling voice, though already certain of what the answer would be.

Cathy was frowning, her eyes rheumy. "Them too. Ximen Judd released a report about what the Runic Guard found within the tower. It all seemed to line up perfectly with your own story about the lab full of pregnant women and the staff of doctors that oversaw them. After that, the news could only assume that all the men in the tower had gone mad and killed everyone inside, before dying themselves." She wiped tears from her eyes. "Those poor women and their children. And to think that I almost ended up one of them. I guess I have Glenda Gace to thank for cutting me up in her jealous rage, unknowingly saving me from such a fate," she added, smiling weakly.

Rekco glanced at the tattoo of a beautiful red rose that concealed the gruesome scar on Cathy's right outer thigh. The reminder of the abuse she suffered at the hands of her despicable caretakers when she was a child set his heart ablaze until his skin felt hot with rage. That fire combated the overbearing guilt that weighed down on him now knowing the fate of all the people he tried to save from Mayor Welzig Retallor's clutches. His whole body trembled as though he could burst at any moment, a feeling that faded in an instant the moment he felt Cathy's soft touch upon his shoulder.

"None of this is your fault, okay?" She assured. "All of this falls on Welzig and his schemes to poison all of Last Thesi with his Ather."

Rekco lifted his head, puzzled. "Huh? What do you mean? And who is that *Ximen Judd* person you mentioned?"

Cathy grimaced with embarrassment. "Sorry! I keep forgetting that you don't know this stuff. I'll fill you in—"

her eyes shot to the radio on the kitchen table. "Or *maybe* I can let you hear for yourself." She got up and flicked the on switch then turned the dial until the gravelly voice of a man played from it.

Together they sat, listening to Ximen Judd's speech that seemed to play on loop all throughout the day on the newly established Runic Radio Station. Rekco's brain felt swollen from all the information it had been trying to process since he awoke. Afterwards, he sat on the couch in silence while Cathy fixed them both a cup of hot cocoa. When he glanced over to her, he let out a gasp that made her jump.

"What is *that*?!" he cried.

Cathy spun around to the window, looking outside at the stars in the night sky for some sort of looming threat. "What is *what*? The stars? Did you forget about those too?" she joked.

Rekco pointed at the pot sitting on the windowsill below where she was looking. In it was a flower, the likes of which he had never seen before. Its six fully blossomed petals were a radiant blue, akin to the haunting color of Ather. Cathy lowered her glance to the exquisite lily sprouted from the pot of soil and gave a shocked cry.

"It's a Hope Lily!" she said excitedly, clapping her hands together with joy. "I've never seen one grow indoors! It's a miracle!" She gave it a sideways glance as she came down from her high. "But why is it *blue?*"

Rekco shifted his lips. "That's what I was saying. It's not just blue—it's Ather-blue." He stood up and approached the pot, extending his hands towards it.

Cathy threw herself between him and it as though the flower were her child. "Nuh-uh! You stay away from it!"

"But—it could be Ather. You were the one just talking about *poisoned Ather mind control bullets*. What if it's not safe?"

She puffed her cheeks out and furrowed her brow. "That's different! The Retallor Corp's Ather was poisoned. *This*—This is a miracle!"

Rekco sighed and backed down, sinking back into the couch by the fire. "Okay, so what does it mean, then?"

Cathy was fawning over the mystical flower long after Rekco's words struck her. She turned to him with a delayed reaction. "Well, I don't know why it's blue, but a Hope Lily growing indoors is supposed to be a miracle of fortune!" Rekco could see the gleaming stars in her eyes as she spoke. "It could be a sign of good things to come!"

Rekco raised an eyebrow. "Things haven't really been good though lately, have they?"

"Now that you mention it, they have! You heard what Ximen Judd said. There hasn't been a single case of madness—even now! Plus, I just spoke to Zeke today about his plans to lead The Underground refugees across the Forgotten Woods to the Redlands and start anew. Things are starting to look up for humanity!"

Rekco's concerns grew the more Cathy spoke. "He's going to take them through the woods? I don't think that's a good idea. And I'm not ready to trust the leader of the Runic Guard either."

Cathy set down the cup of cocoa on the kitchen table, looking annoyed. "I don't trust Ximen Judd either, and that's exactly why I believe Zeke's plan is for the best. I know it's not safe, but he has a band of warriors from The Underground, and he's pretty strong himself, isn't he? I know you want to save Last Thesi, but maybe it's just not possible. Maybe it's time to let it go, for humanity's sake."

"That's not it," Rekco said in a restrained voice through gritted teeth. "I want—I *need* to find my father. He's the key to all this, I know it! And I think maybe my heritage could have something to do with what's happening to me right now."

"Your *heritage?* Because your father is the Eminent? I mean, it doesn't sound impossible—nothing is *impossible*, right? And I knew that would be your stance on the matter. That's—that's what makes this so difficult to say. I want you to do what you feel like you need to do, but that isn't what's best for the world—not anymore. That being said, I'm joining Zeke's cause. He's got a base set up in the slums. I'm going to pack my things and leave for there as soon as you're recovered."

"I told you I'm all better now," he responded out of frustration, without giving his words any real thought.

Cathy's lips thinned and she dropped her glance. "Okay. If you're sure. I'll go ahead and leave for Zeke's in the morning then. I'll send for Bragau to come back for the rest of my things."

Rekco's heart sank into the burning pit of his stomach. The remorse he felt was unparalleled, feeling as though he had just made a grave mistake. A grim silence filled the room and weighed down on his shoulders. He could feel the veins in his forehead pulsing, his mind racked with distress at the thought of Cathy leaving for good. He wanted to say something to try to make her stay, but, "I don't know what to say," was all he could muster.

"You don't have to say anything," Cathy said, shaking her head. "If you change your mind and want to come with, just ask the guys at the Coop for directions to Zeke's hideout. Goodnight, Rekco, and goodbye." With that, she retired to her room while Rekco remained on the couch, his head in his hands, the twin mugs of cocoa sitting on the table had gone cold.

Chapter 7: Beyond Measure

The following day, Rekco woke up to a silent house—Cathy was gone. It was later than he was accustomed to waking up, nearing noon by the time he left his bedroom. His body felt heavy, bogged down by the dread and regret that filled his entire being. *I should go with her. I know the woods better than most. I could help them get through safely. But ... What about my father? What about Last Thesi? Is it right to abandon the city just like the Retallors wanted to?*

Rekco's thoughts plagued him as he scoured the pantry for something to satisfy his rumbling stomach. As he searched, he noticed that Cathy had left the blue Hope Lily behind. A token of good luck, perhaps? Though he felt that she needed it far more than he.

The pitiful breakfast he had sated his hunger pangs, but the loneliness that remained could not be cured so easily. Never had he been left to his own devices for so long. Even after Maven's death, Cathy quickly filled the void of companionship his mentor left vacant, but now that she was gone, all of his anxieties began to rise to the surface. He needed to hear a voice that wasn't his own. The city was too far to be of any help. He worried the long trek to the Coop, accompanied by his troubled conscience, may drive him mad.

Instead, Rekco scoured the house for his communicator, the one Dim gave him so they could reach one another about their missions. Once he found it, buried beneath a pile of unused bandages and the tacky black clothes given to him by the Shadows, he held it up like it was a sacred treasure. Thankfully, it still had some juice left in it, at least enough to make a call to Dim, whose number was the only one saved on the device. He pressed the green button to page Dim and waited.

Rekco paced in a circle around the couch in the living room, muttering to himself, "C'mon, Dim, answer." He waited and waited while the line rang, until at last, the ringing ceased.

"Hello?" Dim's voice sprang from the rectangular device. Hearing his friend's voice sent a surge of life through Rekco's body.

"Hey, Dim. I heard about what happened to Kinnley. I'm so sorry for your loss. He was always a great friend to me. Are you holding up okay?"

There was silence for a moment, and in that moment Rekco's heart dropped, feeling as though he had said something wrong and sent Dim fleeing. Just before it became unbearable, Dim spoke in response, "Oh, it's *you*, Rekco." He did not sound pleased by the realization. "Rekco Curse, son of the Eminent, *hero of the people*. Is that all you called for, to say you're sorry about Kinnley?"

Now it was Rekco who did not know what to say. He did not want to fight with Dim, nor did he expect to find confrontation when all he sought was solace. "No, that's not all. To be honest, I'm having a hard time right now and could really use someone to talk to," he admitted.

"*You're* having a hard time?" Dim's voice rose like the magma in a volcano nearing eruption. "Half of the population is gone! I saw the chaos and calamity on the ground while you were up in Retallor Tower, playing the hero. And not just that, once I brought Kinnley back to the Middle District for the family to pay their respects, I found that I had no family left! They were all gone! My brother went mad and beat my mother until she was unrecognizable, before dying a painful, maddened death—but *you're* having a hard time?"

Rekco didn't enjoy being yelled at, but he held his tongue until Dim was finished. "I didn't know. I'm so sorry, Dim, for everything."

"You should be! I regret ever telling you about the Retallors' plan. I never imagined it would cause something like this."

Rekco reeled, his own anger starting to rear its head. "What does that mean? The Retallors were the ones planning to doom everyone in the city who they considered unworthy. They needed to be stopped!"

"That may be true, but at least we could have survived and come up with a plan to take them down later on, when the world was safer. Now everyone I cared about is gone, and the world is *still* doomed. What a truly heroic deed you've done, Rekco."

Rekco felt pressure within his chest and his breath was hot and irregular. It took all his will to refrain from screaming. "It's not my fault, Dim! I don't understand why—"

"You're wrong," Dim interrupted, his voice shaky. "It *is* your fault. I tried hard not to speculate too much, but now, even the scientists in the Research District are starting to believe that when Retallor Tower went on lockdown, something inside must have triggered their poisoned Ather to detonate, causing the mass breakout of madness. And that wouldn't have happened if you hadn't gone there that day to *heroically* save the city from the Retallors' plan. Truly ... it's as much my fault as it is yours; all because I told you the truth. Now I have half the city's blood on my hands, and the death of my entire family too."

"Dim ... I—"

"Just leave me alone, will ya?" Dim said in a defeated tone before Rekco could finish the thought that he had not yet fully formed. "Leave me to my suffering until this cursed play we're all forced to take part in comes to a close. It's the least you can do for all the damage and heartache you've caused." There was a low *click*, and Dim was gone.

Rekco tried to call back at once, but when he pressed the green button, the communicator powered down; even it had had enough of him. He dropped the device to the floor, his head feeling woozy, eyelids heavy, wanting nothing more than to go back to sleep and try to forget all of his woes. An immeasurable guilt weighed on Rekco, eclipsing all the other negative thoughts in his mind. He felt selfish and childish, and as small as a speck of dust. He fell back onto the couch, wishing to sink in between the cushions and disappear.

Is this how my father must have felt after the great battle for Thesi? Is this what it means to be a hero? To cause pain and suffering for those closest to you for the sake of the greater good? No wonder my father decided to vanish from this world. But there has to be more to it than that!

He sprang from the couch, his mind latching onto a new purpose. Determined to clear the negativity from his head, Rekco decided to get some fresh air and take a lap to the Forgotten Woods and back. As he stood and stared down the dirt path beside his cabin in the plains, he couldn't help from dwelling on Cathy's words. *Do what you feel like you need to do*. "What I need to do," he mouthed aloud, closing his eyes.

He focused his mind as best as he could, allowing the sound of rushing water and tumultuous winds rise within his ears; the sounds that only seemed to toll for him during moments of high stress, when his life was on the line. It was a stream of consciousness he knew he needed to learn to tap into. He thought back on his battle with Welzig Retallor; how he moved faster than the mayor's barrage of bullets, if only for a brief moment. *That is what I need to do.*

Though his eyes were closed, Rekco felt as though the world around him was still, and that the breeze itself had ceased. His eyes burst open, and he sprinted forward with all his might, every muscle within him tensing. In a flash, time returned to normal, and an immense pain ran through his body, starting at his face, before it was replaced by numbness. His vision was eclipsed by a dark brown color. As the numbness in his body subsided, he began to grip his hands, feeling the blades of grass that were eluding his fingers.

He pushed up on his palms, lifting himself off the ground, and glanced to his right to find that he had only dashed the length of his house before falling in the grass beside the dirt path. He sat up and rubbed his sore nose to make sure it wasn't broken. "Maybe this power isn't meant for moving long distances. I need to figure out how far I can go without falling."

Rekco stood again with renewed vigor, determined to master this newfound power. "Is this what Maven was trying to protect me from, from going down the very path my father went?" he began aloud, staring out at the treetops lining the horizon before him. "I'm sorry, Maven. I have to learn to control this power and make it my own. I need to go down the path my father went—that's how I'll find him. I'll disappear, just like he did, if I have to. I know he's the key to saving humanity, even if Cathy doesn't believe it."

He took another deep inhalation, this time focusing on moving only a short distance: the length of his home. He was already kicking off his back foot before his eyes had fully opened, and just as one foot left the ground, his other made contact. He did not fall, but instead, stood on shaky legs in the spot he first took off from when he tried to sprint to the woods. It felt like a mere baby step of progression, but progression it was nonetheless, and he couldn't help but cheer aloud at the small triumph.

*

Rekco dashed this way and that, each time with a *boom* that echoed through the plains. He continued to practice this short burst of godlike speed for hours, which turned into days, and weeks, until he had no idea how long it had been. His obsession with mastering this power made him forget the last time Bragau came to deliver supplies and pick up Cathy's things. He could not recall if they spoke, or what was said, but none of that mattered now. All that he cared about was following in his father's footsteps.

As he practiced, Rekco would occasionally stop to glance at the potted Hope Lily sitting in the windowsill, visible from the road beside his house; the Ather-blue flower seemed to have the power to keep his mind focused on the task at hand.

After countless attempts of trial and error, Rekco became confident in his ability to swing a sword during the swift movement without accidentally throwing it hundreds of feet into some overgrown sward. He noticed that he could travel farther with each burst without the loss of stability, and even veer in directions that weren't straight lines. What was at first an incomprehensible movement, ending as soon as it began, was becoming no more difficult than swinging a sword to hit a motionless target.

He set up a course full of obstacles and goals to test himself and further his mastery. He stared down the makeshift trial he built from the dirt road, ready to take it on for the first time. Without even the need to ground himself, he bolted off, bronze sword in hand. He leapt over a fallen tree then quickly dipped down to avoid a log that he hung from a flagpole, while picking up a stone, before finally swinging his sword at the end.

Rekco let out a triumphant sigh and smiled at his accomplishment before returning back to the start. "One-hundred more times should be good for today."

Rekco found that the more he used this power of his, the stronger he became—and not just in his legs, but his entire body and mind felt as though they were also surpassing their limits. Time itself seemed to pass differently after he became more accustomed to moving at such speeds, making him grow impatient whenever he wasn't training. But he knew that speed was not all that his father was known for.

"Both Maven and Bragau said he was able to lift Bragau's wooden cart above his head single handedly," Rekco said to himself as he scanned through Maven's toolshed for the heaviest thing he could find. What he found was a broken water heater that Maven kept in hopes of repairing it someday. Although it was bulky, he imagined it was something Maven was able to lift on his own. "I need something heavier."

Rekco turned to the plains, trying to remember if he had ever seen any large boulders within the tall grass. It was a fruitless endeavor. The only boulders he could think of were the massive ones he saw that littered the beach, but the last thing he wanted was a potential run in with the Runic Guard that patrolled it.

"There has to be something," Rekco contemplated, sitting with his back against the front door of his house. "Or ... *someone!*" he cried as the spark of a brilliant idea popped into his mind.

He set off at once—for the slums of Last Thesi. The trip on foot took a couple of hours on average but was made far shorter by the explosive speed Rekco could muster at will. He found fun in it, weaving through clusters of rolling knolls and dashing up and over towering mounds in an instant. He loved the feeling of his long, green hair whooshing back as he moved. It reminded him of the exhilaration of riding a motorcycle for the first time with Dim, but without the motion sickness.

Even though he took his time, Rekco arrived at the front gate to Last Thesi in only twenty minutes. Not seeing Kinnley's bushy grey mustache smiling at him there brought him down from his elation in an instant. There was a new guard sitting Kinnley's post instead, one Rekco had not met before. It was an older man, though not quite as old as Kinnley was; he had dark hair and a mustache that drooped as much as his wrinkled jowls. He was sitting at the chair outside of the gate, reading over the day's newspaper until Rekco approached him.

"Hoy there," Rekco greeted, making himself sad with memories of Kinnley.

The guard did not stand, but instead gave a grumble in response as he rustled the newspaper while flipping the page. "That booming sound out there. Was that you?" he said without taking his eyes off the article he was reading.

"Oh, yeah, it was." Rekco blushed, having not considered the kind of ruckus he would cause zipping through the plains in repeated, short bursts.

"Ah, well, try to keep it down next time. I'm trying to read here."

Rekco frowned, though he had yet to wonder until that point if it were possible to use his power without making so much noise. "I'll try. Could you open the gate for me?"

The guard still did not stand. Instead, he kicked his right leg up and crossed it over his left. "Go on ahead. It's already open."

"Huh? Why is it open?"

"It's always open now," the guard said flatly.

Rekco squeezed his eyebrows together in confusion. "If the gate's always open now, then why are you here?"

"Because I'm reading, and you're interrupting that. Now go on." The guard raised the newspaper to conceal his face, as if pretending that Rekco was no longer there. Rekco acted as such and proceeded through the unlocked gate without another word.

He took care not to use his power in the city for fear of what kind of attention it would bring or the damage it could do should something go wrong. The slums were as rotten as ever; the layer of dirt and grime caked upon the cobblestone road was so thick that it nearly looked like it was paved like the ones in the High District. Most of the streetlights were only there for show, casting nothing more than shadows onto the street. The only thing that was different was the fact that the smog overhead had thinned, allowing the sunlight to cascade over the forsaken southern district of Last Thesi for the first time in years.

Rekco saw far less beggars than he was used to. He assumed the majority of the slums' population had migrated to the Middle District to sully the clean cobblestone roads and well-proportioned buildings there. He wondered what other kind of mayhem came to be when the wall between the two districts just up and vanished, a feat he heard on the radio was done by the Doombringers—by Kyoku.

"Maybe things are getting along more peacefully now that the madness is gone, and that ..." he thought aloud, trying to find a silver lining, but stopped his thought before he could try to find anything positive in half the population being wiped out.

It wasn't much longer until he arrived at Barbier's Soup Coop. Rekco wasn't sure what day it was, to be honest. Part of him hoped that Cathy was working, though she was not the reason he came. An unfamiliar short, bulky teen stood outside of the Coop in the place Bugg Zeke always had. The young man greeted him, "Good day. Care to come inside and take a load off?"

"No thanks. Would you happen to know if Zeke is working this evening?"

"*Zeke?*" The bouncer asked, sounding almost offended at the mentioned name. "No. He doesn't work here anymore, unfortunately."

"Ah, I figured as much," Rekco said with a frown. "What about Cathy? Is she here?"

The bouncer raised an eyebrow before shaking his head. "No. She doesn't work here anymore either. Why are you looking for them?"

"Well," Rekco paused with thought. "It's kind of private, actually."

"Private, huh?" The bouncer crossed his muscular arms and scratched the scruff on his chin. "Say, you wouldn't happen to be Rekco, would you?"

Rekco reeled in surprise. "I am! But how did you know?" A worrisome suspicion began to fill his heart.

"Ah, great! It *is* you! Cathy told me to be on the lookout for a guy with green hair. It's a pretty uncommon thing, but I didn't want to assume."

"Oh, she did?" the words fell from his mouth in a hollow sort of way.

"Yeah, she said if you came around asking where she was, to give you this." He handed Rekco a piece of paper. On it was a map and written instructions for how to get to *Zeke's Hideout*.

"Ah, yeah, that's *exactly* what I came for," Rekco lied, though it was only a partial lie. "I'll be off then. By the way, what's your name?"

"I'm Latif! Latif Anselem!" Latif said, putting his hand at his hip and giving a confident smirk.

"Good to meet you. I'm Rekco, though I guess you already knew that," he said weakly before giving a wave and departing for Zeke's Hideout.

The way there reminded him of the route he took to get to the entrance of The Underground, though this was much less treacherous. He passed through an abandoned industrial area on his way to the rundown apartment complex where Zeke and his followers were holed up, where Cathy now lived too. The grey building was covered with railed walkways accessible by rickety metal stairwells. The place looked like it could fall down at any moment, making Rekco worry about Cathy's safety living in such a building.

He searched the place for the great metal door the paper told him to find. Along the way there was no sight nor sound of any of the people who supposedly inhabited the complex. After having to stop and frustratedly reread the directions five times, Rekco was able to find the security door. When he knocked, a voice came calling from the other side, "How do you plan to stop the apocalypse?" It was a familiar, frail sort of voice that he was sure he'd heard before, but the phrase it spoke was one that was most familiar: it was the same question written on parchment papers that were plastered up all around the slums.

"Huh? I'm looking for someone," Rekco said, confused, his mind still trying to remember something. He heard a whooshing sound below his waist and a metallic *clink* that made him jump, followed by a gasp on the other side of the door.

"Oh! Champion!" the voice said in an overjoyed tone before the door swung open, revealing a little old man whose deformed spine made him look like he was collapsing on himself. He beckoned for Rekco to enter the empty room then closed the security door behind him.

"You! You're the guy from the entrance of The Underground!" Rekco cried, relieved to be able to match the voice to the person. "You survived?! But how? I thought the Runic Guard blew up the entrance when they came storming into The Underground."

The old man shook his whole body along with his head. "The Guard, they ignored me, just like everyone else does when they enter. But not you," he pointed his shaking, bent arm at Rekco. "You and that irritable wizard talked to me."

"*Wizard?* You mean Koku? Is he here too?" Rekco asked, still wondering what became of Kyoku since the day he stormed Retallor Tower with the wizard's help.

"No, he's not here. They could use his help, I'm sure."

"If I ever see him again, I'll let him know to come here," Rekco assured. "Do you know where Zeke—er, Bugbear is?"

"The captain," the old man swooned. "He is planning and plotting for humanity's survival. Might be too busy, but I can call, if you wish."

"Please, if you could. Tell him I need his help and want to meet with him outside, if possible."

The doorman hobbled off to the left, to another room where an archaic telephone box was laid out on the floor, the wires protruding from it leading into a hole in the wall where it was once mounted. The hunched man picked up the receiver and turned the dial repeatedly. "Hello, yes, I have an important guest in the front yard—a Champion. He seeks an audience with the captain, outside. What does he look like? Oh, he has green hair and—okay!" He placed the receiver down and began walking back to the reinforced metal door.

"What did they say?" Rekco asked as he followed behind at a snail's pace.

"He'll be right out. You can wait down at ground level." He opened the door and saw Rekco out.

Rekco waited patiently for Zeke to show himself, wondering where the mountain of a man would appear from, and how, considering the size of all the doors on the building appeared much too small for him.

"Hey, Rekco," a deep voice called from behind. Rekco whipped around to see Zeke standing there, as big as ever, dressed in all black. "What do you need?"

Rekco stood for a moment. He had not yet thought on how to word his unusual request to the giant, nor had he figured out exactly what that request was. He spun around and scanned his surroundings while Zeke gave him a confused look. "Ah ha! That would be perfect!" he cried. "Zeke, I need you to do me a favor."

Zeke nodded, thumping his chest with his fist. "Anything for you, Rekco. What is it? And why me?"

Rekco had already gone off to tug at a mess of debris. "Because you're the strongest person I know. Here!" He pulled a massive roll of discarded carpet from the pile, thick with dust and dirt. He then dragged it over to Zeke and let it unfurl at his feet.

Zeke appeared more confused than before Rekco answered him. "What's this for?"

Rekco was too distracted to answer right away, another piece of rubbish having caught his eye. He ran off to grab a sheet of metal and stacked it on top of the carpet. "Okay, here's what I want you to do." As he told Zeke his outlandish plan, likely sounding like an insane person, he spotted Cathy looking down at him from the third floor of the apartment complex, just outside the metal door. Beside her was a dark-skinned young woman with curly hair; she looked familiar to him, but he was far too distracted to search his mind for the answer.

"Are you sure about this?" Zeke said, cracking his knuckles.

"Yeah, I am. What's the worst that can happen?"

Zeke shrugged, and Rekco gave a grin before getting on the ground and climbing underneath the carpet. He laid on his back and poked his head out from the dingy carpet, all the mildew and dust made him want to sneeze. "Are you ready?" Zeke asked.

"Go!" Rekco cried.

At the word, Zeke pushed down on the layer of metal and carpet with all his might, pinning Rekco to the ground. He could feel the pebbles beneath him digging into his back as his body was crushed beneath Zeke's mass. Rekco waited until he couldn't move an inch from where he laid and then tapped into the stream of consciousness that allowed him to move at hyper speed; the sound and sensation in his ears was no longer an eerie conundrum, but instead, the call of his power, coming from a source still unknown to him.

Rekco closed his eyes to listen to the song; it still sounded like nothing more than furious water and wind, raging a storm inside his head. When it rose to its culmination, Rekco's eyes burst open, and he pushed against Zeke's opposition with all the strength he could muster. That strength was more than he hoped for, more so than he could ever have dreamed to achieve. With a single shove, Rekco exploded upright, and Zeke was thrown into the air as high as the second story of the apartments beside them.

Zeke let out a booming howl as he flew through the air and landed with an immense *crash*. When Rekco heard the sound, his heart dropped, and he bolted to Zeke's side in an instant. The gigantic man was sprawled out at the other end of the building. He sat up with a loud groan, looking more surprised than hurt. "Wow! That was incredible!" Zeke bellowed.

"It really was," Rekco said, blushing. "Thanks for helping me test that. I'd ask you to help me again, but I'm afraid you might get hurt."

Zeke let out a guffaw that shook the ground beneath him. He stood up and patted the dust off his clothes. "I'm not hurt! I'd gladly help again if you tell me how you did it." Together, they walked back to the spot recognizable by the decimation left behind on the pavement where Rekco threw Zeke off him.

Rekco stooped down to grab the sheet of metal that had landed a ways from Zeke. "I—" he began, not knowing what to say. He glanced up at the third story balcony to find that Cathy was gone, along with her friend. He set the metal down upon the carpet, shifting his lips as he said, "I have to get going. Maybe we can do this again sometime, as long as you're up for it."

"Of course!" Zeke's voice thundered as he gave Rekco a heavy pat on the back. "Keep comin' back and I'll help you train. As long as you consider joining up with us. We could really use somebody like you when we cross the Forgotten Woods."

Somebody like me? Like the Eminent? Rekco thought, responding to Zeke with a smile and a wave before he made to return home. The power within him seemed to well up infinitely, but what powers within the universe sought to oppose him, he did not yet know.

Chapter 8: The Other Side

Kyoku's mind raced with anticipation for what the world would bring beyond Oglis' portal. The sensation of lightheadedness was akin to what his own warp magic inspired. The key difference between their spells was the color. Though Oglis' conjured portal was as yellow as her beady eyes, blue light filled Kyoku's vision. Unlike with his technique, the azure glow did not abate; it swirled and crackled every which way, like the flames upon a sun's surface.

"Hurry up and cross the checkpoint already," a voice said with contempt.

The sound startled Kyoku, making his body jolt upright. A lone man stood before him amidst a shimmering sea of blue. He had long, stone-grey hair that was kept out of his face by a headband. The purple and silver plated armor he wore appeared far more advanced than anything Kyoku had ever seen or read about. Though the expression of his eyes were veiled behind thick goggles, the way the bow of his upper lip curved with disgust was apparent.

"Can't handle the warp gate, huh? I thought only children had that problem. And they say you're supposed to be a master wizard," the man scoffed.

Kyoku's face became hot with rage. He wanted to blast the man and his sour expression into next week, yet he maintained his composure and remained cautious to the unfamiliar environment. He could not risk the possibility that there were others capable of deflecting his magics like Oglis had. He turned around in a circle to observe his surroundings, only to find that there was nothing to see. At his back was a wall of swirling blue energy, so thick that nothing could be seen beyond it.

Kyoku turned back to face the armored guard, his mind refocused, and his emotions stifled. "Who are you, and what is this place?"

There was no break in the contempt on the man's face. He waved his arm in the only traversable direction, saying, "Name's Vapor. That's all I'm authorized to say, though I wouldn't tell you anything more even if I were allowed. Now go on and get out of here so I can resume my patrol. Oglis is waiting for you." When Vapor turned away and began to walk off, Kyoku could see the unusual weapon on his back: a great cudgel, the length of his torso, that was a shade bluer than Vapor's grey-blue skin; each end was covered with black spines that were as dark as the cloth that was tightly wrapped around the weapon's middle.

Kyoku was quick to realize that attempting to speak with Vapor would be fruitless. Instead, he heeded his word and started down the hallway, ahead of the disgruntled guard.

The tunnel was wide and empty, its walls and ceiling made up entirely of evermoving blue energy. The magic within the walls and floor reminded Kyoku of Ather, but it did not give off the same crude feeling as the magic that ran Last Thesi. This magic felt pristine, as pure as clean water and as light as clouds. He could not help but fawn over the complexities of a place seemingly made of magic and wonder who could have created such a place. *That guard said Oglis is waiting for me. Does that mean this is that foul creature's domain?*

Kyoku followed the tunnel for some time—until it opened to a humongous room lined top to bottom with the same stream of blue energy, flowing like a gentle river. He looked up at the giant chandelier that hung from the ceiling. It, too, was made up of magic, shifting and dancing like the tiny blue flames that sat as decoration on it. It seemed the gaudy chandelier was not the source of light within the room, for a white kind of light basked over it, unlike the blue radiance the walls and ceiling gave off.

Kyoku's eyes were drawn down from above when faint voices pushed their way into his ears. Desks filled the great room as far as his eyes could see. A woman sat at each desk; some toiling away at papers that littered their desktops, others spoke into headsets, having conversations about things that made no sense to him, while few sat unmoving with eyes staring out at the churning magic in the walls. None of the women seemed to take notice of him as he passed through the unending rows of desks.

An unsettling realization came over Kyoku after a moment: all the women looked the same in the face, with skin as pale as the moon and soft, caring eyes. Nearly all of them had golden hair, though many of them wore it in different styles. *Clones? Is such a thing possible? Or maybe they are some kind of automata, variants of a base model?* His heart sank mid thought when a pair of emerald green eyes locked with his own from amidst the sea of distracted workers. The woman staring in his direction was not like the others. She had long, voluptuous, purple hair and was clad in a silver breastplate from which a flowing white dress extended from.

Kyoku gulped at what seemed to be a coincidental glance. He maintained eye contact with her, assuming she would return to her work sooner or later. That was not the case. Instead, she raised her dainty hand and beckoned to him. He squeezed his eyebrows together, addled by her gesture, then proceeded towards her desk.

"Are you lost?" she asked once he arrived.

Kyoku frowned, glancing down at the nameplate that sat upon her desk which simply read: M-9. He raised his eyes from the perplexing plate and asked, "Who are you, and why do none of the others notice me?"

"My name is Melonine. I have been blessed with an amount of free will that far exceeds that of my sisters. Many find it—unsettling, even Dalu himself."

Kyoku gave her a sideways glance as though she were speaking a foreign language. "Okay, Melonine, tell me everything you know about this place."

Melonine shook her head. "You are not authorized for such information."

"What do you mean by that? You don't even know who I am!" Kyoku snapped.

Melonine did not react to his hostility, responding with a straight face, "You are Kyoku, origins unknown, thought to be the Overflow, a speculation that is calculated to be ninety-nine percent accurate."

Kyoku's mind had gone blank to her words the moment she said his name with nary a stutter or hiccup in her voice. "H—how?" The rest of her words caught up with him after a delay, eliciting confusion and frustration to well up in him. He was getting tired of not understanding, having to refrain from destroying this place and be done with its mysteries. "What exactly *can* you tell me then?"

"I cannot tell you what I am authorized to tell you."

His eyelid twitched with fury, the destructive magic within him ready to erupt. "So I have to keep asking you questions in hopes that they are ones you are allowed to answer?" She responded with a nod, but showed no pleasure in his torment, which did well to dampen his anger. "Okay," he said, taking a deep breath as he leaned his palms onto her desk. "What is this place?" he asked, wholly prepared for her to deny his request.

"This place is known as the Core. It is the center of the universe, the center for which Dalu, Creator of All Things, oversees existence."

Kyoku's nose wrinkled, and lips thinned as if he smelled something rancid. He pounded on Melonine's desk, making the mess of papers and trinkets upon it rattle. "Don't toy with me! *Creator of All Things?* Is that the overcomplicated term for *God* you people use here? There's no such thing!"

Melonine shook her head. "You may not like it, but it is true. Dalu created the universe and all things within it; you and I, the thoughts within our minds, and our ability to process said thoughts."

"*Dalu*, huh?" Kyoku scoffed. "And this place is where such a being resides?"

"Correct."

"Take me to Dalu then. Let me meet with this *Creator of All Things*." Even as he spoke, Kyoku already knew what Melonine's answer would be, and the frustration within him began to run rampant again.

"You do not have access—"

Kyoku swept his arms across Melonine's desk in a fit of rage, throwing everything from it, things that dispersed into nothingness before they could reach the ground, only to reappear on her desk moments later. "Who decides what I do and do not have access to?"

"Oglis Inima. Once you report to her and she decides your importance to her mission, you may be granted access to more information."

The name of that blue gargantuan brought awful memories to Kyoku's mind, but also made him remember how and why he was there in the Core. "Oglis Inima. Is she the reason you know who I am?"

"Correct. She discovered you and reported your whereabouts while on her current mission."

Kyoku grumbled at the thought of that loathsome creature spying on him in any way. "Where can I find her then?"

Melonine stood from her desk and turned to the left. "Her chambers are that way. It is the first room in the Hall of Fate. If you follow the wall in that direction, you will eventually find your way there."

The word *fate* made Kyoku scowl, but he was otherwise glad to have found a sense of direction in this unusual place where everything seemed to look the same. "Then I will go now. Will I be able to find you here again when I am done so that you may answer my questions?"

"Most likely. It is rare that my duties require me to leave my desk, but far more common than that of my sisters. Please return as often as you wish and I will address your questions." Melonine smiled in a genuine way that cooled Kyoku's burning heart, transferring the heat instead to his face and ears.

Without another word, Kyoku started off to find the so-called Hall of Fate. While he was passing through the dizzying rows of desks, he was forced to stop, almost crashing into another figure doing the same.

"Pardon me," a man dressed in a peculiar purple uniform said. His silver hair was tied in a ponytail, extending beyond the middle of his back, nearly down to his black pants. His raiment, adorned with black leather upon the shoulders and gold pendants and chains on the breast made him look important. His left wrist rested on the hilt of an unsheathed katana that hung at his side. He gave Kyoku a quick glance up and down and pushed his rimless glasses up the bridge of his nose and continued walking in the opposite direction.\

Kyoku continued to scan the man from behind, his eyes drawn to the sword at his side; its edge was dull, yet the blade appeared polished and pristine. Once the man was out of sight, Kyoku continued, breaking free from the field of desks and making his way in the direction Melonine instructed. He scanned over the sitting women as he proceeded along the wall adjacent to them, their voices blended into an incomprehensible clamor. It seemed that Melonine's statements about them were true—not one of them looked his way.

It will be a pain finding her again in his crowd of droning robots, but I'll have no choice if I want my questions answered, Kyoku thought, frowning at how similar everything in that room was.

At last, Kyoku reached a break in the seemingly endless wall of blue energy. The Hall of Fate, he assumed it to be, was home to a row of ten rooms that were given a generous amount of space between them, each with a number plate hanging above them. Entry to each room was barred by a metal door with no handle in sight, save for the first room, which was left wide open. Kyoku did not know how doors could be hinged to walls made of magic, but he did not bother to speculate. *That'll be another question for Melonine.*

Kyoku began to approach the open room but froze in place the moment he saw something unnerving in his peripheral; far down the Hall of Fate, flitting across the ethereal blue floor, was the golden trim of a black robe. At once, Kyoku turned away from Oglis' room and sprinted in the direction of the figure, his mind unable to do anything but remember the one person he ever knew to wear such robes. "*Master Gofun,*" he thought and said in unison.

He ran as hard as his legs would allow, but he did not feel like he was getting any closer to the robed figure. After a moment, the figure vanished and Kyoku stopped, bending at the waist as he panted. He turned around to find that he had not gotten any farther than the room marked with a 10 above it. His eyes were rheumy with vexation, unable to shake the thoughts of his late master from his mind.

"What are you doing there, running in place?" A smarmy voice full of annoyance called. Kyoku scanned the area to find a short, bald man with skin so blue that he blended in with the walls. He had a large head and big eyes that appeared too big for his miniature stature, a long pointed nose, and wide, blue lips that were darker than his skin. His white lab coat trailed along the ground as he approached Kyoku from the other end of the hall. "It seems that you are forbidden from going any further. How unusual. If you are here in the Core, I see not why you wouldn't have free reign of it. Allow me to remedy that." He snapped his little blue fingers, showing off his perfectly white fingernails in doing so.

Kyoku raised an eyebrow and took a single step forward, his golden boot crossing beyond the invisible barrier that held him back prior. He sped off again in search of the gold-trimmed robes, faintly hearing the words, "No thank you?" When he arrived at the place where the figure disappeared, he turned and saw a metal door with no handle. With no patience remaining within him, Kyoku placed his hand upon the door, and it exploded into a cloud of red ash, revealing the room beyond it.

The massive room inside was even bigger than the room full of desks. It was host to an incomprehensible number of people, all dressed in black robes. Rows of immeasurably long tables were there to accommodate them all as they sat, eating and drinking and chatting with their neighbors. Kyoku scanned the room in haste, trying to find the robes with the golden trim. He found robes lined with green, blue, red, and the occasional silver thread, but none were gold.

His chest rose and fell, and his head felt so full of thought that it could burst. Amidst his disarray, the small man sidled up next to him and said, "What are you looking for? This is the mess hall, but if it's food you're after, couldn't you just create your own?"

"Robes—with—gold—lining. Where?" Kyoku said between breaths.

"Huh? *Gold?* I wouldn't know. It's not my job to keep track of the engineers and their ways of labeling one another. Come now. Oglis awaits you." The blue dwarf turned from the entrance to the mess hall and began back towards the Hall of Fate. After a moment of defeat and angst, Kyoku did the same.

"Do you work for Oglis?" Kyoku asked as he walked alongside the man, having to slow his pace to a crawl so as not to leave him behind.

"My name is Dr. Gavin. I work with all those who reside in the Hall of Fate."

"And I'm sure you aren't allowed to tell me anything more than that until I speak with Oglis?"

Dr. Gavin scoffed. "I do not operate by the same rules as those *dolls*. I will tell you what I wish to, which is that Oglis requires your attention in her room." He stopped at an out of place-looking end table that sat between rooms 3 and 4. It was just short enough for him to reach. "We will speak again, I'm sure, after I've designated which room will be yours."

Kyoku stopped before room 1 and gave Dr. Gavin a confused look, but there was no time for any further exchanges.

"Come in, Kyoku," Oglis' distorted voice called from within the pitch-black room.

Kyoku crossed into the darkness, not knowing what to expect after all he had seen thus far.

Chapter 9: The Ten

The darkness within Oglis' room was suffocating—with no end in sight. The endless fog seemed impenetrable; so thick that it felt as though he were wading through a quagmire. He pressed onward slowly, without any sense of direction, holding his arms out at length to prevent himself from walking into any unseen objects.

"You're almost there!" Oglis' voice called from what sounded like leagues away.

As he went along, Kyoku began to catch wafts of a salty scent, one so pungent that he could taste it. There was familiarity to it, but his mind was far too focused on following the remnants of Oglis' voice to pore over it. A circular patch of light appeared out of nowhere, outlining the center of a table where three figures sat. Kyoku peered up at the spotlight in search of its source and saw nothing but a tunnel of deep blue, as dark as the night sky.

"Take a seat. Anywhere is fine," Oglis said as she rose from her seat and craned her body forward, becoming visible underneath the light.

Kyoku approached the table with caution, his eyes darting from Oglis to the other two figures sitting silently beside one another on the other end of the table. "What do you want from me? What did you mean to show me by bringing me here?"

Oglis gave a cruel, distorted laugh. "I brought you here to show you where you belong! Where all of your colleagues reside—here in the Hall of Fate. We are the Ten!" she proclaimed with pride, raising her hand up at the light.

Kyoku stopped at the edge of the table, counting the ten chairs that circled it. "*Ten?* That's quite a title for *three* people. Where are all the rest of them?"

"How astute of you," she said, the light within her eyes growing thin. "You see, three of your colleagues are indisposed. And the Swordsman, I believe you've already met, is on the way to carry out his mission. The others have yet to be procured, unfortunately."

"*The Swordsman?* What does that make you—the *Ringleader?* What's with all these self-gratifying titles?" Kyoku noticed steam emitting off of one of the seated figures. The heat bended beneath the spotlight, reflecting the light in a way that made it look like it was dancing atop the table.

"That is what some call me, yes, but our titles are not self-given. Such names are preordained, a causation of the binds of destiny, signifying our roles within the cosmos—"

"Why are you answering so many questions after telling me I couldn't ask any? And from a newbie, no less!" A man's voice shot from the heated darkness.

Oglis turned her head to face the voice. "Be mindful of interrupting me, Loch, for I may not be so forgiving next time."

An intense scoff, akin to that of a scolded child came from the darkness, and Loch shifted uncomfortably in his seat, saying not another word as the heat around him began to dissipate. Kyoku held his tongue, not wanting to exacerbate Oglis' annoyance at that moment. Instead, he waited for her to face him again, her unrelenting yellow eyes cutting through the darkness like rays of light breaking the clouds. Her face still showed no expression—she was unreadable.

"As it so happens," she began, touching her long three fingers to the table, "I was just about to open the floor to questions when you arrived, Kyoku. Would you like to ask one?" Her piercing glance bore into him, as though she could see into the depths of his mind with a mere glance. "Anything at all."

It felt like she was baiting him to ask something he was not allowed to know. He did not want to know what repercussions might come should he do so. Instead, he thought of the safest question that came to mind. "How are you able to speak my name clearly? Or rather, why are the people in and around Last Thesi not able to?"

Oglis turned her eyes down at the table as she ran her thick fingers along it. "That was *two* questions," she said, subtle wrinkles forming around the edges of her eyes. "Anyone who comes in contact with the Core is graced with a unifying boon: the power to understand and speak the languages of *all* worlds. So, no matter where you came from, I can speak your name or converse in your tongue because of the knowledge bestowed by the Core."

Kyoku shifted his lips, trying to take every word Oglis said with a grain of salt. He was not yet sure if he could trust the people of the Core and their unusual beliefs. For now, her answer was satisfying enough. *Could this mean that I—am from another world? That means my parents could still be alive somewhere out there. Gofun would have known—if he were still ...* His thoughts trailed off, muddied by grief. He saw the silhouette of a hand go up in the shadows; it was the man Oglis had referred to as *Loch*.

"May I ask a question?" he asked, in a voice that sounded far more restrained than when he last spoke.

"Yes, Loch, you may."

"Could you tell us more about the target? And what might our order of operations be?"

A dainty sigh came from Oglis' voice box. "Again, two questions. Well, I suppose it is yours and Ramirez's first mission, so I can excuse it."

Kyoku furrowed his brow at Loch, unseeable in the dark. *First mission? And he called ME a newbie?*

Oglis leaned closer to the middle of the table, holding her palm upright beneath the spotlight. "This," she said as an orb of yellow light appeared hovering above her open hand, "is our target."

Kyoku reeled when he saw the picture within the globe become clear. *Him?!* It was none other than Rekco Curse, son of the Eminent, and longtime thorn in Kyoku's side. *That country bumpkin is who they're after?!* He wanted to voice his concerns and pose a host of questions, but he abstained, eager to hear the purpose for which Oglis sought Rekco.

"Who is he, and what is his title? The only two that remain are the Eminent and the Dragon, if I'm not mistaken." A woman asked, but it was not Oglis' inhuman voice. This voice came from the figure sitting beside Loch. Her voice was smooth as silk and cunning, with a hint of temper similar to that of the man sitting beside her.

"This, Ramirez, is Rekco Curse. He has no title," Oglis answered.

"*No title?*" Ramirez spoke with a rising inflection. "If he has no title, then he must not be one of us, and if he's not one of us, then why would he be the target?"

"Good question. He is the target because of his connection to another, one who has slipped away from my grasp once before: the Eminent."

That name made Kyoku's heart drop. He had heard numerous stories of the Eminent both in The Underground and throughout Last Thesi. He was considered by many to be *the hero of the people* during the Irol Age, but never had Kyoku imagined he would have a connection to these otherworldly beings residing at the center of the universe.

"If he's not even one of us, then why do we need to go through all this planning to capture him?" Loch asked, sounding annoyed.

"*Capture?* Who said anything about capturing him?" Oglis laughed in a condescending way. "That will come in due time, once he is ripe for the picking."

"What is the mission then?" Kyoku asked, entering the conversation at last, unable to be reluctant any longer.

"To *ripen* him, of course! I want him to face trials unlike anything a mortal should know; to test him to see if he is worthy of becoming one of us—one of the Ten."

"What about The Eminent?" Kyoku asked, confused. "Is he not the main target?"

"Well, that will be up to Rekco to decide."

Loch let out a great, excited sigh. "What's the order then? When is it my turn to test the pipsqueak?"

Kyoku sucked his teeth, feeling uncomfortable at the thought of a group plotting to *test* Rekco's capabilities. Even though Oglis seemed to already accept him as one of the Ten, he wanted to be praised more for his own worthiness. He thought of a scenario in which he would face Rekco and defeat him in whatever trial Oglis conjured up, denying Rekco of ever joining their leagues. *It would be the best for us all, really, wouldn't it? That dirty carrot has no place here, unlike me; I wasn't required to face any trials, after all.*

Kyoku's visions of grandeur and purpose were brought to a screeching halt; a thought had crept into his mind. *Do I even want to be part of this shady organization? Do I want to leave my dying world and join these mongrels in the Halls of Fate? No—at least, not without understanding their grand scheme, and the purpose for which they are being gathered here; not before I find out where I came from.*

While he conversed with his conscience, Kyoku kept his eyes fixed on the projection of Rekco within the globe. It showed him walking along the path outside of his home in the plains. He was astonished that such magics existed, ones that could show live happenings the way advanced technology could. He began to ever realize how much more he had to learn, and that the world beyond his own was far larger than he had imagined.

Loch gave a shocked gasp, heat exuding from his silhouette, which brought Kyoku's attention back to the conversation. "The Swordsman?! He can't go first! That green-haired runt won't stand a chance against him!"

"Calm yourself, Loch," Oglis said, making the globe vanish. "The Swordsman is already en route, so the order cannot be undone. But worry not, the Swordsman has no desire to kill the target. He simply wishes to test his capabilities in his own way—one *swordsman* to another."

"Oglis," Kyoku interjected as politely as he could. "Can you tell me more about the Ten?"

Oglis' citrine eyes narrowed until they were nothing more than yellow lines. She gave a forced chuckle through her voice box that sounded like a strained cough. "It is not my job to educate you. Ask one of the Melonys if you seek more information—maybe the one that you've acquired such a liking for already?" Kyoku's eyebrows furrowed at Oglis' jest, knowing full well that she did not know his mind. "What I *can* do is introduce you to your two colleagues here, since you will soon be collaborating with them." Oglis pointed one finger towards the two shadows sitting beside one another. "They are Loch Standstill and Rebecca 'Ramirez' Standstill, known as the Lovebirds."

"Huh? How is it that they share a title?" Kyoku asked, looking in the Lovebirds' direction, still unable to see them through the darkness.

"*How,* indeed? Our titles are a mysterious thing. These etchings on our souls cannot be changed so easily—and believe me—I've tried to separate them for some time." Oglis gave a hearty laugh that made Kyoku's skin crawl, unable to imagine what kinds of cruel things this alien war criminal did to those two. The darkness itself was intimidated by her presence, as the mood within it became full of sorrow and trepidation, a feeling Oglis promptly cut through. "You will meet the others in due time, I'm sure, once you are needed for the mission, that is."

"What am I to do in the meantime?" Kyoku was weary at the thought of being locked in a room in the Hall of Fate like a toy awaiting its master's desire.

"Do what you wish. Explore the Core to your heart's content, or return to your world if you'd like. I will find you when you are needed, no matter *how far* you try to run," Oglis said with what Kyoku couldn't tell was a playful laugh or a threatening one. Everything about her made him feel uneasy, and it seemed that she went out of her way to maintain such levels of unrest in him.

With that, Kyoku left Oglis' chamber and returned to the vibrant blue Core. Dr. Gavin was nowhere in sight within the Hall of Fate, so Kyoku stood alone for a moment, trying to determine what he wanted to do. He glanced down the hall to his left where the mess hall was, then to the right where the hall opened to the room full of identical women working. His mind was racked with so many thoughts that he could hardly formulate any sort of plan. He was torn between scouring the Core for clues about Gofun, picking Melonine's brain for more information regarding the Ten, or returning home to warn Rekco of the trials he would soon face.

Kyoku chewed on the inside of his cheek, and after much deliberation, started towards the sea of desks.

Melonine's purple hair made her stand out from the other women, so finding her again was not as difficult of a task as Kyoku first thought. When he approached her desk, she was already looking at him with a smile on her pale face.

"Welcome back, Kyoku. I take it that your meeting with Oglis went well?"

"Because I'm still alive?" he scoffed.

"Because you have been granted access to new information," she said flatly.

Is she truly just a doll? he wondered after seeing her lack of reaction to his sarcastic remark. In that moment of unexpected empathy, his mind went to a place he did not predict. "Could you ... tell me more—about yourself?"

Melonine's eyes changed for a second, as though his words had caused her pain. When she spoke, she was as monotone as before. "My name is Melonine. I am the *ninth* of my sisters, created by Dalu himself in an attempt to bring back his lost love—" she stopped, hesitating as though she had said too much.

"How could the creator of all things love something? Was this woman also originally one of his creations, or is it possible that—"

"Forget I said that, please. I, uh—request that you change the subject to things you are authorized to know about."

She told me something I'm not supposed to know? Is that the power of free will? Kyoku's heart raced at the thought. Melonine suddenly became the most important person to him. Her ability to overstep the boundaries imposed upon her could be the key to learning the truth about this place—and finding Oglis' weakness. "That's okay. We can change the subject," he said in a soft tone, while, in his mind, he schemed. *I need to be careful not to push her. I need to remain in good standing with her, so as not to lead her on that I am using her for information for my own goals.* "Could you then, tell me more about the Ten?"

"Certainly. What would you like to know?"

"First, tell me about the Swordsman."

"Very well. He is a man who was born into a war-torn world, where technology and magic never had a chance to advance beyond the ability to craft sharp blades, spears, arrows, and other weapons of death."

"Why not? Were they all really too preoccupied with trying to kill one another?" Kyoku scoffed at the thought of such a barbarous place.

"Precisely. These unending world wars drove the populous to near extinction, and it became evident that the apocalypse was nigh. Instead of banding together to bring stability to their race, the people of this world began to blame one another—and thus, the war continued. One day, a scout reported to his general that one of his most powerful vanguards was mysteriously wiped out. The general suspected an enemy flank or some other form of trickery. He dispatched the full force of his army to that point, in hopes of overwhelming the would-be attacker, but when he and his company arrived, they were met by certain, instantaneous death—by the hands of a single swordsman.

"This was the first time we in the Core observed and recorded such a phenomenon. It became clear that this man was no ordinary mortal. He went on to single-handedly slay every soldier, general, commander, and king on the planet, bringing an end to both the war, and humanity itself."

"What then? What happens when somebody survives until the end of the world?" Kyoku asked, beginning to wonder if such a fate might befall his own world.

"Normally, such a person would be offered a permanent position here, to work for Dalu—but this mysterious, nameless swordsman was no normal man. Because we did not know the full extent of his abilities, we could not afford to give him the opportunity to *jump* to another world and be lost again. We sent a taskforce to capture him, but it was futile. The Swordsman even fought death itself to a standstill."

"Death itself? Such a thing exists?"

"Yes, the being known as the Reaper of Worlds is the master of death, whose job it is to destroy worlds when they have reached the end of their lifecycle. Since this event predated the birth of Oglis, we did not have an established protocol for how to apprehend such powerful beings."

"If death could not take him and you had no other ideas, then how did he come to reside here?"

"It is said that Dalu himself made a deal with the Swordsman—a divine pact, if you will."

"A divine pact?" Kyoku's mind raced at the possibilities of such a thing, though he did not yet believe that a higher power truly existed.

"Yes. The details of the pact were made off the record, and many of the specifics were lost in time. Legends say that Dalu was able to recruit the Swordsman to help him procure others like himself, and in exchange, allow him to roam freely and do as he pleases within the confines of the universe."

"So, does that make the Swordsman the true leader of the Ten?"

"Not quite. He is not a leader, but one who thrives when acting alone. Once Oglis joined the ranks within the Hall of Fate, her leadership skills were quickly realized, and she assumed the mantle of leader of the Ten."

Kyoku shifted his lips. He did not trust this organization, and he did not trust in their god-like cult leader, Dalu. *Ten ultra-powerful beings that God himself seeks to control? It can't be for anything good. I need to come up with a plan, but what can I do if that twisted leader of theirs, Oglis, is impervious to my magics? She said her power was the counter to mine, so maybe there exists a counter to her own.* He pondered for a second, his mind processing as fast as it could, until a single solution came to mind, one that he was not fond of. *I have no choice but to help Rekco. Maybe together we could defeat her. I'm sure he would join me as soon as he found out that they might know something about his father.* "What is the Swordsman's weakness?" he asked aloud.

Melonine raised an eyebrow in hesitancy. "The Swordsman is the oldest and most revered member of the Ten. We don't even know his true name. He has never been defeated in battle, not even by Oglis." She shook her head. "We must thank Dalu for the fact that we have him as an ally. If I were you, I would refrain from speaking such questions aloud, should you be deemed a *traitor.*"

The way she said that word elicited a response that Kyoku had kept locked deep in his conscience. "*Like my parents?*" he mouthed so quietly that he could not hear himself, but the words repeated in his head; those were the last words Gofun spoke to him, in a voice that was not his own, before he vanished in an explosion of destructive magic. "It's nothing. Disregard the question."

Melonine's eyes appeared human for a moment, as if seeing and empathizing with the pain he was feeling. "You're not thinking of giving aid to Rekco Curse, are you?" she asked. Kyoku stared into her eyes, trying to read her intentions before speaking a response, but before he could determine if he could trust her, she continued. "It wouldn't make a difference at this point."

Kyoku furrowed his brow. "Why not?"

"Because—" Melonine began, glancing down at the far end of the room, "The Swordsman has already returned from his voyage to your world—with his bounty."

Kyoku's heart sank into the hollow pit of his stomach. He whipped around to see what Melonine was seeing.

Chapter 10: Hou

Rekco continued to train his body and mind every day, excited by the thought of doing so for the first time since his days as a child training under Maven, when each day felt like a brand-new adventure. He missed Maven dearly. The admiration for his late master served to drive his desire to obtain more power. *I won't let anyone else dear to me to die before their time.*

He thought of Cathy every day he trained. Every time he saw the blue Hope Lily in the windowsill, he was reminded of how she would pick the flowers from hilltops and tuck them behind her ear and the sweet earthy scent that filled the room whenever she walked in with one on her person. There were no Hope Lilies in the slums, he knew. He wondered if she missed the flowers and the grass and the breeze now that she was holed up in that rundown fortress with Zeke and his company.

Such thoughts filled his mind the whole morning. Rekco had become so adept at controlling his powers that even when his mind was distracted so, he was able to complete his morning drills without error. By noon, he found himself halfway to Last Thesi with a basket full of Hope Lilies in hand. He planned to stop by Zeke's hideout and drop them off for her. Even if she refused to see him, he still wanted her to have them.

"Maybe Zeke can run some more strength training exercises with me while I'm there," he thought aloud. He stopped when he emerged from the hills and caught sight of the towering walls outside of Last Thesi. "What the?" He squinted, able to scarcely make out that one of the humongous double doors that led to the Parade Grounds were ajar.

Rekco picked up the pace. Once he arrived at the gate, ready to question the absentminded gate guard, he came to find that the post was vacant. He scratched his head while glancing about the area. An empty chair sat beside the gate with a newspaper tucked beneath its leg. "What was that lazy guard thinking? Opening the entrance to the Parade Grounds then abandoning his post? Kinnley would have never done such a thing." Mentioning Kinnley made his heart ache again, and it reminded him of the scorn in Dim's voice the last time they spoke, which only made the pain worse. He couldn't bear to admit to the possibility that Kinnley's blood was on his hands.

Rekco set down his basket of flowers and proceeded towards the Parade Grounds to see if he could find the absent guard and give him a stern, Kinnley-like, talking to.

The opening was barely wide enough for a person to enter. He shimmied through, feeling like he was sneaking into a giant's home. Beyond the door was the perfectly white brick road that stretched all the way through the city to the beach on the other end of it. The Parade Grounds was a place where fanciful spectacles took place every once in a blue moon. Rekco had only ever been to one parade in his whole life, but it was a thrilling experience that remained vivid in his mind even now.

The grounds were empty, which was no surprise, seeing as there was nothing to see there when there was no parade, aside from the grueling Runic Tower that shot into the heavens at the center of the city. The threatening aura the crimson spire gave off was enough of a deterrent to keep even the most desperate vagrants from trying to breach the grounds—that, and the promise of certain death that came with approaching the Central Tower uninvited.

Rekco glanced around from the entrance. The gate guard was nowhere in sight. "Where could he have gone?" he said as he slowly set foot inside. The wide road ran between the enormous walls that separated the slums and the Research District. The only direction to go from there was forward, so Rekco did just that.

When at last he set his eyes on the Runic Tower, after having tried to ignore it since he entered the grounds, it seemed to infiltrate his mind like the repressed memories of a long-forgotten trauma rising to the surface. *I'm stronger than I was last time I was here,* he thought, and it was true. It took but a moment for Rekco to refocus his mind and dispel the tower's imposing presence from his mind. Feeling more confident after staving off the tower's affliction, he continued deeper into the Parade Grounds in search of the gate guard.

He glanced up at all the empty balconies and spectator's boxes that adorned the brick walls on either side of him but caught no sight of the guard. The more he looked, the more he wondered if the guard had even entered the grounds at all. It was clear that there was nothing to be seen between where he stood and the Runic Tower sitting at the center of the grounds. "Is it possible that he went beyond the tower?" Rekco said, not liking the idea of having to walk all the way to the foreboding tower and circle around it just to find out.

Rekco continued to walk towards the tower, almost aimlessly at times, his mind occasionally going blank, which made him forget what he was doing there for a brief moment. Suddenly, a voice popped into his mind that was as clear as his own conscience.

"You lack *precision*!" it said, a phrase that made absolutely no sense to him.

"The tower's tricks never end, do they—" Rekco began saying, his heart dropping into his stomach as he felt a murderous intent weigh heavily on him.

Instinctively, Rekco kicked off his front foot and threw himself backwards as a thunderous *crack* erupted

Searching for The Eminent: The Collapse of Reality 121

and echoed throughout the grounds. He glanced down, feeling as though time were moving at a snail's pace, and saw an enormous gash appear where he was just standing; pebbles and debris were flung in every direction, drifting through the air as slow as clouds in the sky. Time returned to normal as Rekco landed on his feet. The ground beneath him vibrated from the force at which it was struck, making him wobble in place, his eyes darting every which way to find the source of the attack.

"You're as quick as they say," a meticulous voice called, but Rekco could not discern where it came from. "But you're untrained. You don't even understand your own power."

Rekco drew his eyes from the sky and saw a lone man standing a ways from him. He was an older man, with a long white ponytail and glasses. He was wearing a purple coat with black buttons and shoulder pads. A thin sword hung unsheathed at his hip, looking much like the katana Kaiten wielded against him in the Champion of The Underground Tournament.

Rekco drew the bronze sword from his hip, unsure what to expect from the mysterious swordsman before him.

"A warrior must be as great as the sword they brandish. Though, sometimes the sword is even greater," the man said as he raised his own blade up to the blue, sunlit sky, seeming more interested in it than him.

"Who are you, and why did you attack me? What did you do with the gate guard?" Rekco demanded in a stern voice, pointing the tip of his blade towards the man.

"My blade's name is Hou. I am merely its Swordsman." Hou shimmered in the sunlight, emitting a green glow when the light struck it just right. "I am not here to attack you, but merely to *test* your ability."

"*Test me?* Why? Did somebody send you? The Retallors? The Runic Guard?" Rekco gripped his sword tight, inching backwards, though he was too far from the door to flee from the trap that had befallen him.

"I bring regards from Oglis Inima and the Ten, but I operate under my own motive—to judge if you are worthy of taking up your father's mantle."

The Swordsman's words were like another language to Rekco, but the moment he mentioned his father did the fog disperse from within his brain and it all made sense. "My father?!" He cried at once, the hilt of his blade digging into his palm as he squeezed it. "What do you know about my father?" The brick road beneath Rekco's feet rattled as the mysterious power within him welled up. It would have only taken one false word at that moment for him to strike the Swordsman down as quick as lightning; but the sensation quelled, driven back by the unusual, yet familiar name that his mind recognized after a delay. "*Oglis ... Inima.* I feel like I've heard that name before—wait! I have! It was in a dream—where she spoke nonsense to me, threatened to kill hostages taken from Retallor Tower, and she too, mentioned my father—the Eminent. But that was just a dream. It wasn't real!"

The Swordsman shook his head as he closed his razor-sharp eyes. He looked up at the walls looming over them and the narrow patch of sky visible above where birds once soared. "You will find that many things in this world are not real. *This* is not real," he said, pointing his sword up where his eyes were drawn—but at what, Rekco did not know. "And to answer your question. I know little about the Eminent—only of his importance."

"Oglis Inima said she was looking for him, so I assume you are too. What do you want with him?" Rekco's heart was pounding with anticipation. He had not had any new leads regarding his father since he traveled to The Underground, though he was unable to search for him there before the place was destroyed. All these years that he's searched, news about his father seemed to elude him, yet now, it appeared that it gravitated to his newfound power.

"The Eminent is one of the Ten, being a crucial piece in stopping the *Fleeting Requiem*—that is why we seek such a person."

Rekco grimaced, his face contorting with confusion. "*The Ten? The Fleeting Requiem?* Everything you're saying is nonsense. If you don't want to tell me the truth, that's fine, but don't make up stories."

The Swordsman pushed his glasses up the bridge of his nose with his finger, stone faced in disposition. "The Fleeting Requiem is a cosmic threat. It will destroy everything you know and more if we don't find the Eminent. I will prattle on no longer if you wish not to hear my *stories*. Prepare yourself to be tested!" He widened his stance and held Hou in both hands. It was a stunning blade, one Rekco could not help but admire.

Though the Swordsman's words about a cosmic threat made Rekco shudder for a moment, it was fleeting, muddied by the deception he sensed. He readied his bronze blade, dropping his stance low, while channeling the sound of rushing water within his eardrums. All the while, he could not take his eyes off the peculiar sword. He lowered his blade, which made the Swordsman show emotion for the first time in their encounter.

"To yield is not an option, son of the Eminent," the Swordsman said in a stern tone.

"I'm not yielding! But your sword, Hou, is mesmerizing. I've seen blades like it before; a katana and a wakizashi, I believe they were called, but yours puts those to shame."

The Swordsman gave a gleeful smirk. "You are a true swordsman, just as I hoped. Hou accepts your recognition and praise. She was once a katana herself—but has become much more since her forging."

"As stunning of a blade as it is, I have to ask, why would you wield a dull sword?"

There was a glint in the Swordsman's eye as he spoke, "What you see right now is Hou in a sheathed state." What happened next made Rekco question if he were dreaming again. The silver blade in the Swordsman's hands rippled like water, until the layers of folded steel began to separate and sway every which way, just as the tall grass in the plains outside. The tendrils of liquid metal pulsed and zoomed back into its solid state, and Rekco felt a pain at his cheek; blood trickled from a surgically thin cut beneath his eye before he had even realized what happened. A violent *crack* rang through his ears and his heart sank as gashes formed in the brick walls on either side of him. "You see, Hou is a living being, with a soul just like you and me—and like you and me, she possesses a *gifted* soul, one capable of amazing feats."

At that moment, Rekco realized what dangers befell him facing this nameless swordsman and his enchanted blade. *I can't let my guard down, no matter how friendly this swordsman appears. I need to*—his mind trailed off as he focused his power, knowing now that he must maintain his heightened reactions just in case Hou were to launch another inhumanly quick attack.

"Your trial is simple:" the Swordsman announced unprovoked. "Your blade must meet my flesh before the seventh swing of my sword—which will bring your death. Even the tiniest scratch counts."

Rekco still did not understand the purpose of the trial, or even who the Swordsman was, for that matter—but if failure meant death, then he knew he must succeed. His heart fluttered with fear, but it did not falter. In fact, his vigor redoubled as he launched himself at the Swordsman at top speed, becoming nothing more than a blur of green and orange, ready to strike true with his blade and put an end to this outlandish trial. *I don't care what kind of abilities you or your sword possess, I won't give you a chance to raise your blade!* Rekco thought as he swung his sword, aiming to strike the Swordsman across the shoulder in a nonlethal way.

When Rekco's perception of time returned to normal, his eyes grew wide in disbelief, for his blade had caught nothing but air—the Swordsman was gone. Rekco accelerated again as he spun around to find the sword Hou coming down upon his head; from the corner of his eye, he spied that the fabric on the Swordsman's shoulder pad was frayed. He retreated in an instant from the Swordsman's attack, putting a fair amount of distance between them. The Swordsman did not act surprised when Hou did not find its mark. He instead stood calmly as he prodded the gash in his coat with his fingers.

"Cutting my clothes does not count, son of the Eminent," the Swordsman announced. "And now you've missed your chance to catch me by surprise." The sunlight reflected off his glasses, hiding his eyes. He nonchalantly returned to his wide stance, as though dueling at such superhuman speeds were ordinary to him.

Rekco, still dumbfounded, could not brush off such an occurrence. "*How?* How did you avoid my attack? There's no way you're as fast as me." Even as the words escaped his mouth, he wondered if it were, in fact, possible that there were others like him, like his father, with similar physical capabilities. But if so, what would make his father's power so important to seek out?

The Swordsman's wrists softened, and he shook his head. "I am not as quick as you, far from it, but my decades of experience offer me the anticipation to keep up with an opponent such as yourself. Not to mention, I know your power—perhaps just as well as you; I've watched you train and grow; I know your tendencies and techniques inside and out. You have little chance of striking me as you are now."

Rekco's face went flush. It reminded him of how Maven used to taunt him during their practice duels when he was young. That anger was always a surefire way to push him to train harder, to disprove his master. His temper flared at the thought that he was still so far away from achieving the mastery required to walk out from his father's shadow. "Don't underestimate me—" his eyes went blank as liquid steel zoomed towards his face. He swayed his upper body to the left just in time to avoid being skewered by Hou's edge.

Two. Rekco pushed himself away from the blade, setting his eyes on the Swordsman, who had not moved an inch from where he stood; Hou had merely extended to a length longer than the wide streets in the High District. *Now!* Rekco thought as he closed the gap between them and made to strike while the Swordsman was defenseless—or so he thought. The tip of Hou rippled into ten thin blades that rained upon him like a volley of arrows. *Three.* Rekco used all the speed he could muster to avoid the blades that struck the ground all around him, corralling him towards the unscalable wall that hid the Research District.

With nowhere to go as the storm of blades fell upon him, Rekco leapt at the wall, breaking the ground beneath him from the force. He hit the wall with his right foot and kicked off it, looking down as the liquid steel met at the wall and followed him, cutting up in a perfectly straight line, all the way up to the sky, barely missing him. *Four.* Rekco was breathing hard as he landed upon the ground, not used to exerting himself so much since learning to control his power. He watched as Hou's enormous blade raked across the clouds, rending them into nothing, before retracting back to where the Swordsman stood, still as a stone, without a drop of sweat on his brow.

How am I supposed to hit him when he can do THAT? Rekco racked his brain for an answer, with only two more sword swings to go before the Swordsman's seventh, which promised certain death.

"Your defensive capabilities are quite impressive, son of the Eminent, but that is not what we are searching for. We need someone who can strike true, against all odds, in the face of utter annihilation—in the face of the Fleeting Requiem," the Swordsman said before taking a deep breath. He took a single step forward and, with one masterful movement, swung Hou horizontally. The blade stretched forward all the way to Rekco and curved, sweeping across the entirety of the brick road.

Rekco reacted in haste as he dropped to his knees and slid beneath the attack in a similar fashion to how he would duck under tree branches in his training exercises. He rose and shot straight ahead towards the Swordsman, ready to unleash an attack of his own. He closed the gap between them in an instant and swung his sword with all his might across the Swordsman's abdomen, but his bronze blade was met with resistance; tendrils of liquid metal had shot up from the ground in front of him, creating a cage to protect the Swordsman.

Rekco turned his head for a fraction of a second and saw Hou rushing back from its sweeping attack as if it were a stream of water pouring down the drain. He dragged his blade across the impossible cage with a frustrated grunt and began to backstep as the tendrils before him erupted from the ground like the wild roots of a massive tree being uprooted. The metal lashed erratically, ripping the brick road asunder, forcing Rekco back to a neutral position.

Six.

Droplets of despair-filled sweat rolled down Rekco's chin as he gasped for breath, his heart thumping hard against his chest. His insides were roiling. He could not help but wonder if the Swordsman had been holding back all along, merely toying with him. As a child, he often wondered if Maven was doing the same during their sparring sessions, but was always too afraid to ask, for fear of the harsh truth of the disparity between them. But he was just a powerless child then, so how could this feel so similar?

Rekco recognized at that moment that he had been toyed with all along, that Maven never went all out on him, and that the Swordsman wasn't either. But now—the seventh swing was imminent—the death stroke. He stood there feeling as pitiful as a scorned child, powerless to stop the coming lashing.

The Swordsman looked sullen as well. He hung his head low, hiding the disappointment in his eyes. "Rekco Curse, son of the Eminent, you've failed. It seems that you are not a worthy successor after all. We shall have to continue our search for your father then. I bid you farewell. May you find peace in your next life—" and with that word, he vanished.

The hair on Rekco's neck stood on end and an electric chill shot through his whole body. He heightened his senses to the max, not ready to lay his life down so easily. His every muscle was tense at the sound of furious wind and water raging within his eardrums. It grew and grew, and after a painful *pop* that reverberated inside his mind, the Swordsman became visible. The blade master was soaring through the air, his eyes squinting with tremendous focus. His momentum began to slow rapidly, until he was inching along like a leaf drifting upon a gentle zephyr.

Though the Swordsman was moving at such a slothful pace, Rekco on the other hand, could not move an inch from where he stood; he couldn't even lift a finger. His perception had accelerated beyond what his body could act upon. He gawked helplessly as the Swordsman grew closer, his arm rearing back, Hou rumbling with the intent to kill, its layers of folded steel separating in slow motion.

The blade fanned out until it was a massive tidal wave of liquid metal that would soon crash into him and reduce him to nothing but a splatter of blood.

Even Rekco's roiled insides were frozen, leaving him in a perpetual state of nausea. He wondered if his vomit would come up before Hou's attack ended him, or if it would merely be lost in the bloodshed.

Despite the overwhelming doom he felt, Rekco did not give up. He tried to push himself to act, exhausting every ounce of what energy he could muster. *Move! Move! Move! MOVE, dammit! I can't die like this! Not before I find my—* and just like that, an awe-inspiring thought came into his mind. He imagined finding his father, the one and true Eminent, and joining forces with him to defeat Oglis Inima and her organization called *the Ten*. It was something out of a dream—better than anything he could dream of, really. He wanted that more than anything.

In that moment of pure desire, Rekco felt his left hand twitch. He struggled and strained like his life depended on it, which it very well did, and suddenly, his arm began to move. Rekco winced, feeling pain, anxiety, and fear all at once as he pushed his sword forward at the incoming Swordsman. He felt the veins in his neck and eyes bulging painfully, as though fire itself coursed through him. Hou was so close that his heart couldn't take it. He knew that if he lost focus, that this would be the last thing he saw.

With one last, desperate push, Rekco thrust his arm forward, roaring internally. Time came crashing back to normal, and everything went black. A moment later, Rekco heard himself take a deep draught of air, and all the pain he felt prior came back. He opened his eyes to the brick road inches away from his face, beads of sweat falling like rain as he dry heaved. The sound of metal scraping along the ground reminded him of the sword in his hand, its bronze edge coated red.

Rekco felt the displaced rubble digging into his knees and the stinging pain of debris entering the skinned right forearm he must have fallen on. He held his head up, met by a feeling of vertigo that made him want to vomit even more, and saw the Swordsman sitting before him, clutching his side with one hand, the other resting upon Hou, who stuck out of the ground beside him. His face was pained, yet cheerful.

"You—did it, son of the—" he was forced to stop by a blood-filled cough.

Rekco clambered to his feet, not feeling accomplished just yet. "You're—after—my father. I—can't—let you—get—away!" He held his bronze blade forward with shaky hands.

The Swordsman smirked, despite the blood dribbling from the corner of his mouth. "Don't get—too hasty now. You cannot fell me without a sword—" on that word, Hou lashed out, shredding Rekco's bronze blade like it was paper. "I hope you can find one—that matches—your *determination*."

Rekco let out an exhausted gasp, but he couldn't remember why. Emptiness washed over him, making him feel like the breeze could topple him. He fell to the ground just as the remnants of his sword did.

*

Rekco's eyes cracked open to the white brick pressing against his face. His head was pounding.

A voice rang in his ears, garbled a first, but came into focus as it continued. "... What's going on here? How on earth did you get into the Parade Grounds?"

Rekco turned his head with much fear, expecting the dizziness to make him want to pass out again. No such feeling came, to his surprise. Instead, he saw the aloof gate guard standing over him, looking shocked and annoyed.

"C'mon now, up! You gotta get out of here before the Runic Guard comes and sends the both of us to an early grave!" The guard helped Rekco to his feet.

Memories were slowly coming back into his mind. He glanced around, feeling like there should be someone else there. "The Swordsman!" he cried once he remembered.

"Ah! My ears!" the guard yelped, his face closer to Rekco's than he had cared to notice as he acted as a crutch for him to stand. "What are you talking about?"

"Where did he go?" Rekco was looking around, trying all the while to escape the guard's grasp so he could tear off after him.

"Have you gone *mad*?" the guard cried, that final word struck Rekco like a curse, making him freeze on the spot. "There's nobody else here! Nobody is allowed in the Parade Grounds! That's why you've gotta go! Now!"

Rekco's eyes were desperate to find evidence, but he was astonished to find that none existed. All the destruction their battle caused seemed to have been erased, even the blood that fell from the Swordsman's wound was gone. He raised his right arm that was skinned all the way up to the elbow and covered in rocks and dust. "Here! My arm! It's still hurt!"

"Yeah, yeah. That's because you FELL!" the guard made a point to shout that fact into Rekco's ear as retaliation.

Rekco winced but was not deterred. He patted his side to find his sheath was empty. "My sword is gone! I came in here with a sword and he cut it up!"

The guard grumbled and pushed a bronze hilt into his hands. The blade was all but gone, with only a couple of inches of an edge remaining. "*This?* It was sitting beside you. That's a pretty lousy *sword* if I've ever seen one."

The guard continued to walk Rekco towards the double doors leading to the plains outside.

By then Rekco realized how crazy he must seem. He consigned to keeping his mouth shut, lest he wanted to get sent to an asylum to rot until the end of the world. *It was real! It had to have been! If only Cathy was here—* "Cathy!" he cried out loud, again feeling embarrassed immediately after shouting.

"Huh? There was no girl in there either, buddy. Now that's a better dream, though. I wish there were girls in the Parade Grounds. This gate guard's salary can't afford much at Club Tower, ya know?"

"No, there wasn't a girl in there. But I was on my way to see one. I had a basket of flowers that I set down right by your chair when I saw you weren't there," Rekco pleaded, hoping they were still there.

"A basket of flowers, you say? We'll see about that, nutso. I've been sitting there all day and never saw a soul or *basket* come by."

The guard dragged Rekco all the way back to his post. All the while, he regretted mentioning the basket and what its absence would say about his mental state. He thought to overpower the guard and make a break for his house in the plains, but he knew needed to maintain a friendly relationship if he wanted to get into the city again without any hassle. When at last they both arrived at the empty chair, Rekco's heart fluttered; it was just as he last saw it, with a newspaper stuck beneath one leg, and a basket of Hope Lilies sitting beside it.

The guard's eyes looked like they would fall out of his head. "What? How? What kind of magic is this?!" he shoved Rekco away as if he were cursed. "Take your magic flowers and begone!"

Rekco took the basket without a word and went ahead beyond the open gate and into the slums of Last Thesi. While on his way to Zeke's hideout to drop the flowers off, he recounted his otherworldly battle with the stoic Swordsman. The memories were as real as anything, but so were his memories of all the dreams he's had of Maven ever since his death.

He ran his finger across his cheek where he remembered that Hou had cut him. The gash was gone, though upon further inspection, the blood remained. "That's strange. If the cut is gone, why would there still be blood?" His own words made him wonder about his powers and what they might be capable of. The Swordsman's harsh criticism stuck out in his mind. *You don't even understand your own power.* It made him think. He stole away into an empty alley. Though the slums itself were as barren as ever, he couldn't risk being seen.

Once he felt secure and alone, Rekco leaned his back against the wall and focused his will. Adrenaline coursed through his body as the mysterious power within him was brought out. Instead of bolting off at an inhuman speed or exerting the strength of a mammoth, he simply stood still and watched his injured arm. The wound began to warp and slowly seal, as though time were being sped up for him alone. The rocks and debris were pushed out from his flesh as it closed up and became as if it were never injured at all.

Rekco let out a breath of exhaustion, unable to maintain the acceleration any longer. He slid down the wall, panting and heaving. "Maybe it's too soon for me to be doing that again after such an intense battle. But ..." he raised his right arm up to the sunlight. It was grey with soot and dust, but altogether uninjured, "... this sure is miraculous. I wonder if my father was able to do the same. Maven never told me any stories about my father having healing powers, but I guess he also never told me any stories where my father got hurt in the first place."

Rekco sat, mesmerized by his own feat, wondering all the while what his father's experience with learning to control his own powers was like, and most of all, wondering what became of the man known as the Eminent.

After a long rest, he picked himself up and finished his journey to Zeke's hideout. He missed talking to Cathy about news and developments regarding his search for Rekston, though he knew in his heart that his obsession with finding the Eminent was what drove them apart. "I'll just give her the flowers and go and save the talking for another time."

The hunchbacked door attendant welcomed him through the steel door to Zeke's hideout with a low bow. "It's good to see you again, Rekco. Have you come to join our efforts to save humanity from the coming apocalypse?"

Rekco's lips thinned at the question, knowing already what kind of disappointment his answer would cause. "I'm sorry, but that's not why I'm here, Kree. I just came by to bring Cathy these Hope Lilies from the plains. Could you call and see if she would be willing to come here and get them from me?"

Kree shook his head and his whole upper body along with it. "Unfortunately, Ms. Cathy is not here."

"Huh? Why not?" Rekco tried to poke his head around but there was nothing to be seen in this room made to appear like any of the other abandoned apartments.

"She's gone with Mikayla on a top-secret mission for Champion Bugbear. I would tell you where, but I don't know myself, truly."

Rekco let out a dejected sigh, his body still on the verge of collapse. He stumbled before shaking his head to reinvigorate himself. "That's okay. Could I leave the flowers with you instead?"

"But of course! I will keep them safe until she returns and present them to her on your behalf."

"Perfect. Thanks, Kree. I'll be going now." Rekco teetered out the door, no longer having any interest in asking Zeke to help him with strength training. He'd gone through enough trials for one day, he thought. On that thought, he wondered that if the Swordsman were but one of ten members of *the Ten*, would that mean that nine more trials awaited him? What would they be, and when would they happen? Rekco did not know for certain, but they would come sooner than he could prepare for.

Chapter 11: The Worth Of A World

There had been much clamor within Oglis' war room as she, Kyoku, Loch, and Ramirez watched a recording of the Swordsman's battle with Rekco.

"A stroke of luck!" Loch cried furiously. "Pathetic that the Swordsman would call that a success!"

Oglis snickered eerily, sounding like somebody was trying to blow into a broken kazoo. "But it wasn't luck, was it? Only the strong survive, right, Kyoku?" she said, turning her beady yellow eyes upon him as he sat alone at one end of the roundtable.

The way she spoke always implied that she knew his thoughts. It was a vile form of manipulation that Kyoku did not know how to combat. He simply gave a nod and remained quiet.

"What of the Swordsman's condition? Will he still be able to take part in the trials?" Ramirez asked.

"Unlikely. He's suffered a mortal wound. Dr. Gavin is currently tending to him to be sure his body doesn't enter a stasis."

What she said was true. Kyoku's hypersensitive ears could hear Dr. Gavin's voice coming from farther down the Hall of Fate. "Where are the healers when you need them?! Somebody get down to engineering and pull one up this instant!" There were so many things he did not understand about what those around him were saying. It was as frustrating as it was enticing. His thirst for knowledge rivaled his fear of Oglis.

"Excuse me," Kyoku began politely, "you say the Swordsman has suffered a mortal wound? Are you not worried that he will die? That seems like it would be the worst case scenario here."

Oglis snicker erupted into full blown laughter, the kind of mocking laugh of a pretentious teacher hoarding information from a fledgling student. "The Ten cannot *die*, not truly, not until our goal is achieved and our usefulness has run out." Kyoku raised his eyebrows in disbelief but did not dare to interrupt. "Should one of us be *killed*, our bodies would simply enter a stasis of resurrection. Though, it is said that someone returning from the dead is never truly the same." She glanced in the direction of Loch and Ramirez's silhouette and gave a playful jeer. "Isn't that right, Lovebirds?" Her question was met with grim silence.

"What about you? Have you ever died before?" Kyoku questioned, desperate to know if such a thing was even possible for a being as powerful as she.

"Unfortunately, no, I have not. Now, enough chit-chat. We must continue our mission. Rebecca, you're up next, and Kyoku too, we'll need you to help with this one."

Ramirez stood from her seat without a word. Kyoku was hesitant, not ready to follow the tyrant. He stood as well, but not in silence. "You want me to turn on Rekco? I have not yet agreed to join your efforts in *testing* him, nor have I agreed to join your organization—not without getting something in return."

Oglis' eyes lit up. Kyoku did not know if it was anger, exhilaration, or something else entirely that she was showing. She planted her massive hand on the table, leaning forward so she was basked in the beam of light shining from above. As her long head craned forward, the spiked whips that hung in a line down the back of her neck fell forward and draped over her broad blue shoulders. "No, I don't want you to *turn* on your little friend. Quite the opposite, actually. I want you to remain close enough to him that you can manipulate him to our liking. As for your—" she stopped to let out a short chuckle from her voice box, "—*demands*, I will first assure you that you will receive *many* things if you comply; knowledge, power, and the like. That being said, what is it that *you* desire to get in return?"

Kyoku felt nervous under Oglis' scrutiny. He did not expect her to concede to his wants in any way. "I—" he hesitated, feeling warmth on his cheeks. "I want you to assure the safety of Rekco, Cathy, and all of Last Thesi; that none of your plans will cause harm to any of the people there."

The yellow dots of Oglis' eyes shimmered, then grew a hair bigger. She burst into uncontrollable laughter, pushing herself off of the table and returning to the shadow. Her vociferous howls were inhuman, sounding full of violent intent and cruelty. An abhorrent creature like her was not meant to laugh, Kyoku thought. Her chest did not move as she bellowed, nor did her muscles contract, as though the laughter did not come from deep within her body. She waved her hand about, as if to disperse a cloud of laughing gas that shrouded her. "Rebecca, you can go now. Head to the rendezvous point and await further instruction."

"Aye." Ramirez said with a salute before disappearing from the shadowy table.

"Kyoku—" she said through bouts of repressed chuckles. "You are going to take the long way. Ask that doll of yours to tell you how to get to *Dock-C*, I'll have someone waiting for you there."

Kyoku was red in the face from both embarrassment and the fury he felt in the face of Oglis' mockery. "What if I say no?"

Oglis stopped laughing, and her voice became serious. "Then I will have to alter my plans in a way that might *cause harm* to MANY of the people in that little world of yours."

Kyoku shifted his lips, taking her threat as an adequate answer. "Am I dismissed then?"

"Off with you."

Kyoku left Oglis' foggy room and the Hall of Fate. He still had many questions, and luckily for him, Melonine was just the person he wanted to talk to. He returned to her desk in the vast room full of dolls and their ever busy conversations.

"You look displeased, Kyoku," Melonine said, turning her head slightly as she spoke to him, her purple eyes softer than when last they spoke.

"I'm fine," Kyoku raised his guard. "I wanted to ask you something."

"Oh? What is it?" Her expression seemed less robotic and more genuine. It must have been a long time since she received so much attention. The apathetic look on her face made him hesitate to probe her for his own gain, so instead, he got right to the point.

"Oglis asked me to go to a place called *Dock-C*. Could you tell me how to get there?"

"Of course," Melonine smiled, seeming joyful that he did not ask her a question that walked the thin line of what she was and wasn't allowed to say. She stood up and pointed. "You will want to go that way and—" her lips thinned, and she glanced about herself uncomfortably. "Actually, how about I go with you and show you the way myself?"

"That sounds—perfect," Kyoku said, returning her smile as best he could. His plan to get close to her was coming to fruition sooner than he predicted and he could scarcely contain how pleased he was. *Perfect, indeed. I'll know the truth about this place, the Ten, and Oglis' weakness soon enough!*

Together, they walked out of the crowded room and proceeded through the azure maze that made up the Core. This was the first time he had seen her stand up. To his surprise, Melonine was far taller than he expected, reaching what his height would be without his golden platform boots. The silky white dress that she wore beneath her breastplate extended all the way down to her feet, dancing upon the ground as she walked.

Melonine did not speak a word while they walked, but her eyes told a story of their own; a doll spurned by God himself because of the free will he mistakenly gave her, shackled to a desk for all eternity, now finally free to stretch her legs and wander the catacombs of her blue prison. Kyoku left her to her own thoughts, choosing to align to his theory that she could defy her makers if given enough time to ponder. His own mind kept to memorizing the patterns within the maze carved into this sea of Ather-like energy.

They traversed a plethora of narrow, winding hallways, gaping ballrooms, and unusual slopes and inclines that could not be seen, but instead felt when walking upon them. The areas they passed through were all but empty, only occasionally crossing paths with an armor-clad warrior, the likes of the guard Kyoku saw when he first entered the Core.

"Here," Melonine said at last as she went on ahead at a faster pace, and eventually stopped before a wall of faint blue energy that trickled down like a babbling brook into the fierce current of energy that made up the floor below them. "From here you will be able to see outside."

Outside? he thought as he approached the wall. Now closer to it, he noticed the energy grew weaker until it was all but translucent. What he saw beyond the window was scarcely a sight at all. All that could be seen were waves of black and white crashing into one another like a current of water streaming into an opposing torrent of oil. The longer he watched the two forces battle, did they blend into a grey static; chaotic and unrelenting, slamming each other into the window.

"What—is *that?*" Kyoku asked, unable to take his eyes off the pulsing black and white entity outside. Feeling uneasy about how safe it was to stand so close to the window, he began to retreat, stopping as he bumped into Melonine's reassuring hand at his back.

"This is the *Sturm*, or at least, that's what we call it here. It is one of the few unexplainable phenomena in the universe; a seemingly unending war between *light and darkness*, two forms of energy that little is known about. Master Zerus, the Worldmaker, who resides at the edge of the universe, has been researching them for some time now, taking samples from the Sturm that surrounds the Core."

"That thing is alive? And it has The Core surrounded? That doesn't seem safe."

Melonine nodded but did not appear as concerned as he. "It is said that the Sturm has existed as long as the Core itself, and despite that, it has never breached its walls. What it wants is a mystery to us all, but it continues to thrash the outer walls evermore. It is concerning, at most."

"What do you think it wants? There has to be something valuable in the Core if it is still trying to get in after all that time."

"What do *I* think?" Melonine looked confused, almost bleary-eyed at the thought that someone would ask her opinion on something rather than seeking factual information. She tucked her lower lip under her teeth, giving his question much thought. "It could seek the artifacts sealed within the Archives of Time. But to me, the answer is clear: I think it wants Dalu."

"*Dalu?* The so-called Creator of All Things?" Kyoku nearly scoffed while uttering such a title.

"Yes. He is the most valuable thing within the Core, so he must be what the Sturm seeks."

Kyoku shifted his lips. "Astute reasoning, I suppose. But wait—Dalu is *here?*"

"Yes. Where else would he be?"

"I don't know, somewhere watching over all the cosmos or something."

"He *is* watching over all the cosmos—from here. I have heard that Mel-one and Mel-two are the only ones who have seen him in person, while others merely speak with him at times through telepathic communication. I have done neither."

"Doesn't that make you feel—bad?" Kyoku prodded, in hopes of getting her to open up more and divulge her secrets. "If you're the ninth, I'd think you must be important, but it doesn't seem like they treat you that way here."

Melonine's posture slumped slightly. She was becoming more human to the wizard by the moment. She turned from the Sturm and looked at him with eyes full of kindness and confused emotions. "It does—but—I can't fault anyone for being put off by my ability to express free will. You—on the other hand—why are you saying these things?"

"Because I—feel the same as you here. I'm told that I'm one of *the Ten*, given reign to dwell within a place so prestigious that it's called the Hall of Fate. Yet, nobody tells me anything more than the bare minimum and I'm threatened more than I'm praised. I feel like a—"

"Prisoner?" Melonine finished for him. "I know that feeling. I always thought it was just my ill-mannered programming that made me feel such things. But now—I'm not so sure. You're one of the sacred Ten, only under Dalu in terms of importance here within the Core."

"It certainly doesn't feel that way," Kyoku scoffed.

"Let me—let me help you. Ask me anything! I'll tell you anything you wish to know to help ease your mind." She got terribly close. Kyoku could smell the faded perfume on her clothes, something that he imagined had been lingering on her for eons. It was a woodland scent, full of earthy tones and the sweet fragrances of dried flower petals and herbs.

Kyoku instinctively inched back from her, his heart sinking, whether from her presence intruding on his personal space, or from the prospect of her words, he did not know. *Anything* was exactly what he wanted to hear, but he knew he could not so bluntly ask for Oglis' weakness. He needed to feign innocence for a while longer. "There is a lot of talk here of destiny, fate, prophecies, and what have you. I want to know—what is my destiny? What is it that the Ten seek to do with me?"

Melonine's eyes gave away what her mouth had yet to; it was a grim response. She, too, shied away, clutching her arms to her armor and tucking her chin to her chest. "No. You don't want to know that. I want to help you— but—*that* won't. I'm sorry. I can't answer that." Her lack of response didn't leave much to the imagination. Kyoku's heart raced as he pondered what kind of maniacal scheme Oglis and *Dalu* had for him. It made him want to run, yet he knew such a thing would be futile while Oglis lived. Before he could respond, Melonine started off, beckoning towards a narrow hall left of the great window. "Dock-C is just through there. Please go now. You *don't* want to keep Oglis waiting." Her eyes were harsh, and her voice was as robotic as the moment they first met.

"Okay," Kyoku conceded. "I'll go now. Thanks for talking to me. Maybe we can talk some more when I return from the mission?"

Melonine gave a stiff nod, not saying a word as he passed in front of her and entered the hall.

The corridor had a steep slope. Kyoku imagined he could sit on the floor and slide down if he really wanted. At the bottom was a straight landing that jutted out into the storm of light and darkness, protected by the same thin veil as the window in the room above. Kyoku proceeded towards an idle craft sitting at the end of the platform. It was shaped like a bird and made of some foreign metal that was a greyish bronze in color. A glass dome covered the small cockpit that appeared to be room enough for only two people.

Kyoku approached the vessel, his eyes scanning over its lack of wheels and exhaust pipes, things even the Ather-powered carriers in his world had. His mind could not help but be curious how such a machine operated. Amidst his wonders, a man appeared from the other side of it, his forehead smudged with dark soot and the jumpsuit he wore stained with grime.

"Hey there," he greeted while waving. "Name's Maxwell Haunts, I'll be your chauffeur for today," he said with a grin, extending a gloved hand to Kyoku. The glove in question was even dirtier than the rest of him. He looked down when Kyoku did not reciprocate and quickly retracted his hand. "Oh, sorry! I'm a bit mucked up. I was just doing some work with the engineers below when I got the call to fly."

Kyoku took his eyes off the golden-haired man and set them on the craft beside them. "You'll have to show me how this thing works."

Maxwell let out a laugh, "Any time! I wouldn't get *too* interested though! Engineering isn't for everyone, ya know?" he swayed his right hand, emitting a faint red glow, and the glass dome over the cockpit opened.

Kyoku's eyes grew wide. The magic was so subtle, but he recognized it at once. He stared at the glass dome, raising his own hand to it. The luminescence from his hand was blinding in comparison to Maxwell's, but the machine reacted just the same, closing down to its original position.

"Woah!" Maxwell gasped. "You can do that?! Can't put anything past one of the Ten, huh?"

"What exactly is *that?*" Kyoku questioned, his voice sounding dire and angry when it came to the mystery of his origins and powers. He was so distracted that his hand was unknowingly still glowering with red magic as he got closer to Maxwell, whose audible yelp made him notice and undo the spell.

"Well, we don't really have a name for it, to be honest. We just call it *engineering*: the magic used for creating, manipulating, and destroying things. Everyone down in the engineering wing can do it, but that's because we were made to. It's an otherwise, incredibly rare skill, from what I've been told. It's no wonder you're so taken by the spaceship here! I bet you could fly this baby yourself with that kind of output!" Maxwell slapped the ship's metal exterior. "Whew, I can only imagine what kind of help you'd be to those working on the Waylynx II right now. But enough jabbering. We should be off. I don't want to get on Oglis' bad side."

There was so much to take in that Kyoku relegated himself to silence for the time being. It did not help that Oglis was expecting him to arrive by a certain time, it seemed. He would have wanted to probe Maxwell's brain to learn everything he could, but he figured there would be time in the future for such things. Maxwell opened the cockpit again and hoisted himself up into it. Kyoku followed behind and sat in the plush seat beside him.

It was a cramped contraption, allowing two to sit inside, but likely was only made to hold one person comfortably. The interior was far more lackluster than what Kyoku expected. The dash was barren, save for a circular dial that tracked the speed of the craft and the engine's heat levels.

"Buckle up and we'll be off," Maxwell said as he clasped a safety belt across his chest.

Kyoku found the belt and mimicked the pilot. A moment later, the glass dome closed down over their heads and the ship began to hover off the ground. Kyoku felt an unusual weightlessness as the ship coasted gingerly towards the wall at the end of the landing. He braced himself for impact, but to his surprise, no such thing came. Instead, the pointed nose of the carrier pressed into the magic wall as though it were made of rubber.

After some resistance, the membrane broke, and the ship zoomed through it all at once. Awfulness was the next thing Kyoku knew when they entered the black and white entity called the Sturm; terrible feelings were being injected into his mind from every direction as the ship wobbled back and forth within the mass of static. A crimson barrier surrounded the ship in its entirety, protecting it from the Sturm's onslaught. It was a nightmare come alive; sorrow, anguish, confusion, and hatred all buffeted in an endless volley against the ship's shields.

Kyoku slowly turned to face Maxwell, only to find that he appeared unaffected by the Sturm's imposing presence.

"First time through the Sturm, huh? You get used to it, I promise. It's a wild thing, but I assure you, it's perfectly saf—"

The ship was struck hard, like it was a fly being swatted out of the sky. It spun out of control, making Kyoku's insides roil and brain pulse with pain more so than it already had. Everything became a blur as the ship spiraled; downward or upward, he wasn't sure. After a chaotic moment that felt like an eternity, the ship steadied itself and began to fly straight again.

Kyoku grabbed his bulbous hat off the dash and set it back upon his head, turning to Maxwell with a face of contempt. "You were saying?"

"Ah! Just a bit of turbulence!" Maxwell said with a weak laugh. "I'll be honest though, I've never seen *that* level of turbulence before. The Sturm must be feeling rowdy right now. But no worries, we'll be through it in just a moment."

Maxwell was right about that, at least. Not more than a minute later, they exited the cruel amalgam. The emotions his mind was exposed to were gone like a dream the moment they were clear from the Sturm, but Kyoku was left feeling torpid. It took him a bit longer than it should have for him to react to the scene outside of the Sturm because of that. When he came to, he jolted upright, unable to contain the gasp that came forth.

"First time seeing it, right? Not what you had expected, I'd imagine," Maxwell said as he steered the ship left from the Sturm, out into the vast universe.

It was, in fact, far from what Kyoku had imagined the universe would be like. The array of colors scattered throughout the cosmos were magnificent; greens and blues, reds and purples, stars upon stars, so many that they formed spirals, all upon the black void that seemed to stretch farther beyond any of it. From where the ship had exited, Kyoku felt like he could see the entirety of the universe, unmoving; still as a painting, all the cosmic dust and stars were, and without a planet in sight.

"What's going on here? This cannot be *it*," Kyoku demanded an explanation. His mind needed it.

"Well, you see," Maxwell began, scratching his head in the face of Kyoku's scrutiny, "the universe isn't quite finished."

"*Finished?* Finished, what? Being made?"

"Ah, yeah! That's the right way to put it," his eyes shied away, acting as though piloting the ship suddenly required more attention than it had prior.

Kyoku furrowed his brow. *Nonsense. There must be more to this than I am allowed to know.* "So, you're telling me that Dalu, Creator of All Things, isn't done creating *all things?*"

Maxwell didn't respond, his eyes seeming focused on something out in the empty, eerily still reaches of space. His eyes weren't lying though, it seemed, as Kyoku too noticed the unusual object they were approaching. It appeared to be a semi-circular platform made of metal with a ring of silver acting as a guardrail around it. At the center of it was something too small for Kyoku to tell what it was from so far away.

He kept his eyes on the center of the semi-circle as the ship began to decelerate. The small object looked like a snow globe, though it did not depict a cheery scene like those he had seen in Last Thesi. Instead, it housed a grey light and nothing more. The glass globe's base was made of a dark grey stone which sat upon a metal platform attached to the semi-circle.

"We've arrived," Maxwell announced as the ship touched down softly on the metal landing. The glass dome lifted, and he sat with anticipation for Kyoku to exit the craft.

"Where have you taken me?" Kyoku asked, not ready to be left alone on some stationary platform lingering in space.

"Uh," Maxwell stammered, "home?" He looked as unsure about his answer as Kyoku was. "World One, right? Don't tell me I got it wrong. Oglis will send me to the *endless nightmare*," he shuddered.

"No," came a hollow-sounding voice that sent a chill down Kyoku's spine. He spun around in his seat and saw Oglis standing over the ship, having seemingly appeared out of thin air. "You're quite right, albeit a little slow in arrival. Come now, Kyoku, we've much to discuss."

Kyoku's body seemed to move on instinct, heeding the monster's will. The moment his golden boots touched down on the platform, the glass dome on the ship closed and it sped off, back towards the miserable Sturm that could be seen writhing at the center of the universe.

Kyoku adjusted his black and teal vest before turning his sights upward to Oglis.

"Now that you've seen the universe for what it truly is, I imagine you have a lot of questions. That is why I allowed you to see it," Oglis said, looming terribly over Kyoku.

"You want me to ask questions?"

"I want you to *understand* what is at stake here. The universe's growth is stunted for a reason."

"And what is that reason? Because it is destined to do so?" Kyoku gave a quiet scoff.

"Because there is less to get attached to, less lives on the line when it comes to stopping the Fleeting Requiem, and most importantly, less places for such a threat to hide."

"What exactly is *the Fleeting Requiem?* Is it another group like the Ten?" Kyoku questioned, his eyes drawn to the peculiar snow globe sitting before him.

"It is an entity with the power to destroy the entire universe. That is all you need to know about it, and that we, the Ten, are the only ones capable of stopping it."

"Why? What makes *us* so special?"

Oglis snickered sinisterly. "Because, in truth, each of the Ten harbor a piece of Dalu's power." Kyoku furrowed his brow, his eyes becoming unfocused at the thought, but did not speak. "When Dalu sought to create the cosmos and everything in it, he wanted to create *ten* disciples to help him watch over it. But something went awry; a distraction, an attack upon him, or maybe he simply exhausted more power than he needed to—we'll never know. Amidst the great *overflow* of energy that the universe began to unfold from, ten pieces of his power flew out into the cosmos, hidden among all the souls of the beings that were meant to fill it.

"At that moment, it is said that Dalu stopped the flow of time, halting the expansion and creation of the universe in an instant. Within the same very moment, all the prophecies and destinies were born, and Dalu knew what the true purpose of those ten would be. Now we live within this eternal second, while Dalu attempts to locate those ten fragments of himself and bring them to defend the universe from annihilation."

"That is a lot to take in," Kyoku said, trying to play scenarios in his mind where such a thing was possible. "So, you're telling me that my being one of the Ten was random? It could've been anyone else?"

"Maybe," Oglis said with a glint in her beady yellow eyes. "Perhaps Dalu's power is attracted to souls with a strong will, souls destined to become great beings, worthy to house such a power."

Kyoku glanced at the glass globe full of shimmering grey light that sat at waist height. "And what of *this?* —" he extended his arm towards it while pointing. The moment his finger got within a certain proximity from it, he felt an intense gravitational pull coming from it that made his body jolt. He reeled back at once, looking down at his hand to see if it were unharmed, then back to the globe, more questions swirling about his mind.

Oglis slowly cupped her large, three-fingered hand around the glass bauble; her fingers trembled against the tremendous force while it tried to pull her inside. She broke free from it and took a step back, a stiff-sounding breath coming from her voice box. "Inside this orb is a world—*your* world; the sun, the moon, the stars, and your little blue planet, all existing within this tiny sphere. I could crush it within the palm of my hand, and all within it would be lost; that little city of yours and all the people in it, all living under glass. Such a fragile existence."

Kyoku's face became messed up with confusion. He got as close as he could to the small globe, staring at it with focused eyes, but he could see nothing within it beyond the grey light. "How is such a thing possible? Better yet, *why?*"

"Magic is truly a miraculous thing, is it not? This is the handiwork of Zerus, the Worldmaker. There are four other stations like this one set up around the edges of the universe, all observed by Dalu's chosen *Overseers*. Each of them contains a vast galaxy and at least one planet bearing life."

"Why create such a large space for a miniscule amount of life? Why not create a galaxy *full* of life?" Kyoku questioned, still trying to come to grips with the startling new information.

Oglis shot a husky scoff from her voice box. "My people traversed the stars for eons, searching for planets to conquer, to assert our dominance within the galaxy; and all that time, we never once found the edge of space, let alone Dalu's Overseer. I imagine the Overseer of my world got a good laugh out of that. We were fearless flies who never found the great light to zap us from existence—no matter how hard we tried." Kyoku gave her a sideways glance, only halfway understanding what she was rambling about. "*That* is why."

"So it's all just to keep us from learning about the truth? About this world beyond our own, frozen in time?" Kyoku spat, insulted by the thought of pompous gods deciding such things.

"Precisely. Which brings us to *your* why." Oglis' eyes became devious. She craned her long neck so she could watch Kyoku's expression as she unveiled the harsh truths to him. "These worlds are no more than a simulation—an illusion of life, the purpose of which is to allow beings to be born in an unending cycle of life, until another one of the Ten shows themselves. Then, the observer of the world relays that information to me, and—well, I think you know the rest."

Kyoku's heart sank at the thought, his chest rising and falling. Terrible thoughts came to his mind, regarding the worth of life and its purpose. He brushed those thoughts aside in an attempt to retain control of his emotions. "That's *why* life exists? All the suffering, and sadness, and death; just to find the Ten? And what fills these globules full of life? Dalu? Some other crony of his?"

"Why, Dalu has already created all life. I think you've already seen it," Oglis stretched her long arm and pointed out into the cosmos at a great swirling mass of stars. It was something Kyoku had already noticed on his way there. It was easily the biggest celestial body in the universe; a massive whirlpool, full of shimmering stars, moving slower than the hour hand on a clock. Now that he thought about it, it was the only thing, aside from the Sturm, which moved within this existence frozen in time. "I can see the gears turning within your mind. And your thoughts are exactly right. That thing, known as the Great Whirlpool, is the source of all life. Those stars you see swirling inside it are not stars at all—those are *souls*. That place is overseen by the Reaper, said to be Dalu's most powerful disciple."

Kyoku had had enough of Oglis' threats, mind games, and fabrications. He let out an exasperated sigh. "Enough of your nonsense, monster!" he boomed, raising his hand to her. But before he could say another word, a thin veil of light, the same color as Oglis' eyes, surrounded them, and Kyoku's body seized up.

"I knew it would be too hard to make you believe me with words alone. That is why I brought you here—so I could *show* you, so my words could be undeniable. Now, come with me." At her final word, the barrier that had surrounded them began to move, bringing them closer to the world-bearing globe, until Kyoku felt heavy as a boulder, yet light as a feather, and they were both sucked inside.

Everything was black at first, but the tiny speckles of stars became visible moments later, painting his vision with their light. The sphere of energy that held Kyoku and Oglis zoomed through space faster than he could process. The stars that he first saw became nothing more than trails of light cutting across the black void of space. Not long later, their celestial carrier came to a halt, and Kyoku's blurred vision began to regain focus.

"Look familiar?" he heard Oglis' voice ask.

Kyoku could still not make out what he was seeing, aside from various shades of greens and blues that melded together to fill the entirety of his vision. He squinted, trying to force some clarity. It worked enough for him to recognize that they were sitting idle outside of the atmosphere of a planet. "Is this—"

"Correct. This is the doomed planet you and your friends reside on."

Doomed, her voice echoed in his already swimming head. "*Why?* Why does it have to be doomed?" His body was trembling with anger, with no place to direct it.

"Because it has already served its purpose, and should it continue to thrive, it would be that much harder to locate the Eminent. You fail to understand that the souls of those that do not house a piece of Dalu serve no purpose; their lives are meaningless, only awaiting death, in hopes that they could return again with something more to offer. If I had it my way, I would kill all the *worthless* beings to speed up the process. What do their lives matter when the fate of the universe hangs in the balance?"

That word and the venomous way she wielded it, stuck with Kyoku; *worthless*. He could not help but think of those few he cared about; both those lost and those still living. Two in particular came to mind: Gofun and Mandie. They both believed in him and treated him with the utmost kindness, despite his often dour demeanor. Knowing that they were both gone made his heart feel like it was in a vice—yet to Oglis, they must seem as inconsequential as specks of dust on the wind. The thought made rage flow all throughout his being. He wanted to attack her, to unleash every spell he could manifest before his body was lost to the vacuum of space. But he could not allow his hatred for her to get in the way of trying to save his world. It took all his concentration to stifle such desires, leaving him silent before her. Oglis seemed to read his convictions and looked to press him more so.

"You wanted to know *your* purpose in all this?" She began, her voice conniving. "Yes, I was listening to your conversation with the doll. I hear *everything* within the Core. Allow me to tell you the truth your *darling* was so afraid to. Your soul, Kyoku, the Overflow, will serve as the catalyst to create a new, *perfect* universe once the Fleeting Requiem is defeated. So, take solace in knowing that, even though you won't be able to see it yourself, your sacrifice will be for the greater good; finally, you'll be a real *hero*—albeit, unwillingly. THAT is your destiny!"

Kyoku's shoulders and head slumped forward as turmoil took root within his mind. *It can't be true. But— none of this should be true. A universe, untouched by time, worlds being raised as cattle, its inhabitants serving no purpose other than to die, and a galactic threat that scares even the creator of the universe itself.* It all was nearly too much to bear. His desire for knowledge had never hurt him so, not since he greedily destroyed the magic tome Gofun left for him as a child while trying to probe its forbidden pages.

"Your silence speaks volumes, Kyoku. Do you believe me now? Good. Do you have any last questions for me before I send you off? Remember, we have a mission to uphold," Oglis said, acting nonchalant despite the damage she had done to Kyoku's psyche, visible on his face.

He had plenty more questions—of course he did—but he could not allow the tyrant to know his deepest desires: the search for his origin and parents. Kyoku knew that she would use it as leverage against him if he were to show how much it meant to him. Yet, one other question had lingered on his mind for some time; a mystery born from Rekco's search for his own father. "I have one last question," he said through gritted teeth, abating his own malice as best as he could.

"Well? What is it?" Oglis asked, sounding both intrigued and impatient.

"Did you kill Irol Retallor?"

And just then, for the first time, Kyoku saw it: the most subtle shift in the muscles around Oglis' eyes and contractions of the leathery mesh that lined the rectangular voice box that extended from below her eyes down her neck. Such a simple question, yet it elicited so much more than he knew her to be capable of. "Why, yes, I did," she responded coolly.

"Why? To end the Irol Age and quicken the extinction of man so you could snuff out the Eminent?"

The lights in her eyes thinned. It must've been the closest thing to a smirk that she could manifest. "No. In fact, I did not have any plans for the Eminent at that time. I killed him because he, too, is one of the Ten. He is now in our custody. A tricky bugger, he was," she raised her left arm up, or rather, what remained of it. "He made me lose my arm. Though, I can't complain. I have since repurposed it and have grown quite fond of its new *function*."

Kyoku's eyes grew wide at the thought. He had always wondered how a being that could regenerate more quickly than she could be destroyed would be missing an arm. Finding out that Irol Retallor was one of the Ten was nothing compared to learning that Oglis' immortal body could actually be harmed—somehow.

"Nothing else, then?" Oglis asked as though she were a train conductor preparing to take off. "I will send you down to the rendezvous point now. Rebecca is already there waiting for you."

The yellow veil that surrounded them began to encroach upon Kyoku alone, leaving the alien floating in space. Bright lights filled his vision, and a feeling of weightlessness washed over him. The mission at hand was far from his mind. He had much to ponder, far too much.

Chapter 12: Apocalyptic Acquaintances

There was plenty of daylight left to burn by the time Cathy and Mikayla reached the border between the slums and the Middle District. There wasn't a gate guard in sight to attempt to thwart riff raff from entering the *pristine* western quadrant of Last Thesi. Cathy couldn't help but stand and stare at the quiet town that mirrored the rotten slums; they were so similar, yet so different all the while.

"The air is so clean here," Cathy said, taking in a deep draught of fresh air into her lungs. It reminded her of the plains, a place she missed terribly. It had been a month already since Zeke's hideout in the slums became her new home. It was so much more cramped than she was used to, but it was no surprise since she was sharing quarters with a host of refugees from The Underground.

"Yeah, it is," Mikayla agreed, showing a forlorn expression of her own. "The last time I was here was as a Doombringer, along with Marcus and our good friend Beal, and Koku." She pointed at the Runic Tower in the distance; the red and blue spire stuck out apart from the homely buildings like a sore thumb—a fiction within reality. "Beal died there, killed by the Runic Guard."

"That's terrible. I'm so sorry for your loss. We don't have to go any further if it will only cause you pain to be here."

Mikayla shook her head. "No, it's fine. It could have been me who died that day, or Marcus, or Koku. It could've been Beal standing here with you today. I—I have to cherish the life that I have—for those who could not be here today," she said, clutching the medallion around her neck in her hand, her voice breaking. Cathy sidled up next to her and squeezed her tight, fighting the tears behind her eyes. "So," Mikayla began as she wiped her reddened eyes. "What do you want to do first?"

"Well, as much as I want to see the sights and shop for gifts to bring back to Zeke's, there's something far more important for us here. We can have our fun after that."

"Business first. I like that," Mikayla smiled. "What are we waiting for then?" She took Cathy by the hand, who returned the smile, and the two of them tore down the cobblestone road.

Even the roads were clean. The same cobblestone that ran through the slums was scarcely recognizable with the years of dirt and grime caked onto it. As wondrous as the Middle District was to Cathy, seeing it made her sad for the people forced to live in the slums for all the years leading up to when Kyoku recently tore down the wall between them.

"It's strange," Cathy began, and the two of them stopped in the street. "Seeing the same buildings as the ones in the slums, but these ones full of life, really aggravates me. And to think that the Retallors that ran this city for decades left that place for dead."

Mikayla frowned. "Not anymore. But, speaking of buildings *full of life*," she pointed at a row of desolate homes to the northeast. "Not all of them are."

Cathy gasped when she noticed an entire cul-de-sac was as rundown as the slums were; abandoned homes with broken doors, boarded up windows; some even had caved in roofs or gaping holes in the exterior brick walls. "Don't tell me," she began to say within a breath as she scanned the forsaken homes.

"Looks like it," Mikayla confirmed. "Vagrants from the slums have already taken over that once quaint little street. They'll run rampant through the whole Middle District like a disease, I'm sure, now that there's no barrier to stop them. Should we go drive them out?"

It saddened Cathy to imagine that this homely little town within Last Thesi could be a replica of the slums within a year's time. But that thought was merely a distraction to humanity's new goal. "No. That's not why we're here. It won't matter if they level this whole town once we're gone. Let the walls crumble on top of their heads and bury this whole place for all I care. We'll make our own homely town—elsewhere."

Mikayla gave a nod of comradery. "It's the harsh truth, but I'm glad you can see it. Let's keep going."

They went ahead beyond the depressing sight, to a shabby marketplace where some of the surviving townsfolk gathered. There were carts and stands set up all around the market square; some full of vegetables, others selling handmade clothes and jewelry, and various other makeshift shops for people to haggle and trade goods. It was a pleasant sight to see people talking and laughing in broad daylight—something Cathy was not used to seeing.

As Cathy walked to the center of the courtyard, all sorts of heads turned. Not only was her pink hair a sign that she was a descendant of those beyond the Forgotten Woods, but she and Mikayla were the only women there. She could hear the murmurs regarding her hair and tried not to lash out at the host of eyes upon her; she often forgot how uncommon it was, and wondered if Rekco would have drawn just as many eyes with his green hair.

"Look at this," Cathy said to Mikayla, who trailed just behind her, shooting dirty looks at the rubberneckers all the while. There was a stone monument that stood taller than her. Plastic flowers littered the ground around it. Upon the slab names were etched—far too many to count. Cathy knew immediately what it was.

"A memorial?" Mikayla asked as she looked it up and down.

"Seems so," Cathy's voice became full of sadness the longer she looked at it. She knelt down and ran her finger along the row of names that were in alphabetical order, starting with the family name. Mikayla followed her finger as it slowed on the S's.

"That's a lot of Smithy's. It looks like the whole family was wiped out by the halvening," Mikayla's tone became deflated at the thought.

"All but one—" Cathy began but was startled by a loud *slap* against the ground behind them. Her and Mikayla spun around defensively, only to find a young man in overalls standing there, a thick layer of sweat at his sun bronzed brow. It appeared he had dropped the sack of grain he was carrying to the ground.

"Sorry. I didn't mean to startle you. Nobody 'round here seemed to know you two, and with it being such a small world now because—you know, I thought maybe you were new to the area. My name's Ply. Ply Griffith. Is there anything I can help you find? There's a mess of vacant homes nearby. Nobody would mind if you squatted a while, or settled down there, even."

Cathy cracked a weak smile, pleasantly relieved that the man was not there to stir up trouble the way aggressive beggars in the slums would. "I appreciate the offer, but we're not planning to stay. Actually, we are looking for someone, though." She pointed at the family name on the stone monument.

"Smithy? They're good people. But unfortunately, as you can see there, they're pretty much all gone. I did hear that at least one of them survived, though. Sad thing, really. They must be lonely in that big house—the Smithy family house."

"Did they all live together?" Mikayla asked.

"Aye. Three generations, all in the same place—all gone in an instant. The Smithy family had been in that house for as long as I know, but now—I just hate to think about what is becoming of the world." The man seemed to go limp at his own words. He crouched down and picked the sack of grain off the ground then pointed west of the marketplace. "You'll find it thataway. It's the big one with a yellow roof."

Cathy's heart ached hearing the sorrow and hopelessness in Ply's voice. She wanted to extend an offer for him to join Zeke's company, but knew it wasn't her place to do so. Instead, she wiped her eyes before any tears could finish forming and said, "Thank you, Ply. We'll be going now."

Cathy and Mikayla left the square, heading westward in search of the Smithy house, catching glares from the onlookers as they did. Heads peered out of windows as they passed through a residential area. Cathy wondered just how rare it was to see a woman in broad daylight nowadays. She wondered how much more screwed up their faces would get if they saw the horde of women holed up in Zeke's hideout.

Mikayla leaned in close and spoke quietly, "Sad, isn't it?"

"What's sad?"

"Everything. Everyone. They're all either scared witless or just plain hopeless husks of themselves."

"Yeah," Cathy said with a dejected breath. "It makes me want to try to help them all, but I know I can't."

"Exactly why we need to leave and start anew. Maybe once we get settled in the Redlands, we can start evacuating more people out of Last Thesi."

Cathy nodded and smiled. When she turned her eyes back forward, she stopped in her tracks. "Look! The yellow roof!" she pointed, having spotted it a ways ahead.

"Let's go!" Mikayla started up again and hurried ahead.\\

Both of them stopped when they arrived before the quaint wooden fence that circled around the Smithy house. The latch meant to hold the front gate closed was busted, and there was a bloody handprint smeared on the picket fence. Mikayla went first, handling the gate with care with one hand, the other firmly gripping the knife hidden at the waist under her loose shirt.

The sight of the blood made Cathy woozy, so she shied her eyes from it as she passed, keeping her gaze focused on Mikayla's back. The enclosed yard was spacious. There was an old tire swing hanging from a tree in the yard and a weathered picnic table beside it on one end and the remnants of a broken down carriage on the other. The front door to the home was ajar, and there was no light coming from the open windows, only the faded, salmon-colored blinds whipping in the breeze.

"Anyone home?" Mikayla called through the cracked door.

Cathy wiped sweat from the front of her neck as Mikayla slowly pushed the door open, afraid of what might jump out. The heavy wooden door creaked and scraped against the stone floor, pushing a layer of dust as it opened fully to a black room. Cathy could see the outline of shapes in the shadows; a long couch sat in front of the dark void of a fireplace, a toppled lamp beside it, bent over a plush armchair.

They both entered the home with caution. Sunlight shone through one of the windows on a writing desk at one of the walls. The floor near it was littered with newspaper pages from the day of the halvening, some with bloody fingerprints still visible. Cathy turned her crossing vision from the pages on the floor to find that Mikayla was no longer at her side, and nowhere in sight, for that matter.

She wanted to call out for her but was deathly scared to do so. A touch upon her shoulder came from behind that made her jump and yelp.

"Sorry," Mikayla said abashed. "It looks like nobody's home."

"Really? What should we do now?"

"He's got to be somewhere else if he's not here. Do you have any ideas? Is there anything he likes to do that you know of?"

Cathy made a quick exit from the abandoned Smithy home. She could feel the ominous presence that loomed on her shoulders leave her the moment she got in the sunlight outside. She stood in the front yard, pondering Mikayla's question. She thought back to the night she first met him with Rekco and Kyoku at the Coop. She remembered how playfully drunk he was, and how they had to wait the night out for him to wake up before going home.

"I think I have an idea," Cathy announced.

"Oh? Shall we then?"

Cathy was about ready to leave, longing to escape from the horrific aftermath left of the Smithy family's massacre, when her eyes were drawn to the tire swing hanging from the tree in the yard. It swayed gently in the wind, unaffected by the calamity that overtook the world around it. She watched it with thoughtful eyes, as though she were in a trance.

"You know," she began, with a deep sigh, "... when I was a little girl, growing up in the slums, in that wretched orphanage, I used to imagine what the world was like beyond the walls; all the kids would, really. We all liked to make-believe that there was this mystical world out there, where people were free, living without pain or suffering or hunger. I remember imagining riding on the wings of a huge bird and flying over the walls to see that golden endless beauty.

"Now, seeing what lies beyond the slums, beyond Last Thesi—the way people struggle and hurt just as we did—now I know there is no paradise out there to save us from the woes of life. Instead, it's up to us—we have to make our own paradise."

Mikayla gave a nod and a warm smile. "I couldn't have said it better myself!"

Cathy turned her gaze from the tire swing to Mikayla beside her, who looked out at the vacant homes down the street. "How about you? You grew up in the town beneath the city, right? Did you dream of what life must be elsewhere?"

"Not really, no," Mikayla said, shaking her head. "Many of my elders showed such scorn to those living above ground when I was growing up. They cursed the Runic Guard and the bloated bureaucrats that ran the city. The dreams people down there had were of our homeland, far away in the Gendoli region. I won't lie and say I remember the history that well, but the ones who did, swore against Ather because of what it did to our homeland."

Cathy looked down in thought, remembering Ximen Judd's speech about poisoned Ather and the Retallors' would-be schemes involving it. "I hope things aren't as bad up here as your elders said they were."

"Not *quite* as bad," she responded with a smirk, giving Cathy a gentle pat. "Everything will be better once we get out of this place, right?"

"Right!" Cathy lifted her head with eyes refocused on the task at hand: humanity's survival. "C'mon. Let's continue. I have a good idea where we could find who we're looking for."

On Cathy's assumption, the two of them searched the nearby area for a pub, hoping to find Dim there. Eventually, they found their way to a stone building with a sign hanging above the front door that read, "Snake Edge Pub."

They walked in without a hitch. Neither of them were of legal drinking age, but with the state of the world as it currently was, the staff did not seem concerned. Fewer heads turned than they had previously within the Middle

District, though many such heads may have been too drunk to notice the two women enter the building.

"Do you see him?" Mikayla whispered.

Cathy glanced around. The place wasn't very big; nowhere near the size of Barbier's Soup Coop, and not even half as welcoming. There were more patrons there than shoppers in the market square, all drowning the sorrows of their losses and numbing their minds from thoughts of the madness that ravaged the city. A row of stools lined the countertop where the bartender hastily refilled pints of beers and shots of liquor. There, among the tired and the belligerent drunks, Cathy spotted the shabby scholar, sitting all by his lonesome, his face full of a mug of beer.

"There he is," Cathy whispered back to Mikayla, pointing, "sitting between the construction workers and the old guy who looks like he's asleep."

"I see. Shall we, then?" Mikayla asked with a smirk.

Cathy approached the row of drunkards, all reeking of booze and tobacco and sweat. She tapped Dim on the shoulder and said, "Hey Dim, it's me, Cathy."

He turned to her with a dumbfounded expression, as if she were a hallucination created by his drunken stupor, then turned back to face the bar without a word. He sipped away at his drink, paying no attention as Mikayla prodded his other shoulder.

"He's far too out of it," Mikayla said. "Plan B, then?"

Cathy shifted her lips uncomfortably. "I suppose so," she said with reluctance.

Mikayla shoved Dim from behind, knocking the drink from his hands. "Albright Smithy! You're under arrest!" she said in an aggressive voice full of conjured authority.

Dim shuddered at her words and threw his hands up high, giving a nervous yelp. "Sorry, ossifer! I'll talk, I'll talk! Just don't hurt me," he said guiltily. The nearby patrons were far too busy in another plane of existence to question what was happening.

"Good. Now come with me. I'm hauling you off to the dungeons," Mikayla asserted, taking him by the wrist and drawing him away from the bar.

Cathy cringed, slinking away from the bar while covering her face in embarrassment, unable to believe Mikayla's plan was working. When they got outside with Dim in their *custody*, she turned to Mikayla and said, "How did you know that would work?"

Mikayla shrugged. "People who think they've done wrong are just waiting to be snatched up and punished for their sins, aren't they?"

Cathy frowned, knowing the guilt Dim felt for helping the Retallors capture those young women from The Underground. She wondered if he also blamed himself in some way for the widespread madness and the halvening that took his family from him. She could see the reproach on his face as she held his head low, avoiding all eye contact. "Okay, well, let's hurry up and get him somewhere safe so he can sober up."

"How about the Coop? It'll be a little bit of a walk, but it's not as far as trying to haul him all the way back to Bugbear's like this."

"It'll have to do. I'll help move him," Cathy said, forcing Dim's arm over her shoulder. He smelled like a wild animal and didn't look much unlike one with his unshaven face and disheveled hair.

Together, they hobbled Dim back through the market square, acquiring a host of new, queer stares. It wouldn't be much farther until they arrived in the quiet and empty slums and would be home free. Such a task proved it would not come so easily when a voice shouted at them as they passed by the vagrant-infested cul-de-sac from before.

"Ay! Why don't you little ladies ditch that chump and join my gang of survivalists?" A burly bald man called from the porch of a ransacked home. He had an intense underbite and was dressed in tattered, mismatched clothes that were all either too big or too small. He must have plundered them from the houses he and his gang had taken over. "We could really use the help *repopulating*, if you know what I mean," he cackled, and his cronies joined in, flashing what little remained of their rotten teeth. They were all dressed similarly to their leader, in clothes not suited for their wiry, withered bodies. The lower ranked henchmen could be told apart from the rest, as they were left to wear children's or women's clothes or tattered hand-me-downs.

The band of miscreants funneled out of their broken playhouses and were quick to surround Cathy, Mikayla, and the drunken Dim.

Mikayla, unimpressed and unintimidated by the would-be gang, dropped out from Dim's armpit and struck the nearest approaching assailant in the throat. She stood over the fallen man and shot a devious glare at the ringleader, saying, "Sorry, you're not my type. I prefer a person with *teeth*, who knows what soap is."

The bald man scowled. "I ain't into a dark-skinned runt meself, but I'll take your friend there!" He cried as he lurched towards Cathy, who was stuck shouldering Dim's deadweight.

Mikayla moved to get between them but was taken from behind by a gangly gremlin of a man. She grunted and cursed, shouting, "Cathy!" as she tried to escape.

Cathy's mind shut off for a second, staring blankly at the contorted face of the bald man barreling towards her. She felt Dim slip off her shoulder and crumple to the ground with a *thud,* and a loud *pop* followed. The overbearing man was thrown onto his back, gasping and groaning in pain. She looked down to see the steam gun she carried at her hip was in her hands, her finger trembling on the trigger. It whirred and clicked, signaling that it was ready to fire again. She spun and shot the man trying to grab her from behind, then spun again at the sound of an ululating shriek.

A trail of blood spurted through the air as Mikayla freed herself with one quick slash to her attacker's chest. The sight of the blood made Cathy's mind swim, her legs wanting to buckle. The howls and cries around her filled her ears as a dark circle tightened on the edge of her vision.

"Get back!" Cathy heard Mikayla cry but could not turn to see what was going on. "Yeah! Get out of here! Run back whatever hole in the slums you crawled out of!"

The next thing Cathy knew was Mikayla's hand taking her own as she helped her to her feet. She didn't remember ever falling to the ground amidst the commotion, but her scuffed knees told the tale. "Are you okay?" Cathy asked, seeing Mikayla's face come into focus.

"I should be the one asking *you* that," Mikayla chuckled. "I'm fine. Thanks to your help I was able to drive them off, even though I know we agreed we wouldn't do that," she said with a grin.

"Oh. Good. I'm glad," Cathy heard herself say, the blood returning to her cheeks and limbs, bringing pain to the more badly skinned knee.

"Since when are you afraid of blood, anyways?" Mikayla asked, still holding her hand tight and supporting her to stand up with her other hand.

"I'm not sure. I never used to see blood. But lately, with all that's been going on in the world—the destruction of The Underground, the slum-dwellers trying to take over the Middle District, and—the halvening, I can't help but imagine so many gruesome things. It makes me sick to think about them, and I wish I wouldn't. I don't want to see *anything* like that, so I guess, maybe that's why seeing a little bit of blood triggers me so."

"It's okay. Just try to relax your mind a little." Mikayla pulled Cathy in close. Her warm embrace was calming.

When they broke apart, Cathy looked into Mikayla's eyes and smiled; her bold, hazel eyes were a touch more green than normal. "Thank you, Mikayla."

"It's no problem. You're the one who saved us just now, after all! They seemed a lot more scared of your gun than me," she said with a lighthearted laugh. "Just let me know when you're good to go."

A groan came from the ground. Dim was splayed out on the cobblestone road. His eyes creaked open to the two women standing over him. "Huh? Who'er you?" he asked before passing out again.

"I think I'm good. I'd rather get to the Coop sooner so we can rest and recharge after all this." Cathy knelt to Dim's side. Mikayla mirrored her and together, they hoisted him up to his feet and began again on their trek back to the slums.

*

When Dim awoke, he found himself seated at a wood roundtable with a bowl of steaming soup sitting before him, a glass of water beside it. His bloodshot eyes detested the well-lit environment, but his gurgling stomach couldn't resist the hearty soup. He finished it quickly, and just before he was about to stand up from the table and leave, Cathy and Mikayla sat down with him.

"Glad to see you're awake and sound enough to feed yourself," Cathy said, eyeing the empty bowl.

"Hum, so this isn't a dream then?" Dim asked, rubbing at his bleary eyes.

"Who dreams about food?" Mikayla questioned, giving Dim a weird look.

Cathy got red in the face, reminded of the dreams she had of eating grilled fish by the beach, only to wake up and find drool on her pillow and lint in her mouth.

"How did I get here?" Dim looked around, seeming to recognize where he was.

"I needed to talk to you," Cathy said in a stern tone.

"You could've called? You didn't need to go and kidnap me," Dim pouted, crossing his arms.

Cathy pulled a communicator out of her pocket and wagged it before placing it on the table between them. "I tried. Look, it's important. We need your help."

Dim leaned back against the chair, rolling his eyes. "If it's about Rekco, I'm not—"

"*Rekco?* What? No—I—actually haven't spoken to him in a while now."

Dim's expression became stony, and he came back to bring his elbows on the table. "*Really?* I won't pry as to why, but I'd imagine something serious must have happened."

"A lot has been happening, as you know. And that's why we came looking for you. Will you hear us out?"

Dim furrowed his brow in thought. "I guess I have to, since you gave me this free meal and a piggyback ride." He shifted his sights to Mikayla who had been sitting quietly up until then. "Who is your friend? I don't think we've met," he extended his hand to her from across the table. "Albright Smithy, but I go by Dim."

Mikayla took his hand firmly, which seemed to take him by surprise. "Mikayla Reyland, *Doombringer*." Dim gave a look of shock and rescinded his hand at once. Mikayla snickered at his reaction and said, "*Former* Doombringer."

"Introductions aside," Cathy said as she pulled out a rolled up piece of parchment that was tucked into her belt. She unfurled it on the table, revealing the crudely drawn map of the region. There was a red line going from Last

Thesi, through the plains and the Forgotten Woods, and ending up in the Redlands on the other side, where a circle was drawn.

Dim looked it over with a frown on his face. "What is this supposed to be?" he asked.

"This is our plan for humanity's survival," Mikayla answered. "We have a band of warriors and refugees who escaped the destruction of The Underground and are now planning on relocating to the Redlands to start anew."

"Huh? You'll never make it through the Forgotten Woods. There're monsters in there, ya know?"

"I know. Bugbear, or *Zeke*, as you know him, says he has a *secret weapon* for if we have trouble getting through," Mikayla said, ducking down as she mentioned Zeke, as if he were some kind of criminal. Cathy shot her a glance, it being the first time she had heard of such a thing.

Dim scoffed, "It better be something fierce, because you're not going to get by peacefully, that's for sure. Anyways," he pointed his finger at a section of the line running through the woods, "you won't make it through here with a huge group of people, especially if you mean to take any carts or supplies with you."

Mikayla loomed over the map, squinting at Dim's finger. "Why not?"

"Because there's a steep ridge here where your path is going." He dragged his finger south and looped it through the woods and back up to the Redlands. "You'd have to go around it. This way."

"How do you know that?" Mikayla asked, sounding unconvinced.

"The Retallors took satellite images of all the places they wanted Remote Scholars like me to investigate. The Forgotten Woods happens to be one of them. I've seen that place inside and out, despite having never gone there. That's also how I know how dangerous it is."

Cathy's beamed at Dim, which made him reel uncomfortably. "*That* is exactly why we need your help! Having somebody like you with us to lead the company would be a godsend. You're a Remote Scholar, for crying out loud!"

Dim grew red in the face, turning his nose up and looking away in the face of Cathy's compliments. "That is true. I *could* be instrumental in assuring your company safe passage—as long as I don't have to fight any monsters."

Cathy waved her hands, saying, "No, no. No fighting. We'll leave that up to Zeke and his warriors."

Dim's face was starting to show signs of life the more he mulled it over. "I—could really make a difference then?"

Cathy nodded. "A big difference. Right, Mikayla?"

Mikayla picked up on Cathy's cue to lay it on thick, though, what they were saying was still true. "Right, huge!"

Dim slumped for a moment, as if reflecting on a burden which weighed on his conscience. "It was partially my fault that the Retallors got away with so many atrocities. I may have even had a hand in causing the halvening. Knowing that, would you still take me?"

Cathy and Mikayla nodded in unison.

"Then—I'll do it—to atone for all that I've done—both directly and indirectly."

Cathy stood and put her hand on Dim's shoulder. "Thanks, Dim. You're going to make a big difference in helping us. I mean it. If we can reach the other side of the woods, we can put everything that's happened behind us and start again."

Dim nodded, wiping the tears from his eyes. "*Start again,* huh? That sounds—pretty good."

*

Later on, the three of them returned to Zeke's hideout. Kree was there, as always, supervising the door and relaying vital information to the depths of the repurposed apartment complex. Though, he had more than greetings for Cathy this time around. This time he bore gifts.

"For me?" she said, looking at the basket of Hope Lilies in wonderment. She missed those flowers so, and had a good idea where they came from before Kree said a word on it.

"From Master Rekco," Kree said with a bow after he passed the basket to Cathy.

"*Master*," Dim scoffed, still sour towards Rekco, especially after Cathy told him how he wouldn't be joining them in their quest to save humanity.

"Shush," Cathy hissed. "How thoughtful." She twirled one of the flowers between her fingertips before tucking it behind her ear. It seemed to bring warmth to her heart. She pined for Rekco to join them, not just for the sake of their survival, but because she missed him as much as she missed the flowers, if not more so.

To Cathy's surprise, Kree did not vanish from sight after handing over the basket. He waited until she turned her sight from the heartwarming gift back to his misshapen face. "There is one more thing," he said when at last their eyes met.

"Oh? What is it?" Cathy wondered what else Rekco could have possibly given her.

"This one wasn't from Master Rekco," Kree assured, dashing her imaginative thoughts, but also sparking her curiosity more so.

"Huh? Who's it from then?"

"I don't know. It was left outside with your name upon it. Here." He pulled a sealed envelope out from under a stone on the floor and handed it to her.

The envelope was made of sturdy, teal paper that was sealed shut with the charred imprint of a thumb. After seeing it, Cathy had a pretty good idea who it was from, and it made her heart race to finally hear word from the wizard.

Chapter 13: The Glass Sword

Tired swords were strewn about the grass and soil, some with dull edges and cracked hilts. After returning home from his battle with the Swordsman, Rekco searched high and low for a new blade after his other had been reduced to scraps by Hou. He stripped every blade off the weapon's rack and scoured the depths of the storage shed outside of his home to no avail. All the while, the Swordsman's words resonated within him, "*A warrior must be as great as the sword they brandish ... I hope you find one that matches your determination.*"

Rekco found himself repeating those words aloud whilst thinking of the magical blade the Swordsman wielded. It made him wonder what kind of sword his father once used. Whatever kind it was, it wasn't here.

He sat in the grass, surrounded by swords that were unworthy of his grasp. He glanced at the sky above; at the clouds passing by, and the majestic yellow star shrouded in a blue tint that always came out far before the sunset. "Maven never told me about what kind of sword my father used. It couldn't have been anything out of the ordinary. But if that's the case, how could he stand up to foes like the Ten? Maybe I'll just have to find my own way again—my own magical blade." Rekco's own words made him think. "*Magical* blade, huh? What if ..." he stood up and sped off towards the hill westward, towards the dark abandoned cabin; the once home of master wizard Gofun and his protege, Kyoku.

It was quite the stretch to imagine that Gofun left behind any sort of magical relics or tomes that might be able to conjure such a weapon. Rekco wished Gofun were still around to give him advice on his situation, and Maven too, for that matter.

Rekco arrived at the broken down cabin. It had no front door, save for a stretch of green tarp that stopped the rain from getting in. The roof still had some holes in it, things he meant to have fixed over the years but never got around to. The interior was not much better. His eyes were immediately drawn to the crater in the wooden floor to the left when he entered. That was where a maddened Gofun attacked Kyoku as a child and left the young wizard no choice but to defend himself.

The battle resulted in the destruction of their home, and the loss of the master wizard. Nothing had even remained of Gofun to be buried, and Kyoku never bothered to make any sort of grave for his late mentor. Rekco didn't know if it meant that Kyoku refused to believe his master was truly dead, or something else. Either way, it seemed a touchy subject to bring up to the wizard, so Rekco often refrained from speaking of Gofun around him.

Rekco steered to the right, where a hallway extended from the wreckage within the empty living room. Down that hall were two doors: one on the right side went to Kyoku's tiny, childhood bedroom, and the other at the far end of the straight hallway that led to Gofun's study. One thing was amiss from the last time he had snooped around the dark cabin: the magical door leading to Gofun's room was gone. Rekco remembered the purple aura that resonated from the door was so intense that it deterred him from ever approaching it.

"I wonder if Koku got through it already and searched the room for its secrets," he said to himself as he approached the doorway.

A single peek into Gofun's study answered his question. It looked like a hurricane had blown through the room; shredded paper, scraps of wood, and other debris were scattered about, bookshelves were toppled, and the floor was cracked and splintered. The only thing that appeared untouched within the room was a single desk pushed up against the wall between the two fallen bookshelves.

There were only two things on it amidst the dust and debris. One was a single glass leaf, golden and green, and perfectly transparent. The other was a peculiar sight: a snow globe, but unlike any that Rekco had ever seen. This one had no water or sparkles or little houses inside. In fact, there appeared to be nothing in it at all. And unlike the leaf, the globe did not have any dust on it.

Rekco smacked his lips as he glanced around the small room. "It doesn't look like there's anything else here. I wonder if Koku tore the place up out of frustration once he realized that there was nothing out of the ordinary here."

Amidst his ramblings and imaginative recreations of what could have happened here, Rekco nonchalantly reached for the snow globe, his hands habitually looking for something to do. An odd sensation came over him as his fingers got close to it, and a sudden fright filled his mind. He turned his sights to the glass orb and could not believe what he was seeing. The light around his hand was bending and stretching, making it look the length of his arm. An unknown force seemed to be drawing him in, like some otherworldly gravitational pull.

Rekco let out a warped cry that elongated like his entire body seemed to as it was sucked into the tiny globe. His vision got so messed up that his heart sank with fear, and the next moment, everything went black.

Out from the blackness came a single light that shone out in the void. The spotlight was set on a single point, highlighting a floating object that Rekco could not distinguish from far away. He turned back to find that there was nothing but darkness behind him. With nowhere else to go, Rekco proceeded towards the light, in hopes that it would lead to an escape from the magical trap.

As he got closer to the spotlight, he heard a voice. Where it came from, he did not know. "Kyoku," the unfamiliar man's voice began. Hearing the name filled Rekco's ears with an uncomfortable sting. He knew it was Kyoku's, but he could not understand it. "I am pleased to speak with you on your eighteenth birthday. I hope that under Gofun's tutelage you have grown into whatever it is you desire to be. I am sure you have questions, and all will be answered in time by Gofun. In the meantime, I offer you a gift that is more than words, should you choose to take it."

The voice became louder and clearer as Rekco approached the light. A transparent rectangular case floated within the beam. Inside the case was what appeared to be a sword, but one far from anything Rekco had known: it was as see through as the case it rested in, with a grey hilt that had two prongs that looked to extend and protect the wielder's hand. He furrowed his eyebrows at it, for it looked more like an ornamental blade than one used for battle.

Once Rekco stepped into the light, the voice continued, as if it were programmed to do so. "I do not claim to know your desires, but I know you have an aptitude for magic—it's in your blood. But since we do not always go down the paths carved by our parents and our mentors, I wanted to provide a tool to you—had you decided to study the blade instead of magic alone." The case slowly opened, revealing the transparent sword in all its glory. "Whoever touches this blade will have it bound to them until their dying day. It is an ancient relic, said to be as old as time itself. Fret not where I got it from, for that is a consequence I will have to deal with when and if the time comes. This blade, while bound to its user, will resonate with the magic in them and channel it into its edge."

A blank piece of paper materialized out of thin air and floated beside the case. "Should you decide that this weapon is not suited for you, please place your hand on the paper here and you will be sent outside, and this place will be locked by a spell that only Gofun's words can undo, so if you are to change your mind in the future, he may unlock it for you."

Rekco stood in an awkward silence, waiting to see if the voice would say anything more, but there was nothing. He glanced up at the sword levitating before him, then down to the paper that floated at waist height. At that moment, he was stricken by guilt.

"So, this place was meant for Koku to find, but if I was able to stumble into it, that means he never did. And if Gofun is ... then that means nobody will ever be able to get in here again?" His voice trailed off. He could not in good conscience take what rightfully belonged to Kyoku, but at the same time, if he didn't, then it would be lost forever. "I—I don't know what to do," he said, his eyes fixed on the sword as he remembered what the voice said. "I—I'm sorry, Koku," he said, closing his eyes as he reached up and grabbed hold of the grey hilt.

At that moment, his head became woozy, and the voice spoke again, "Be cautious, be curious, and remember that, despite all the difficulties and trouble we've put you through, we'll always love you, Kyoku. We hope to see you soon, love Endu and Elliane." The two names were unintelligible to his ears.

On that word, Rekco felt his body grow light and the world warped around him until he found himself standing back in Gofun's study, the desk before him. The snow globe on it was unmoved. Rekco reached out with his right hand, full of trepidation, and grabbed it and held it up to the sunlight pouring through the holes in the ceiling.

At that moment, it was just an ordinary, empty snow globe. He set it back down and turned to leave the room but felt a resistance; the sword in his left hand was caught in the doorway.

Up until then, Rekco had forgotten he was holding it. It was so weightless that when he tossed it back and forth between his hands, he could only tell he was holding it by the texture against his palms and fingers. The once clear blade now housed a faint blue glow—his glow. He ran his finger up the blade's edge. It was sharp in a way that was uncanny, yet the sword itself felt like it was made of glass, making him worry it would shatter if he tried to swing it.

Rekco left the cabin in a hurry, eager to test it, yet nervous about it breaking. He picked a dense rock out of the tall grass outside, it felt oddly heavy compared to the sword. He tossed the rock into the air and swung at it, expecting it to knock it away and chip the sword's edge. But instead, the blade passed through it like it was fog. The stone fell to the ground, perfectly cut in two, and the blade showed no sign of damage.

"Wow," Rekco gasped, holding the glass sword up to the sunlight. He tried not to feel guilty about claiming what was rightfully Kyoku's. But on the other hand, seeing the blue light twist and swim within the transparent blade made his heart race; it made him know it was his. He grinned as he gripped it with confidence, bending his knees to get into battle stance. "We'll see whose blade cuts through who's next time we meet, Swordsman."

After having his fill swinging the weightless blade about, Rekco turned his sight to his hip and frowned. "How am I supposed to sheath this thing?" he said to himself, trying to find a way to tuck the blade into his belt without cutting himself. He fumbled and the glass sword slipped from his hand, then seemingly vanished.

Rekco's heart fell into his stomach at the thought that he lost the mystical blade he only just discovered. "No no no don't do that to me! Where did it go?" He got on all fours and searched the grass for the blue shimmer within the sword. There was nothing to be found. He shot up to his feet, and in his frustration, clenched his fist tight. From his fist came an eruption of blue light that shot upward towards the sky, the surprise of which made him reel his head back, and good thing too, for when the light faded, the glass sword was in his hand again.

"Huh? How did I do that?" He turned the weapon in his hand, giving it a thorough look over. While staring at it and holding it up high, he opened his hand to release it to the ground, but it did not fall. Instead, it vanished within a faint blue glow, leaving behind the particles the size of gnats that drifted and dispersed in a second. His heart jumped again, but this time it was full of excitement.

Rekco gripped tight again and watched with awe as the glass sword appeared within his hand as if it had never left. "Amazing!" he swooned. Once the child-like excitement wore off, his mind became stricken with worry. "Wait, this could be dangerous." He imagined all the situations where he might clench his fist but NOT want to summon the sword. "Let me think. There has to be a way to control it." He cleared his mind of all things involving blades and battle and tried to make a fist again. This time, it did not appear. He lit up like a neanderthal discovering how to make fire for the first time, letting out a joyous hoot.

"It really is *bound* to me then, huh? Just like the voice said ..." he trailed off, lost in thought. "That voice was— Koku's father?!" Rekco gnawed on his thumb as he contemplated. "Darn, that means I *have* to tell him. I couldn't withhold that kind of information while he's still so concerned about where he came from." He recalled all of what the man's voice said, trying to keep the memory fresh for when he might see the wizard again.

At that thought, Rekco realized that it had been quite some time since he had, in fact, seen Kyoku. "Since Retallor Tower ..." his mind began to go to dark places, full of uncertainty. "There's no way he's—dead, right? Could it be possible that he went mad during the halvening?" Fear overcame him at the thought of what a maddened wizard could do. He thought of Gofun, who was only stopped because of the power of another wizard. "If he had, I feel like the whole world would know. We'd probably all be dead." It was some consolation to his troubled mind, but he couldn't help but wonder where Kyoku could have gone since then.

Rekco returned to his cabin on the other side of the hill. At first glance, his eyes caught sight of something stuck to his front door. He rushed to see what it could be. "What is that?" he said as he approached it. "A *letter?*" The teal envelope was stuck to the door via a weak magical imprint that took a single gentle tug to dislodge. He turned it over to see the burnt thumbprint that sealed it. "Speak of the devil, huh?"

He opened the letter without reluctance and removed the single piece of paper from within that simply read, "Meet me tomorrow at the west end of the beach at noon. You can get there through the Middle District. I've invited Cathy as well. I need to speak with the two of you."

"Signed, Koku," Rekco read aloud. His interest was piqued, wondering what the wizard would talk about. "Why the beach, I wonder? It sure is a long way to go just for a meeting, but, at the same time, Cathy will be there." He pondered for only a moment before he made up his mind.

Chapter 14: Ruby Bullet

"You've arrived. Took you long enough," Kyoku heard a woman's voice say, his vision and mind still clouded by the yellow energy that had sent him back to the planet.

He opened his eyes when they came to focus, relieved to find that Oglis was not there. He was standing in an alley between two brick buildings. The cleanliness of the area told him that he was somewhere in the Middle District. He straightened his vest and adjusted the hem of his puffy teal pants, still feeling somewhat disoriented from the warp.

The woman that stood before him was Ramirez. It was the first time Kyoku had seen her clearly and not shrouded in shadow. She was a tall woman, standing nearly a head taller than him, though she was still small compared to Oglis. Long locks of dark brown hair poked out from beneath the white and red patterned cloak she wore over her head. Her reddish brown face appeared far softer than her rigid personality.

"What are you looking at?" She demanded, her piercing brown eyes staring daggers at Kyoku.

"Oh, it's nothing. This is our first time meeting face to face, isn't it?"

"Correct. And hopefully it'll be the last. I'd prefer to take missions alone, but this is a special case, since you know the target so well." She reached into her cloak and Kyoku caught a glimpse of the white button-up shirt beneath it, along with a pale white axe strapped at her hip. She drew a rustic-looking gun from the back of her belt and a single bullet from her pocket and loaded it. "Is there a problem?" She asked defensively, still seeming uncomfortable to be looked upon by Kyoku.

"No. I was just looking at your gun. It is—*interesting.*"

"Huh?" she sounded offended. "How so?"

"It's just," Kyoku shifted his lips, "looks a bit *dated.*"

Ramirez scoffed. "Shows how much you know about me and my power." As she held the gun in her right hand, she glided her left over it and a red glow trailed behind her fingers.

What she didn't know was that Kyoku was playing coy with her. He knew everything he needed to know about her, thanks to Melonine. "You're right. I don't know much about you, or about the *others* in the Ten," he lied, stoking the possibility that Ramirez could divulge some knowledge to him that he did not know, specifically about the tyrant Oglis.

"Ask what you wish, if you're so curious. But just because you ask doesn't mean I'll answer you."

"Well, since you and I are together on this mission, how about I ask more about you? What's with the two names? Oglis calls you Rebecca, yet everyone else seems to call you Ramirez, which isn't your family name if you've taken Standstill from Loch."

Ramirez gave a cruel smirk that reminded Kyoku of Maneuvers. "Back in the world I came from, it wasn't smart to be a woman in broad daylight. And women who wanted to work or pick up a gun would sooner be stoned than taken seriously. Thanks to my stature, I was able to take on the name Ramirez and play a man without a hitch. The rest is history."

"That sounds a lot like how things are in this world, though maybe a bit worse."

"There's always something worse somewhere," she said, cocking back the hammer of her old-timey gun.

Kyoku knew she wasn't lying about her past, since it mirrored the intel Melonine gave him. Half of his perception recalled the conversation with her as he continued to speak with Ramirez.

"What can you tell me about Ramirez?" He asked Melonine.

A reenactment played within the confines of his mind, depicting the details of her life, as told by Melonine. Rebecca was raised on a desert planet; born the youngest, and only sister to six boys, all of whom were gunslingers. Being brought up in such a family, it was only natural that she'd become enamored with guns like all her brothers. Unfortunately, she was forbidden to take one up, being that she was a woman.

Despite that, young Rebecca did not listen to the laws, nor did she fear death. Her desires could not be stifled. She often *borrowed* her brother's guns and practiced shooting each night, sometimes staying out until the sunrise reminded her of what trouble would come if she didn't return them on time.

By the time she was an adult, Rebecca was a better shot than most, or so she thought. In fact, she was the best sharpshooter on the planet, thanks to the god-like perception instilled in her by the fragment of Dalu's soul inside her. Veiling her gender and identity, Ramirez became the most sought after gunman in the land, taking jobs only from the highest bidder. Finally, she was leading the life she always dreamed of, until—she was hired to kill a man—a man named Loch Standstill.

The mission went awry when she saw him; something in her soul burned to know him and knowing him only seemed to make her soul burn hotter. Her failure to kill Loch resulted in a bounty on both their heads. Eventually, Rebecca and Loch went on the run together, but they didn't mind. The closer they got to one another, the more their powers grew and developed, until nobody could dare challenge them, nobody from their world, at least.

Once their true identities were discovered by the cosmic being that oversaw their world, and word made it to the Core, Oglis was sent to convince them to join the cause and offer them a place in the Hall of Fate. Oglis' ways were *deathly* convincing.

It was a fate Kyoku wanted to avoid. Oglis seemed to be treating Rekco far more tenderly than those that came before him. Perhaps that would cease once he completed the trials she planned out for him.

Kyoku turned his eyes to Ramirez's gun. The pistol's barrel was long and grey, and the wooden handle was marvelously lacquered and polished. It may have been an old gun, but it seemed good enough for Ramirez. "Is it not a weakness to wield a gun that can only hold one bullet at a time?" Kyoku asked, having noticed that when she loaded it.

"To a normal person, perhaps. But to me—" Ramirez pointed the gun straight up and fired it into the sky. While the explosive sound still rang in the air, she pulled the hammer back and fired it again, and again, and again, all the while the gun gave off a faint crimson glow. Kyoku could tell right away what he was seeing.

"You're creating a new bullet every time you fire, aren't you?" he asked, impressed at the thought.

Ramirez smirked slyly. "How perceptive of you. You're only half right, though. I won't pretend to have the same mental fortitude as you to be constantly creating things in the heat of battle. I'd prefer to relax my mental stack as much as possible at such times." She unloaded the bullet from the gun and held it between her fingers. It, too, had a red glow to it. "I've enchanted both the gun and the bullet. Once together," she said, loading the gun again, "they'll be bound to one another, and continuously attract one another."

Kyoku furrowed his brow in thought. "So, it's the *same* bullet each time, warping back to the gun after it's fired?"

"Correct. It warps back after it has used up all of the kinetic energy. My enchantment increases that as well. This gun can inflict severe damage on a target from leagues away."

"And you can aim it accurately from that far away?"

"Yes," she assured with confidence, her brown eyes gleaming. "I use my powers to the fullest, much unlike the *target* we're going to test today."

Her words made Kyoku wonder what the extent of his own powers were, and *what* they were, specifically. *If Gofun taught me basic, elemental magic, and the power to create and destroy is something I inherited from my parents, then what exactly makes me one of the Ten? What did Oglis see in me that made her know?*

Amidst his thoughts, he turned to Ramirez, who seemed to be waiting for something. "What is the plan then? Oglis didn't tell me much; only to meet up with you here."

"The plan is simple. Once the target arrives at the designated place, you'll distract him while I get in position, then—" she pointed her gun and imitated it firing, "*bam!*"

"You want me to lure him so you can get a cheap shot at him?" Kyoku asked, giving her a sideways glance.

"Oh, no. I'm not going to shoot *him*," Ramirez answered with a devious smirk.

"Wait," Kyoku reeled at the terrifying realization. "Don't tell me you're going to shoot—"

"The girl," the words fell from Ramirez's cruel lips and sank into the pit of Kyoku's stomach, making his insides boil.

"Oglis promised me that Cathy wouldn't get hurt if I complied with her plans!" he said in a rage.

"Oglis promised you that your friends wouldn't be *killed*. Hurt is a temporary thing. Plus, I'm an expert shot. I'll make sure only to graze her hip, just for you. I'm sure it'll leave a cute little mark."

Kyoku could feel the hairs on the back of his neck standing up. Magic welled up within him, making his eyes burn red with the destruction he wished to rain upon Ramirez at that moment. It took everything he could muster to refrain, fearing that Oglis was nearby; watching; listening. *Could this also be my trial; to test my loyalty? I have to stay my resolve. I can't let her know how to better manipulate me. But the idea that I have to allow Cathy to be hurt ... it angers me almost beyond what I can control.*

"I'll just have to take your word for it then. But remember this: if you miss, I'll kill you myself," Kyoku assured, his eyes still glowing red.

Ramirez scoffed. "If I miss, I won't fight you on that. My word is as true as my aim." She held her hand aloft to him. He took it and gave it a firm shake, feeling the calluses on her palms.

"What is the trial then? With the Swordsman, he had a goal. I imagine this would be similar, assuming Oglis likes to keep these things theatrical."

"Indeed, she does. He succeeds in the trial should he disarm me. Simple as that."

"You know, that doesn't sound all that difficult for someone with the powers Rekco possesses currently. I think you'll be lucky to fire more than a few shots before he finds you and closes the gap."

"Well, I'll admit, he's probably not the best matchup for my skill set. But I won't lose to an underdeveloped newbie like him."

Kyoku sneered at her. "I don't find your skillset all that impressive, to be honest. This trial would be even *easier* for me than it will be for Rekco."

Ramirez's gaze burned hot, but she did not lose her cool. "*Really* now? Care to make a wager on that?"

Kyoku scoffed. "Right here and now?"

"And why not? We've still got some time. Or are you feeling scared now that I didn't back down?"

Kyoku took a few steps backwards, putting distance between them in the narrow alley. "One shot," he said, raising his index finger. "If I disarm you after one shot, you'll miss your shot on Cathy."

Ramirez tucked her hands into the pockets of her slacks and gave a quiet snicker. "Very well. On your command."

"No need. Fire at will—" as the words escaped his mouth, Ramirez performed a perfect quick draw and fired her pistol at him. Kyoku felt electricity coursing through his arms at the sound of the gunshot, amplifying his reaction time to an inhuman level. Moving on instinct alone, his hands rose and cupped around the bullet when it was an inch from hitting him in the abdomen; a field of crimson energy poured from his palms, creating a sphere around the bullet, stopping it dead in the air. The electric sound buzzed a moment after the explosive sound of the gunshot finished, whisking up the black and grey spiral pattern on the fabric of his full-body tights.

The red enclosure sat between his bare palm and the other covered with black and grey swirls all the way to his fingertips. Kyoku took his hands off it and let it float and bob in the air like a balloon weighed down by a bullet tied to its string. "There," he said definitively.

Ramirez kept her gun pointed at him. "Gee, you stopped it. As impressive as that was, it doesn't matter—" she pulled the hammer back on her pistol and squeezed the trigger, but nothing happened. "Huh?" She turned her gun and opened the chamber to find there was no bullet inside. "What did you do?!"

Kyoku swayed his hands around the floating crimson prison. "See for yourself." He pushed it with his hand, serving it to her gently like it were an overblown beach ball.

Ramirez eyed the sphere, her bullet still inside it. "I see," she said flatly, swatting it back to him. "Better than I expected. You created a pocket dimension to make my bullet think that the gun it's bound to doesn't exist. That's the kind of magic only the gods that oversee the worlds know. How did you learn that?"

Kyoku released his spell and let the limp bullet fall into his hand. He walked it back to Ramirez and handed it to her. "I don't know. My mind—just—knows these things. My mentor used to tell me that I got it from my father, but I don't know who he is." Ramirez shifted her lips without a word. Her eyes didn't seem to know anything about it, so Kyoku didn't press her. "I have your word then that you won't hurt Cathy—that you'll miss her on purpose?"

"Yes, you have my word. And don't worry, I can miss a shot just as well as I aim them. Come now, it's about time that the target arrives." Ramirez began to climb up on the roof of the building, leaving Kyoku to make his way to the beach.

*

Rekco's trek through the Middle District had been pleasant enough. Without much direction, he decided to just continue to head west, in hopes that he would eventually reach the beach at the edge of the city. The place was not as marvelous to him after having spent so much time in the High District, where technology thrived, and the buildings shot into the sky.

All through his travels, he could not dispatch the loneliness from his mind. He wished he didn't have to be alone in seeing the Middle District for the first time. He would've loved to have gone with Maven or Kinnley, or

Cathy and Dim, even Kyoku's company would've been better than nothing, he thought. He couldn't fathom living a life alone. *Once I find my father and put an end to whatever is ailing this city from behind the scenes, my life can return to normal. Maybe I'll move somewhere like here, where the ocean breeze wafts through the town, where the buildings are clean and roads maintained, where the people seem happier.*

Such dreams were torn to shreds by the thought of Cathy leaving the city for good. He tried to imagine what life could be like if he joined her and sought to begin civilization anew somewhere far from the great walls of Last Thesi and the plains and the threatening woods. He could vaguely remember a dream he had as a child, one which seemed to be a message from his father. In it, he saw the tavern just on the other side of the woods that Rekston Curse and his allies frequented. Rekco wondered if that building still stood, or if it had been blown away or ravaged by the foul creatures of the forest, seeking to expand their territory. The thought of those giant flowers with mouths full of thorns and the trees with screwed up faces that commanded them, pouring out from the wood to conquer the empty world made his skin crawl. He hoped they would all stay in their sanctuary for eternity.

The gloom Rekco felt was pierced by a shimmer that caught his attention from the corner of his sight. He turned and saw a motorcycle store amidst the row of shops along the boulevard leading to the beach. A wide window displayed three of the newest models, all of which appearing similar to the Ather-powered ones he rode with Dim when they were still friends. The sight made his heart both rise with glee and fall into despair.

He wanted to exclaim about how cool they were and daydream of owning one, but such imaginings only reminded him of the friendships that he'd lost and would likely continue to lose on his quest to find his father. His eyes shifted to the shopkeeper inside, who was making sure the bikes kept a certain level of polish. The grizzly man looked tired and distraught, a sentiment Rekco empathized with.

As much as he wanted to go inside and get a closer look, he didn't want to risk missing his chance to repair his friendship with Cathy and learn why Kyoku wanted to see them. "Maybe another time," he said as he turned from the window and continued westward.

The beach became visible as the street grew wider. Rekco often forgot that there was no towering wall on the west end of the city. All that stopped anyone from going outside was a thin brick wall that any adult would have no trouble scaling over. There was one opening in the short wall where the street ended and was replaced by a path carved out of the sand outside.

Rekco glanced around curiously. There were plenty of people at the edge of the city, many shopping or chatting, but none seemed to dare step outside. *Why?* He became nervous that the Runic Guard's siren would blare the moment he set foot on the dirt path, and that his life would soon be put on the line. No such thing happened, though he did feel an odd lightness in his head once he crossed the threshold.

Rekco looked back for a moment on the bustling Middle District one last time, unable to shake the peculiar feeling that something was amiss, before he went ahead towards the empty beach. He scanned the golden sands and the shallow edge of the water but saw not a soul. He became worried at what seemed to be an impossibility. *I thought the Runic Guard opened up the beach to the public? Why wouldn't there be anyone out here if that were the case? Cathy and Koku aren't here yet either. What if this is a trap? Could it be possible that somebody used Cathy and Koku's names to lure me here?*

Rekco whipped around fearfully, and his heart fell into his stomach at the sight of two figures approaching. His eyes were so unfocused from the stress that he became woozy, unable to discern who they were. A familiar voice broke through the fog in his mind, and the world began to become clear again.

"Rekco? What are *you* doing here?" the woman's voice called, its host nothing more than a blob of spring colors, shifting and swaying in the sunlight. The light twisted and bent around the figure, until it wasn't only their voice that was familiar.

"Cathy!" Rekco exclaimed as though she were in danger. She wore a yellow blouse with frilly ends and white shorts beneath it. Her eyebrow shot up in response, and another shape appeared by her side. The dark colors blended with various shades of off white and tan, becoming the young woman, Mikayla from The Underground. "What is she doing here?"

Cathy shifted her lips with annoyance while Mikayla looked away uncomfortably. "The letter didn't say anything about coming alone."

"*Letter?* You mean, *this?*" Rekco pulled the folded letter from his pocket.

"Yeah. I got one just like that. From Koku."

"So did I. Did yours not mention I would be here?"

"No, it didn't. It just told me to meet here at noon."

"I see," Rekco said with a dejected breath. "Would it have made you not want to come if it did?"

Cathy's expression softened a bit. "No, of course not! Rekco, I have no ill will towards you. You're still a dear friend to me—but—we're just not on the same path anymore."

"Why not though?" Rekco asked, his emotions beginning to flare. "Because your new friends want to abandon Last Thesi?"

"No, because *I* want to abandon Last Thesi!" Cathy answered back, matching his tone. "This city is cursed. It's caused you and I nothing but pain—and not just us, but everyone who's been forced to stay here."

"Well, I think *everyone* else in the world has had it a bit worse, seeing as they're all gone now," Rekco said sardonically.

"And you don't find that coincidence strange? Especially if there were people here with the power to wipe out half the city in a matter of minutes. You don't think they could've done the same thing to the rest of the world outside the walls?"

"Do you think you can just run away from something as powerful as that? I know I can't. That's why I have to stay and fight."

Cathy shook her head. "The fight's over, Rekco. The Retallors are dead. The Runic Guard will own this city in a year's time. I don't want to be around to see what the new tyrants want to do with us."

"I think you're wrong. I think the fight's just begun. I have a new lead, a massive one."

Cathy tilted her head, her interest piqued. "*Really?* What is it?"

Before Rekco could open his mouth, a distorted whooshing sound cut him off, followed by a crimson glow that appeared between them. When the light faded, Kyoku stood there. He wore the same unusual attire as when Rekco last saw him, flecks of red ash dissipating in the air around him.

"I'm glad you two were able to make it," the wizard said before turning his eyes to Mikayla. "And it's good to see you are well too, Mikayla."

It had been some time since Rekco had seen Kyoku, but still he could sense that something was off. He seemed much unlike himself; there was urgency in his yellow eyes, the eyes he usually kept hidden behind dark shades. His voice sounded far more restrained and polite than usual.

"I'm glad you're alive, Koku," Cathy said. "We've been worried about you." She turned her eyes to Rekco, as if signaling for him to speak.

"That's right," Rekco joined in, taking her cue. "What happened to you outside of Retallor Tower? Why have you been gone for so long?"

Kyoku's eyes shied away for a second, darting to the buildings at the edge of the city then to the sand and back again to them. He swallowed hard before speaking. "There's no time. I have to tell you—" His voice was cut off by a loud *pop!* The sound was like a cannon firing in the distance. An eruption of sand burst by Cathy's feet. The moment it did, another pop came, and another torrent of sand flew into the air.

"Something is shooting at us!" Cathy yelped, trying to inch backwards, but Kyoku rushed to her side and stopped her where she stood.

The sand flying through the air kicked up dust, making it hard to see. Rekco charged forward through the cloud to try to see where the attack was coming from. Another cannon fired in the distance. His ears weren't sharp enough to tell where it was coming from, but he knew someone who might be able to. "Can you tell where it's coming from, Koku?"

"Northeast from here, on top of a long building facing the beach." Kyoku answered at once. He didn't move an inch, standing as still as stone in front of Cathy with his arms spread, as though he were creating a barrier around her. Rekco was grateful for that.

Rekco could scarcely see what the wizard was talking about. While he was staring, another pop came, but it did not sound the same—this one had struck flesh. A scream echoed from behind him, and he spun around, his heart racing with fear. There he saw Mikayla laying upon the ground, blood dripping from her abdomen, staining the sand beneath her.

"Mikayla, no!" Cathy cried out, rushing to her friend's side. She looked as though she would faint at the sight of the blood. Kyoku caught her as she fell to her knees. Her head bobbed for a moment, as though she had lost consciousness, before the will to save her friend overcame her fear. "Koku! Create some bandages. We need to stop the bleeding right away!" she said as she turned to the wizard.

Rekco backtracked instinctively, his vision becoming crossed as he started towards Mikayla. Kyoku threw his hand up and cried, "No! Go stop the attacker! I'll take care of things here."

Rekco's vision came back into focus at Kyoku's assuring words and he turned his sights back on the buildings northeast. All he could muster was a nod, as it felt like a stone was obstructing his throat. He swallowed down the terror and anxiety and focused his mind. The next moment, he bolted off northeast.

To Rekco's surprise, the cannon continued to fire, even while he was moving at top speed—much unlike the bullets the mayor once fired at him that seemed to halt in the air before his power. The popping sounds rang all around him, as if they were aiming solely for him. It stoked the fire burning in his chest and made the suspicions in his mind grow. *It has to be ... one of them*, he thought as he stopped before the buildings outlining the border between the beach and the Middle District. A lone figure could be seen atop a long building with a slanted brown roof.

Rekco saw the figure's arm raise and he made sure to move swiftly to continue his approach. He zoomed forward as another shot struck where he had been standing. The next moment, he was standing with his palms upon the building, ready to scale it with one quick movement. He focused his strength and kicked upward against the wall while pressing his hands in and throwing himself up. He flung himself to the roof with ease, catching the side of it and pulling himself to his feet.

"Not bad," a woman's voice called. It was not the distorted voice of the alien Oglis, but it was a threatening voice all the same. She took a step closer, and pulled the cloak off her head, letting her long, wavy brown hair flow over her shoulders. Her dark brown skin glistened under the sunlight.

"Who are you, and what do you want?" Rekco demanded, standing vigilant, in case the woman was to fire again.

She looked him up and down and gave him a disappointed, sideways glance. "*Really?* You came unarmed? I guess you fail then—" she said, pointing her gun at him and firing it.

The gunshot made Rekco's ears ring so bad that he could scarcely hear the whooshing within his eardrums as his power escalated. He gripped his hand tight, summoning the glass sword and swung it hard at the coming bullet. It burst upon impact, exploding into a cloud of red dust.

The woman's eyes lit up with excitement, raising an eyebrow at the feat. "*That* wasn't in the dossier." Her old-timey gun glowed red. Instead of reloading it, she pulled the hammer back and fired again. "You lack precision!" she yelled as though it were a battle cry.

Rekco swept the bullet away with ease. "I think you're the one who lacks precision here. I'm far too quick to be hit by your projectiles. You can't win. Just tell me what you want and give up."

She cracked a rage-filled smile. "You're still a guppy! I like the scorn in your eyes though. I wonder how you'd be acting if I had hit the girl you like instead."

Rekco bared his teeth, grinding as he spoke, "That's enough!" He made to move forward again but was stopped by another *pop!* Shards of stone scattered about as the bullet pierced through the roof where Rekco sought to step.

"Not so fast!" the woman said with a taunting chuckle as she made to fire another shot, this time pointing the barrel of her gun at him.

Rekco swung at the bullet with annoyance, but his blade caught nothing. Just before the bullet struck the glass sword, it exploded, pelting him with a barrage of glowing red shrapnel. It burned like a hot fire on his skin. He reeled back and let out a sharp cry, the burning pain coursing through him.

She cackled at Rekco's agony, shifting her weight to one side as she stood, basking in it. "My name is Ramirez Standstill, but many people call me *Ruby Bullet*. I'm sure you can see why. I'm surprised you didn't learn from your encounter with the Swordsman—not to underestimate one of the Ten."

Rekco grimaced as he glanced from the shining bits of metal stuck in him back to Ramirez. "So, you *are* with that monster. Hunting for my father too, I assume? I won't feel bad about hurting you then."

"You won't be the first to kill me, and you won't be the last," Ramirez scoffed, a cruel, crazed gleam in her eyes. "Maybe we'll kill each other endlessly until the end of time? And for your information, I could care less about your father. I'm here for my mission alone."

"And what is that?" Rekco asked, breathing hard against the pain.

"To test you. Your trial is simple: disarm me, or *die!*" she cried, pointing her gun at him yet again.

As she readied it, Rekco felt the holes in him loosen; the shrapnel had disappeared! He braced himself for another volley of hellfire to rain on him, but to his surprise, Ramirez pointed the gun upward. She fired it, and suddenly, an intense flame licked at Rekco's back. He toppled forward onto his knees from the impact, his back burning, feeling blood drip from the many holes caused by more shrapnel.

It warped! Rekco thought, now realizing the extent of her unique abilities. He knew then that he could not underestimate her any longer; that he needed to end this swiftly before she could unveil any more deadly tricks. He tried to pull himself up, but Ramirez kept the pressure on him.

"Nuh-uh!" she said, pointing and firing her gun again.

The weight of the shrapnel digging into his back vanished. At the signal, Rekco shielded his eyes and face with his arm, trying to protect himself from the blazing shards of metal. But this time, the bullet flew straight and struck him in the side; it burned far worse than the chunks of metal he felt prior. He let out a howl that could be heard all the way to the shore, crumpling to the ground as he breathed heavily.

Rekco's mind raced. He had not trained using his explosive speed from a downed position, but he had no choice but to try it. He grabbed the shingles on the roof with his hands and tucked his knees to his chest, then with one motion, flung himself the same way he did when he scaled the roof. Speed enveloped him as he moved. He could feel the tiny holes on his back, chest, arms, and face seal up all at once as he raced towards Ramirez, swinging his blade.

Her expression was frozen at that moment. Rekco used his sword to wrench the gun from her hand and sent it flying into a nearby cluster of buildings. Time returned, and they were face to face, Rekco feeling triumphant.

"There," he panted. "You're disarmed. I've won. Now give up."

Ramirez's expression was not that of a woman defeated. Instead, the fanatic look in her eyes was that of exhilaration. She swiftly reached into her cloak and pulled an axe from her hip, as white as a cleaned bone. "Not yet!" she yelled as she raised it up and swung it down like a hammer.

Rekco raised his glass blade to the white axe. When their weapons clashed, the whole roof quaked. Rekco could feel that the tremendous force Ramirez was exerting was beyond what any human could output; far stronger than anything he'd ever faced. It weighed him down, cracking the shingles beneath his feet. He thought quickly and moved quicker, spinning to the right to shrug her weight off. She came forward and swung sideways at Rekco as he drew himself backwards, parrying her.

He accelerated as much as his body would allow, and in that perfectly still moment, he saw that her chest was wide open, her red and white cloak trailing behind her, frozen in a fluttering motion. Rekco pushed off his back foot and leapt up, rearing his glass sword back to stab it downward and claim victory, even if it meant killing her in the process. Something in the adrenaline-haze he was in made him feel as though he, too, were moving in slow motion. As the muscles in his right arm tightened, Rekco began to see a blue light out of the corner of his eye, growing brighter and brighter.

Warmth seemed to envelop him as the light burst into a flare. Rekco turned his head slowly and was shocked by what he saw. The glass sword was shining, but not only that—from it, a vortex of Ather-blue energy was spinning around him, as though he were passing through a tunnel. The sight made Rekco's mind swell with fear. *What is this? What's happening?!* He lost his focus, and lost control of his power as well. Time came crashing back to normal, and his arm seemed to slip forward, sending the incomplete vortex along with it. The energy converged beyond the tip of his blade, decimating the roof where Ramirez stood.

Rekco's heart dropped; it beat irregularly as time continued to fluctuate between normal and slow with each passing second. Debris shot into the air every which way to the point that he could not see beyond the carnage. His gaze went everywhere it could, until finally, he found Ramirez with both feet in the air; she was falling backwards, having stepped out of the way of the attack just before impact. There was a look of sheer terror on her face, unlike her usual smug appearance. For a being who showed no fear towards death, what could she have seen that affected her so?

Ramirez's cloak flitted as she fell in slow motion. Rekco tried to move to grab her, but his body would not heed his commands. The mysterious, terrifying attack he unleashed had drained him of everything, and left nothing in its wake. So, instead, he was forced to watch the woman fall from the rooftop, until she hit the hard cobblestone below with a ghastly *crack!* Blood pooled beneath her, stretching upon the ground the way the slow tide crept up the shore. Rekco turned his head away, unable to face the lifeless look in her brown eyes any longer.

The feeling in his limbs began to come back after a moment, allowing him to stand, though his legs were still shaky. He stumbled to the missing chunk of the building, looking as though a giant had taken a bite of it. A sigh of relief fell from his gaping mouth as he noticed that the building was vacant—seemingly used for commercial storage.

Rekco struggled to climb down the side of the building and made his way back to the beach. There he found Cathy sitting alone, her shoes off, the tide nipping at her toes. Beside her was a patch of bloodstained sand that the tide was slowly drinking. Her eyes that had been so bright before were now dark and sunken as they stared off at the endless ocean.

Rekco sat beside her. "What happened to Mikayla and Koku?"

"He took her back to Zeke's to rest," Cathy said, not taking her eyes from the azure horizon. "He said that he thinks she'll be okay. The bullet didn't hit anything vital, but at first, it wouldn't stop bleeding, as if it were sucking the blood out of her. She bled so much that I started to get over my fear of blood—I started to get used to it." Tears streamed down her cheeks. "I don't *want* to get used to seeing blood!"

"I'm so sorry, Cathy," Rekco said, the guilt eating away at him.

Cathy wiped her face with her arm and turned to him. "Why would you need to be sorry about that?"

"Because—" he choked on his words, imagining he was feeling what his father was afraid to express when he decided to disappear, "it's my fault. It's me that person was after. And even though I stopped her before she could do any more harm, she won't be the last person who comes after me. Anyone near me is in danger from now on."

Cathy looked confused. "I don't understand. What's happened since I left?"

Rekco told her of his encounter with the Swordsman and how it pertained to the dream he had about the blue creature. He told her what little he knew of Oglis and the Ten, and their divine plan for him. It was so confusing to him that he couldn't imagine what Cathy would think of it. She seemed to ponder in the silence that followed his tale, the tide now soaking the hems of her white shorts.

Cathy stood up amidst the silence, as though she were done thinking, and extended her hand to Rekco. He took it and she helped him to his feet. "Maybe it truly is best for us to be on separate paths then, at least for now, right?"

"I think you're right," Rekco responded, his voice sullen, still trying to accept the fact that he must go on alone, just as his father had done before him.

"I think if there's *anyone* that can help you now, it's gotta be Koku. We should go back to Zeke's and talk to him right away."

"Good idea," the hollow words escaped his mouth.

Cathy gave Rekco a gentle smack on the shoulder. "Don't worry. We can still meet up in the end, right?" she said, giving as warm of a smile as she could, given the circumstances.

Her words did always have a way of cheering him up, even in the direst of times. He smiled back at her. "Yeah, and we will."

"You promise?"

"Of course."

Chapter 15: Club Tower

When Rekco and Cathy returned to Zeke's they would find that Kyoku was already long gone. The wizard doubled back to the beach in haste to find what had become of Ramirez. He had only caught a glimpse of the explosion that occurred during her battle with Rekco, but he feared for the worst. His fears came to fruition when he stood upon the rooftop where they battled and saw the blood splatter where Ramirez fell. *Where is the body? There's no way she survived a fall from this high. Could it be that Oglis already took her body back? If so, then what of me? How long until she comes back for me?*

Kyoku stood there, biting his thumbnail, paying no mind to the onlookers gathering from the beach to see what the commotion was about. His mind filtered out the murmurs and accusations being slung about him, because they were, as Oglis said: *worthless;* their opinions and their hopes and their dreams, even their lives, all worth nothing in the grand scheme of things. They could do nothing to him, so they did not deserve his attention.

One voice was so close that it could scarcely be ignored by his sensitive ears. "Hey! You! Get down from there!" The voice of a man dressed in the blue uniform of the gate guards called from the ground below.

Kyoku glanced down at him, then turned his sight to the crowded beach, his eyes soaring over the horde of civilians in their bathing suits, then off to the ocean that stretched on what seemed forever. He wanted to run away, fly out into the blue horizon and keep going until it ended, or never stop at all. But he knew that no matter where or how far he ran, Oglis would always find him. Her grasp was inescapable. The hopelessness that such thoughts caused latched to his mind, and all the other negative thoughts he had prior flooded in behind it.

His life felt forfeit.

Without another thought, Kyoku vanished. He whisked himself far away to the peak of a skyscraper in the High District, a place where he could be alone with his thoughts. The only sound that could be heard was the humming of the Ather extractors floating at height with towering buildings. His mind wrestled with itself to find a solution to his predicament.

I can't risk going back to Rekco and Cathy at a time like this. Oglis might think I am plotting against her if I reveal her plan to them. What then? Just wait until she decides to snatch me up and haul me back off to the Hall of Fate? What if I'm blamed for Ramirez's death? What if I truly do get imprisoned there? What if I never get another chance at freedom?

Kyoku's worries only escalated from there. He desperately searched his mind for an answer—even a hint would do. Amidst his memories, something odd stood out: a snow globe, sitting idle on the desk in Gofun's quarters. It seemed innocent enough to him when he was last there over five years ago, but now, after having seen the truths of the universe outside his world, that simple object could be a clue.

Without hesitation, Kyoku warped to the dark cabin outside of Last Thesi. He crouched down in the tall grass that surrounded it and scoped out the area. *There's no way Rekco would have returned home by now.* The coast was clear. He entered the ruined cottage in a hurry. Being there again brought back painful memories of his childhood and his late master. He shook the thoughts from his mind and proceeded down the hall in the right corner of the living room, all the way to Gofun's room.

Everything there appeared just as he had left it years ago. It was a mess of debris and broken things. Kyoku shifted his eyes away in reproach for his childish actions. When he mustered the courage to bring his sights back up and face what he had done, he saw the very snow globe from his memories. It sat on the desk, untarnished, with nary a scratch on it. He was thankful he hadn't accidentally destroyed it in his adolescent fury. It appeared empty, sitting atop a stone base, much like the orb that contained this world.

Kyoku reached for it with reluctance, expecting to feel the same kind of gravitational pull he felt when he approached the one leading to his own world. As his hand drew closer, his mind raced with excitement and wonder, eager to see what kind of secret world the glass orb might contain. He closed his eyes, but all he felt was the slippery glass upon his fingertips. He opened his eyes in disbelief.

"No, it can't be," he said aloud as he picked up the globe in his hand and held it up. "It looks just like the one that contains this world. There has to be some kind of magical protection cast upon it! Of course there is! Gofun loved puzzles, so there's no doubt he left one for me to decipher." Kyoku shook the globe, put it down, spun it around, poked it, and even cast spells on it, but nothing came from the seemingly ordinary snow globe. He folded over the desk, leaning on his palms, his morale in shambles. "Gofun ... were you really just a man? Then ... What about my parents? Is it possible that they were just people too, living on this cursed planet, doomed to die before their time? Could they already be ..." his mind wandered off to terrible places and sorrow began to overwhelm him.

Amidst the vortex of hopelessness that engulfed his mind, a glimmer of hope shone through, someone who might know how to defeat Oglis, someone who was not *just* a man. Kyoku vanished within a cloud of red. When he bent upright, he stood in the dark and desolate lobby of Retallor Tower. There were streaks of dried blood on the white tile floor all about the room. He drew his eyes from the carnage and walked to the far end of the room where the receptionist desk was. Behind the desk were a host of pictures, newspaper clippings, and other decrees of the Retallor families' excellence, all in golden frames.

Kyoku scanned the array of awards. *There has to be something here that dates back to when Irol Retallor was killed by Oglis. If Irol was one of the Ten, then he would have left a magical trace on something when he severely damaged her arm. I must find that trace and follow it back to that fateful encounter.* He began stripping the pictures off the wall one by one. Each one carried feelings of triumph and a certain kind of smugness only the late mayor, Welzig Retallor, could have left behind, but Oglis was nowhere to be found.

Kyoku stopped his hand before an old black and white photo, one depicting Irol Retallor shaking hands with a rugged man. There was a striking resemblance that he could not place, until—he gasped, "Rekco? No, not quite. It must be—his father! The Eminent!" He suppressed his elation and excitement, though it felt like he was about to strike gold. Carefully, he pulled the frame off the wall and gently pried it open. His fluttering heart stopped the instant he freed the picture from the frame.

He frowned. The picture was merely a photocopy of the original. There was no trace on it beyond what the man who printed it had for lunch that day. With a sigh, Kyoku tossed the frame to the ground. It shattered atop the pile of bent golden outlines and shards of glass. "That was the last of them," he said dejectedly. The defeat that crept into his mind was relinquished quicker than it began the moment he turned and saw his final lead across from the desk: the golden bust of Irol Retallor. It sat at the center of the room, untouched by the blood splattered on the ground around it.

Kyoku stepped to the seemingly ordinary statue, eying it up and down all the while. "Might as well try," he said as he nonchalantly reached out to touch it, not even looking at the thing as he did so. To his surprise, his hand caught nothing but air. He turned his gaze to the gaudy statue and made to reach for it again. He watched as his hand veered away from Irol's face just before it would make contact.

His eyes lit up, "This is it! This statue must have some magical trace left from Irol Retallor, but it seems he's cast some kind of protection spell on it, making it impossible for me to touch it. *Impossible,*" Kyoku scoffed. "Nothing is impossible for my magic," he said as a crimson aura coated his hands. "Now, reveal your secrets to me, Irol Retallor. Show me how you almost outwitted that monster."

With his hands encased in the destructive red magic, he reached to touch Irol's face. A sizzling sound rang as the invisible field shrouding the statue burned up around his hands as they drew closer. He could feel how intensely the statue resisted, how it pushed back against his palms with a ferocity that pained Kyoku's wrists. "Almost," he winced, "there!" His hands clapped on both of Irol's golden cheeks, and right away, colors and sounds whooshed into his mind, taking over all of his senses.

The prism of colors spiraled, drilling through any thought he had, and the warping, bending sound pierced his conscience until all he heard was a high-pitched screech. It happened so fast that Kyoku didn't have the time to feel woozy or weightless as he fell to the ground unconscious.

*

When Kyoku awoke, the room was nearly pitch black, save for the glow of the streetlights just outside. He sat up and glanced around, having forgotten where he was or what he had been doing. The dream he had was beyond vivid; it had felt like an entire lifetime had passed, but not his own—it was the life of the whole universe, from the big bang erupting from the dark void, up until the end of time, where everything returned to said void. He glanced up at the pristine bust of Irol Retallor and it all came back to him. He came to realize that the magical trace he felt when he touched it did not encompass Irol Retallor alone, but every being within the universe; every life from start to finish, every outcome that has or will happen—*everything*.

"That ..." Kyoku began with a winded breath, "... was *infinity?* But how? What exactly *is* Irol's power?" He picked himself off the floor and patted the dust from his clothes, feeling both exhausted and vexed. He felt no closer to an answer, and on top of it all, he had wasted the whole day away. "At least I didn't wake up locked in a room as a part of Oglis' collection. But ... how much longer will that last?"

He warped away, returning to the rooftop in the High District where he knew nobody would be. The high-tech district was like a different place at night. Bright lights shone all through the streets and just about every skyscraper and building was glowing with the colors of their company logos, all illuminated by the Ather that powered much of this city. One sky-piercing tower was unlike the others, standing out like a sore thumb by how vibrant its lights were, even when compared to the others around it. Spotlights shot into the night sky all around it, moving in strobe-like patterns that changed colors every few seconds.

The candescent tower stood taller than every other building around it, it's only rival in the High District being the blacked out Retallor Tower that was invisible behind the curtain of the night. Kyoku had overheard gossip about a place untouched by the apocalypse, where all that was felt was ecstasy, a place called Club Tower. "Could that be the place?" He imagined it was merely a place for adults to numb themselves from the truths of the world by burying their head in the intoxicating sand. It was a feeling he was quite jealous of at the time.

He didn't give his next decision much thought, for the more he thought about anything, the more the sorrow and hopelessness would allow themselves to steep in his mind. He appeared out from a cloud of red ash across the street from the entrance of the bright building. There wasn't a person in sight. He scoffed, "Were all the lights just for show, then?" Kyoku sauntered up to the glass doors; they slid aside at his presence.

The base floor was lit by a warm, homely kind of light that was far dimmer than the blinding lights outside. There was an array of cherry-colored plush couches scattered about the room with little wooden end tables at their sides. Kyoku scanned the room. The only person was a burly man in a black suit standing in front of a brass elevator door. Kyoku crossed the empty lobby and approached the man.

"Going up?" The man asked in a deep voice as he eyed Kyoku's unusual attire.

"Yes, I am," Kyoku said in the tone of a royal who was beneath speaking to such a commoner.

The man held his hand out. "ID?"

Kyoku sucked his teeth. After all his magnificent travels, between descending deep below the city to The Underground and to the center of the universe itself, he had forgotten that the legal age to enter bars and clubs was twenty, and that he was only seventeen. Even if he had an ID, it would do him no good. "I don't have one," he said as if offended that the man would ask such a thing from him.

"Can't let you in without an ID. Sorry."

Kyoku furrowed his brow in anger. "Have you not seen the state of the world we live in?" he asked, twisting his body and gesturing to the empty street outside, likely still covered in blood stains from the halvening that were now baked into the pavement. "Just let me in."

"No can do," the man said sternly, shaking his head. "The moon could be about to fall onto the city, and I still wouldn't let you up without an ID. Do you know why?" Kyoku raised an eyebrow in response. "Because this place would be swimming with filthy vagabonds otherwise. The fine people upstairs want to forget about the troubles of the world, not *see* them up close. If you want to party without ID, go find some rancid back alley in the slums."

Kyoku frowned but was not deterred. "You leave me no choice then." He swayed his hand in front of the man's face, and a red glow followed behind it. The man's eyes grew wide and glazed over by the magical hue.

"No ID? No problem!" the man said, his tone joyous. He pushed a card into a key slot beside the elevator and it opened up. "Step right in. I'll send you somewhere *good!*"

Kyoku walked into the elevator without a word and the doors closed behind him. *Mental Manipulation*, as he had coined it, was a volatile spell he came up with over the years he spent researching the madness that spread throughout Last Thesi. He had deemed that magic was what made people affected by the madness act against their will, becoming chaotic and violent. Through some reverse engineering, Kyoku learned to replicate that thought-controlling ability using his own magic.

It was a spell that only seemed to work on the lesser, feeble minds of *worthless* mortals and only lasted a few seconds. If he were to put forth any more magic into a person's mind, he risked the spell killing them, just as the madness would. His many test subjects for the spell were all people who had already gone mad, so they would die no matter what he did, even if his spell canceled out their animalistic behavior.

The elevator stopped with a *ding*, and the light above the door read 66 in acid green font. A fog carrying the scent of alcohol and cigarettes hit him right in the face the moment the door opened. Kyoku stepped out and was greeted by another man in a black suit. "Welcome to Club Tower floor 66. Enjoy your stay." The man gave a bow and stepped aside.

The shady room outside of the elevator was small. Soft, pink light spilled from the next room as if to lure men into its depravity. Kyoku followed the light. There, he saw people lounging on circular couches, sitting close and cackling like hyenas, while others crowded around a long bar where two men and a woman served them drinks. Either the pink light distracted from his unusual, custom made clothes, or all the people in there were too far gone to pay him any mind.

Kyoku walked through the room with a look of disgust on his face; everyone around him bumbled drunkenly, cheering and singing in slurred speech. The voices were all incoherent, drowned and muffled by the loud music that played from the speakers hanging overhead. An adjacent room was overflowing with pink suds and bubbles. A man with a woman on each arm emerged from the fluffy miasma, laughing and panting their way over to the bar for another round to renew the numbness in their minds.

It was then that Kyoku noticed just how many women were there; for nearly every man was a woman at his side, scantily dressed and peppering him with compliments. He had become so accustomed to how things were in The Underground over the years, a place that had been seemingly untouched by the plights that made women so rare in Last Thesi. *Has this place hired all the women remaining in Last Thesi? Have they no dignity?* He circled around the crowd and found an empty row of seats at the bar that was likely only empty because there was no bartender there.

Kyoku sat down and bent forward over the glossy counter, resting his head on his arms. This world was doomed. He imagined all the death and destruction that was caused solely to flush out the Eminent. He envisioned Oglis destroying the whole city once he, Rekco, and Rekco's father were captured and taken back to the Hall of Fate. And even if that were not the case, how much longer would this place last as it was now? It was maddening to think about—how no matter what Kyoku tried, he would not be able to assure that the people he cared about would live full, peaceful lives.

Amidst his troubled thoughts came a tap at his shoulder. He turned to find a short man standing behind him wearing a white suit that seemed to absorb the pink light above. He had a smug face that was exceedingly punchable, appearing to be in his thirties; clean shaven, save for a thin mustache outlining his upper lip with pockmarks on his cheeks that were so severe that his face looked like it was made from aged leather.

"Hey, buddy. You look rather down. Ya know, this is a place for fun, not for *glum!*" He clumsily rhymed his words as he extended his hairy-knuckled hand and said, "My name's Wally Rattford. I'm one of the managers here at Club Tower. What's yours?"

Kyoku looked at the hand, then back to Wally and responded coldly, "You can call me Koku."

"Ah, Koku! Now that's a name. You see that guy over there, Koku?" Wally pointed at the man covered in suds wearing two women upon each of his shoulders. He was a stocky kind of young adult, with auburn hair that was tousled from all the partying. "His name is Barnov. *He* was glum like you, but Wally here doesn't stand for that, not on my floor. I hooked him up with the *two for one special*," he said with a deplorable chuckle. "Now look at him!"

"Are you going to bring out some half naked women like those to cheer me up?" Kyoku sneered.

The smile on Wally's face did not fade. He shook his head. "Nah, you're different, aren't ya, Koku? You got sharp eyes and sharp—uh—*ears*, huh?" He turned sideways and beckoned with his arm. A petite woman stood from her seat on the other end of the room and hurried over. She had fair skin with luscious black hair cascading over her shoulders and erratic freckles on her nose that spread to her cheekbones.

"Yeah, boss?" she asked in a nasally tone.

Wally took her hand in his and bent to kiss it, then turned back to Kyoku. "You look like the type that is only interested in the *real deal!* This here is Tiffany. She's one of the few *real* ones around here. I'll let you take her for a spin in one of the private lounges, on the house, if it'll put a smile on your face." He led her by the wrist, acting to hand her off as if she were a pet on a leash.

Kyoku flared his nostrils in disgust, having realized the truth about this place. He swatted Wally's hand away, saying, "*Real?* Are you saying then that all the other women here are not? What are they then?"

Wally's eyes skewed deviously. "Some boys have a real knack for it, while some others just have to be dolled up and keep their traps shut. I think *you* could pull it off, personally. If you're ever desperate and need to get rich quick, I'd let you join the squad here on 66."

The muscles in Kyoku's face tensed. He nearly blew Wally away for his insolence but didn't feel like dealing with the aftermath in such a crowded place.

"No dice? No worries. I hope I didn't offend. We at Club Tower just really care about keeping people happy during these troubling times." He released the girl from his grimy clutches and sent her back to her seat. "You just wait, sweetie. I'm sure I'll find you *something* to do," he said with a smirk before turning back to Kyoku. "How about you come with me so we can have a chat?" He beckoned as he began to walk away. "C'mon, I'll show you the executive suite."

Kyoku stood and followed the sleazy man back to the elevator where the man at the door gave a gracious bow.

Searching for The Eminent: The Collapse of Reality 217

"Where to, sir?" The door attendant asked without making eye contact.

"I'm goin' on break with my new friend here. Gonna show him the lap of luxury," Wally answered, pointing back to Kyoku.

"Very well! I'll send you two up."

The elevator opened and Wally and Kyoku stepped inside. Being in close quarters with the man alerted Kyoku to the musky scent that he gave off. It was a mix of sweat and long faded cologne trying to mask his need for a shower. He welcomed the door opening, ready to be free from the tainted smell. Wally walked out first into a sea of strobe lights. Kyoku followed and was struck by a cold wind and the much-needed smell of fresh air, the air of the clear night sky.

"Here we are! Come take a look at the sights!" Wally said, spreading his arms and doing a twirl.

The *executive suite* must have been code for the roof. Nobody else was up there, implying that it was off limits to normal patrons. Such commoners would have likely fawned at the opportunity to see the city from so high up, but Kyoku had seen it from far higher. The spotlights atop the roof glided their beams across the cloudless, dark blue sky, obscuring any stars they passed over.

"What do ya think? This here is the tallest *occupied* building in all of Last Thesi." Wally was glancing at the pitch-black floors of Retallor Tower in the distance, which stood slightly taller than Club Tower. Wally's point was moot, Kyoku thought, looking at the central Runic Tower which stood leagues taller than the two skyscrapers combined, extending so high into the sky that its peak could not be seen.

Kyoku was teetering between rage and tears, and nothing or no one seemed to be able to change that. His mind, amiss with what to say, made him turn to Wally and blurt out, "How can you be happy at a time like this? This world is doomed to end any day now."

Wally gave a deep, thoughtful sigh. "Even if it did, that's just how it was destined to be, right?"

"*Destined?*" Kyoku asked, his blood beginning to boil.

"Yup. *You can't change the stars, nobody can,* is what I always say. That's why I live how I do—not carin' about nothing. Why care about what you can't control? I just sit back and let destiny do its thing. See how well it worked out for m—" the air was ripped right out of his mouth and lungs, creating a lasso that bound his arms to his waist and lifted him up.

"Destiny?!" Kyoku roared, sending Wally higher. "Let me *show* you destiny!" He held the man, scared witless, over the edge of the Club Tower. The ground was so far away the street lights looked like stars. "Just because *you* can't change the stars doesn't mean it can't be done! I could rip the stars from the sky and sunder the heavens, revealing the cosmos for what it truly is!" Wally drifted away from the roof, dangling in thin air by the rope made of his own fetid breath. "If I dropped you right now, would you call that destiny?" Wally was aghast, seemingly not processing the wizard's words. He screamed and shouted and babbled, making no sense. "Here, your destiny—created by me."

Searching for The Eminent: The Collapse of Reality 219

    Kyoku released the spell and Wally plummeted, his sharp scream cut and began to fade. While he watched Wally fall farther and farther, Kyoku bounced his knee anxiously, as a plethora of thoughts spiraled within his mind. *Save him. Save him. Warp and grab him before it's too late. Don't do it. He's worthless, just like Oglis said. Let him die like the fodder he is. Nobody will care that he's gone. They'll all be gone too, soon enough. No! Save him! There's still time! He can change! The world can change! It's not over!*

    But it was—over. Wally hit the pavement below, making an indiscernible red splotch. Kyoku stared at it for a moment, his vision crossed, hearing nothing but the whistle of the wind. All the voices within his head had gone, leaving nothing behind. He felt no emotion; no anger, remorse, or sadness. He was as numb as the patrons of Club Tower at that moment, if not more so.

    Just then, as if awakening from a cruel dream, Kyoku bellowed at the top of his lungs, cackling madly as he raised his arms up, sending electricity flying through the sky. His magic tore through the strobe lights. Through the sounds of their explosions and the fire and lightning strewn about, it began to rain on all of the High District. "Is *this* your destiny?!" His voice boomed, amplified to match the thunder overhead. "Is this what you wanted, monster?! For me to see and accept my world for what it is—worthless?! Worthless! Worth! Less!" He laughed and laughed, unable to control his emotions any longer. Tears ran down his cheeks alongside the stars streaking across the sky, popping like fireworks—flecks of crimson stardust, depleting into nothingness. It all mixed into the pouring rain he created.

To him this world was doomed.

Chapter 16: The Day After The Storm

The intense rain the night prior left the streets in the High District looking like the face of a pock-marked vagrant; the potholes were surely not to be fixed anytime soon, considering the state of the unions that maintained the roads. Workforces that had all but crumbled were only now slowly being pieced back together after the good news from Ximen Judd and his Runic Guard that the madness was gone.

Everyone had been acting as though they'd survived the end of the world as of late. Sara, on the other hand, felt that it was only beginning. Something was stirring still, behind the scenes—she knew it in her heart, but she couldn't yet prove it.

Barnov arrived to meet her outside of her apartment complex riding an Ather-bike with a bucket seat to keep the camera he loved so much safe. It was a sight that made her light up, only to grimace a moment later when after he parked it, it burst into a cloud of dust. He stepped to her; sweaty, with dark bags under his sunken eyes, looking altogether unkempt—which had become his new norm as of late.

"Another drunken night for you at Club Tower, I take it?" Sara scoffed playfully.

"How could you tell?" Barnov asked as he fanned himself with his wide opened, unbuttoned denim jacket, beads of sweat falling off his rounded chin.

"I know a hangover when I see it, trust me," she responded with a half-smile. "I hope it was worth the headache. How were *the boys?*"

Barnov shied his eyes away from her, looking abashed at her question, his face turning red. "They're fine."

"Good. Did you get caught up in that ungodly storm?" She asked, staring at a puddle in the street; shards of broken glass glittered atop it like diamonds.

"No, thankfully," he said with a sigh of relief as he looked up at the adjacent buildings with their broken windows. "It got so bad that the folks at Club Tower let everyone stay the night, free of charge. I saw hail at one point that was falling so hard it cracked the glass on a nearby building. I heard some people saying they saw fire spinning in the clouds and stars fall and burst, but I wouldn't trust the word of a junkie."

Sara laughed. "Does that mean I shouldn't trust your word either, then?"

"Hey, now! I've been clean ever since *that day*. A little high isn't worth the risk of getting Ather poisoning from smoking that crystal stuff, now that we know that's what caused the madness. Alcohol is good enough for me, thank you."

"Right, because I'm sure there's no Ather in that bougie stuff they give out at Club Tower," she sneered. "I still don't trust that whole *Ather poisoning* spiel either, but that's another story."

Barnov switched his hefty camera to his left side and checked his watch. "Say, where's Mindy? I thought she'd be here by now."

"She better. If we wait on the side of the street any longer, we might look like a couple of panhandlers."

"Me? Sure. But you, no way. You're still dressed to the teeth, even at the end of the world. I admire your strength, ya know?"

Sara blushed at Barnov's unexpected words. *Fake it 'til you make it*, was what she always told herself when she was first starting out as a reporter. Those words seemed to pop up in her head more often as of late. She shot a surreptitious glance at the necklace dangling against Barnov' sternum. It was a puffy foam ball, the kind that sat at the end of the pole Psilen always carried around to record audio with. That token of the friend he had lost showed the true courage he had that Sara envied. She would do anything to forget the events of that day, even if it meant forgetting all the people around her that she lost.

Just then, a loud metal *thunk* sounded, and a white news van pulled up on the road beside them. The side door slid open, and Mindy leaned out, looking perkier than when Sara had last seen her. She turned her head towards the front of the van and shook her fist and cursed, "Hey, I told you to watch the potholes!" before she turned to face Sara. "How's it going, Ms. *Cracked Earth?* If you don't keep those cracks in check, Ronaldo might hit *you* next time I tell him to avoid the potholes," Mindy said with a playful smile.

"Watch who you're calling *cracked earth*. You're starting to develop some yourself," Sara responded with a smirk of her own, tugging on the side of her eyelid. Normally, she would have had Mindy's head for a comment like that, but nowadays, appearances seemed so inconsequential. She was just happy to be alive.

The two of them shared a laugh before Mindy beckoned them, saying, "Come on, let's get going," and swung back inside the back of the van.

Sara and Barnov climbed into the spacious back compartment of the news van, and after closing the door behind them, it sped off at Mindy's signal. As they drove through the High District, it became clear that Sara's apartment complex was not the only area that had been affected by the storm. Some of the boulevards they passed by had it far worse; their broken windows and decimated pavement made it look like a mirror of what Sara imagined the slums to be like—though she had never been there to say for certain.

Mindy leaned in close as they sat huddled on the cushy long seat behind Ronaldo. "I'm excited about your lead, Sara," she said with excitement in both her tone and youthful eyes.

"Same," Barnov chimed in with a thumbs up. "But why do we have to go to that creepy graveyard first?"

"Because," Sara began with an authoritative breath, "I've never seen the Eminent's grave before, and if we really want to unearth this scandal, it'll be important that I do—that we all do."

Mindy nodded in agreement. "Leave no stone unturned!"

Sara smiled, a smile that warped into a scowl when she caught sight of something through the tinted glass window in the back of the van. Barnov saw it too, though he might have reacted to her change in expression and assumed something foul caught her eye.

"Ah, more fanatics," Barnov said aloofly, gazing out the window as they were forced to slow down for the mass of people gathered in the street.

The crowd raised wooden signs and flags displaying a myriad of messages, all of which were in support of the Runic Guard. Many wore paint on their faces to tint their skin to match the shade of Ximen Judd's ghastly blue and grey complexion. Some wore custom-made patches embroidered on their clothes of the Runic Guard's insignia, the blue greatsword with angelic wings sprouting from its hilt. Their shouts were out of sync, making it difficult to understand what drivel they were spewing.

"What do they want now?" Mindy frowned.

Sara got closer to the window, thankful that the swarm seemed to show no interest in their van. "I've heard rumors that they are pushing to get the Runic Guard to erect towers in *every* district in Last Thesi. Even the rotten slums."

"Ew. I'd hate to have a tower here in the High District. It's bad enough that we have to see the Central Tower from here."

"Crazy how the public's opinion on the Runic Guard could shift so much so quickly," Barnov said with a weak chuckle.

Sara shook her head. "It's not crazy. The people here are no different than they've always been. They just want somebody to lead them and tell them everything will be okay. Now that the Retallors are gone, Ximen Judd is swooping in to claim the city. The timing is all too coincidental." She continued to stare at the rowdy protestors, even after they broke free from them. She watched as they faded into the distance of the road behind them.

"Well, we're going to figure it out, right?" Barnov asked with as much of a smile as he could muster.

"How about a little more enthusiasm?" Sara joked with a scoff.

"We will!" Mindy cheered, closing her eyes tight. "This story could save the city—the world, even!"

Sara smiled and lowered her head, looking down at her exposed knees sticking out of her pencil skirt. This world really needed saving still, she thought, despite what many of the brainwashed citizens of Last Thesi believed. It seemed that Ximen Judd was mere steps away from tyrannical rule, the kind that could spread the world over and repopulate it in his name. She wouldn't allow that to happen.

After a period of steady cruising, the van slowed again, this time coming to a complete stop.

"What is it now?" Barnov asked, trying to look out the window.

"Checkpoint," Ronaldo said from the front seat as a guard approached the driver's side window.

They had reached the border between the High and Middle District, where guards were posted at all times to check the credentials of anyone coming or going. It was an archaic ritual, Sara thought, a sour expression on her face. "Even with so few people remaining within their walls, those petty guards feel the need to police us," she said, refusing to look in the direction of the guard.

"We're all press, sir," Ronaldo assured. "I can vouch for their clearance."

The guard hummed in thought, giving the driver a lengthy stare. Mindy popped her head out from the backseat window and the guard's expression flipped in an instant. "Oh! You're with *the* Mindy Chakrabarti?" He seemed to turn bashful at the sight of her. She gave a wink and he nearly fainted. "Oh my! Go right on ahead, and good luck with your report!"

Ronaldo flicked his wrist out the window, flashing a two fingered gesture, and drove through the checkpoint. Mindy swept back into her seat with a grin on her face. "Looks like these cracked eyes and smile of mine still got it!"

With some effort, Sara forced her scowl into a smile. "We would've been cleared either way, but thanks for saving us the hassle of having to get out of the van."

"Anytime." She turned back to Ronaldo. "Just a straight shot from here to the graveyard, right?"

"That's right, Mindy. We'll follow this road along the northwestern edge of the Middle District and exit out the corner of the city. You all can take this chance to check out the newly opened beach to our right, if you want."

They all turned their attention to it. There was no towering wall on the back part of Last Thesi where the beach sand mingled with the end of the cobblestone road that worked through the Middle District. Instead, a brick wall, short enough that an able-bodied adult could scale it with ease, was all that separated the citizens from the beach. Before, when the Runic Guard seized the southwestern side of the beach, trespassing was punishable by death, but now, the people flocked to the warm sands in droves.

There were a few intersections that were newly created for pedestrians to cross the road, forcing them to stop multiple times on their way to the far edge of the city. Barnov seemed enamored with the sight of the golden sands, as though he'd never stopped to look at them before.

"Man, that looks like a lot of fun! How about a little detour?" he asked slyly, like an adolescent plotting to ditch class.

"Absolutely not," Sara said, bursting his bubble, though her eyes, too, were drawn to the many broken and fragmented families enjoying the sun in an attempt to dampen their losses.

"Bah, I should've known you'd say that. All work and no fun, right?" he whined.

Sara shifted her lips, at first in annoyance, but after some thought, her expression calmed. She put her hand on Barnov's knee and said, "We can all come back here—together, once we finish this story."

Barnov seemed to light up like a festive tree. "Really? You mean it?" Sara nodded in response. "How about we go to Club Tower together after that?"

"Now you're pushing your luck, kid," she said with a laugh.

"It was worth a try," he smiled.

The sightseeing and playful banter they all exchanged made the time pass far too quickly. Sara felt like she was having fun for the first time in a long time. She wished it could have lasted forever. But nothing lasts forever, she knew. The van came to another stop, this time before the gate to the graveyard. There were three other vehicles ahead of them, one was a stretched out black hearse carrying a coffin in the back.

Once they were let through to the grassy cemetery beyond the west wall, they all seemed to look in awe. There were nearly as many people there as there were at the beach. Friends and family stood mourning their loved ones and delivered flowers to their freshly plotted graves. Sara and crew passed by at least five services as they drove slowly to the parking area. She could hardly imagine how busy the priests and the gravediggers had been since the halvening, and how many of themselves they had to bury and perform services for.

Ronaldo parked the van in a vast dirt lot. Sara wondered if that lot would have to be plowed and primed to house new graves, or if the overflow of bodies would simply have to be burned to ash. She stepped out of the van, shielding her eyes from the sun overhead. The air was cooler outside the city and the scent of greenery wafted along the breeze.

There was a man standing beside a wooden wagon in the parking lot. He looked much like a ghoul, with dark sunken eyes, pale skin, and ragged clothes. The back of his wagon was full of flowers, mostly plastic ones with a sign below that read: ONE FOR A COPPER—TWELVE FOR A SILVER. Beside that was a basket of freshly picked Hope Lilies. Sara had never seen one up close before, only ever in pictures or stories.

"Fancy those, eh, lady? One for five silver, five for twenty. They're the best way to pay your respects," he said in a voice that was as shabby as he.

"No thanks—" Sara began, only to be cut off by Barnov's meaty paw stretching out before her.

"I'll take one," Barnov said, holding out a single silver coin to the man.

The man snatched the coin and gave it a good eyeing before handing over the pristine white Hope Lily. "Thanks ya."

Barnov turned and handed the flower to Sara, "Here."

She blushed, taken aback by Barnov's gesture. She'd spent years barking orders at him, slapping, and throwing things at him, and yet he still risked his life to save her. She took the flower in one hand and shielded her watery eyes with the other. "Thanks, Barnie."

"No problem. Go ahead and lead the way, Sara," he said, hoisting his camera up on his shoulder.

Mindy and Ronaldo joined Barnov's side, and all waited for Sara's lead. It made her feel good to be in a position of power again, yet there was a hint of sadness all the same. She beat back the negative feelings and found her journalistic excitement, saying, "Okay, this way."

Sara started southeast through the cemetery. Blades of grass tickled her exposed ankles, and the faint sounds of sobbing filled the air. Barnov appeared uncomfortable, but he kept his focus. A group of onlookers pointed at Mindy and murmured, while others seemed to scowl at the possibility of the news impeding on their private memorials. Sara heard bits and pieces of sermons as they trekked by, the priests' powerful voices seemed to give her courage.

Eventually, they made their way to a lonely row of graves, tucked away in the shadow of the massive wall to the left of it. There, none mourned or stood paying their respects. Sara looked down at the four headstones beside each other. "Here," she pointed.

"Which one? Maven Verse?" Barnov asked, pointing his camera at the stone.

"No, this one," she pointed again to the one beside it.

"Rekston Curse, huh? What a name." He knelt down before the grave of the fabled hero.

Sara joined him, looking over the stone. The shabby headstone was a mere slab with the name amateurishly etched into it. It was nothing compared to the gaudy stones of wealthy men and retired bureaucrats. She stood up and gazed out at a tall stone monument in the distance. She knew what it was without even getting near it. It was the Retallor memorial gravesite. All around it their whole family was buried. Amongst them were the late mayor, Welzig, his brother, Cecil, and even Irol Retallor himself, the former king of the fallen empire.

"It's sad to think that the *hero of the people* who once helped save this city is remembered in such a way, while those dogs are buried in the sun." Just then, Sara noticed something she hadn't before. She stooped down again before the grave. There was a single Hope Lily sitting atop the mound of dirt. It looked as fresh as the one she held in her hand. "Look! Someone has been here recently!"

"Woah, you're right!" Mindy said, poking her head between them. "But *who?*"

Sara turned her eyes from Rekston's grave to the one beside it and her eyes widened, and heart fluttered. The stone had the name *Charlotte Curse* on it, a name she had never heard before. Suddenly, all the puzzle pieces in her mind began to shift into place, and everything was beginning to make sense. "Could it be?" she gasped.

Mindy was as sharp as ever. She took notice and realized just what Sara was thinking. "A *child?* They could have had a child!"

"Child of the Eminent," Sara said through a wispy breath, as if reading from a book of mythos. "What are the odds that they could have turned out—"

"Like their father," Sara and Mindy both finished.

After the brief moment of realization, Sara jolted upright, turned to Ronaldo, and commanded, "Ronaldo, go get the van. We have to go there, now."

"Aye, boss," Ronaldo said before he ran off.

"What exactly was the lead you had, Sara?" Barnov asked, standing up.

"One that could bring us hope," Sara said, setting down her Hope Lily beside the one on Rekston's grave.

Chapter 17: Cosmic Flesh

Sara laid out a row of pictures on the metal floor inside the back of the news van. They all featured the same young man with long, green hair. Some were taken from security footage in the R.D Hospital, some from the library cameras, and even from the street sensors in the High District.

"How did you get these?!" Barnov gasped as he eyed them in detail.

"The power of privilege, of course," Sara smirked. "I've been calling and asking around everywhere I could to see if anyone had seen a man with green hair. Thankfully, some people who are still alive to tell their stories were able to give me firsthand accounts—from there it was history." She turned to Mindy beside her who was already grinning, as if waiting to be called upon. "But it was Mindy here who really pulled through in the end."

"How so?"

"Well, all these pictures and accounts weren't enough for me to actually find this guy, and nobody I talked to seemed to know where he came from. It wasn't until I showed Mindy the pictures, then she got to work in her own way, going directly to the streets for answers—even going as far as to take to the slums."

Mindy seemed to be unable to contain herself any longer. She went on and continued the story on her own. "Gross, I know! But I had this hunch! I'd heard about this trendy place deep in the slums that people came from all over Last Thesi to check out, some even coming all the way from the High District!"

"Woah! What kind of place is it? A new party spot?" Barnov asked with a glint in his eye.

"No, no. Nothing like that. It was a restaurant called Barbier's Soup Coop, where, get this, they serve free food. And not just some slum dumpster slop—this is gourmet food we're talking about! They even have real chicken there!"

"Seriously? Chicken costs an arm and a leg in the High District."

"It's true! They have fish too; the kind thought to be extinct. It's incredible. To be honest, I think that place is a story and a half itself."

"Sounds like it. You're making me want to go there now."

"As good as it sounds, this story we have here is the motherlode. Tell him the rest, Mindy," Sara said.

"Oh yeah. I got caught up thinking of that mouthwatering fish stew I had there. But anyways, while I was there, I decided to ask around and flash some of the pics. To my surprise, just about *everyone* there knew the guy! They said he goes by Rekco, and that he lives somewhere outside the city, just off the dirt path."

"And that was all I needed to hear," Sara concluded. "I always thought it was Rekston Curse hiding under an alias, but after seeing the two graves, I'm almost certain this Rekco guy is Rekston's son."

"I can see why you'd think that. This guy is a spitting image of him," Barnov said, flapping one of the photos in his hand. "That's where we're headed then?"

"Yup, we'll go all the way down to the Forgotten Woods and search all over the plains if we have to."

"What if we find his house and he's not home?"

"Then we wait—" Sara said but was nearly tossed from her seat when the van began to shake. The ride became incredibly bumpy, as though they were driving over a street covered in potholes worse than those in the High District.

"Hold on everyone!" Ronaldo called over the sound of cracking dirt beneath them. "It seems that my van isn't meant for this kind of terrain. I hope it doesn't get too dirty. I just washed it."

"I *hope* it doesn't break down and leave us stranded way out here!" Sara scoffed. She glanced out the window at the vibrant green hills outside. Many of them were covered in Hope Lilies, which made scorn rise up in her heart for that flower salesman.

"Don't worry, I'm sure it's just a little turbulence," Mindy said, trying to stay cheery, though she was starting to sweat.

"I really don't want to have to push this thing all the way back to town," Barnov complained.

The van teetered and warbled, as if its frame were trying to escape its wheels. The constant shaking was making Sara nauseous to the point that she considered jumping out and walking. Just as she felt she wanted to scream for Ronaldo to stop the van, he did, on his own accord.

"There! I can see a cabin!" He cried. "That's gotta be it!"

"Thank god," Sara sighed, clambering out of the seat and out the door. "Let's just walk the rest of the way."

It wasn't far, and the earthy air was a relief to her swimming head. Her heels didn't like the dirt road, but it was better than losing her lunch. After a short walk, they arrived at the wooden cabin. They all stood before it, exchanging nervous glances at one another as if waiting for someone to lead. Sara took the opportunity to do so. Forcing her courage to the surface, she walked right up to the front door and gave it a firm knock. There was no response.

"Uh oh," said Barnov, looking around the cabin to see if there was anyone outside. "I'm not seeing anyone around the sides or back, and there's no vehicles parked around it either. He could be gone."

"That's fine," Sara said through a depleted breath, having to swallow a mouthful of saliva to calm her stomach. "We'll just have to wait then—"

There was an immense *boom!* that shook the ground, making the grass sway and the trees in the distance shudder. Before anyone could speak, a man was at their flank. He had long, dark leaf green hair that whipped at his cheeks as he approached them. Barnov stood to bar his way, but even he seemed to tremble before the young man's presence.

"Hey, who are you people, and what are you doing here?" He raised his empty fist at them and light sprang from his hand as if it were an illusory trick, then suddenly, he was pointing a sword upon them! It was a mesmerizing blade, unlike any Sara had ever seen or heard off; the diamond-shaped edge was transparent with a blue light living and writhing beneath its surface.

Sara crossed in front of Barnov and took initiative, raising her arms up high in the sky. "We mean you no harm! We just want to talk to you. My name is Sara Stone, and this is my crew. We're with the news."

The man lowered his sword and it vanished into thin air. "You sure this isn't just another one of Oglis' *tests?*"

Barnov spoke next, though he could only raise one arm in the air while keeping hold of his camera. Patches of sweat were starting to form on his undershirt. "I have no idea who that is. We definitely aren't working for them. I promise!"

The man gave a sideways glance, the sharpness in his emerald eyes dulling. "I'll trust you for now. What is it that you want to talk to me about? And why me?"

Mindy stepped forward to Sara's side, her knees were quivering. "B—Because—we know—who you are, Rekco Curse, son of Rekston Curse—the Eminent."

Rekco's eyes grew wide with surprise and Sara and her whole crew tensed up as though he would attack them. Just as he began to open his mouth, something incredible and haunting happened: a vociferous howl shot through all the plains, and behind it, a voice followed.

"REKCOOOO!" It screamed, elongated and full of anger, like a raging mad god about to smolder the land. "COME OOOUT!" The man's voice alone shook the earth and sky alike; even the air seemed to grow hot and thick at its command.

At this unearthly call, Rekco's demeanor changed completely. He whipped around with dire haste, looking fearful. He seemed to sense something Sara and her fellows could not, for without another word, he took off down the road.

"Wait!" Sara heard herself cry out as she bolted after him, kicking her heels off so she could make chase. The purple shoes laid in the grass before Barnov, who reacted a moment later and followed her, Mindy and Ronaldo too.

Rekco did not respond to their calls for him to stop. He continued down the dirt path towards Last Thesi. Barnov pointed and cried out when Rekco tore from the path and went off into the grassy plain. He was awfully fast, creating a larger gap between them by the second. Still, Sara remained vigilant, her eyes sharp as her wits, following the green haired man—until—

"He's—"

"Gone?!" All of them gasped at once.

There was nothing standing between them and the woods in the far distance, yet Rekco had seemingly vanished, as if he'd traversed another plain of existence. The notion was not as far-fetched as Sara had thought.

*

Rekco thought it strange that the voices of the news crew chasing him had suddenly ceased. He turned back from where he stood in the grass to find that they were gone. It both perplexed and worried him. He pushed onward towards the booming mad call for him in hopes that it would provide an answer to their whereabouts.

Not far from the path, Rekco saw a figure standing alone in the wild grassy flatland, with nary a boulder or tree about him. Rekco slowed his pace, approaching the lone man with caution. "Are you the one who called me?" He asked. "What have you done with the reporters?"

"Yes, I am. And don't worry about them. They're safe outside. It's just you and me here," the man snarled, lifting his head to face Rekco, who reeled at the sight of him. He was unlike any human he'd ever seen, with skin as grey as ash, blue-tinted sclera around his red eyes, and brown hair that seemed unnaturally spiky, as though it were made of stone. He wore a simple black tank top and loose slacks but seemed to carry no weapon.

Rekco's heart burned before the otherworldly adversary. "You're one of them, aren't you? One of the Ten, come to find my father—"

"YOU LACK—RAW POWER!" The man bellowed from deep within his belly. His voice made the air vibrate and caused Rekco's ears to ring. It reverberated back and forth as though they were in an underground cave.

"I'll take that as a yes," Rekco said with a wince. "I'm getting tired of you all and your games."

"Good," the man sneered, "because I'm not here to play games. My name is Loch Standstill, and I will make you pay for killing my wife! I WILL end you!" He pounded his fist on his chest, which gave a sound like two boulders slamming into one another.

"Your *wife?*" Rekco looked confused. "That woman from before, with the gun, she was? —"

The next second, Loch was standing face to face with Rekco. He felt a force strike his stomach and the ground beneath him seemed to vanish. Loch steered Rekco into the air with his fist alone, digging deep into his gut, then threw him across the grassy plain. "Yes. She is. And I'll make sure you pay for hurting her!"

Rekco tracked mud all over his clothes as he tumbled through the soil, his insides throbbing with pain that seemed to reverberate throughout his body just as Loch's voice had. He clambered onto his hands and knees, his vision crossed. "That was a cheap shot," he muttered. "I won't let it happen—"

"Again?" Loch finished in a condescending tone, appearing over him and delivering a swift kick to his side, firing him further across the plain as though he were a leather ball. Rekco felt his ribs crack on impact, sending an electric pain to the organs behind them.

The whole world spun in circles as he rolled violently through the dirt. He imagined his back would soon be to the trees of the Forgotten Woods, and that maybe he could use their cover to his advantage. Impossibly enough, when Rekco sprung to his feet, he stood exactly where he first met Loch, as though he'd never moved. He glanced around in distress, unable to find his opponent.

Rekco heightened his senses, forcibly mending the broken bones in his side. *Any second, he'll pop up, then he's mine.* His thought was correct. Loch appeared with a flash, but did not move right away, as if he were frozen in time. Rekco took the opportunity to push his body to act even quicker than his ruthless opponent, summoning his sword and striking him across the chest with one seamless movement. But something was wrong; though Rekco's sword had caught flesh, it felt as though he had dragged it across the face of a mountain—and then—a pain struck him again in his gut.

Rekco was sent flying again before he could see what came from his attack. He heard Loch laughing, his jeers bouncing off the air itself, making it sound as though it were coming from all angles. "Nice try, quick boy, but not even that magic sword of yours can cut me."

Rekco was laid out on his back while Loch's mocking comment sprang from ear to ear, echoing in tune with the ringing in his ears. He lifted his head up and saw the hardened man standing across from him, a black gash across his chest. All around the slash mark were a prism of colors and sparkling lights. The skin around the wound looked just the same, appearing the way the cosmos of space was depicted in picture books he'd seen at the library.

The gash faded away, lost in space, and Loch's skin returned to normal. "See? Not even a scratch!" He walked up to Rekco and bent down slowly, reaching for his collar. Rekco accelerated and sped away but was unable to create much distance between them. No matter how far he ran, Loch would always be standing no more than twelve feet away from him. "You can't escape me, not until the trial is done."

"And what is this *test* then? What do I need to do to win your game?" Rekco asked, panting from the exertion and the lingering pain.

Loch gave a great guffaw, seeming to thoroughly enjoy Rekco's distress. "The funny thing about that is: there *is* no goal! You'll just have to fight me until you either beat me—or die!" He continued to laugh. "I'll even give you a hint: my weakness. You see, my people were born with a deadly toxin in our brittle bones. When I was little, I almost died from a hairline fracture. To make up for it, our bodies grow hard as stone as we enter adulthood. But unlike them, I've been blessed with godlike power: my skin is as dense as the cosmos itself! So, no matter how hard you try, you'll never pierce me!"

Rekco did not react to Loch's condescending nature or his laughter. His expression remained calm, yet serious. Loch was just another opponent, another puzzle standing in the way of him finding his father. "But Oglis did pierce you, didn't she? That's why you're here."

Loch's smile faded, and he began to fume. The air all about them became hot with his rage. "I hope she does worse to you. In fact, I'll make sure of it by bringing you back so she can set you up in the Endless Nightmare."

Rekco shifted his lips. "And what is that? Some alien torture device? Is that where they plan to take my father?"

"Oh, of course not. The Eminent is far too good for that. But you—you'll be forced to experience wretched things; seeing your loved ones killed before your eyes in the most awful ways, only to face their killer and find that he is invincible and that you are helpless to die at his hands—over and over, and over again. Oglis will invade your mind and find what hurts you most, and make you live those things, never knowing what is real or not, yet always hoping that the death you find at the end of it will be final."

Loch's words made Rekco shudder with fear. He knew if he couldn't escape, then he'd have no choice but to win. "What constitutes a *win* against you then? Do I need to make you yield?"

"*Yield?*" Loch repeated with a chuckle then erupted into boisterous laughter. "I'd never. You'll have to kill me—just like you killed my Rebecca."

"I didn't kill her," Rekco said with annoyance. "She jumped off the roof of a building and fell to her death."

Loch's expression soured. He appeared disgusted at Rekco's recounting of the tale. "You really are stupid, aren't you? A know-nothing guppy, born into power, without any idea what it does. It's no matter. *This* will be the end of the line for you."

The moment Loch shifted his weight to move, Rekco acted. He accelerated and launched himself at the fearsome man, slashing him relentlessly with his glass blade as he circled around him. Loch raised his arms and lowered his chin behind his bent elbows while Rekco showered him in blows. Rekco swung and swung, until both his arms and legs were tired, only for Loch to bust out of his defensive curl and strike him, throwing him onto his back.

"Is that all you've got?" Loch mocked. His whole body was covered in galactic patterns and stars and cuts that slowly faded. "What happened to that brilliant attack you tried to crack my sweet with? I want to beat your ultimate attack so you can feel utterly defeated before I send you to hell!"

Rekco coughed up blood and wiped it on the back of his hand as he stood. He thought back to the spiral of blue energy that surrounded him and his blade, and the massive explosion that followed. "I—I don't know how to do it."

Loch scoffed. "Maybe I can beat it out of you then." He zoomed to close the distance between them. Rekco slowed time and struck Loch all over his extended right arm and shoulder, then took a swift left hook to the ribs for his efforts.

Rekco crumpled to the ground, feeling as though his ribs were going to collapse onto his insides. He focused the mysterious power within him as Loch bent down to grab for him again, but this time, nothing came. His wounds did not heal, and he could not dash away from Loch's grasp. Rekco kicked and struggled, dropping his sword into thin air as the chiseled man grabbed him by the collar and lifted him up high. Loch was taller than him, though not quite as tall as Ramirez.

"Out of juice already?" Loch complained. "I won't accept that! Not after what you did to Rebecca! What you ..." he trailed off, and Rekco noticed something peculiar—tears streaking down his stony cheeks; red as his pupils and viscous as molasses. It was a disturbing sight that made him wonder if there was more to the fiery man than he led on. "It can't ... be left ... uneven!" Loch shook Rekco furiously.

Rekco struggled to free himself, but he was spent, battered, and beaten. He expected Loch to punch his head off amidst his fury-filled babblings, yet the blow never came. "I don't understand what you're talking about!" he cried as he kicked Loch's hard body. It made as much difference as kicking a mountain. Loch didn't budge. Instead, he continued raging.

"If I go back there—Rebecca—she—won't be the same. They'll say she is—but I'll know!" Loch's voice broke. Rekco could feel his captor trembling, though it did not aid in escaping his grasp. "That's why ... we always promised to die together—reset our souls together! That's why—I can't go back there alive! But—I can't let you get away with what you've done!" He sent his fist into Rekco's midsection repeatedly, while holding him up like the punching bag he made him out to be.

Rekco coughed up blood onto Loch's shoulder, his vision crossing and flickering, threatening to lose consciousness. He needed to find a way to escape. Loch was beyond reasoning with, and nigh impervious to his attacks. Loch reared his arm back to punch him again. As Rekco stared down into Loch's hate-filled eyes in a stupor, his gaze fell and was drawn down, and just then, an old memory burst into his mind.

He was reminded of the teachings of his old master and caretaker, Maven. "Ya see this bone here, green lad? It's called the *clavicle*, or better known as—the collarbone. It's one of the easiest to break, only needin' a few pounds of force to do so. If ever you're in a pinch, don't feel bad about aimin' there. Livin' is more important than honor, got it, green lad?"

A tear formed in Rekco's eye, remembering Maven, remembering the long life that was taken from him. He had to go on for his sake, no matter what. Rekco reared back his right arm to match Loch's, the glass sword appearing in his clenched hand. As his emotions welled up, so did it seem that his power did as well. In that moment of desperation, driven by the will to live, an azure light began to glow about his arm.

Loch's eyes grew wide with anticipation, and he stayed his arm. "Yes! Yes! Hit me! Hit me with the last ounce of life you can muster before it gutters out! Let us both die together!" he cried as he cackled madly.

Rekco abided. He did not wonder what otherworldly force was forming around him, nor did he fear what it would bring. The magical energy spiraled around him, forming a celestial tunnel. Without hesitation, he drove the blade downward, aiming directly for Loch's collar bone. The spiral spun and whirred, converging into the point of the glass sword as it made contact with Loch's bone. It made a terrible screeching sound, like metal grating against stone.

Rekco felt an intense pain as Loch struck him in the sternum with a heavy blow, pushing his stone fist into him as though he meant to push it through him like a sword, howling all the while. Loch's insane cry reached its peak as a blinding light exploded from the tip of Rekco's blade, freeing him from his grip and sending him flying.

Amidst the light and wonder sounded a tremendous *crack!* When the blue hues dissipated from Rekco's vision, he found himself flat on his back again. He bent upright and saw that Loch had fallen to his knees, his once haunting eyes, now appeared hollow and lifeless. The cosmic pattern upon his flesh was spreading all over his body, as if trying to defend him from an attack that wasn't there. The stab wound on his collarbone was white and cracked, unlike the rest of his thick armor.

The black void and stars and prismatic celestial bodies proceeded up his neck, washing up onto the top of his head and down beyond his ankles. Once his whole body was covered, Loch let out a deep, dry sigh and fell face first into the grass. The crash of his stony body sounded like an avalanche that shook the plains.

Rekco's mind did not entirely process what had just happened. He simply let out a sigh of triumphant relief and let his head fall back onto the plush grass while a dark circle closed upon his vision.

*

A voice roused Rekco from his sleep, crying out, "Here! I found him!" It was a greasy, stout man wearing an open jacket.

Soon after, others rushed to his side. One yelled, "Get his legs!"

Another said, "Let's get him inside."

Rekco was too tired to be bothered. He closed his eyes again.

The next time he opened them, he was staring up at the ceiling in his home, feeling the soft couch cushions beneath his tired back. It was an eerie feeling of deja vu that he didn't have the energy or patience to place. A dark-skinned woman with long black hair stooped beside him, a cup of water in her hand.

"Here. Can you lift your head?" she asked, trying to help him up while guiding the cup towards his lips.

Rekco shifted upright, feeling his whole body ache as he did so. He felt like he had been run over, and he wasn't far from the truth. "It's you again," he said before glancing around to find the news reporters from before, each standing at different ends of the couch.

"What the hell happened out there?" The golden haired woman, Sara asked.

"It's—" he began, cut off by the sharp pain of broken bones that went unmended after he exhausted his power. "Nothing." He looked around at all their concerned faces, yet he was the one concerned about them. He didn't want them getting mixed up in the dangers of his *trials* like Mikayla had. Instead, he thought to do as they wished so he could be rid of them for good. "How about we have that talk you guys wanted?"

Sara rounded to the front of the couch and sat beside the other woman, looking both eager and unsure at the same time. "Okay. As long as you're up for it."

It was a long-winded discussion, but Rekco told them everything—or just about *everything*; from the Ather mines hidden along the coastline, to the underground city, the Retallors schemes, and finally, how he assailed their tower. He felt a bit self-conscious sitting before their cameras, having every word of his written down as he said them, but he didn't care as long as it kept them out of harm's way. He didn't know what they planned to do with the information he provided them, and he didn't care. It seemed that what he said was sufficient for them.

Sara continued to ask him questions about his father, his whereabouts, and his connection to the Retallors.

All the while, the other woman, who he had learned was named Mindy, got a call on her communicator. She reeled at what she was hearing and burst into Barnov's shot to interrupt the interview. "We need to go, now!" she said, distressed in both tone and expression.

"What? I don't care what's going on. *This* here is the most important thing we could be doing right now," Sara said, shoving Mindy back.

"Nuh-uh! There's something bigger!"

Sara's expression became dire, and her interest peaked. "Like what?"

Mindy gulped hard before speaking, "Something is going down outside of Central Tower. I got a call saying there's a TON of people gathered around the tower—and—they all—have eyes that are *blue and glazed*."

Everyone gasped, including Rekco.

"If what you heard is true then—"

"Yeah, the madness—it's back."

Chapter 18: Keeper Of The Hall

Dr. Gavin was the keeper of the Hall of Fate; it was his sole purpose and the reason for his creation. But at times, it was as though his purpose was to tend to Oglis' every whim. He tended to her more than to the hall itself. But times were growing stranger as of late, and Oglis was growing more distant, requiring less and less of him. He wondered what was amiss; what about the Eminent made her act so?

Dr. Gavin had just finished in room seven, the Swordsman's room, making sure he would receive the medical attention needed to stop him from entering a stasis. *Those dolts better handle it! We can't have the Swordsman out of commission too. What if the Core were to come under attack? What if the Fleeting Requiem comes to destroy us all? Our defenses are always lower during these missions where we must allocate such heavy resources.* He spat at his own thoughts. *Just throw all of the newcomers in the nightmare, I say. It's not worth molding them and testing them if it puts our defenders in stasis.*

He flared his large nostrils, warbling back and forth as he piloted his shrunken, blue body down the hall towards room one, Oglis' room. Along the way he stopped to check on each of the rooms. "Six," he said aloud, looking up at the VI above the sealed doorway. "Irol Retallor. That troublemaker. We must keep that one shut. He'll ruin us all if he ever gets out." He hobbled on and looked at the next doorway. "Five." It was closed, but not locked. There was a window that was far from Dr. Gavin's eyes. He waved his hand and commanded it to come down to his level. He peeked inside where two bodies lied upon tables beside one another, shrouded in red magic, indistinguishable. "Lovebirds. Dead. Killed before they even got to face the Eminent. Disgraceful," he cursed and moved on. Next up was, "Three." The door was lifted, and the room was black and empty. "Per'cei is already in position. His turn shall be next, no doubt."

Dr. Gavin proceeded past the room labeled II without looking at it or saying a word. It was another empty room—one that did not require his attention. Rooms eight and nine were reserved for the Eminent and Kyoku, the Overflow, while the tenth was still out there in the universe—somewhere, eluding fate. Dalu's will, which lingered within his mind, reminded him not to worry about *that one,* the one known as *the Dragon.*

As Dr. Gavin approached room I, a voice could be heard. The thick essence within that room muffled it beyond recognition. He proceeded inside anyway, as it had been some time since he spoke to Oglis, and he had concerns he wished to address. He walked slowly through the dense blue fog, which made it hard to breathe if idled within it for too long. The way the fog pressed back against him each time he tried to enter the room made it seem as though it were alive, but being that it was Oglis' magic that created it, it was no surprise that it caused such a tremendous force.

At last, after sifting through the indomitable fog, the pillar of a woman came into view. Dr. Gavin was so small that he couldn't see her head or face unless she bent down, but he could tell her front side from her back based on her legs alone. Right now, she was facing away from him as he approached, seeming uninterested in his arrival.

"Madam Oglis, may I speak with you?" he asked in the tone of a humble servant, much unlike his title.

"Why, hello, Dr. Gavin. You may speak *to* me, if you wish, for I am rather indisposed."

Dr. Gavin looked up as best as he could to see what she was doing, but her upper body was the top of a tower piercing through the clouds to his stature. "Oh. My apologies. Should I return later—"

"No. Soon, there will no longer be a *good* time for me to speak with you, so better now to get on with saying what you intend to."

Dr. Gavin's blue face went flush, though he was but an insect before her that he doubted she took notice. "Very well, then. I just—wanted to alert you that the Lovebirds are both dead. It will be some time before they awake from their stasis."

"*So?*" Oglis responded coldly, not even turning to face little Dr. Gavin.

"Well—and Kyoku never returned after fulfilling his role in Ramirez's mission."

"*And?* The Overflow knows he cannot escape me now that I have felt his magic. I could follow his trace across the whole universe, if need be."

"Ah, yes, but—don't you think it unwise to allow someone with such an important power to roam freely about the universe? What if he were to accidentally—"

"He won't," Oglis interrupted. "He's terrified of his fate. He'll do anything to avert it. Just let him wallow and brood like the petulant child he is. One day, he'll return here. I can assure you of that."

Dr. Gavin shuddered at the imaginings. "What if when he does, he seeks to fight?"

"*Fight?*" she chuckled. "No chance. Not while he thinks his magic is useless against me."

"What if he finds out the truth?"

"And who would tell him? Nobody knows other than those who are in the room right now. I trust you'll keep to yourself, Dr. Gavin. You know what consequences would come if you do not."

"Why, yes. You can count on me, as always, Oglis."

She hummed aloud, making tiny vibrations in the fog from her voice box. "To think that such an intelligent creature could be fooled so easily. That boy, Kyoku, wields the most powerful type of magic in the universe, yet he thinks that it is worthless against my regeneration. It makes me laugh every time I think about it."

"Well, it seems that your brilliance is greater than the Overflow's then."

"For now," she said. "Is that all then?"

"Well, not quite. What about Rekco and that mysterious weapon he wielded against the Lovebirds? It looked like something out of the Archives of Time! It can't be safe to allow him to continue using such a thing. He's already shown energy outputs capable enough to crack a soul with it. Who knows how much more powerful he could become if left unchecked."

"The Archives of Time, you say? Have you ever been?"

"Oh—no, I have not. But still, that blade far exceeds the armaments of our own soldiers here in the Core. It can't have come from his world."

"Indeed. Still, that is not to get in the way of his trials, or the mission at hand," Oglis said, sounding distracted.

Dr. Gavin tilted his body back and forth, trying to see what her hand was doing. "Say, Oglis, what is it that you are so busy with?" At his question, there was a metallic screech from above, as if a lift were triggered, followed by a loud *thud* that hit the ground with such force that it dispersed the fog around them. Oglis stepped aside and Dr. Gavin shrieked at what he saw standing before him. "T—that's! —"

"My latest experiment. A possible solution to this *Eminent problem*."

Dr. Gavin stared at it flabbergasted. Before him, tied to an upright examination table, was a man with long green hair and emerald eyes that looked devoid of life. "He's—Rekco?! A spitting image of him! But *why?*"

"You see, Dr. Gavin. I have a hunch about the Eminent's unique abilities, one I decided to test myself. To do that, I recreated an exact replica of the boy using his DNA and implanted all of the combat footage we have of him into his mind. I've removed all of his worthless, human functions; speech, the need for sustenance, or desires. And to make it complete—" Oglis placed her hand on her chest, and it began to glow. From the light came a small orb of golden energy. She took the orb and held it to the clone's bare chest, which seemed to long for the light. It sucked it into the place where a human's heart would be, then suddenly, its whole body convulsed, eyes flickering and fingers twitching. "There! Now, he's alive. My own creation—but what shall I call him?"

Oglis began to ponder and mutter to herself, no longer paying any mind to Dr. Gavin. He took that as a signal that their conversation had reached its end. He guided his way back through the dark blue fog and showed himself out. When he returned to the Hall of Fate, he stood there for a moment and gave a heavy sigh. *Something is amiss. Something's not right with Oglis. I hope for her sake that the boy will fail, so that we may put this Eminent business behind us.*

*

Rekco woke up in a haze, unsure how long he had been asleep for. The sun was still out, but was it the same day's sun that was there when he let his fatigue take him? The news reporters were gone, he noticed. He wondered if they had actually been there at all, or if they, too, were a figment of his distorted reality.

He got up off the couch, expecting to feel groggy, but to his surprise, he felt unusually revitalized. The intense battle he had with Loch that pushed him beyond his limits seemed as if it had happened ages ago. While inspecting himself for bruises, Rekco noticed the holes in his shirt from the shrapnel Ramirez assailed him with.

He lifted the shirt off his head and found that the wounds were all gone, leaving not even a scar behind. It was one of the wonders of his newfound powers, powers he had now been told multiple times that he did not understand. He was starting to believe those claims more and more as he fought against the Ten. "I bet my father could help me understand this power more. But I still have no clue where he is," he said to himself as he pulled out a faded orange shirt from the box Bragau recently delivered to him. Seeing the box of clothes reminded him that Bragau also took Cathy's belongings some time ago, leaving the home feeling empty and lonely.

Rekco wondered how she was holding up, and if Mikayla was doing better. The medics at Zeke's hideout said she would be okay, giving praise to the haste in which Kyoku brought her to them. He didn't know how Kyoku knew about Zeke's hideout, although it didn't surprise him that he did.

After a quick bath, Rekco returned to the living room and sat alone on the couch. The longer he sat in silence, the less silent it seemed to become; a strange, low buzzing sound vibrated within his ears. He looked around the room to see where it was coming from and eventually took to the kitchen to continue his search. The sound grew louder, as though it were calling to him.

He scoured the kitchen, but soon realized the buzzing was coming from something in plain sight. "That old radio," he said, staring at the black void at its core that once housed a brilliant blue light. Seeing it always reminded him of Maven and his final days, where he was obsessed with the radio, taking it everywhere he went and treating it as though it were his child. It was no wonder Rekco often chose to overlook the thing.

Rekco walked over to the buzzing radio and turned the dial, only to find that it was already on the lowest volume. Annoyed, he decided to turn the volume up instead, hoping that some music might drown out the sound. Instead of a melodic tune, the beginnings of a news broadcast played from it.

"Hello, my name is Sara Stone. I'm coming to you live from Central Tower, at the heart of Last Thesi, where something unfathomable is happening. It appears that a large crowd has gathered around the Runic Tower, but not just any crowd; every one of them is showing the telltale sign of *madness*: foggy blue eyes. Despite this, the seemingly maddened group has shown no signs of hostility ..."

Rekco's vision blurred for a moment as he listened to the woman's voice, remembering that it was she who he spoke to before he passed out. He remembered the other woman talking about *Central Tower* and *madness* before they all left. "So, it's really true then. But *why?* And how?" His skin crawled at the thought that such a terrible affliction would rear its ugly head again. "Does it mean that Ximen Judd was wrong about what caused the madness? Or could it mean that the Retallors, or somebody connected to them is still alive?" Rekco did not have much time to speculate, as the tone of the broadcast took a horrifying turn.

"Reeekco," Sara's drawn out voice called out of the radio, sounding weak and distorted. It sent a jolt throughout his whole body. "Y—Yo—Y—You—laaack—faaaiii—faaaii—faaaiiith—" she droned on in a monotone for an uncomfortably long time, leading up to a bone chilling *crack*, followed by a static-filled silence.

Rekco was sweating and breathing hard after hearing the ghastly broadcast. The shadows within his dimly lit house seemed to grow darker, until he thought his eyes were closed. He felt dizzy as the world burst back into focus. His knees were bent to a crouch, with eyes staring at the wood floor, mind blank. The Runic Tower at the center of the city had seemingly been calling to him for years every time he looked at it, but now it made its call public. He knew there was no choice but to heed it.

Rekco left his home at once, leaving the staticky broadcast to play. He sped through the plains as fast as he could, only stopping once the towering walls surrounding Last Thesi were in sight. There, he saw that the two double doors leading to the Parade Grounds were wide open. He bolted off again towards the beckoning doors, and a moment later, he was standing within the doorway to the pure white grounds.

There wasn't a soul in sight around the entrance. He didn't bother to check if the gate guard was at his post; there wasn't any time to waste. Rekco proceeded through the empty grounds without a hitch. The foreboding Runic Tower that loomed terribly over the city was silent for once; it made no attempt to enter his mind or impede his progress, as though it were opening the way for his embrace. Rekco started towards it in haste, eventually stopping once he caught sight of shapes gathered about the Runic Tower.

He wondered if the fanatics had attacked Sara during her broadcast, just like they had murdered his mother when he was a baby. The thought made Rekco's blood boil, until he remembered how much unlike herself Sara seemed at the end of the broadcast; she had sounded eerie and inhuman, which made Rekco fear something more sinister was afoot. He expected to find the group chanting prayers to the Runic Guard around the tower but saw no such thing. Instead, what he saw was truly horrific.

Bodies were strewn about the foot of the tower, all laid out on the ground with stiff arms that looked still as statues, reaching desperately up towards the heavens. At the forefront of the crowd, he saw Sara, laying on her back, her neck twisted and broken. She laid in the arms of the bulky man, Barnov, who sat on his knees—both of them cold and lifeless.

Rekco's vision blurred at the sight, recalling just moments ago how excited they were to be meeting him and finishing their story, now were meeting their fate instead. He knelt down beside Barnov to see if he or Sara had any visible wounds. Rekco became nauseous upon closer inspection of the horrid scene. What first looked like tears streaming down Barnov's cheeks were actually strands of a pale blue, yarn-like substance. The same threads were pouring out of the corners of Sara's gaping mouth as she laid broken.

"Is this madness too?" Rekco muttered, unable to take his eyes off the threads. "But—I thought it wasn't supposed to affect women?"

At his words came a grinding sound, akin to that of the giant doors to the Parade Grounds opening. Rekco turned back to see that the doors in the distance were not stirring. He looked forward again and saw that the base of the Runic Tower had an opening where no visible door had been. From the opening came three glittering clusters of blue light, fluttering over the pile of corpses that surrounded their home. Each of the ethereal figures wielded a great sword that shone as bright as they, blue as Ather.

"The Runic Guard," Rekco said scornfully as he stood to face them. "Is this your doing?"

They made no response, and it was unlikely that the featureless figures could formulate words at all. Instead, they zoomed towards him all at once and raised their blades up high. Rekco knew the Runic Guard were quick, as he had seen their fearsome powers on display when they decimated The Underground. But now, he far exceeded them. He acted quicker than they, summoning and swinging his blade with one swift movement, striking the three guards at once. Their bodies burst into clouds of stardust, and their swords all clattered to the ground, splintering like glass when they hit the brick road.

With the Runic Guards felled, Rekco started towards the opening in the tower, all while hoping it would remain open long enough for him to enter. Along the way, he stepped over the mass of bodies that littered the ground, trying to shoulder the tremendous guilt he felt about the horrific ends they met. "I'll avenge you all. I promise," he said as he crossed into the Runic Tower.

A foul stench struck him in the face the moment he entered the crimson spire; it was like rotting death, coming from every direction, but without any visible source. All the walls about the ground level of the tower were lined with bookshelves. Upon them were thick tomes on the history of places Rekco had never heard of. Were they books on the history of other worlds, or civilizations long lost to the passing of time? Rekco didn't have the time to discern such things—his goal was clear: reach the top of the spire and confront the ruler of this wretched place.

A wide staircase wrapped all around the inner walls of the tower, spiraling up higher and higher, beyond what Rekco's eyes could see. He bolted up the stairs at top speed without wasting any time. He did not stop, not even when more soldiers of the Runic Guard floated down from the tower's heights like apparitions and tried to assail him. His glass sword vanquished them with ease with no more than a flick of his wrist.

Up and up, he went, and the higher he went the worse the stench of rot became. It only took a few minutes in the foul, stuffy tower for him to begin to forget what fresh air was like. The bookshelves and the books upon them grew more decrepit as he ascended higher, and eventually the walls appeared as though they were covered in scabs. Given the fetid scent and the disgusting, crusted walls,

Rekco might have thought he was climbing up the throat of some enormous beast.

All the while he climbed, Rekco saw not a soul, save for the occasional luminescent body of a Runic Guard. There were no floors or breaks in the stairway, making it obvious that this place was not meant for people. He feared that the terrible smell would make him woozy and cause him to trip and fall all the way down the tower. Despite his fears, he fought against it and persevered, continuing his trek towards the top, thrust far into the heavens. He had no idea how long it would take to get there, or what would be waiting for him when he did.

Chapter 19: Blue Dress

While Rekco raced to the top of the world, Kyoku was living in the lowest portion of hell—at least, within his mind. The wizard awoke on a rooftop in the High District, a light reflecting blanket of his creation draped over him. He rolled over, his body aching and mind racing. He wanted to return to sleep, as it was the only way to quiet his mind; the world of dreams was the only place he could be free of his inescapable fate.

He was but a pawn, to be sacrificed for a greater good that he did not understand nor consent to. It was too much for him to bear. All his life, Kyoku wanted to be free of the burden of being a magical prodigy, or whatever it was that he was being raised to become. He wanted to lead a normal life, even if it meant being *worthless*. He wanted to be praised for his deeds, not his heritage—sought after for his intellect, not his powers.

It was all a dream now.

Soon, this world would end, he knew, and he would be forced to meet his fate as kindling to spark the creation of a new universe. "What is there worth doing in the meantime?" he said through a breath of dejection. Just as the words escaped him, thoughts of the pain and suffering of those around him popped into his mind. He was reminded of the blood pouring from the wound in Mikayla's belly, and the agony she went through because of him. "But—that could have been Cathy, bleeding out before my eyes, mind full of fear and uncertainty." His thoughts were derailed. "Cathy," he heard his voice speak, though he wasn't sure when he commanded his mouth to utter her name in such a longing way. "Is there no hope for her either? Is her destiny entirely out of her hands, bound to the suffering that all wretched mortals are doomed to feel?"

Kyoku looked to the sky. From his perch, high up above the city, he could scarcely see the green tops of the trees in the distance. He knew of Zeke's plan to cross the Forgotten Woods in an attempt to preserve humanity elsewhere. It was a good idea for those ignorant of their hopeless struggle, without any idea of how little their world was worth in the grand scheme of things. "But still," he began, "I could help them. I could warp every last one of them across to the Redlands. I could supply them with magical seeds and technology to help get them on their feet. I could make a difference."

His heart fluttered at the thought, though his heart also seemed to skip a beat at the thought of Cathy's smiling face as a reward for his deed. He wanted to leave this world in the best shape it could be in—for her, and everyone else. At last, he had found some hope to latch on to, even though his own life was still forfeit. He stood up and prepared to make for Zeke's hideout in the slums.

Within the next breath, Kyoku was there before the abandoned apartment complex tucked away in the quietest part of the slums. Just outside, at the base of the building, he recognized a wooden wagon that was parked there. "That deflated plum is here?" he questioned aloud, referring to Bragau, the delivery man who often brought supplies to Rekco's house in the plains.

"Koku!" a voice cried excitedly, making his ears ring. He turned quickly to find Cathy walking towards him with an empty crate in her arms. "You're back! I'm so glad! We could really use your help around here."

For some reason, seeing her overjoyed at his presence did away with his ability to respond. Instead, he simply glared at her. She put the crate down and shifted her weight, putting her hand on her hip.

"Sorry. I didn't mean to be so forward. It's just that—you tend to disappear quickly, so I feel like I need to blurt out what I want to say while I can."

Kyoku shook his head, feeling guilty for his abruptness for the first time. "No. It's okay. I just have a lot on my mind as of late. How is Mikayla doing?"

"She's doing better, thanks to you!" Cathy beamed. "She's been asking about you. You should go inside and see her. I'm sure she won't be the only one in there happy to see you; almost everyone here is somebody you helped evacuate from The Underground. While you're there, I could show you around the place too, if you want."

Kyoku shifted his eyes away. "That's part of the reason I'm here." When he looked forward again, his heart sank. Cathy had gotten incredibly close. She was staring at something.

"You're not wearing your dark glasses anymore. I think you look better that way. You have such unique, yellow eyes. They're beautiful, ya know?"

Kyoku's insides seemed to lurch about. The way he looked at her must have come off as disgust, because she took a step back, looking reproachful for her comment. "Still blurting things out?" he said in a sarcastic tone, trying to lighten his expression, though he could feel his body temperature rising.

"Oh, yeah, sorry. I didn't mean to offend you."

"You didn't offend me. It was just an unexpected thing to hear." Kyoku found himself looking more closely at Cathy's eyes as well. Usually her soft, pink hair was the only thing he noticed about her, not her plain, brown eyes. But upon further inspection, her eyes weren't so plain. Amidst the shades of brown were other, more subtle colors; reds and greens and yellows, all mixed into the hues, showing more when the light struck her eyes a certain way. They reminded him of the giant clusters of stardust frozen in the cosmos, stuck in a state of uncertainty, never knowing what they might become should time return to the universe.

Cathy smiled, as though she could read the thoughts he would never dare say aloud to her. She reached out to grab his wrist, saying, "C'mon, let's go inside," but before he could feel her touch, she was yanked away. She yelped as her body was wrenched into submission. The cart driver, Bragau, held her tightly from behind with a wicked grin on his face and eyes that were glazed over with blue clouds.

Kyoku's eyes widened, and nostrils flared as he reached for her. Bragau pulled her back farther out of his grasp, snickering all the while. "He's gone mad!"

"Koku! Help!" Cathy cried as he struggled to free herself, punching and kicking the rotund man, but to no avail.

Bragau opened his mouth, but the words that came out were not his own. They sounded twisted and full of pain and elation at the same time. "I'm sorry to interrupt your precious reunion, but I'll be taking the girl now."

"What?" Kyoku responded in disbelief. "What is this? The mad don't speak!"

Bragau laughed a wispy laugh that sounded like a hiss. "Come, you. Let us leave this *traitor* to his wonderings."

That word: traitor. It brought back a host of memories that Kyoku kept locked deep in his mind. Suddenly, a sense of deja vu hit him. "Just—like my parents?" The hairs on the back of his neck stood on end and his blood began to boil. He raised his hand to Cathy's captor without a thought.

"Exactly! You remember now, child. You've grown to be an even bigger traitor than them, though—a traitor to the Ten—to Lord Dalu!"

"*Dalu?* Just who are you?" Kyoku asked through gritted teeth, holding back his rage and will to attack; his vision wavered as he started to see red.

The being puppeteering Bragau did not act coy, to Kyoku's surprise. "My name is Per'cei. I am one of our lord and savior Dalu's chosen followers!"

"So, you're one of *the Ten* then?" he asked, still looking for an opportunity to free Cathy from Bragau's grip.

"Koku," Cathy gasped weakly as Bragau clasped his hand across her throat.

"I am done entertaining this *traitor*. I came to seek *collateral* to ensure cooperation from the green haired boy, but it seems that what I found counts for the both of you! How splendid!" Bragau's face twisted into a

Searching for The Eminent: The Collapse of Reality 263

terrifying, toothy grin. Out from the side of his neck, a pale blue thread broke free. As it did, Kyoku's eyes widened with fear, his eyes drawing next to Cathy.

She writhed in pain as the pores on her neck began to shift. Kyoku saw her attempt to mouth a word and made to reach out to her without a thought or plan fully formulated. Bragau sniggered, gripping her tighter, the thread protruding from him bouncing all the while. Thoughts of fear, and of loss, and all other miserable things spiraled within Kyoku's mind faster than a normal person's mind could process. He cried out, "Let her go!" and the world seemed to bend to his will.

Bragau burst into a cloud of red ash, as though he were a rental vehicle reaching its time limit. When the particles blew away in the wind, Kyoku gasped to find that Cathy was gone too. He rushed forward to find the pale blue thread on the ground where they both stood. Beside it sat a peculiar marble. Kyoku bent down and picked the thing up; it fit perfectly in the palm of his hand.

It was black as the void, with tones of white skirting beneath the surface, flowing like a river at times, swirling and dancing like leaves on the wind the next moment. He stared into the void with eyes unfocused. A familiar warmth pulsed through his hand that made tears well up behind his eyes. "*Cathy?*"

"You're lucky she didn't crack! You risked her soul just to ruin that fat man's! Ha! How bold of you!" A faint voice bounded out of thin air. Kyoku's eyes darted about, ready to strike wherever it was coming from. "Can't find me so easily, can you? You've become so accustomed to my trace that it feels akin to breathing air! You've searched for me for the last five years, yet here I've been, all along!"

Kyoku's sophisticated ears picked up on where the sound was coming from. He drew his eyes down to the blue thread by his knee. It wriggled like a worm before it stood up on end to greet him. He snatched it up in his free hand and held it up high, his balled up first flowing with red, destructive magic. "What did you do to her?!"

The thread emitted a laugh. "You think I'm afraid of you? I am resistant to your magic. You should know that after the years you've experimented on me! But as far as the girl goes—I've reduced her to a more *portable* form, turning her inside out. Now where her body once was, her soul exists, and her body remains on the inside."

"Undo it, now!" Kyoku demanded, sweating and exuding a terrible heat.

"Not so fast! How about you come and make me, traitor? I'll kill you for your efforts and haul both of you back to the Hall of Fate!"

"Where—are—you?" he seethed, hardly able to speak through his anger.

"North. In a region called the Shattered Coast, in what remains of a little settlement known as Benton."

The home of the Awakki? Could this person be the one who ruined them?! he pondered as he held the thread so tight that his fingernails bore into his palm. "Just you wait, then. I'll be there to end you shortly."

"Lovely!" The thread vanished from Kyoku's hand along with the voice.

With Per'cei gone, Kyoku fell back off his knees, and sat for a moment. He cradled the marble in his trembling hands, feeling guilty to the point of nausea that he was not able to save Cathy from this fate. "Don't worry, Cathy. I'll find the one who did this to you and make him turn you back." He placed the marble in his pocket while wondering if she could hear him while trapped inside her own soul, or if she were instead stuck in a perpetual dream. He hoped, for her sake, that it was the latter.

*

Kyoku reappeared in the small settlement of Benton in the Shattered Coast. It was a ghost town, forsaken long ago after its people were driven out by a legion of undying wolves marked with the eyes of madness. He stayed on guard as he walked about the tired and broken huts on the off chance that some of those wolves were still lurking around these parts.

There were bloodstains both inside and out of many of the abandoned homes. Tattered remnants of clothes mauled by ruthless fangs littered the streets, though there were no other remains in sight. Kyoku was surprised not to find any bones or mangled corpses anywhere in Benton. "Could those wretched beasts have gulped down every last bit of them?" His words reminded him of the way their jaws unhinged and how their pulsing innards could be seen beyond their maw of razor-sharp teeth. It was an unsettling thing that he'd rather forget.

It didn't take much searching for Kyoku to have an idea where Per'cei might be. At the center of the settlement was an enormous crater. It gave off a vile aura that made him feel like bugs were crawling beneath his skin. He began to scale down the steep crater, his eyes scanning it in detail. The ground was soft, as though Benton had recently gotten a fair amount of rain.

Where are you? Kyoku wondered as he went further down. Was Per'cei hiding, biding his time to execute a sneak attack on him? His eyes spied something as he got closer to the deepest point of the crater. It was the body of a man, lying dead upon his back. The old man was covered in small, circular wounds, as though he had been stabbed all over by needles.

Kyoku felt his insides roil the moment he noticed one detail in particular about the fallen man: his ears, long and pointed like the tip of an arrow. "Old man Nomak ..." Kyoku said solemnly beneath his breath. "You came all this way back to Benton, to your home ... just to—" A rustling sound interrupted his thought, making him tense up. He scanned Nomak's body for the source of the sound, his ears wiggling all the while.

Kyoku followed the faint vibration in the air and saw something peculiar, sitting within the deepest point of the crater, just a few paces away from Nomak's corpse. It looked like a meteorite from afar but became much more the closer he got to it. The child-sized thing pulsed and throbbed, as though it were a slab of some abominable flesh. Grey and pallid it was, with bulging veins and pustules all over it.

Kyoku stopped in his tracks as it began to shift, like an egg about to hatch. And hatch it did, birthing a sleuth of tendril-like strands of pale blue thread, the very same kind that madness always left behind. These threads were far longer than those that sprung from afflicted humans. It continued to flow into the dirt, spilling all about the crater.

Kyoku began to pace backwards as he kept his sharp eyes on the dastardly thing spewing yarn in every direction. Soon, the fleshy meteor rose high into the air, held up by the ever flowing strands of thread that dug into the ground. The chaotic current of blue began to shift and mold, until it formed insect-like legs for the meteor to walk with. The abomination shifted downward, as though it were an eye gazing at Kyoku on the ground before it.

"How timely of you. And here I thought you would simply run away, as you did from Oglis and your duty to the Hall of Fate," a small, yet sinister voice called from within the meteor.

"Is this your true form—the true form of madness?" Kyoku asked in disgust, staring up at the abysmal thing.

"*Madness*. What you call madness, I call divine purpose! These worthless creatures serve no purpose. They are so ignorant of their creator that they are unable to praise his existence—to worship and cherish the life he has given them! I gave them purpose, and knowledge to take to their graves, so that they may someday be reborn as one of the Ten and serve him!" Per'cei preached.

"You're insane!"

Per'cei lifted one of his legs and stomped down hard towards Kyoku. The massive culmination of interwoven threads made it look like a gigantic spear. Kyoku dodged as it plunged into the ground where he had stood, sending dirt flying through the air. When he landed again on his feet, Kyoku slung fire, ice, and lightning at the suspended meteor. Per'cei warbled as it struck him, but the huge creature did not topple.

"You wretch!" Per'cei shrieked, sending forth another leg.

Kyoku would not be crushed so easily. He rolled out of the way and bolted back upright, though his balance was shaken by the uneven terrain. This time though, when the spool of thread struck the ground, tendrils of thin yarn separated from it and sprung at Kyoku. He tried to move, but lost balance for a split second and felt as though daggers had cut him all over. The string flew as straight as arrows, striking the dirt all around him after nicking him.

Kyoku's protective leotard shredded like paper against Per'cei's spines. He quickly warped to safety, reappearing on the other side of the crater. The warmth of his own blood was hot on his sides, arms, and legs, but the pain only fueled his rage. He sent a blast of red magic at Per'cei, the likes of which would destroy anything in its path—normally.

Per'cei reacted quickly and a curtain of thread fell over his meteoric body. The pale blue drape blocked the spell with ease, leaving behind not even a trace of it. "Your magic cannot best mine!" he cried triumphantly.

Yet he fears it making contact with his body. If that's the case, then— Kyoku thought as he sent himself flying into the air upon the trail of a conjured zephyr.

"It doesn't matter where you fire from! I will always block it!" Per'cei squealed as he sent another volley of spines upward towards Kyoku.

Kyoku watched the sharp strings zoom at him, waiting until just before impact, then—he vanished. The next moment, he reappeared in the air directly above Per'cei. A gust of wind pushed him downward as he summoned a blade of ice around his arm. Per'cei raised a barrier of thread around himself that broke Kyoku's fall. He thrust his blade down, maneuvering it through the wall of elongated threads. He could feel the tip of his blade scratch against the meteor on the other side.

"A sword like that cannot harm me!" Per'cei's voice rose as a wave of pointed strings did, ready to crash down upon Kyoku.

"When fighting a wizard," Kyoku began to say, the ice covering his arm beginning to glow red, "nothing is ever what it seems." Following his final word, an explosion triggered, and a crimson light erupted from the crater. The blast sent him flying. He landed on his feet, though not gracefully, stumbling to fall on one knee before picking himself back up again.

Kyoku focused his sharp, yellow eyes on the center of the explosion as the red light dimmed and faded entirely. He came to find that Per'cei's tumor of a body remained intact, though there was a chunk missing where his attack struck. Per'cei released a laugh, proclaiming his victory. The creature raised one of his monstrous legs, ready to squash Kyoku once and for all, but the movement made cracks spread from the missing chunk and cover his entire body.

Per'cei faltered and let out a sharp gasp just before his body crumbled and burst, sending granules of meteorite all over the crater below him. Beneath his protective shell was a heart of pale blue yarn, and without a body to stabilize it, the ball began to unravel wildly. It only took a second for the massive pillars of thread to come crashing down and for Per'cei's core to burst just as his body had, sending strands of string flying in every direction.

Kyoku watched on as Per'cei's downfall unfolded, while keeping enough caution about himself not to let his guard down in case he still had a desperate trick up his sleeve. His gaze darted between each of the miserable piles of seemingly harmless yarn, ready to strike if anything were to emerge from them. Nothing came—nothing other than a voice.

"Curse you! I underestimated you, but I won't let it happen again!" Per'cei's voice was small and frail, but Kyoku could not see where it was coming from.

"*Again?* You've lost. Now, give up and return Cathy to her former self and I'll spare you."

Per'cei laughed in the face of Kyoku's proposition. "You claim victory, yet you've never laid eyes on my true self. And so it shall remain! You've merely severed my connection to this planet, though my work here is already done! I have already dwindled the population to near nothing, while making sure to kill every newborn baby girl after they left the womb."

"So, you're the reason for the unexplainably low birthrate of women? And the genocide of the Awakki as well? For what purpose—to entrap the Eminent? Was all this suffering all for one man?"

"For the Eminent alone? No. I do what I do because it's *fun!* Why have pity for worthless creatures who contribute nothing to the fates?"

Kyoku was beginning to seethe again, his eyes still searching for Per'cei amongst the scraps of his fallen puppet. *If he's here, I can't allow him to escape! But if he's not, then where is he? Why would he lure me away from the city—unless!* Kyoku swayed his arm and sent a gust of wind across the bottom of the crater. All of the yarn was swept away, revealing nothing.

"That's right. I'm not here! But you've realized it too late! Until we meet again, *traitor!*" Per'cei said with a snicker that too was swept away by the wind.

Kyoku reached into his pocket and pulled the black marble out. He stared at it as darkness filled his heart and mind alike. "Cathy ... I—wanted to give you something before I left this world." From his other hand he conjured a magnificent cloth that was the color of the deep blue ocean. The long dress was woven from silk, the same as the scarf they found when they traversed the Shattered Coast together. He became dedicated to learning to recreate that material after seeing how it made her eyes light up that day. He had held off on giving it to her, though he didn't know why. And now it was too late.

Kyoku wrapped the marble in the blue dress, feeling utterly lost. Clouds as black as the ones that encroached upon his thoughts began to circle above and rain began to fall on Benton, though it could not touch him or Cathy, for the magic his body emitted scorched every droplet. When he turned around, he was standing on the northern wall of Last Thesi, looking back on what little remained of civilization.

The storm he left in the Shattered Coast was slowly shifting, making its way to Last Thesi. He separated the marble and the dress, allowing the latter to dissipate into a cloud of red ash as he placed Cathy back in his pocket.

His eyes focused on the terrible Runic Tower at the center of the city, wondering how he would explain Cathy's fate to Rekco, should they ever cross paths again.

Chapter 20: Do Parasites Pray?

The stairs seemed unending. Rekco wasn't sure if he had been climbing for minutes, hours, or days even. The Runic Guard did not put up much of a fight when it came to trying to stop him from going higher. If anything, it was the scent of decay and death that seeped from the walls trying to impede his progress. Nothing appeared itself in the higher reaches of the Central Tower; the bookshelves were decrepit and deteriorating, while the books upon them seemed nonexistent, maybe having wasted away and decomposed—even the stairs themselves were browning, feeling brittle beneath Rekco's hurried steps.

He had no idea that he was nearing the spire; he simply pushed on with indomitable determination. Eventually, after what seemed like an eternity, the winding staircase came to an end. What they led to was an open, circular room, where a large, magnificent blue and silver throne stood opposite of the stairs. A man sat there alone, high up, above all the world in a room with no windows and nothing adorning its walls. The man was Ximen Judd, the very man who gained Last Thesi's trust in a matter of minutes the day he revealed himself on live TV.

After his first public outing, Ximen Judd became the new, unofficial leader of the city. Many citizens looked up to him and his guard as a beacon of hope for humanity, but something was amiss—the madness had returned, lingering at the foot of his tower, leaving a host of dead bodies in its wake. Rekco needed to know the truth, even if it meant confronting the king of the world.

"I've been waiting for you, young man," Ximen Judd said in his hoarse, gravelly voice. He looked much unlike himself from his TV appearance. Instead of appearing as a rugged commander, he was draped with a gaudy blue robe that trailed from his throne all the way to the floor beneath it with a golden crown on his head. Was this what the man had become—a king?

"Waiting for me? Why? Did you know I would find the bodies splayed about the foot of your tower, stricken with madness? Just who are you, Ximen Judd, and what do you know about the madness?" Rekco spoke in a brash way, though his lungs were still adjusting to the high altitude and the rotten air. Despite having reached the top of the tower, the foul scent did not cease, in fact, it seemed to be worse there than below.

"I know many things," Ximen Judd began. "Some of which mean more to you than others. But where to begin? Yes, that's right, I remember now! I have something *for* you."

"What is it?" Rekco was on guard, ready to draw his blade at the first sign of unfamiliarity.

"A question," he said simply, then paused, as though waiting for Rekco to respond.

"Stop playing around!" Rekco responded with impatience. "The life of the land is at stake here! If the madness has returned, and it's *your* doing, I'll put an end to you where you sit!"

"H—How ..." Ximen Judd's face contorted terribly as he stammered, his voice warping to match it. "How do you plan to stop the apocalypse?" he finished, in a weak monotone while raising a shaky finger to point at Rekco below his high perch. He looked rather gaunt and brittle all of a sudden, having transformed from the hardened old veteran into a withered geriatric.

"W—What? What are you talking about—"

"HOW?" Ximen Judd repeated loudly, his voice echoing. "HOW HOW HOW HOW HOW HOW HOW?" His whole body trembled and quaked as he shouted. His voice made the walls around them shake until Rekco thought he was hearing voices from within the walls themselves. At that thought, thin panels along the walls were raised, revealing a mass of cages, each with a person trapped inside.

Rekco reeled, "What is this?!" He whipped around to look at Ximen Judd's captives, the same rotten scent wafted about the room, amplified tenfold. Rekco's eyes just about popped out of their sockets at the accursed sight. All the people behind bars at the top of the tower were like living corpses, their flesh soggy and black with mold and infection. Their eye sockets were caked with scabs and hardened pus that ran down to seal their noses and cover most of their mouths. Their rancid disfigurements made them indiscernible, yet they all spoke in unison, parroting Ximen Judd's ululating question.

"HOW HOW HOW HOW HOW HOW HOW HOW?" The words minced together, firing from every direction. The captives pounded their rancid fists on bars that held them within the walls of the tower, slinging the crust and sludge of decaying flesh with each violent movement. As they raged on, Rekco noticed a peculiar detail about them: they all had wispy white hairs growing out from their pores, out from the scabs and erosion. Rekco had seen such a phenomena before, multiple times, in fact; he recalled the dead bear in the forgotten woods and the corpse within the mines at the edge of the beach.

"Who are these people? What are you doing to them?!" Rekco turned back to Ximen Judd in a rage-filled stupor, only to witness the king of the tower collapse into a pile of dry bones that rolled down the steps leading to his throne. Terror filled Rekco's heart and mind alike, wondering what kind of nightmare had befallen him. The prisoners in the walls let out a horrid screech all at once, the force of their own cries enough to fracture the softened bones in their necks, causing them to fall limp within their cages.

"Those tormented souls are apt to ascend from their mortal shells, soon become members of the Runic Guard—or at least they *were*," a small, mousy voice said from somewhere in the room. The room fell silent as the dead prisoners, leaving Rekco with nothing but questions and a dreadful feeling in his gut.

Amidst the petrifying silence, Ximen Judd's throne began to rumble. It shifted and folded itself into the floor beneath it, revealing one last cage behind it. The bars lifted, and from it, a man emerged. Rekco nearly fell to his knees at the sight.

"*Father?*" Rekco called, hearing his own voice come from his mouth, sounding as though he were a young boy again. "W—what are you doing—" he stammered, unable to believe what he was seeing.

Rekston Curse, *the hero of the people*, looked as though he had stepped out of the old photos hanging in Rekco's childhood bedroom—virtually untouched by time. His dark green hair was longer than his son's, extending beyond the green stubble that lined his jaw. Though he appeared as old as he was when he left Rekco as a baby, his eyes did not reflect the age of his body; they were sunken and bleak, as though he had just witnessed the destruction of all things.

Rekston continued forward without a word and bent down to pick up the drape and crown Ximen Judd had worn. He threw the blue drape over his bare back and placed the crown atop his head then finally met eyes with Rekco. Seeing his son for the first time in almost two decades did not seem to affect him; his eyes remained cold and horror-struck. A voice began to speak, but the words were not coming from Rekston's mouth.

"I was expecting a grander reaction. Where are the tears, son of the Eminent?" a tiny voice asked. The voice seemed to come from everywhere at once. Rekco looked around at all the dead prisoners trying to find where it was coming from but saw no movement. "You won't be able to find me so easily with eyes alone. Have you no sense for magic?"

Rekco was coming back to his senses by the moment, no longer awestruck by the presence of his father, and his frustration was growing. *If that truly is my father, and not some kind of trick, then he's clearly under some sort of spell.* "Who are you and what have you done to my father? Show yourself!" he cried, drawing his glass blade from thin air.

"I prefer rage over tears anyway!" The small voice declared. Just then, Rekco saw something moving on top of Rekston's head. A strange, pale blue thing emerged from the inner circle of the crown he wore. It looked like a rectangular piece of cloth using tiny strands of string at its four corners as legs to move and climb up on top of the crown. There, Rekco was able to get a good look at the peculiar creature. It had two black dots for eyes that sat just above a slit between two of the edges where the cloth looked like it wasn't sewn tight. The loose slit moved like a mouth as the thing continued to speak. "My name is Per'cei. You look at me as though I am a monster, yet I am a perfect being—once but a microbe living in a pool of rainwater, but God's destiny had greater plans for me. He blessed me with a fragment of his soul, and I grew to this size and attained true clarity, the likes of which a fleshy mortal could never comprehend!"

The way Per'cei was speaking sounded all too familiar. It made Rekco's blood boil further. "God's destiny? And a fragment of his soul? Does that make you—"

"Yes. I, Per'cei, am one of the Ten! Just as the Eminent here before you!" He proudly stood on his hind legs, each of them gripping tightly to the crown beneath him.

"B—but why then—I thought you were all searching for my father, yet you've had him all along?! Rekco asked, gasping for air all the while as his heart seized in his chest from the anxiety.

"That is where you're wrong. We are not searching for your father—we are searching for the Eminent."

"B—but—he's—" Rekco stammered, pointing at Rekston while his mind came to a separate, grim realization.

"He's not. Not anymore," Per'cei confirmed what Rekco suddenly feared.

Rekco collapsed to his knees, his sword clattering from his hand and disappearing the moment it touched the ground. He was at a loss, feeling utterly defeated in his quest to find his father, the Eminent, and join forces with him to bring down Oglis. "Then *who?*"

Per'cei's little specks of eyes gleamed. "That is what I plan to find out!"

Rekco glanced up and took notice of a great tapestry spread over the ceiling in a spider web-like pattern. It sank like a pale blue hammock, one made of a very familiar looking kind of thread. The more he glanced at the tapestry devoid of detail, the more his mind began to piece Per'cei's evils together. He stood up, his eyes ablaze, and drew his sword once more, this time pointing it at the small creature atop his father's head. "It's you, isn't it? You're the true source of the madness!"

"My, how studious of you!" Per'cei laughed, reeling his upper body backwards and flailing like a centipede.

Rekco turned his sights downward to the bones scattered about the floor. "Then all the stuff Ximen Judd said to the people of Last Thesi about the Retallors and their poisoned Ather was a lie?"

"Not quite. What I said was true, minus the *source* of the Ather. You see, it was *my* Ather fueling your city all this time—my power, giving light to your buildings, nourishment to your babes, transportation for your burdens, and clothes for your backs, ready to be triggered at any given moment!"

"So, it was *you* then?" Rekco asked, trembling with pent up rage. "*You* killed the pregnant women in Retallor Tower ... *you* killed Kinnley and the rest of Dim's family ... *you* killed Gofun ... *and* Maven."

"Their fates were sealed when they became intertwined with *yours*," Per'cei responded sternly, his words stinging Rekco's heart.

"But why? What was the point of it all?" Rekco's voice broke, unable to accept the cruel creature's answer. "If you had my father all along, then why kill so many innocent people?"

"*Why,* you ask? At first, it was simply to ensure that your father had nowhere in the world to escape to. But, once he turned himself in, revealing that he was nothing more than a *man*, that is when I began to kill the people of this final bastion for humanity—to punish him for his treachery. I spent years trying to get him to reveal his true self to me and make him use his powers again, but it was no use. I thought maybe if he watched you die before his eyes then he would finally listen, but then came a spark of hope! You survived, not once, but twice! And finally, *you* used the very power he once possessed! Albeit, unrefined and immaturely, it made me reconsider my plan. That is when master Oglis decided to intervene—now here we are."

There were tears in Rekco's eyes, but not from sadness. Though he did feel bad for the torture his father went through, he knew now was his chance to free him and be the hero his father once was. "If you don't need him anymore, then you'll let my father go!" he said as he steadied his blade.

"You will have to help me determine that answer—yourself—for *that* is your trial!" As Per'cei spoke, a stream of blue thread forced itself into Rekston's hand, forming a blade. Rekston held it aloft, almost mirroring Rekco's posture, his eyes developing a foggy blue glow.

"No!" Rekco cried, being all too familiar with those eyes.

"Worry not, son of the Eminent. Greater beings, even those without their full power, do not die when I touch them. Now, let the true Eminent rise up and claim victory!"

On Per'cei's word, Rekston lunged forward and struck at Rekco. He wasn't impossibly fast, nor was much faster than a normal person was, really. Rekco blocked the attack with ease, but seeing his father's face in a madness induced rage stopped him from fighting back. Rekston continued his assault, not acknowledging the fact that he was outmatched, and paying no mind to the tears in Rekco's eyes.

"Father! Snap out of it!" Rekco cried, pushing Rekston back. He grabbed his father and tried to shake him but was met by a sharp pain as he was cut by his pale blue blade.

Rekston snarled as he broke free from Rekco's grip, swinging his blade wildly all the while. Rekco zoomed at him and swung hard, aiming for the thread blade in hopes to break it and end their cruel duel. The force from

Rekco's strike Rekston skid backwards, but his blade itself was unscathed. *There has to be a way to free him without hurting him!* Rekco thought quickly while he continued to block his father's attacks.

His eyes locked onto the crown on his head, noticing that Per'cei was no longer mounted on it. *That's it! Maybe Per'cei went back inside the crown. If I destroy it and separate them, he'll be free!* Rekco moved with a *boom!* appearing behind his father in a flash, swinging his sword horizontally across the golden crown. The glass sword cut through it as though it were water, sending shards of gold all over. Rekston slumped forward lifelessly the moment the crown was gone.

"Yes!" Rekco cried out. His joyous cry abruptly became a sharp gasp that took his breath away as a burning pain was felt in his gut. Rekco glanced down at the blood seeping on the blue blade that was stuck in him, following its edge to Rekston's hand holding it backwards in his slumped position. The old hero stood up and turned around, his eyes still glazed over by blue fog.

A tiny laugh echoed throughout the room. "You thought removing me would release him from my grip?" Per'cei appeared out from Rekco's peripherals, climbing across his shoulder. His feet felt like blades of grass and his body lighter than a cloud. He sprang up and latched onto the tapestry, blending into it, as it was the same color as his flesh. "While my connection to this world remains, I can enter any living being that carries my Ather at will!"

Rekco instinctively gave his father a swift kick, ejecting both him and the blade from his belly. The pain was just as bad on exit. Rekston gave him no assuage before he lunged forward to attack again. The slightest of movements made Rekco feel like he would pass out from the pain alone. He accelerated to both parry Rekston and begin to mend his wound. The damage was so severe, that one bout of acceleration was not enough to repair it, leaving a feeling of searing flame within his insides.

"Is he not enough of a challenge for you, boy?" Per'cei's voice asked from a hidden place high above. "How about I give him a little *boost?*" On his word, Rekston went on the attack again, but this time, the spectral blue hue in his eyes was amplified.

Rekco grimaced as he struggled to fend off Rekston's sword, as it seemed his father's strength was amplified tenfold. Rekston's veins bulged, throbbing with Ather, and he let out a ghastly, painful cry. That painful cry being the first time Rekco ever heard his father's voice was almost enough to break his mind, nearly sending him into a blind rage, explosive enough to destroy everything around him.

"Stop! You're hurting him!" Rekco pleaded, taking a split second to scour the web of tapestry above for the parasite, to no avail.

"No, it is *you* who is hurting him by delaying the inevitable! *You* must cut your father down if you wish to free him from his torment!" Per'cei's voice rang, coming from every direction—both close, yet so far at the same time.

It was a frustrating realization that seemed to hold true. Rekco was running out of options, seeing no way around Per'cei's cruel trial. His body was growing weary after countless clashes with Rekston, empowered by Per'cei's Ather. He knew that if he stalled for too much longer, he would be the one to die, leaving his powerless father with blood on his hands and the fate of the city on his shoulders.

Just as Rekco gulped down his hesitation, whilst choking back tears, ready to do what must be done, a faint rumble came from below that echoed until it cascaded up the entire tower, all the way to Per'cei's tapestry. The quake caused both Rekco and Rekston to lose their balance for a second, but Rekston did not return to posture. Instead, the hero fell onto his backside as the sword dropped out of his hand, his eyes returning to normal, looking full of both terror and relief.

"Father!" Rekco cried out, lurching forward with his hand extended.

Rekston looked up at him, and in that brief moment, Rekco saw his father's true eyes for the first time.

"No!" Per'cei screeched as he leapt from his web, the whole intricate tapestry crumbling and collapsing as he did. He landed on the back of Rekston's neck and dug his wispy legs into his skin. Rekston's eyes fogged over again, and he rolled backwards while picking up the thread blade. "My connection—it's been broken! Damn that wizard traitor, turning his back on the Ten! I knew Oglis should have locked him away!"

Rekco gave Per'cei a sideways glance. "*Wizard?* Don't tell me—does this *wizard* have teal hair and pointed ears?"

Rekston's eyes mirrored the parasite's sly expression as Per'cei piloted the hero. "Why yes, your fears are true. It is exactly as your mind is screaming at you. Your own friend has betrayed you, only to in turn betray the will of

God himself—a double-cross true to his traitorous nature!"

Rekco was speechless; seething while also on the verge of hyperventilating, his mind stricken with grief. He was mentally at his breaking point, teetering towards insanity. He knew that he could not afford to think too deeply on Kyoku's connection with Oglis and the Ten, not while his insides were still scarred and his father was not free. He took a deep, shaky breath, his lungs trembling just as much as his hands, and did his best to focus his mind on the obstacle at hand.

Rekston frowned at the lack of emotional eruption then readied his pale blue blade. Kicking off his back foot, the legendary hero propelled himself at Rekco with renewed strength, imbued again with Per'cei's Ather. The two traded blows in succession. With each swing, Rekston's strength seemed to grow; the fog over his eyes transformed to flames, shining like a pair of sapphires. He struck with an attack so fierce that it sent Rekco skidding back even after blocking it with his own magic blade.

Rekco's hands were tingling from the shockwave. He lowered his blade and saw with horror what his father was becoming. Blue threads were protruding through the veins in his neck, looking dreadfully painful and tiny white hairs were starting to sprout from his pores. Rekco was running out of time. If he didn't end this battle soon, his father might be lost for good.

"If you wish to give your father a proper burial, you better strike him down! Otherwise, he will ascend into one of my guards and be nothing more than a cloud of

Ather," Per'cei jeered, his voice playing out of Rekston's mouth.

Rekco zoomed back into the fray at full force, leaving Rekston no choice but to defend. While he rained blows against his father's defenses, he stared at the deplorable creature holding tight to his neck. *How can I remove him without the risk of also severely hurting my father?* He searched for a solution, for some kind of opening, but none presented itself. He was scared that if he removed Per'cei with his bare hands, that the creature would take control of him instead.

Rekco's mind was made up at that moment. He swung his sword hard and Rekston reeled back as his guard was broken.

"Yes! Do it now!" Per'cei cried with joy.

Rekco rushed forward, aiming the tip of his blade at Rekston's chest. At the moment his blade would meet flesh, Rekco accelerated to the maximum speed he could muster. He reappeared behind his father in a flash and thrust at Rekston's neck instead. He finessed the tip of the blade, scooping it underneath the middle of Per'cei's body and flung him into the air as if he were flipping a pancake.

The tiny being spun in midair for less than a second before being pierced by Rekco's sword and driven into the wall like a piece of parchment paper faster than the time it took for Rekston to fall to the floor. Per'cei let out an ear-piercing cry as Rekco pinned him to the wall.

"I'm taking my father from this tower, *alive*—no matter what!" Rekco said, holding his blade tight.

"Don't think you've won!" Per'cei's eyes glinted as he tore himself free, leaving a nasty gash in his paper-like body that no blood spilled from. He jumped up into the tattered remains of the tapestry above that looked like a mess of tangled vines.

Rekco's eyes could not follow Per'cei's slippery movements. The creature was lost to him in a matter of seconds. Instead, he turned his sights onto his father laying at the center of the room, unmoving. He rushed to his side and knelt down. *Good! He's still breathing!* He looked around fearfully, expecting that Per'cei was still slinking around, waiting for the opportunity to possess Rekston again.

Rekco glanced up at the tapestry again. It was far too high for him to reach, and though he imagined he could power his legs to jump high enough, he couldn't risk leaving his father unattended. He thought back on the magnificent attack he used against Ramirez and Loch. He'd only ever conjured it by accident thus far, but he was desperate enough to try.

He reared his blade back the way he remembered he had done, while focusing the magic within him; from his shoulders, to his bent elbow, and all the way down to his fingertips. Nothing came. There was no torrent of energy surrounding him and his sword wasn't glowing any brighter than it already was. He stared at the faint blue glimmer within the glass sword, how the magic swayed and turned as though it were alive. Just then, he was reminded of the voice of Kyoku's father when he first explained the mysterious weapon.

"... while bound to its user, will resonate with the magic in them and channel it into its edge," Rekco repeated to himself under his breath. It was something that never crossed his mind before. The glass sword was no regular sword. It was bound to him—an extension of him, no different than his limbs.

He focused again. This time when he sent power to his arm, he did not stop it at his fingertips, instead, sending it beyond, into the glass sword in his hand. His eyes grew wide when the blue light beneath the blade's surface flared. It burned bright as flame. A vortex of magic, blue as Ather, surrounded him, and for the first time, he did not fear it.

Rekco stared up at the web of tattered thread spread across the ceiling with blazon eyes. He aimed the tip of his sword upward and said aloud, "Are you sweating up there, Per'cei? *Can* you even sweat? Either way, I won't miss!"

Rekco did not know exactly the extent of the power he was wielding, but he let it fly anyway. He thrust his blade towards the heavens, unleashing the vortex that surrounded him. The pillar of light he fired tore through the tapestry and the top of the tower alike. It blasted into the sky like a spotlight, destroying everything in its wake. The force of the attack was felt throughout the entire Runic Tower; when the tremendous tower shuttered, it shook all the foundations beneath it and sent a shockwave that spread under the surface of the whole city.

When the blue beam dissipated, Rekco saw the purple dusk above—and nothing else. The top of the tower was gone in an instant, and Per'cei was nowhere to be seen.

Despite his magnificent feat, Rekco did not yet feel triumphant, not until he knew the conniving creature was dispatched. He scanned over the sky above, straining his eyes in search of the tiniest of movements. *There!* An alarm blared in his mind when he spotted the piece of cloth flitting about in the clear sky above.

Rekco took a deep breath and reared the glass sword back once more. "Nowhere to run. It's time to finish this and free Last Thesi from your poisonous grip!" He focused again, letting the glass sword drink the power within him. The moment the vortex came forth, Rekco fired it upward without hesitation. The beam enveloped Per'cei and ripped apart the clouds beyond him.

When it was done, a single thread fell gently like a leaf from a tree in autumn, back to the open tower.

Another shockwave cascaded down the tower and shook the earth far below its spire. It rang like an echo of Rekco's victory. He caught the pale blue thread between his fingertips and gave it a twirl before blowing it away with his lips. The sigh of relief that escaped him was a short respite, and though it was much needed, now wasn't the time to relax. He stooped down to his father's side as he lay unconscious.

Rekco patted away the white hairs that gathered atop his skin like moss. "It's time to get you out of here—" he began to say but was cut off by a roaring sound coming from below. The sound was accompanied by what felt like an earthquake. The whole tower shook, and dread filled Rekco's heart. "Don't tell me—"

There was an enormous *crack!* Just then, the whole world seemed to tilt, and Rekco knew that his fears were coming to life. The shockwaves that circulated through the tower before must have caused an instability somewhere and the base was beginning to give way. The crack that rang throughout the top of the spire was the sound of the tower bending like the knee of a giant, ready to tumble down onto the city below.

Rekco grabbed hold of his father in a panic as the two of them slid across the tile floor as the tower went sideways. He planted his feet against the wall with Rekston unconscious in his arms. From there he could see out the newly created skylight and watch as the tower plummeted through the clouds. Only a moment later did the tall buildings of the High District come into view, racing closer and closer by the second.

All the voices inside Rekco were screaming for him to jump. There was no time to think on it. He severed ties with his fears and leapt from the falling upper half of the Runic Tower. His powers activated on instinct, amplifying his perception of time to the point that the falling debris halted in midair. Without any thought or questioning, he reached his foot out to kick off a hunk of red clay suspended in the air.

Rekco used it to catapult himself to the next nearest piece of debris, not stopping to imagine what might happen should his foot miss or his resolve falter and his powers betray him. He gracefully propelled himself down the falling wreckage as though it were a stairway with gigantic gaps between each step. The city below looked as bleak and dark as ever, still some minutes before the automated night lights turned on throughout the High District—would they even get the chance to? He was still so high up that any people in the streets looked no different than ants. He prayed that they would get out of the way in time, but he knew they wouldn't, for only he was untouched by time at that moment.

He could not allow his mind to wonder what kind of lives would be cut short because of him—what kind of families would be broken because of him—what kind of hopes and dreams would be ruined because of him. Instead, he simply quickened his pace and steadied his steps for his and his father's sake. The tops of the buildings were getting closer, though none were close enough for him to jump to safely. The scattered stones, broken tiles, and books were growing scarcer by the moment and Rekco's heart sank at the realization that he was traveling faster than the tower was falling. Soon, he would run out of frozen objects to step on. Soon, he would reach the end of the line and fall into a tunnel of blackness.

*

Rekco opened his eyes to the sound of gravel scraping against pavement. He looked up from where he laid on the ground and saw what appeared like a mirror of himself facing away. The green haired man was gazing up at the darkened sky where all the stars were starting to come out, to be scared witless by the horrific aftermath of the scene they just missed. Rekco was bleary-eyed and fatigued, yet his mind was alert and full of worry.

He pushed through the pain he felt throughout his body and shot upright, sending bits of red clay covered in dust flying. "F—Father, is that really you?"

The green haired man turned around, the gaudy blue robe Per'cei had draped him in was gone. Rekston's expression was pained, one of guilt and sadness. He approached without a word and extended his grime-covered arm to his son. Rekco took it and felt himself be lifted to his feet. Rekston did not look him in the face, unable to take his eyes off the wreckage around them. "Thesi ... is ..." he muttered in disbelief.

It was then that Rekco took notice of his surroundings. All around them were collapsed and ruined buildings, having been smashed by the fallen Runic Tower. It looked like what Rekco imagined the end of the world would be. The air was filled with dust from the crash and the street they stood on was indiscernible. He scraped the side of his foot against the ground to reveal a painted line on the street beneath a layer of dirt. This was certainly the High District—or what remained of it, at least.

Rekco looked at his father, unable to feel any sense of victory or relief. He had finally found the man he sought after his entire life, but at what cost? Would the city actually be able to rejoice and rebuild now that their long forgotten hero had returned, and was that hero even the same man as he once was?

"I—I didn't mean—for this—" Rekco stammered, weighed down by the guilt for what he'd done in a greedy attempt to put his own desires before the wellbeing of the city. "I just—wanted—I just wanted to bring you back." Tears fell from his eyes—tears for all those who died for his selfishness.

"I'm—" Rekston began to say, looking down at his hand clutching his side covered in blood, "sorry." He collapsed onto a pile of rubble, where Rekco rushed to his side, beginning to feel feverish.

Rekco stared at the grievous wound on his father's side that was staining his skin red. "No! Wait—can't you—just?!" He babbled, unable to express his panicked thoughts properly. What he meant to ask was why wasn't he healing—why weren't his powers healing him? But Rekco already knew why. He sobbed at his father's side. "You can't die! I've been trying to find you my whole life. I have so much I want to ask you—so much I want to tell you! I need you! You—can't just die now!"

"I—I've—always—been with you," Rekston said, his voice weak and shaky. He pointed at Rekco's heart. "In there. I left some of my magic behind—to protect you and guide you—but—I didn't know—it would grow. I tried—to keep you—away from the tower. I always sent signals—for you to—turn back—but you—you got too strong. I wanted to keep you—safe—and separate from my—burden. I endured that monster's torture—for years—hoping I could buy you enough time—to lead a normal life. I failed you in that regard."

Rekco took his father's hand and placed it back down gently on his bloody abdomen. "*You?* You were the one making me feel that way whenever I looked at the Runic Tower? I thought it was the Runic Guard trying to keep me from saving you." He hung his head down shamefully, feeling like all of his life had been for nothing. Out from the dark reaches of his mind came one last spark of hope. He lit up at the thought. "Wait! Ramirez and Loch *both* told me that the Ten never truly die, not until their duty is fulfilled—whatever that means. But still! You're one of them! You're the Eminent! It means that you won't die! You'll just fall asleep for a while, right? Then you'll wake up and we can finally talk—about *everything*—"

Rekston raised his hand to stop Rekco. "I'm not the Eminent—not anymore. *You* are—now." Rekco's heart dropped at those words, just as Rekston's eyes began to close. "I—wish—I could—leave you—without—regret." His breath faded along with his last word. *Regret.* It was all Rekco felt as he sobbed by his father's lifeless body. His mind was in shambles, unable to process that it was now he who was bound to the Eminent's fate.

Thunder cracked in the distance and a flash of lightning painted the sky. Dark clouds were closing in, and with it came a dreadful feeling. It was magic. The likes of which he experienced when he was a boy—the kind of chaotic magic driven by emotions gone mad. It was Kyoku. He was near.

Chapter 21: Memories Of A Dream

Rekco found himself walking aimlessly through the ruins of the High District, his mind distraught with grief and rage, opposing one another as equals. He could sense the wizard was nearby, though he didn't know how. It was nothing like the rest of the senses his body expressed—this sense seemed to come from deep within his being, deeper than his heart, in a place that he did not understand. Was that thing he felt radiating within him his soul?

He did not bury his father and did not know if he would ever get the chance to. At that moment, his life felt forfeit—doomed to be bound to things he did not yet understand; Oglis, the Ten, and their righteous duty to defend the universe from some cosmic threat were so far from his mind that they seemed a dream—yet, he couldn't escape it.

Rekco was intent on confronting Kyoku about his connection to it all, and if need be, draw his sword against him. For his own sake, he could not see the wizard as a distant rival or even a friend. Instead, he assumed Kyoku an enemy—a barrier on his way to defeating Oglis and changing his fate.

There was no doubt in his mind that he was getting nearer to where Kyoku was. A heavy rain began to fall, and the wind blew something fierce. Rekco shielded his eyes from the constant debris that berated him while he searched for the center of the storm. Along the way, he found no survivors within the wreckage of fallen skyscrapers and ruined streets. It was a stark reminder of the consequences of his actions. The only way he felt he could repent at this point was to rid the city of godlike beings—himself included.

To his surprise, Rekco's muscles did not ache, nor did his wounds burn. He did not feel depleted even after firing off his ultimate attack twice in succession. It seemed a mystery at first, but then he came to a shocking revelation as he saw something peculiar—or rather, felt it. The crumbled remains of the High District exuded Ather; every fallen building and broken streetlight gave off the faintest taste of it, and his body drank every last bit of it as though it were air. Though the Ather seeping from wreckage revitalized his body, it could do nothing to soothe his troubled mind or broken heart.

Eventually, after wandering through the waking nightmare that was the High District, Rekco came to a place where the rain did not touch. It was a wide street cluttered with chunks of concrete, bent metal railings, and rubble—the innards of the adjacent buildings. A vortex of clouds swirled overhead, just as they did on that fateful night over five years ago when Rekco stood as a thirteen-year-old boy, on shaky legs, outside of a dark cabin in the plains.

This time he did not face the storm alone. A figure sat atop a pile of debris built up like a throne in the middle of the street. He was folded at the waist, head hanging low, with a wall of teal hair obstructing his face. He held something in his pale hand—some kind of ball that was blacker than the clouds in the sky. The wizard did not pay any mind to Rekco as he approached, seeming far too distracted by the object he held.

"What are you doing here?" Rekco asked. It wasn't until he spoke did Kyoku raise his sullen gaze. His yellow eyes were bloodshot and puffy, the petulant expression he often showed gone from his face, instead replaced by the look of a tormented soul.

"Waiting for you," the words fell from Kyoku's mouth along with a dejected breath. "You arrived sooner than I expected. Have you finally developed a sense for magic?"

Rekco nodded. "Seems that way." His eyes were as red and puffy as the wizard's, but he did his best to beat his emotions back. It seemed that Kyoku could sense his grief.

"You've really lived up to the name 'Curse', haven't you? You destroyed a quarter of the city—and for what? You're still alone, so I take it you didn't find the Eminent?" Though the wizard's words stung like hot daggers, his tone was not full of contempt like it usually was.

Rekco gulped down his desire to shout and scream. "I did—find him, that is. He's dead now."

Kyoku's eyes grew wide then became skewed and saddened. "That is unfortunate. Now you'll be bound to his fate in his place, I imagine."

The mentioning of *fate* brought a dark memory to mind, one Rekco had been trying to repress. Remembering Per'cei describe Kyoku as a traitor sparked a fiery rage in his gut that he could scarcely hold back. When he spoke, his voice was shaky and restrained. "That creature—Per'cei—he said that you've been working for Oglis—all this time. Is that true?"

Kyoku did not look away in the face of Rekco's question. He stared at him for a moment before responding, as if he were processing his answer carefully. "It *is* true. She picked me up that day you scaled Retallor Tower, and I've been in leagues with her ever since."

Rekco hung his head low, his clenched fists trembling at his sides. "But—you also betrayed them, right?" He was searching desperately for a reason behind it all, for some redeeming factor in Kyoku's actions, a reason not to draw his blade upon him.

"I did. I did what I had to in order to gain their trust and went against them the moment I found out what Per'cei had been doing to the people here."

Rekco lifted his head and his eyes lit up, feeling like a weight had been lifted off his shoulders. "Right! Of course! You were never on their side! It was all an act! C'mon then! Let's go fight Oglis—together! Let's put an end to all this!"

Kyoku stood up atop the pile of rubble and drew a yellow-rimmed card from the breast pocket of his black and teal vest. "You lack—*intelligence*," he said, his voice full of scorn and sadness. He tossed the card into the air. From it came a single bolt of lightning that struck the ground before Rekco's feet.

"Hey! What's your problem?" Rekco took a step back from the sizzling hole in the street at his feet, not taking his eyes off Kyoku.

"I won't join you. There's no sense in fighting Oglis. We can't beat her. She'll kill us both and take us back to the Hall of Fate. There she'll stick us both in that nightmare and torture us and break our wills until we're *ripe* enough to fit her needs."

Rekco scoffed. "What are you planning then?"

Kyoku pointed at him with the hand that held the black orb. "I'll strike you down here and take you back to her myself. I'll play off my betrayal of Per'cei as a double cross—as part of my plan to subdue you. With that, I'll beg her to return Cathy to her proper form, and hopefully she'll heed my wish."

Rekco looked at the wizard sideways. "Have you gone insane—wait, *Cathy?* What's happened to her?" Fright seized his chest at the thought that Cathy was in danger—or worse.

"Have a look for yourself," Kyoku said, turning his hand upright and holding the abyssal orb aloft. "Per'cei meant to take her back to the Hall as collateral—for you. I tried to stop him, but instead, she ended up like this: a soul without a body."

Rekco felt dizzy. Kyoku's words seemed to echo within his ears as he stared at the object Cathy had been reduced to. *It couldn't be ... my fault?* His mind quaked with guilt and rage. Now, more than anything, Rekco had a goal, a reason to fight—even if it meant fighting Kyoku. "There—there has to be another way! We can confront Oglis together and force her to turn Cathy back!"

Kyoku shook his head. "I already told you. We can't beat her. My most powerful magics are worthless against her regenerative powers, just as your sword will be. The only way is to cooperate with her plan. If you come peacefully, I'll give you a painless death and you'll awake in the Hall of Fate. I'll make sure Oglis turns Cathy back in your stead."

Rekco frowned. "I won't concede! I won't let them win! Not after all they did to the city and the people here; to me and my father, to my friends, to Cathy, even to you and *Gofuhn*."

Kyoku's sullen expression turned to one of disgust at the mention of his late master's name. He too, seemed to restrain himself as he spoke. "You do not yet know the worth of a world—but you will, in time. Then you'll forget about everything we left behind. This place will be reduced to nothing more than dust once we're gone. The best we can do is bring Cathy with us. You should be happy and accept that."

"NO!" Rekco cried, swiping his arm and conjuring the glass sword in his hand. "I won't compromise! I'll save Cathy *and* Last Thesi! If you don't want to be a part of that, then you're just an obstacle in my way!"

Kyoku smirked. "You know if you cut me down, I'll simply be sent back to Oglis. She'll mold me and send me back here until you lose. You'll never escape her. You'll never escape your fate."

"I don't care. I'll defend this place until my final breath!"

"So be it," Kyoku said as he drew the entire deck of cards from his vest. He hurled it into the air. They fluttered about over Rekco and then all lit up at once.

Bolts of lightning rained down from the flurry of cards. Rekco's heightened senses allowed him to dodge and maneuver around the barrage, though not easily. He swept away the streams of electricity that he could not dodge and sent them back up into the sky above. The spells continued to fire in random intervals, leaving Rekco little time to think.

He darted this way and that, sweat forming on his brow and back from the exertion, until—he saw an opening, a clear path to Kyoku. *There!* he thought as he sent all the power he could muster into his legs. He kicked off the ground and shot through the endless volley of lightning, feeling a fiery pain in his side as one grazed his flesh. The pain didn't dampen his resolve. Rekco escaped from the electric prison with his sword at the ready. He swung it hard as he approached the wizard but was met with resistance.

Kyoku moved far faster than Rekco thought was possible, raising his arm to defend himself. It wasn't until they clashed did Rekco realize Kyoku's arm wasn't an arm at all; it had become encased in magical ice, creating a blade like he used in The Underground tournament. Sparks of an electrical current danced atop Kyoku's arm, from his hand all the way up his shoulder. The blade exuded such an intense cold that it caused the air around it to grow thin, making it difficult for Rekco to breathe when he was near it.

"I know your tricks," Kyoku sneered. Rekco wanted to cut the condescending look off the wizard's face and show him that he wasn't the same anxious boy as when they met. He broke from the clash of blades and swung horizontally at Kyoku's mid-section. His blade caught nothing but air—literally! Kyoku's body dissipated into a cloud of vapor that surrounded Rekco. The veil was so thick that he couldn't see through it. "But you don't know mine!" Kyoku said with a snicker, his voice amplified by a spell that masked his position outside the veil.

The cloud of grey smoke turned white and grew frigid. Rekco could feel his joints ache from the simplest of movements. Against his instincts, he spun around in a circle using his blade in an attempt to clear the cloud. It hurt like nothing else to move in the harsh cold, and to make matters worse, the veil did not disperse. Instead, Rekco had created a circle within it, which only gave him a mild amount of relief from the freezing temperature.

Then, without warning, came another array of lightning bolts from beyond the cold entrapment. They homed in on him from all sides at timings that were ever so slightly different. Rekco dodged as best as he could, feeling pain with each move his body made.

"Hurts to move, doesn't it? It looks like my guess was correct, after all; your power doesn't boost your metabolism or body temperature, but only your perception. Let's see you dodge this!"

Rekco turned towards Kyoku's voice and saw a flash of light. He raised his sword to deflect the attack, but no such thing came. As he stared with eyes focused on the light ahead, he felt a tremendous, burning pain at his back. The electric shock coursed throughout his body, sending him to his knees.

"You're as naive as ever!" Kyoku taunted from somewhere outside of the cloud. "How you've managed to best the other members of the Ten so far is beyond me!"

Rekco thought back on his encounters with the Ten and felt like there was some truth to be found in Kyoku's jeers. He glanced up at the sky, where a single star could be seen at the center of the vortex. It was that same star that always seemed to elude the clouds, which came out before nightfall, and was always there when he looked up at night. It seemed to lock eyes with him, as if peering into his soul. It gave off the same intimidating, vile presence that the blue creature did the first time he met her in a dream. At that moment, Rekco realized something that nearly broke his mind.

"Oglis," he muttered aloud, still staring up at the sky in disbelief.

"What are you on about?" Kyoku asked. "What about her?"

"She's—here. She's always been here. Watching us—watching our every move—ever since we were both boys."

"Nonsense. She was looking for your father until *you* showed potential to take his place."

Rekco shook his head. He pointed up at the heavenly star in the sky. "Look—there!" It shifted in a way he had never seen before. It looked just like Oglis' beady yellow eye shrouded behind a layer of blue aura. The center of it moved, steering towards Rekco then to Kyoku, before winking and disappearing from the sky.

Just then, Kyoku began to fume, raging and huffing in frustration. The frozen veil around Rekco vanished and the numbness in his joints began to fade along with it. Rekco saw the wizard, keeled over clutching his head.

"It's not—possible! Has my whole life really been—*preordained?* Has Oglis been watching and controlling my every move since I was a child? Have my struggles thus far been—meaningless? But—why? Why?!" He bent upright and raised his arms to the sky, looking crazed, his yellow eyes gleaming eerily. "I won't allow her to control me anymore! I'll show her! I am the one in control! I'll ruin her plans—even if it means destroying myself!" Kyoku cackled madly.

Rekco watched with caution, unsure what he could say or do to calm the unhinged wizard. He lowered his sword and stepped forward, but the moment he moved, he felt as though his limbs were made of stone. He grew faint and weary all of a sudden, unable to do anything but stand and stare. His sense for magic erupted, filling his gut with a roiling sensation, as though the chaotic storm above had entered him.

Kyoku's skin began to shimmer with a white light. It became brighter by the second, until all of his body was engulfed by it. The light slowly expanded and began to overtake everything around him. Rekco's heart sank as it stretched towards him. He tried to move but his body wouldn't listen. He closed his eyes and saw that even the blackness behind his eyes was glowing bright. The light sucked him in, consciousness and all.

*

It was a bright, sunny day in the High District. Rekco walked down the street amidst a crowd of murmuring people dressed in business attire. None of them looked at him, despite him sticking out like a sore thumb—a carrot within a sea of khaki and black clothes. He tried to remember where he was going, but his mind was foggy.

Instead, Rekco continued on, in hopes that he would remember. He stopped at a crowded intersection where a red light told pedestrians to wait before crossing. A pure white bird soared through the cloudless sky above. It swooped down so low that Rekco could see its beady black eyes. He loved seeing birds, but for some reason, he couldn't remember what that one was called.

Once the bird was out of sight, Rekco turned his eye back to the red stop light. At last, it turned green, and as it did, all the world around it flickered, transforming into an empty, ruined city where the sky was dark and dreary. It was a terrifying vision that was gone in a flash. Rekco looked up, feeling a strange haze in his head, and saw that the light was still green.

He walked across the street behind the crowd. None of them seemed to see what he did, so it must have just been a figment of his imagination—he wasn't feeling himself, after all. He placed his hand against the building on the other side of the street; the concrete was warm from the daylight bearing down on it. He longed for something, yet he couldn't place what that something was.

Rekco looked around at all the foot traffic. Everyone had somewhere to be, it seemed, and in a hurry, too. That wasn't unusual in the High District. All those workers kept the city alive. *Alive?* he thought as he turned his nose up to the clear afternoon sky. Something felt not quite right about it. Thinking about that made him shudder, so he stopped thinking and continued down the street.

Some ways from the intersection, a host of business people were all funneling around a right-hand corner. Rekco was drawn there as they were. He met up with the crowd, packed to the gills on the sidewalk, but despite that, none of them pushed or shoved—they all were content to wait their turn. Rekco waited too. He wanted to see where they were all going, almost desperately so.

Once he got close enough to the corner, he squeezed tight against the building and pushed his way through. As he rounded the corner, his heart sank. All the crowd had gone, and all that he saw before him was a desolate street that the sun had forsaken, and the birds had fled from. It went on farther than his eyes could see, and for some reason his eyes *needed* to see more.

Rekco walked alone down that dreary street, a cold wind blowing at his back. The air became thick, and he began to feel feverish. This was a place he was not meant to see. He turned around with the thought of going back but the street seemed to stretch on infinitely behind him just as it did in front of him. His mind was too full of haze to think, so he continued not to.

The world would flicker at times while he was pacing his way down the street and the bright, cheery world he came from would bleed through. He missed the warmth of it, though he couldn't remember what it felt like anymore. Not after long, the birds were gone from his memory too. All that was left was the lonely, dark street that knew no end—and though it knew no end, something appeared in the distance: a man.

Rekco burst into a full speed run once he saw the man, his salvation. As he got closer, he found the man was no man at all, or at least, he was no kind of man Rekco had ever seen before. His body was made up of white smoke. A black orb sat where his heart would be, emanating the smoke that comprised his form. The details of his face became clearer with each moment as the veins of wispy smoke funneled into his being. He looked shockingly familiar at first, until Rekco recognized him and gasped.

"Father!" Rekco cried, extending both arms out, still running towards him.

"No, Rekco! Stop where you stand!" The ghastly specter of Rekston hollered, his voice echoed in an inhuman sort of way.

Rekco heeded the man's word, stopping on the spot, though his heart ached for his father. They stood at arm's length from one another, Rekston unmoving. Rekco looked his father up and down in surprise. Memories poured into his mind as though he were remembering a dream. "W—what are you doing here? I thought you—*died*." He could hardly believe his own words. His brain was feeding him information that all seemed new and foreign.

"I did die. It seems some powerful force has drawn me back to this world before my soul was able to depart."

"Some ... *force?*" Rekco was perplexed. His father's words were gibberish to his befuddled mind. "I don't understand what you're saying. I ... I've been—trying to find you? Is that what I was doing in the High District?"

Wrinkles of concern formed in the smoke that made Rekston's brow. "Rekco, this powerful spell must be scrambling your brain. You need to try to focus. I'm afraid something terrible will happen to this place if you don't."

Rekco racked his brain. *Powerful spell. Wasn't I just—fighting?* Suddenly, he remembered the freezing cold of Kyoku's conjured blade, the burning pain from his electricity, and—the white light that engulfed everything. Rekco turned away from his father and saw the great white nova in the distance, slowly creeping closer to them, while all the buildings along the way were lost within it. "I remember now!" He cried, turning back to face Rekston, though now the image of his dead father was even more chilling.

"Good! Do you know what caused this?"

"Yes, I do. The wizard, *Koku*. He is often rude and cold, but he seems to really want to help people deep down. I once considered him a friend of mine. But now I'm unsure. It seems as though he's going mad."

"A friend? You should go to him then. Even if he is no longer the person you once knew, it is your duty as his friend to save him—from himself, if need be."

"Save ... him? B—but—I—I couldn't even save you." Tears began to roll down Rekco's cheeks, overwhelmed by the guilt flooding back into his mind. "I did everything I could. I went up against the Retallors, the Runic Guard, and the Ten. I ... destroyed the city trying to save you. What good could I do now?"

Rekston shook his head, leaving behind trails of smoke with each movement. "You can't save *everyone*, son. That's not what being a hero is about. But it takes a special kind of soul to *try* to. You've done your best thus far, despite the mess I left you with, and you're still growing. I never meant for things to end up like this for you. I wanted to shield you from my legacy, not pass it on to you."

His father's words warmed Rekco to his core. He sought his father's praise all his life, though he never imagined it would come from him in the afterlife. It was bittersweet. He gave a stiff nod and wiped his eyes. "I'll do my best! But even if I stop the spell from sucking up the city, what about Oglis? Koku said she is unbeatable."

Rekston's mouth curved into a frown. "That is what Irol Retallor once told me when I suggested that we take her on together. He knew more than I about the matter, since I had not encountered her before like he had."

"Wait, really? Is that what you two talked about when you had that famous duel outside Retallor Tower?"

"That's correct. He told me that Oglis had approached him, asking that he and I join her side to defeat some *cosmic threat*. When he refused, she said she would return to change his mind by force."

"Why didn't she just strike him down right then and there?" Rekco asked.

"My guess is that she didn't know how at the time. Just like me."

"So, you *did* lose the duel then?"

"Unfortunately, yes. Though it was a friendly contest, and an excuse for us to meet and speak, I still gave it my all."

"Irol must have had some crazy kind of power if he was able to beat *you!*" Rekco fawned at the thought, trying not to get lost in his imaginings.

Rekston looked as sullen as his spectral shape allowed. "His ... power changed *everything*. He told me to go into hiding, saying that he would deal with Oglis, and *free* me from my fate. Shortly after the news of his death reached the plains, your mother was killed—by a group of men with eyes shrouded in blue flames."

"Per'cei!" Rekco cursed, clutching his fist at the thought. "That's when you gave yourself up to him? But why didn't it work?"

"Because ... by then, I was no longer the Eminent."

"I don't understand. You gave me some of your power to protect me, but then ended up losing it all? How?"

"Irol Retallor. His power ... is the ability to change someone's *destiny*."

Rekco gasped. "Really?! So that's—"

"Exactly. That must have been what he meant when he said he would free me from my fate. After that, I would unknowingly transfer my powers to you before I left you in Maven's care."

"Maven ..." Rekco said in a sad tone. "Was what happened to him—"

"Part of my punishment, yes. Per'cei made me watch as he turned Maven against you. When I saw you move, that was when I knew you had taken my power. I kept that a secret from that horrible creature, no matter what he did to me."

"I'm sorry you had to endure all that ... But—what about Irol Retallor? If *you* couldn't beat him, how did Oglis do it?"

Rekston glanced up in thought. "To be honest, I have no idea. He could change his and his opponent's fates to the point that no weapon could touch him. Despite that, I knew Irol was still growing into his abilities, so maybe he had not yet mastered it, allowing Oglis to find a way around it."

Rekco pondered on that thought for a moment before speaking. "If that's true, and she was able to find a way to defeat someone with a power like that, then there *has* to be a way to do the same to her!"

"I think so, too," Rekston said with a nod. "Maybe if you and your friend put your minds to it, you can figure it out. I believe in you." Rekco began to tear up again. He reached out to his father. "No!" Rekston cried. "You must not cross this threshold. We are on the edge of the mortal realm. If you come any closer, you'll surely die."

Rekco let his hand fall limp. He would have given anything to hug his father one final time, but it seemed that the fates would not allow it. He turned his head back and saw that the light from Kyoku's spell was still spreading. There was so much more he wanted to talk to his father about, but he knew they were out of time. "Thanks, father. I have to go now, don't I?"

"Unfortunately, yes." Rekston hung his head low and spoke in a somber voice. "One last thing, son."

"What is it?"

"I must know how you feel—about all this. I would not blame you if you resent me for the life I have thrown you into."

"I—" Rekco opened his mouth, taken aback. He had never considered the guilt his father must have been feeling all these years, knowing what his son was being set up for. "I don't resent you—at all. I wish things could have turned out different for both of us, but still, I'm happy that I finally got to meet you and talk to you. I'll miss you, and I'll always love you—no matter what—you'll always be my father."

Rekston's face contorted with a mix of emotions. He looked like he would cry, though his form wouldn't allow it. "I'm relieved to hear you say those things. I'll be able to leave this world in peace now. I'll always love you too, son. Now go, save your world!" Rekston crossed his arm and clapped his hand across his elbow in salute.

Rekco gave a teary-eyed thumbs up before turning back to face the ever-encroaching light. He sprinted down the street towards it, and all the while the world around him flickered between the vibrant Thesi of old and the dark reality of today. At times, the twisted clouds would turn into a pack of birds soaring in the sky, and the broken remains of buildings became full of people, the confused souls of those recently past, unable to make their final departure from this world while Kyoku's spell persisted.

Not after long, Rekco reached the dome of white light. He took a deep breath and crossed the threshold into it, wholly expecting to be whisked away to another world, or blown to bits by a torrent of magic—neither of which came. Instead, he stepped into an empty white void, where, in the distance, Kyoku could be seen floating in midair. The wizard looked asleep, his back resting upon the infinite white void. Rekco tried to get closer but was being forced back by some unseen force.

"Koku!" he cried as he pushed with all his might, trying to breach the invisible membrane that separated them. "Snap out of it!" His pleas seemed to go unheard, and no matter how much he exerted himself, he could go no further. "There—has to be—something!" he thought aloud, still struggling to move forward.

Rekco stopped to catch his breath and gather his thoughts—something there was little time for. He clenched his fist, conjuring the glass sword in his hand.

Searching for The Eminent: The Collapse of Reality 313

There was only one desperate thing left to try, and it was his only hope. He reared the blade back with one hand, aiming the tip of it at Kyoku, suspended in the distance.

Ather coursed through his body like blood through his veins, and the glass sword was his heart. He sent all the magic he could into the blade until it swelled and spilled forth, spiraling all around him. "I'm sorry. I couldn't save you either—but I won't fail to save this world!" Rekco announced as he thrust the blade forward, along with the vortex of Ather that surrounded it.

A beam of energy erupted from the glass sword and raced towards Kyoku. Rekco closed his eyes the second before impact. When it did, it exploded, creating a shockwave that made reality itself quake. The sound of the explosion echoed through his ears as he felt the ground beneath him vanish and his heart leap inside his chest. His eyes burst open, and he saw the white light was being ripped asunder, revealing the black storm clouds that were shedding tears upon the city.

Chapter 22: A Rivalry Ended

Mindy ran for what felt like an eternity, the high heels that she wore long broken and left behind. Her legs were burning with fatigue and cramping, screaming at her to stop, but she couldn't. She did not dare. Nor did she dare to turn back and face the horrific Runic Tower behind her. The images of the crowd gone mad had burned into her mind, their bodies contorting in inhuman ways, until each of them fell to the ground with a *crack*, where they became still as statues with hands still reaching up towards the heavens. Sara's haunting, distorted voice still played in her ears along with the gruesome snapping of her neck as she, too, fell to the ground outside the tower.

That madness was like nothing Mindy had ever seen or reported on before. It seemed to spread like a disease. Ronaldo had keeled over behind her, his voice straining as though he were being choked from the inside. Barnov was taken too, the moment he fell to his knees and cradled Sara's broken body in his arms. Tiny threads of blue fabric poured out of his tear ducts and Sara's mouth like worms from a cadaver. Once Mindy saw that, she ran. She didn't say a word or even let out a scream—she simply ran for her life, around the tower and towards the beach behind Last Thesi.

She clutched the tape recorder close to her chest, holding onto it as though it were her very soul. *I have to get this story out—for Ronaldo, for Barnov, and for Sara. The people must know that this city isn't safe!* Mindy wished it would all blow away and that humanity could begin anew, the memories of this cursed place wiped from existence.

In the distance, she caught a glance of the blue horizon, peering through the western end of the Parade Grounds that was always kept open. Mindy never imagined she would ever have to sprint the whole length of the grounds. The idea of her car breaking down and leaving her stranded in a place like this was once a nightmare to her—but now, her mind knew horrors that were far worse.

Dusk was setting in by the time she arrived at the end of the Parade Grounds. She wanted to cool off her throbbing legs and feet in the ocean waters so badly, a thought that was promptly ripped from her mind the moment she heard a *crack* louder than any thunder she ever knew. She turned back for a split second and instantly regretted it. Her eyes nearly burst from her skull when she saw the Runic Tower collapsing onto itself, the upper half of it appearing out of the clouds as it leaned forward and fell towards the High District. The terror that coursed through her entire being seemed to slow time itself. It was a calamity she could not avert her eyes from.

The tower came down on the wall around the High District like the deadweight arm of a drunken giant. The sound it made knocked her off her feet. That, or the tremendous force of the impact. For a fraction of a second, as her body was tossed through the air along with the debris, Mindy felt at peace—then her mind went blank.

"What's a girl doin' 'ere at this hour?" a voice called amidst the endless ringing within her black dreams.

"Don't ya matter with that right now! C'mon an' help me pick 'er up!" another voice joined alongside it. Their voices were terribly close and loud, as if their mouths were shouting right into her ears from both sides.

"Hey! She's still breathin'!" the first one cried.

"Dang ol' miracle, ain't it?" the other responded.

Their words assured her that she was alive. She didn't feel alive, though. Dread seized her heart not after long, as the world never seemed to come into focus. Everything remained black and painful and loud. She wiggled her toes, which was all her body seemed capable of. It didn't seem that the two men carrying her noticed.

Mindy's breathing became more frantic with each failed attempt to pilot her useless body. *Please, no. Please, I can't be blind! I can't be broken! I must just be so weak that I can't open my eyes, just like how I can't move my body. I'll be okay! I have to be! I have to! Wait, the tape recorder! Where did it go?! I can't feel my hands. Please, tell me it survived. Please, tell me they picked it up with me. I can't be paralyzed ... for nothing. Please.*

Her mind raced, screaming at itself, wishing that the crash had killed her instead of leaving her broken and worthless. The pain she felt was impossible to manage. It was shattering her mind. She wanted the darkness to take her again, so she could wake up, back in her bed in her apartment, to find that this was all a bad dream. The terror kept her awake, forced to ponder the anxiety-filled unknown regarding the condition of her tape recorder.

She could scarcely feel the touch of the men carrying her, though she could not feel the warmth of their hands. For all she knew, ghosts were carrying her along the beach. Their awestruck voices painted a grizzly picture of what became of the city after the tower fell.

"You see any other survivors?" one man asked.

"Nah, nothin'. We're lucky to be survivin' ourselves, I tell ya."

"I hope the farm is okay."

"Gosh, the farm! I sure hope so."

The breeze grazing over her burning skin dissipated, a signal that the men carrying her had stopped.

"Ayo, what's that there?"

"Ah, *this* dingy? I found it on the girl here. Looks like some kind of old-timey recorder. Still works. See?" The man clicked the button and Mindy could hear Sara's voice play from it, playing the last, awful words she spoke as her voice droned on and on, hung up on the word *faith*. The sound sent painful shivers down her torqued spine and the hairs on her neck stood up on end. Despite that, her spirits rose somewhat.

The recorder! It survived! Yes! Don't bother with me now—just make sure that recording sees tomorrow!

"No, not that—*that!*" Mindy felt her body shift slightly, as though they were turning while holding her up.

"Woah, now! What's that big ball of light doin' eatin' up the city?"

"I don't want to find out!"

"Looks like it's movin' slow."

"For now. Let's hurry—"

Before the man could finish his thought, something happened—a great *boom* sounded that made the ground mimic the ringing sensation within Mindy's ears. Even though her body was mangled, she could feel it too. The sensation it caused was intense and frightening, making her feel as though her whole body was plunged into a frozen bath. The jolt made her think she wasn't paralyzed, if not for only a moment. Her mind went blank and swam in the frozen sea until her brain throbbed as if she'd eaten ice too quickly.

She wondered what was happening. She wished her eyes would work.

"Hey, now! Why'd you go 'an drop her?" one of the men cried.

"You dropped her too!" the other argued. "Did you feel that just now? It was like ... my blood turned in'ta boilin' water. Everything burned an' ached. It was so bad that I thought I'd die!"

"Nuh-uh. It was like my skin turned to stone 'an all of my insides became rocks, all rubbin' against each other. It hurt like hell. I thought I'd keel over!"

"Sounds like you had it easy! I was on fire!"

"Ay, shut it, will ya? Go on and help me pick her up so we can get a move on."

Mindy felt hands grab at her again and the semblance of ground she felt on her back disappeared. That terrible feeling had gone to the point that she could scarcely remember it. The only thing she knew was that whatever it was, it seemed to put her mind at ease enough that she could feel herself fading out of consciousness. She was

Searching for The Eminent: The Collapse of Reality 319

soon met with a dark reprieve, not caring where or when she would awake—if at all.

*

The great white light that nearly engulfed all of the High District was gone, and the chaotic storm was too. The purple sky was full of stars and a bright moon, all illuminating the lightless city; Oglis' star was there too, watching the scene below as a curious eye would. Rekco stood in the middle of a ruined street, his mind still hazy as though he had woken from a dream. He peered about, whilst wondering if Kyoku had been obliterated.

The sinking feeling in his gut that he had just killed his most powerful ally against Oglis was put to rest when a figure rose from a pile of rubble in the distance. Rekco ran over at once and cried out, "Kok—" his voice fell just as he did as he quickly crouched beneath a bolt of electricity that flew at him. "Hey! Cut it out! We have to work together—"

"No!" Kyoku snarled. "I—won't!" He looked crazed, with eyes shining like rubies and long strands of tangled hair floating every which way. He raised his pale hand, pointing it at Rekco; sparks of red electricity danced upon it.

Without warning, Kyoku sent a bolt of lightning, as crimson as his eyes were, hurling towards Rekco. It was faster than any of the spells the wizard had cast previously. It took all of Rekco's speed to raise his blade against it. It reflected off the Ather-filled glass sword and blasted through the bones of a collapsed building nearby. Instead of blowing the metal and stone debris into bits, the spell vaporized it entirely, leaving nothing behind. It was then that Rekco knew the danger he was in.

He's totally out of control! I'll have to stop him by force—there's no other way, he thought as he deflected a second bolt. Luckily for him, it seemed that Kyoku was so far gone that he lacked any strategy beyond a head-on assault. The wizard sent bolts of lightning imbued with his destructive red magic continuously, no matter how many times Rekco deflected them.

Rekco was thankful for the glass sword at that moment. The magical blade seemed to be the only thing standing between him and annihilation at that moment. That thought seemed to make something click in his mind—a plan had risen to the surface. *Wait! The glass sword! That's it!*

"This sword—" Rekco began with a strained grunt, pushing his body to block the onslaught of spells, sending them off to destroy what little remained of the High District, "—I got it—from—your father!"

Kyoku stopped just then, frozen in thought. "My father?" His voice sounded cruel and ill convinced.

"Yes! *Endu!*" Rekco cried out, having just remembered the name, as though it had been sitting on the edge of his tongue until then.

Kyoku reeled at the name, nearly falling over. "*How?* How did you—say that name?" The lunacy on his face did not cease, but instead, his expression only seemed to become more twisted.

Rekco did not know how he said it, actually. He had never tried to before. It made him wonder. The next thing he did, he did without any thought or intention, but it would go on to change everything. "Ky—*Kyoku!*" He shouted the name aloud, though his ears could hardly understand it.

Kyoku's eyes returned to their former, yellow color and grew wide with shock. The destructive magic coursing through him ceased. He simply stood, still and dumbfounded.

Now! Rekco's conscience cried, and his feet abided. He closed the gap between them in an instant and swung his blade upward, across Kyoku's chest. "I'm—sorry," he said to his friend as blood sprayed through the air along with tatters of cloth from his vest and tights. Kyoku fell onto his back without a sound, his mind too broken to express pain. Rekco fell forward after him, seeking to drive his blade into his heart. He let a torn cry out from between his gritted teeth and closed his eyes.

A green flash of light erupted and eclipsed the darkness behind his eyelids.

When Rekco allowed his eyes to creak open, his heart was racing with anxiety and guilt, yet he came to find that—he had missed. The glass sword was stuck into the ground beside Kyoku's left side, between his arm and ribs. The wizard lied there with eyes closed, appearing to be in a peaceful slumber, despite the blood dripping from the gash across his torso. Rekco rolled over, letting the blade disappear from his hands and laid beside Kyoku. He looked up at the clear sky in all its wonder and watched as Oglis' star faded away; she had seen enough.

The High District, a place only a few hours ago was the noisiest and most bustling place on the planet, was now silent as a tomb. All the murmurs of passing business people, the Ather-powered vehicles roaring and revving through the streets, and all the fantastic lights had been replaced by the labored breaths of the two life-long rivals. Rekco closed his eyes and nearly fell asleep from the exhaustion that ladened his body and mind. Just as he teetered on the edge of consciousness, he heard a loud gasp that shook the reprieve from his tired muscles and renewed the adrenaline in his veins.

Rekco sat up abruptly to find that Kyoku was awake beside him, though his eyes appeared non-threatening. The wizard turned his gaze upon him and weakly swayed his hand in a dismissing gesture, maybe meant as a sign to disperse Rekco's anxiety. Despite not understanding, Rekco took note of how useless Kyoku seemed, and his body relaxed a little.

Kyoku gazed up at the sky with searching eyes. "Why didn't you do it? Why didn't you kill me?"

"I—" Rekco stammered, both abashed and ashamed by the blunt question. "I tried. I don't know how I missed when I tried to drive my blade into your chest, but—I think it was for the best."

"Why?"

"Well—because, now we can go after Oglis together, right?"

"I told you it won't work. You can go and throw your life and freedom away, but I won't. If you leave me, I will find a way to leave this world and elude her grasp until the end of time."

"Well, unlike you, I don't have that option. I have no choice but to fight—for my father's sake, and this city."

Kyoku's nostrils flared slightly. "Why fight and throw your life away for something that is gone?"

"I'm not fighting for what's gone," Rekco said, shaking his head. "I'm fighting for what could still be—a future for the survivors who had no say in being caught up in all this."

"You're naive," Kyoku spat. "You're still treating the people here like they're any different than cattle being raised to slaughter, when in fact, they're less than that—they're *worthless*. You'll learn soon enough, once Oglis claims your for her collection."

"Is that what you actually believe now?" Rekco asked. Kyoku was silent at the question. "What about Cathy? Is *she* worthless too?"

Kyoku frowned as he drew the orb that she had become from his pocket and held it up against the dark sky. Beneath the black glass, her soul shimmered smokey and white, like the fog that made up Rekston when Rekco last saw him. His glare softened at the sight of it, and that was answer enough.

"Do you plan to take her with you?" Rekco asked, looking at the orb in Kyoku's pale palm.

He didn't seem to have thought of that, as it took him a moment to respond. "Yes. I'll scour the universe for someone who can return her to form."

"That's nice of you. I hope you find a way to do that."

"Maybe I'll even come back to save you from the Hall of Fate," Kyoku mocked. "If I can ever figure out that wicked creature's weakness."

That very riddle still strained Rekco's mind. He had pieces to the puzzle, he felt, but the answer was not yet clear. "If only you could have talked to my father about it before he died, or in that weird dream world you created."

Kyoku turned, his eyes full of curiosity. "What do you mean? Did he know something?"

"Maybe. He told me briefly about his meeting with Irol Retallor. He said that Irol had found a way to hurt her."

"Yes, but he's already been taken and will probably never see the light of day again if he's that dangerous."

"You're probably right. With a power like *that* I doubt Oglis would ever let him move freely."

"A power like what?" Kyoku asked, as if sensing that Rekco knew something he didn't.

"The power to change destiny. That's his power—or at least, that's what my father told me."

Kyoku's ears perked up. Rekco expected to feel the wizard's searing hot gaze before being interrogated about the information, but it didn't happen. Instead, Kyoku did something Rekco had never seen him do before: he began to laugh. He stretched his lanky arms up over his head, still holding Cathy's soul in his hand, and laughed. "Of course!" he said, sitting up. "What a cruel joke that is!"

Rekco stared at the wizard as though he had gone mad. "What? Do you think Oglis is so powerful that she can go against fate itself?"

"Unlikely," Kyoku began, sounding much like himself again. "I'd wager that Irol Retallor's capabilities were not yet fully realized, much like our own abilities. Oglis must have found a way to exploit that ..." he trailed off and began to murmur to himself.

"An exploit? How can you exploit somebody who is able to make you destined not to touch them?"

Kyoku's eyes lit up. "Maybe—because Irol was using his power to protect only himself!" Rekco furrowed his brow, his head beginning to hurt from thinking too much. "What if he was killed by an attack that wasn't directed at him, but one—directed at Oglis!"

"You think she hurt herself to kill Irol? How?"

"It's possible. She is very secretive about her abilities. Beyond automatic regeneration and reality-altering illusions, I don't know what else she can do."

"She can shoot lasers," Rekco blurted out.

"What? *Lasers?* How do you know that?"

"Because she shot one at me in a dream—or well, it felt real, but I think it was a dream. Anyways, she can shoot a beam of destructive energy out of her shorter arm."

Kyoku appeared deep in thought. He sat slumped over with his thumb at his teeth. "She did mention that she lost her arm while fighting him. Maybe that has something to do with it? Maybe she cannot regenerate what she herself caused?"

Rekco's spirits rose the more they discussed. "*See?* We *can* figure out her weakness and we *can* beat her!"

The simple movement of Kyoku shaking his head made Rekco's stomach go hollow. "No, it's still too risky. We don't know for sure if that's what happened between her and Irol. Maybe she tricked him with her illusions, and maybe her arm has always been like that."

Despite Kyoku's valid concerns, Rekco was still about ready to march off and confront the tyrant, though one question still remained. "We also don't even know where she is or how to find her."

"I know where she is," Kyoku said without hesitation.

"Wait, really? Where?"

The wizard turned his face, pale as the moon, westward, towards the beach. "Out in the ocean; out where the water is as dark as the night sky. She's down there beneath all that fog—somewhere."

"How do you know that?" Rekco needed more convincing before he jumped in the ocean, swinging his sword madly.

"It took a while to deduce. You see, there was once a race of people called the Awakki that could feel the presence of the planet itself and hear what it had to say. Once the world outside of Last Thesi began to die, the Awakki felt a foul presence out in the ocean; far worse than anything they could imagine. The last of the Awakki once told me to never go out there. I know now that the thing they felt wasn't that parasite, Per'cei, because he was operating out of the Runic Tower and fettered to the earth via a body hidden in Benton.

"But that's not all. Within Oglis' quarters, in the Hall of Fate, is a peculiar place, full of water vapor frozen in time. All around it is a dark blue, endless abyss, where the ground has a sandy texture. I believe that room is connected to—or hidden deep in the ocean."

Rekco stood up at once and turned his gaze to the shattered wall in the distance. "And you're for sure not coming then?"

"No. Even if I did, I would be of little use. I depleted most of my power when I lost control. I could create a simple raft for you to ride out there, though, if you truly have a death wish."

"Do it," Rekco said, his eyes ablaze.

Kyoku waved his hand, though nothing seemed to happen. "There. It's done. You'll find it tied up on the shore. It'll be some time before the tide takes it."

"Thanks. See you, then." Rekco began to walk away slowly, keeping his eyes on Kyoku, as if waiting for the wizard to say something or stop him. Instead, Kyoku simply slumped forward, holding tight to Cathy's soul with both hands. Rekco stopped and turned back, saying, "Hey, you aren't going to ask how I was able to say your name? Or about your father?"

"Endu? No, I'll find him on my own—I have a fairly good idea where. As far as you being able to say my name: I already know how." Rekco reeled, for he himself did not yet know the reason. Kyoku noticed his reaction and decided to continue. "It's because you're the Eminent now—for certain; which means you've got a part of *Dalu, the creator of all things*, inside of you. It gives you the ability to comprehend things not of this world, say, *myself*. When your father passed is likely when you fully developed that power. It's a shame you'll run off to the slaughter with it."

Rekco smiled, in spite of the wizard's cruel comment and lack of confidence in him. "Well, thanks again—for everything over the years. I don't think I would have been able to grow into what I am today, or even survive to this day without your help."

"Don't thank me," Kyoku scowled. "If there's anyone you should be thanking, it's Gofun. He was the one who saw something in you—probably saw you for what you really were." His voice became calm and still for a moment. "I wonder—what it was he saw—in me."

"Gofun," Rekco said with an air of reminiscence, while also feeling as though the name was new to his unlocked mind. "I'm sure he saw what good you could do for the world. Maybe that's why he brought you here to a place like this." Kyoku curled up and rested his head on his knees with eyes closed and did not utter a response. Rekco understood that as the end of their conversation, potentially their last conversation. He took it as his way of saying goodbye—and thus, a rivalry ended.

Chapter 23: Deep End

The wind along the shoreline was cold, and the water was colder, as if acting to deter Rekco from proceeding out to sea. But he could not be turned away. He longed to unleash the culmination of his rage upon Oglis after all she had done to him, his friends, and the city. Even so, Rekco was relieved he did not need to plunge head first into the freezing ocean.

He found the raft Kyoku conjured for him after little searching. The magical wood it was crafted from was held together by sutures far more intricate than a man could make with any tool or machine. It was light enough that Rekco easily dragged it by the rope it was tied up with—out to the calm tide.

"There's no turning back now," he said to the quiet beach full of massive chunks of stone from the shattered wall. He glanced back at Last Thesi one last time, feeling remorseful for the state in which he was leaving it.

With nothing left to say or do, Rekco pushed the raft into the water with his foot and let it drift until it proved its stability. He took a deep breath of the cool, fresh air, and jumped atop it. There was a thin, yet sturdy oar fastened to the back of the raft that detached with a single tug. Rekco dipped it into the cold water and began to paddle out into the dark blue ocean.

Despite the generous light the moon cast upon the world that night, all the ocean looked dark and dreary. Rekco worried that he would not be able to find the shadow Kyoku spoke of. That worry left from his mind only a moment after it entered, for Rekco began to feel a sensation within him. It made him sweat to the point that he had to gulp down his anxiety and fear and steady his arms so as not to drop the oar.

"That's her—Oglis!" He said to himself, still shocked by his new ability to sense magical presences. What he felt from the distant stretch of water made him wish he couldn't, though. It was a terrible sort of feeling; dreadful and hopeless, like the kind of things the people on worlds Oglis conquered long ago most likely felt.

Rekco focused his thoughts on his desire to defeat her, and it helped a little to do away with the awful feeling. He knew that she had a power that could invade the minds of her foes, something that Kyoku had reassured him of. Because of that, he tried to stay as aware of himself as possible and protect his mind. All the while, Rekco rowed, driven by his hatred for Oglis. The fire burning in his gut kept him warm amidst the frigid breeze that seemed to grow colder the farther he got from land.

Rekco kept his eyes forward, never truly knowing how far away he was from shore. He didn't care. All that mattered now was making Oglis pay, in hopes once she was gone that life would not gutter out entirely from this world and that those who remained could go on.

The little raft groaned as it sailed over turbulent waves out in the silent, black ocean. Rekco's heart jumped with each bump that ran beneath the raft, fearing that it would topple, and the dreadfully dark water would take him. The moon continued to climb up the night sky, where Oglis' watchful eye was nowhere to be found. Rekco did not wonder whether there was a trap set in place for him, but rather *what kind* of trap Oglis had in place for his arrival. He did not have time to speculate that thought, for the raft came to a sudden halt, nearly throwing Rekco into the water.

He glanced about himself. *What's happening?* All the ocean around him was black, with shadows dancing beneath its surface. There was a loud, metallic *thud* from below that echoed throughout the sea, and the world seemed to give way beneath the raft. Rekco fell for only a second, but he let out a scream all the same.

His feet touched down on a metal platform that was so cold that he could feel it through his shoes. His first instinct was to look up at the great big hole he fell down. Waterfalls surrounded all the edges of the opening, yet water did not pool at his feet, or anywhere around him, for that matter. The hole was getting smaller by the moment, and Rekco turned his sights to the ground on which he stood for answers.

"An elevator?" he asked aloud when his eyes saw the circular, metal platform moving with the pace of the water falling around it. As miraculous as it was, Rekco knew that he was in danger. "Oglis!" he yelled, summoning the glass sword in his hand and raising it up. "I know you're here! Show yourself!"

Her eerie, distorted voice called back from everywhere around him in response. "I await you at the bottom—should you make it there alive, that is."

At the sound of her voice came an intense magical presence that Rekco could not ignore. He whipped around but saw nothing, then turned his sights above, where a massive spiral of Ather was coming down the elevator shaft. Rekco squinted, trying to make out what he was seeing; the blue light it gave off reflected off the waterfalls and illuminated the entire pit.

"What is that?" he shouted.

"Some friends, some foes—those are your people—the people of Last Thesi, all condensed to their most primitive, ethereal forms. I believe you refer to them as: the Runic Guard."

Rekco's eyes grew wide. He had just recently learned the process in which a person could be turned into a being of Ather. He remembered the rotting, living corpses Per'cei kept in cages within the Runic Tower. The memory sparked hatred and rage within his heart, yet he did not let it dull his senses. He readied his weapon as the storm of Ather drew closer.

"I'm sorry, to all of you," he said in a somber tone, closing his eyes and taking a deep breath before letting his blade fly. Despite how threatening the enormous storm of Ather was, his body seemed to feed off it. Its presence alone bestowed a magnanimous boon upon him that amplified his powers. His arm moved faster than his mind could perceive, yet he knew exactly where he was aiming. Each sword stroke let off a wave of blue energy that tore through the spiral of lost souls, rending it until nothing was left of it but the fleeting remnants of Ather streaks upon the sky.

A surprised scoff came from the air itself, taking the form of Oglis' voice. "No hesitation, huh? I thought you would think twice about striking down your townsfolk."

Rekco ignored the voice and slowly glided his feet across the icy metal elevator to exit his battle stance. He let his head hang low for all those lost, while also praying that there were still people on the surface who managed to escape such a fate. He lifted his head, eyes full of contempt and said aloud, "You may have watched me my whole life, but you don't know me. You don't know what I'm capable of. I'll show you—soon enough."

"Well, not *too* soon," Oglis laughed. "*That* was only an appetizer. Your real challenge begins *now!*"

Rekco felt a sharp pain in his side that jolted through the back of his ribs. The swift kick he received sent him flying across the platform. He tumbled to the edge of the ring, where water splashed all over him. He sprang up, shaking droplets from his drenched hair. What he saw standing at the center of the platform made him rub his eyes with confusion: it was a mirror of himself.

He was wearing the same orange shirt and brown pants. He would have thought the man to be his father had he not known him to be dead. The saltwater burned his eyes as he rubbed and wiped them. Once his vision came into focus, Rekco realized that the man standing there truly was himself.

"What do you think? The stunned look on your face would lead me to believe you're impressed."

"What's this supposed to be? Some kind of illusion or trick?" Rekco asked, looking his mirror image up and down.

"A trick? No, *this* is my creation—a solution to your impudence. Once I figured out that the power of the Eminent could be transferred to another, at least within the same bloodline, I decided, 'why go through the trouble of training you if I could just *make* a new you to inherit the power?'"

"A new *me?*" Rekco squinted as he stared at himself. The other Rekco began to move, turning to face him. A blade formed in his hand; yellow as Oglis' eyes, mimicking the look of the glass sword he wielded.

"That's right. An Eminent without any dreams or desires, morals or convictions, one whom I pull the strings for. I have decided to call him Ocker—a fitting mirror, I think. Why don't you test him out for me?"

Rekco pointed his sword at Ocker, who did just the same back. He didn't know what to expect, but preferred to take the initiative while he had the chance, opting to dash forward with his blade at the ready. Ocker moved just as he did, meeting him halfway with a sword stroke of his own. Their blades clashed; one, two, three, four times, before they slammed into one another and tried to push the other off balance with raw strength.

Rekco scanned his mirror while trying to hold his sword steady against Ocker's. Ocker's form was an exact match of his own; everything from his footing to the way he held his sword was the same. Their eyes met and Rekco recognized that as the only discernible difference between them. Ocker's eyes were grey and hollow, despite the strain and passion on his face. Rekco could tell he was nothing more than an empty doll, made to look and act like him, and at that moment, he knew he couldn't lose to such a thing.

Rekco accelerated, focusing the Ather within him not only into his limbs, but into the glass sword as well. The clear blade swelled with what looked like blue fog. Rekco saw, amidst the blue in his sword, a strange, red tint as well that was faint and guttering. With all the power he summoned, and then some, he pushed his blade forward and split Ocker's yellow sword into pieces; the beam sword flitted away like fireflies after sunrise, and Ocker fell backwards.

Before Rekco could rush forward and finish the clone, he felt his body seize up, and Oglis' voice rang from the waterfalls. "That sword again," she said with a clicking sound that was much different than a human clicking their tongue; this sounded far less organic, almost mechanical. "Is that all that separates you two? I wonder. What if I—"

At that moment, Rekco's glass sword vanished from his hands, and he regained control of his body. Within the moment he stumbled, Ocker returned to his feet. He tried to resummon the glass sword, but it wouldn't come. Ocker dashed at him with his fists up and began sending blows towards his head. Rekco ducked and dodged, still confused, but adapting all the while to the precarious situation.

Rekco got as low as he could beneath one of Ocker's straight rights and drove his elbow into his sternum, throwing the clone back. His heart was racing fast, yet his mind was brought back to a time many years ago when Maven first taught him hand-to-hand combat.

"Don't ya ever think ya've lost just 'cause ya've lost your weapon. *Anythin'* can be a weapon if ya use it right, especially your hands!"

He smiled at the thought and memory of Maven's voice, clear as day, within his head. He didn't know a thing about the afterlife, but he hoped that wherever Maven had gone, that he could see him now, putting all the training and hardships he's gone through to use. Ocker picked himself up without bothering to pat the dirt off his clothes. He seemed incapable of confusion, doubt, or the basic concept of knowing that he was losing. He simply threw himself forward and fired off a string of punches again, none of which hit their mark, until—

"Enough!" Oglis' voice cried, shattering whatever magical restrictions that were placed upon them. Ocker reacted far faster to it than Rekco, who was still new to sensing magic. The mindless mirror summoned his yellow sword and thrust it towards Rekco's chest without hesitation. Tried as he might to dodge, the surprise of it was more than he could manage. The beam of yellow energy both cut and burned him at the same time as he passed through his side.

Rekco keeled over in pain—pain that lasted all but a second before the adrenaline kicked in and the instinct to retaliate took over. With one hand on his side and the other summoning the glass sword, he stood up and spun around to dodge another quick thrust. While Ocker's sword caught nothing but air, Rekco swung his with furious might, causing an explosion of purple magic to resonate from his blade. It was as though the blue and red light that danced within it had melded together and rose to the surface.

The magical eruption cut right through Ocker's sword arm, separating it from his shoulder with ease. The arm spun into the air, still tightly gripping onto the yellow energy blade. Flecks of red ash danced through the air between the wound and the arm before it landed on the metal platform. Ocker did not react in pain, though he was thrown onto his back by the explosion. Yellow blood dripped from his shoulder and splattered all about as he landed on his back.

Rekco leapt forward to land the finishing blow, but the air suddenly became thick as a brick wall. He fell to the ground before the invisible barrier and quickly glanced about himself. "No more tricks! Your doll has lost!" he cried out in frustration.

Just then, the elevator came to a stop. Not only did it stop, it disappeared entirely, revealing the sandy ocean floor, dark as the abyss and full of menacing shapes. The only light came from Rekco's sword, which gave off a white glow when he wasn't channeling Ather into it. He glanced around, looking for Ocker, but the clone was nowhere to be found. He had gone just as the elevator had.

A moment passed before Rekco's heart dropped and the fear that he would drown blared into his mind. But to his surprise, the water did not act like water at all. He reached out to wade his hand through the still water, and when he retracted it, he realized his hand was not wet, nor was any of his body. It was a peculiar phenomenon that he did not have time to question. Instead, he paced onward along the bottom of the sea.

The sand crunched beneath his feet, much like at the beach, though it was denser beneath the ocean's weight. The tremendous weight of the water made no impact on his movements, though; in fact, it was light as air, and as breathable as it too. Rekco proceeded towards the black shapes in the distance, looming like evil monuments made of twisted stone. Along the way, he passed by smaller natural rock formations that were just as intricate.

It was a marvel to see such things up close. The porous mounds of rock were full of caverns, both shallow and deep, beyond what he could see. Some had reefs about their feet or fantastic fish swimming about that eventually fled at the sight of a human walking through their home.

Rekco remained vigilant, despite the alluring sights, just in case Oglis were to try to ambush him or had some other trap prepared. No such thing came. It was peaceful to the point that Rekco began to feel the intense pain biting at his side again. Luckily, the wound wasn't bleeding, for the heat from the beam sword had cauterized it. He wished the water surrounding him would soothe it, though he was thankful not to be crushed beneath the weight of the ocean all the same.

As Rekco walked onward, a thick fog began to block his vision. It enveloped everything in sight not after long and felt full of magic. Oglis wasn't far off. He paced slowly through the sea of clouds, doing his best to waft it away with his hands, until he saw a light in the distance, yellow and bright. The sight of it made Rekco tense up and ready his blade. It was unmoving and seemingly non-threatening, but he proceeded with caution anyway.

The closer he got to it, the more vibrant it became. An enchanting, blue hue became visible around the yellow light. At that moment, Rekco realized why the light seemed so familiar.

"The star!" he called out, his voice unaffected by the water. He pushed onward, drawing closer and closer to it, until, at last, he broke free from the fog and exited to the other side. It no longer seemed like he was under water. It wasn't quite as dark, and the air was thick with an unusual scent—like a mix between new plastic and old leather.

The formations of rocks there were humongous, looking like black, warped castles. There was an intricate-looking cavernous tunnel that wound all around the base of the mass of stone. The star was there too, sitting before the monument, but it wasn't a star at all—it looked more like a portal. The yellow energy swayed and pulsed in a way that nearly matched the rhythm of Rekco's breath.

Just beside it stood a towering figure, back turned, gazing into the celestial portal. It was none other than Oglis, the tyrant—the monster who orchestrated all the pain and suffering Rekco and Last Thesi endured over the course of his life. Seeing her, even from the back, made him see red. He was ready to face her, no matter what the outcome—he would do everything in his power to make her pay.

Chapter 24: All Things

Oglis was as terrible of a sight as when Rekco first laid eyes on her; gargantuan in stature, with a fleshy cape flowing from the back of her neck down past her shoulders, dark azure and leathery as her skin, and of course, her voice, haunting as could be, exuding from the mesh-like voice box that ran down the front her of face, below her eyes, down to her neck.

"My, Rekco, you have done yourself quite a disservice by coming down here. You could have ran far away, which might have worked for a while to postpone your fate—or even waited to team up with your *friend*, whom I was hoping you would have killed—you know, to save me the trouble of tracking him down and doing it myself," she said, not turning to face him.

Rekco's anger rose with each word she spoke in her spine-chilling, inhuman voice. He was on the cusp of lashing out and stabbing her in the back, for whatever good that would do against a seemingly infallible being. "Kyoku's long gone by now. You'll *never* find him—in fact, I'll make sure you don't leave here alive."

"Really now?" she said in an amused tone. "I am eager to see how you plan to pull that off."

"I'm not playing!" Rekco burst out, pointing the glass sword at her, ready to close the gap between them in a moment's notice. "No more tests! No more games! I'm putting an end to all of it, right now!"

Oglis gave a slight chuckle. "You haven't been playing the game for quite some time now—ever since you dropped that tower on the city, killing thousands of people, if not more. *This* was never part of the plan, but I welcome it all the same. A little disruption can be a good thing, you know?"

Rekco became red in the face, clutching the hilt of his sword so hard that his arm trembled with rage. "*A little disruption?!* Your plan to capture the Eminent has cost more lives than I can even imagine! Thinking of all the plans, dreams, and love that's been lost—all the people who never had a chance to grow or change or know happiness—it makes me so—"

"Is that why you've come to face me? To exact revenge for all the souls long gone? Souls that would have never known your name, and will never know it—the souls of *worthless* beings, who serve no purpose but to help ME find YOU." She was beginning to growl as she spoke, her voice full of confused frustration as she pondered Rekco's reasoning for defending a dying world.

Rekco wiped the tears from his eyes—tears brought on by Oglis' cruel words. He couldn't help but think of Cathy and Dim and Bragau, Maven, and his father, and everyone else she deemed *worthless*. A being like her could never understand his plight—could never understand what it meant to have a friend to care about and protect. "Yes, *that* is exactly why I've come—" he sniffled and fumbled his words as he tried to hold back the melancholy. "Someone like you could never understand what I'm feeling. You don't know what it means to have friends you hold dear, friends and family you'd do anything to protect, and to have them taken from you. A—All I ask is: why? Why are you doing all this? It can't be as simple as *a divine plan*. I can't believe that! There has to be something more!"

Oglis turned her elongated neck ever so slightly and Rekco caught a glimpse of her yellow, beady eye, shining like a brilliant amber in the dark. "*Why?*" she repeated aloud, emitting a vibrating hum from her voice box before continuing. "Nobody has ever asked me that before. Nobody has asked me what MY plan is. You're right in thinking that my goal has little to do with my divine purpose. I am a conqueror. Should the eyes of the gods shy from me, I would set off to conquer all the worlds in the universe. I would strip the gods of their powers and feast on their fattened souls. I strive for that purpose, while adhering fate's design and function within it. One day, I'll outsmart that straight, golden line they call destiny, and learn to cross it. That day, all the universe will become MINE."

Rekco felt a sense of relief that there was a reason for all the chaos she caused in his life, albeit he was also appalled by her passion for cruelty. His composure became steady the more he recognized her as a villain; not just to him, but to all living things throughout the world and beyond what he could comprehend. He gave a slight, anxious chuckle of his own. "Okay. I feel better about killing you now, though I suppose it doesn't matter if it's true that the Ten never truly die. Maybe when you come back, you won't be the same monster you are now."

"You've learned a lot, it seems. Allow me to treat you to a special piece of information, not that it will help you." Oglis reached her three, long fingers out to touch the pulsing portal before her. It yawned, crumpling and folding into a ball of light and shot into her arm, illuminating the veins throughout her body for a brief moment before guttering out. Once the light was gone, she turned to face Rekco at last. "I, unlike the rest of the Ten, do not enter a stasis when I die."

Rekco looked at her sideways, not fully trusting her words. "What? Why not?"

"*That* is my power," she touched her hand to her bare chest that jutted out like a big triangle of flesh that looked as hard as metal armor. A liquid-like, yellow light poured from her hand and cascaded over her front before seeping back into her flesh and fading. "My body and soul are so intertwined that I can control it at will. But because of that, were my body to die, my soul would also."

"What would happen to the piece of that guy's soul then?"

"You must be speaking of Dalu, Creator of All Things. I'm surprised you remember that much. Normally, that fragment of power would go back to the whirlpool of souls and be lost again. But in my case, who knows? Maybe it would be gone for good."

Rekco didn't understand enough of what she was saying to know what kind of consequence her permanent death could have on the universe, and at that moment, he didn't care. He bent his knees and lowered his head, entering his battle stance. He was ready to put an end to this story. Oglis, on the other hand, did not seem so eager. She raised her hand and made a gesture to pause.

"Is that truly your final decision? Might I offer you one last chance to concede and come back peacefully with me to the Hall of Fate? I'll even restore that girl of yours to her proper form so you can bring a little friend with you."

Rekco furrowed his brow at Oglis' mere mention of Cathy. "And then you'll suck the power out of me and put it in that clone of yours?"

"Of course, but having seen what happened with your father, we both know that such a transfer of power wouldn't kill you. It would simply make you mortal again. Wouldn't you like that? I'm sure I could find a nice place where you and that girl could lead peaceful, mundane lives, just like you've always dreamed."

Rekco's brow trembled and ached terribly from the rage he held back. "You don't know *anything* about my dreams! I'll cut you down and save this world! Then, I'll find a way to bring Cathy back myself." He remembered as the words left his mouth that he did not know where Cathy was anymore, and that it was likely she was long gone from this world by now—stolen away along with Kyoku to some distant corner of the universe.

"Suit yourself," Oglis said with an amused sigh. "Shall we begin then?" She relaxed her shoulders, her great claw of a hand dropping low at her side, fingers flexing with anticipation. "You lack—"

Before any more venomous words could exit her voice box, Rekco closed in on Oglis and tore his sword across her chest with such a tremendous force that the ocean floor shook. Blue tinted sand, stones, and time-locked water flew all about and remained suspended in midair even after the quake stopped. Oglis showed no sign of pain, let no shriek or howl escape her, and did not topple. The attack simply caused her to lose balance and forced her onto her back foot. In retaliation, she slammed her hand down, which would have squashed Rekco like a bug had he not zipped away.

Oglis laughed a haunting sort of laugh as the gash across her chest mended itself. "You wish to skip the formalities now? So be it. Die." She raised her left arm and pointed it like a cannon at Rekco. He knew what was coming. He'd seen it before. His whole body tensed up, ready to evade the beam and strike.

The pillar of yellow light burst from the stub of her arm and raced towards Rekco. He saw it coming, watched how it slowed as he sent Ather to his legs. He kicked off his foot and began to circle around her. Oglis' beady yellow eyes moved along with him, as did her arm, and the beam followed just behind him, cutting through all the darkened, underwater mountains in the distance. Rekco could hear them crumbling and falling to ruin behind him, though he did not take his eyes off his target.

He took a deep breath the moment before he decided to attempt to close the distance. With one burst of godlike speed, Rekco dashed forward, ducking beneath the sweeping beam of death, and delivered another powerful blow across Oglis' chest. This time, she was ready, already reaching for him as the sword seared her flesh. Rekco felt her repulsive, leathery finger graze his arm and side, his heart racing with fear, as he reacted on the spot to retreat again.

That was too close. If she gets a hold of me, I'm a goner, he thought to himself, huffing and heaving from the exertion. *But how am I supposed to hurt her? My sword seems useless against her.* Rekco was feeling more tired than he thought he should have after only using his acceleration and swinging his sword twice.

Oglis' wound was already healed by the time she spoke, as if in response to Rekco's thoughts. "You'd need to hit me with a hundred of those in succession to do any sort of damage to me. But I don't think you have that in you. You're already tired, aren't you? Do you know why?"

"Why?" Rekco asked between gasping breaths. "Is this another one of your tricks?"

"Good guess. But unfortunately, no. My *tricks* cannot be done in an area where my physical body is. *This* you're experiencing is *fatigue*. You're so used to fighting in places where Ather is abundant; in the buildings, the streets, even the air itself. But here, far away from civilization, there is no errant Ather to permeate your being. It's a marvelous power, but you've been taking it for granted thus far."

Rekco glanced around in a panic, still trying to catch his breath. Was it true? Have his feats thus far been attributed to the vast amounts of Ather around him? Could he already be running on empty after a couple of brash attacks?

"You won't be able to run forever, nor will you be able to attack me forever. It's only a matter of time before I catch you; one single mistake, one slightly late reaction, and you'll wake up in the Hall of Fate, never to see the light of day again." Oglis said in an increasingly threatening tone.

Rekco tried to think up a plan quickly. He shifted his eyes to the glass sword in his hand. *You might be my only hope here.* He took in as much air as his lungs could manage and widened his stance. Oglis remained an unmoving bastion, raising her arm yet again. When the beam fired, Rekco did not move. Instead, he raised the glass sword against it.

The ray of energy struck the clear blade and pushed Rekco's heels into the soft sand. It reminded him of their first encounter; how helpless he felt before the immense pressure of her unending torrent of destructive power. This time, he had a far easier time deflecting the beam. It spread across the sword like light from a flashlight and curved around Rekco.

The heat from Oglis' assault was dreadfully hot and was getting closer to his limbs than he would have liked. He took one hand off the hilt of the sword and carefully slid his fingers up the back of the blade. To his surprise, the glass sword itself was not absorbing any of the heat and did not burn his hand as it rested on the opposite side of the blade. *Okay, it's now or never!* Rekco tilted the blade with both hands, wincing as parts of the beam grazed his skin as he moved, but was eventually able to position himself in a way where he was able to begin steering the beam back towards Oglis.

It's working! It— Rekco's mind went blank with terror the moment the beam disappeared and he saw Oglis' talon-like foot appear before his face, coming at him. He fell back against the sand, pinned by the weight of her massive, long leg. For a split second, he saw her shimmering eyes narrow as she brought her claw of a hand down like a hammer. His heart beat a single time; so loud and deeply that he felt it in his head and heard it pierce his eardrums.

Rekco sent all the Ather he could muster into the glass sword and thrust it upward into the sole of her foot. The thrust sent a spiral of blue that enveloped all of Oglis' body and rocketed to the surface of the ocean. The ground around him erupted, giving him a chance to roll away and leap back to a safe distance. When his ultimate attack lapsed, Rekco saw that Oglis was still standing; her entire body was covered in burns that made her already leather-like flesh look even more dreadful.

She raised her foot from the hole in the ocean floor and set it down on the ground beside it. "That stung," she said with an annoyed inflection, her voice box rattled as she spoke—it, too, seared and scabbed. Oglis' whole body shuddered, like a dog shaking the water from its fur, and all the gruesome burns and scars melted away. "That was a nice try. I know that you know my weakness. It'll do you no good if I don't give you a chance to exploit it. Too bad."

Rekco cringed, shifting his lips in annoyance. *She has a plan for everything. I'll just have to find another way. Wait—what's that?* His eyes were drawn to a few burn marks on Oglis that did not regenerate like the others. The strange sight made him look at his sword with curious eyes. There, he saw something most peculiar: a tint of yellow floating beneath the glass, swirling within the calm blue Ather. *That's it! The sword must be able to take in magical attacks and, what—redirect them into its edge? The same thing happened when I fought Kyoku; there was a faint bit of his red magic trapped in there that got used up when I fought that clone of me.*

The startling revelation was enough to turn the tide of this seemingly impossible battle, Rekco thought. The problem, though, was that he was beginning to feel desperately tired after that last attack. That, and it seemed unlikely that Oglis would be easily coerced into using her beam attack again. *Think! Think! What can I do?* The image of her yellow, soul-infused energy running through her body played within his mind, and with it, an idea rose to the surface.

Just then, Rekco made a break for the nearby caverns at the base of the intricate mountain. Oglis did not follow him right away. Instead, she scoffed and began to walk slowly towards where he had gone. "Run and hide all you like. You won't goad me into using my beam. I know you're spent and have no other way to win." Rekco heard her say. He did not respond, but instead continued to traverse the complex caverns. "Do be careful in your attempt to flee. If you get *too* far, you'll leave the protection of my domain and be crushed beneath the ocean. I guess that wouldn't be too bad, though—*for me*," Oglis laughed.

Rekco stopped to shake his legs and roll his neck. He was far out of Oglis' line of sight. *I know you're tired, body. This is the last thing I'll ask you for, okay? Then we can finally rest.* He started off again, through the twisting and winding maze where impossible-looking sea creatures dwelled; things with elongated, limbless bodies, bug eyes, and stubby noses. They did not stir or move in response to his presence. They simply watched him pass by.

Magic sense don't fail me now! Rekco thought as he exited from the caverns to a side of the mountain where Oglis was not. He was reminded of her cautionary words and proceeded with hesitation. *I don't see anything. I can feel it is close, though!* He scoured the seabed with desperate eyes, until, at last! *There!* Using the flat side of the glass sword, Rekco nudged the object, an arm, sticking out of the sand.

His heart leapt when he found that the arm was not attached to anything. *Damn! Nothing! Did the beam sword he was holding disappear?* The feeling of hopelessness and defeat were closing in on Rekco's mind. He feared that he would turn back to find Oglis' dark silhouette towering over him, her beady eyes gleaming as she dealt him a killing blow. Amidst his grave thoughts, a glimmer of light appeared out from the sand—or rather, a glimmer of *liquid*, yellow in color; the same as Oglis' energy. It was trailing in the dirt beside Ocker's severed arm.

Rekco touched the tip of the glass sword to it while gulping down his hesitation. When the clear edge touched the droplets, they seemed to be vacuumed up into it, making the edge shimmer as though it were coated in stardust. His eyes grew wide at the discovery, and a new hope appeared. He dipped down on all fours and began to shovel through the sand with his bare hands.

He dug with haste, for it was not just his life that depended on it, but the life of all things in this world. Eventually, he felt cold flesh against his fingertips and nearly jumped with joy. After throwing the dirt off of Ocker's body, Rekco raised the glass sword high over his head with both hands. "Sorry about this," he said as he closed his eyes and drove the blade down, directly into the clone's heart.

The glass sword must have lit up like a supernova, its intense light piercing through Rekco's eyelids. When he opened his eyes, his gaze was immediately drawn to the blade. He held it up high, dazzled by the magnificent glow of the yellow energy swimming within it. It seemed to light all the ocean around him, like a single blazing star in the darkest night.

"This—this is it! This will work!" Rekco said, still awestruck by the beauty of the yellow dew swishing about inside the glass sword.

"Will it now?" an ominous voice called.

No! Rekco thought as he tried to turn to face it—but reacted far too late. His torso and arms became squished by the fleshy talons of Oglis' foot. It took all his strength to resist being squeezed to death. He squirmed well enough to free his sword arm and quickly swung at Oglis' extended leg that held him like the long arm of a giant. He expected her to reel in pain from being struck by the glass sword infused with her power, but when she didn't, his heart sank lower than the bottom of the ocean.

Oglis began to laugh. "Did you think that would work?"

Rekco could feel the hot air on his neck from the guffaw that came from her voice box. The smell that came with it was like old leather sprayed with the scent of fresh plastic. He turned his head enough to see that the gash upon her leg mended without a hitch. He stared up at her, dumbfounded, feeling without hope.

"It's time to go home now," she said, bending her stiff torso forward and reaching her hand out, as if to grab his head and smash it like a grape.

Rekco saw her spiked, whip-like hair fall over her shoulders and drape upon her chest. Seeing the white braids next to her unblemished skin made him think, made his mind race as though he were desperate to remember something that the pain was making him forget. *That's it! The burn marks from my last attack mixed with a little of her energy—they're gone!* A hazy sensation washed over him, making his eyes lose focus as he stared at the place where he knew she was hurting, and he began to question the pain he was feeling.

"It's not—real!" Rekco grimaced, feeling as though his head would pop off with how hard Oglis' talons were constricting him. Just as her long finger was about to make contact with his head, she vanished. Rekco fell to the floor, coughing and hacking, the pain in his sides gone.

"Well done," Oglis' voice called from far away. "Come then, let us finish this." She sounded far more serious than she had prior.

Rekco picked himself up off the ground and gazed up at the tower-like spikes that rose out of the top of the mountain before him. He shook the woozy feeling from his mind that Oglis' illusion caused and started back to where the true Oglis was.

The enormous tyrant stood at the entrance, having never left, her arms folded over her midsection. Her tiny eyes were like a pair of golden earrings glistening in the dark. Rekco held the glass sword aloft; it matched her eyes in color but shone far brighter. Without another word, he threw himself at her and cut across her front.

The mystical blade was met with resistance, and Rekco noticed that his was not the only yellow-glowing blade. Out from between Oglis' thumb and middle finger erupted a beam sword, shining just as bright as his own. Rekco used Oglis' weight to push himself back before going on the attack again. For a massive creature, Oglis was quick, and Rekco was far too tired to accelerate any more to attempt to outdo her. She shifted side to side and stepped hard as she spun to avoid contact with his sword, all while letting a few swings of her own fly.

Rekco felt somewhat enthralled by the battle, though the stakes were far too high for him to fully revel in it. They danced with one another, speaking only with their weapons. Rekco caught a burn or two in the brief instances Oglis' beam sword grazed his flesh. He was numb to the pain at that point, his body running off the faintest fumes of Ather that he was exuding. He set all of his hope in the borrowed power, trapped within the glass sword.

They clashed again, blade on blade; the sound it made was unreal, like two suns colliding. Rekco felt the ground give beneath his feet and he stumbled from the force of Oglis' attack and his own weariness. She swept his arm aside in riposte and thrust hers forward. The beam of yellow light was aiming right for his head, moving ever so slowly, yet his body felt like it was truly underwater.

Rekco's life flashed before his eyes; all his thoughts and ambitions, all within a fraction of a second. Amidst it all, he saw his father's face as he died within his arms in the ruined city he failed to protect. Next, he saw Cathy's smile; how it twisted and warped into a ball of blackness, never to smile again. He wanted to cry for his failures, but there was no time. His eyelids closed down slowly as the blade neared so close that he could feel the heat upon his face. Then suddenly, a pulse echoed deep within him—a desperate spark.

This pulse awakened all his muscles at once and his eyes burst wide open. *I can't let her win! Even if it kills me—I'll defeat her!* Rekco mustered every bit of Ather he could, to the point that he felt like his physical form was becoming unstable. A blue glow overlapped his skin—skin which seemed to deteriorate and become somewhat translucent. He paid his ghastly appearance no mind and simply allowed himself to move, unfettered from the fear of death.

Rekco ducked beneath Oglis' blade in an instant and lurched forward. He slashed across her torso, unable to feel the weight of his own arm or the force behind it; yellow and blue lights merged, overlapping with one another as they rent Oglis' armor-like, dark blue flesh. A hollow gasp sounded from her voice box as she bent upright. While she reeled, Rekco zoomed behind her and struck at her right leg, nearly making it buckle. Before she could react, he glided to her other leg and did the same while taking in a deep breath of the Ather-filled air that enveloped him.

Searching for The Eminent: The Collapse of Reality 355

Oglis staggered and wobbled this way and that—but ultimately remained unmoved. "I—won't fall!" She raged, raising her beam sword. She spun around and swung her sword, moving more clumsily than before, her legs looking like chopped trees, barely holding themselves upright.

Rekco reared his own weapon back, letting it take in all the Ather that surrounded him. The glass sword seemed to grow thrice in size from the overflow of energy that spiraled both inside and out of it. He had no choice but to take Oglis' blade across his chest as he thrust his swollen sword up at her. The corridor of light that it fired was unlike anything he'd ever seen. Soundless and brilliant, it blotted out Oglis' entire body and burst from the ocean floor, all the way up into the sky. It was so bright that it was all Rekco could see, lighting up the ocean like a supernova.

Moments later, the light dispersed, and all the pain set in. From the light, a giant shape emerged, looming over him. Oglis stood there, unmoved, her body covered in burns that made her leathery, blue skin look rotten. Her eyes were still ablaze, shining as the only light within the ever darkening ocean. Rekco eyed his sword in disbelief—it was empty, a mere glass shell with an edge sharper than folded steel. His hand gave out and let it go, causing it to vanish.

A deep sigh came from Oglis' voice box, and she began to fall backwards. She hit the ground with such a loud *thud,* that it jolted Rekco's senses enough to keep his exhausted eyes from shutting. He dragged his feet, slowly inching his way to the fallen tyrant. As he reached her head, Oglis began to laugh like a mad woman.

"He—really did—it," she said, her voice distorting like the sound of a broadcast on a dying radio.

"Huh? *Who* did *what*?" Rekco bent down to her. He had no use for caution anymore. He didn't have the strength to run or resist if she were to suddenly attack again.

"I—Irol—Retallor," her husked voice trailed off slightly.

"What do you mean? What did he do?"

"He—changed my—destiny," she answered with a weak chuckle. Her face showed no sign of pain, as though it were impossible for her to express such a thing, yet it seemed that she was dying all the same. The light in her pebble eyes flickered. "We—can—still—win."

Rekco stared at her as though she were speaking another language. "I don't understand what you're saying!" He cried in frustration, just about ready to collapse over her dying body.

Oglis continued to stare out into the blackness where the sky was, leagues and leagues above them. Rekco wondered if her eyes could see that far. She paid his confusion no mind. She simply continued to laugh, the distorted sound growing weaker and fainter by the moment. "Good—luck. See you—nevermore." With her final word, Oglis' eyes went dark, and her body became lost in the darkness.

Rekco clenched his hand in an anxious frenzy, summoning the glass sword to act as a lantern. He was prepared to die instantly the moment Oglis' safety barrier

Searching for The Eminent: The Collapse of Reality 357

were to break and let all the water's mass back into reality. He glanced about, trying to see if he could spot the elevator nearby, in hopes that he could ride it back to the surface—assuming that it was real in the first place. When he focused his mind, he could hear the faint sound of the waterfalls coming from the elevator room.

He turned towards the sound and saw that it wasn't that far away, but there was one major problem: his legs wouldn't move. *C'mon, move! One more time!* A dreadful possibility filled his mind; a scenario where his body was lost in the deep, waking from his deathly stasis only to die another painful death, over and over for eternity. That horrific image was motivation enough for Rekco to command himself one step forward.

As his foot touched the ground, the sound of rushing water came at him from every direction, and his world went black.

*

Kyoku eventually made his way to the beach. He tore the tattered, bloodied remains of his vest and threw it to the ground where he sat in the cold sand fidgeting with Cathy's soul in his hands.

"What is a soul, really?" he remembered asking Melonine some time ago.

He saw her face as clear as day within his intricately stored memories. She did not hesitate to answer what most would consider a deeply profound question. "It is an incredibly dense shell that contains a person's essence—everything that makes them who they are; emotions, nuanced traits, and even memories are stored inside.

They're nigh unbreakable, yet nobody knows how they are made—aside from Dalu, I suppose."

"Is that all you know?" Kyoku asked, not fully satisfied with her answer.

Melonine nodded. "Little else is known about souls."

"So, all that stuff stored inside—what happens to it after you die?"

"It all gets erased—or cleansed, rather. It has to be done manually so that it can harbor new life."

Reflecting on the memory of that conversation with Melonine gave Kyoku hope as he gazed upon Cathy's soul. "I know you're still in there. I'll never let anyone erase you."

Such thoughts made him feel woozy. He touched the back of his hand to his forehead. He was clammy and feeling altogether unwell. He checked the makeshift bandages he had conjured to see if he was still bleeding. The gash on his chest still throbbed terribly, but it was his pride that was hurt most of all. Bitter defeat and hopelessness were all he could taste, and there seemed to be no end to it.

What am I waiting for? Kyoku thought to himself as he gazed out at the calm sea pushing its tide against the shore beneath the night sky. He was all set to leave this world, yet something compelled him to wait. Did he want to confirm Rekco's fate, or was he simply afraid to take the leap and embark out on his own? A piece of paper formed between his fingers, and he curled up to look at it. It was one of the few things that he could find solace in during these accursed times.

Searching for The Eminent: The Collapse of Reality 359

Kyoku stared at the paper, contemplating it deeply. It was a page ripped out of an old picture book he once read as a boy. The page depicted a world where everything was bathed in a golden hue, where animals frolicked through lush gardens, where the flowers never wilted, and the people all smiled. At the top of the page, in golden letters, read the word: PARADISE.

"*That* is where I want to go," Kyoku said aloud, his voice longing for a freedom he knew was unattainable. "Once I find someone who can turn you back, we'll go there, okay?" He held Cathy's soul up to the page before folding it up and putting it away. He was just about rested enough to depart from this world and set off to explore the universe for Cathy's sake, until—

A magical beam shot out of the far reaches of the ocean, violent as a volcano erupting. It exploded before it reached the sky, lighting up the whole beach and all of Last Thesi behind it. The sight of it made Kyoku gasp. He sat, stupefied by the magnificent spectacle, watching as particles of light trickled down the night sky like shooting stars and faded away when they dipped back into the dark sea. Before he could even contemplate what he was seeing, something far worse began to happen.

Out above the ocean, the sky was ripped asunder. The tears spread all the way to Last Thesi, and from them appeared chains, chains the size of skyscrapers. Each of them had massive hooks at the end. Kyoku watched in awe that quickly changed to horror. He pounded his fist in the sand before standing up, saying, "That must be—the Reaper of Worlds! But why?" He gazed out at the ocean. There was only one explanation, one he could scarcely believe. "Rekco ... He ... won? But that means—the Reaper has come to finish the job. That means—it's too late for me to leave," he said, the hope gone from his voice.

The chains lowered slowly at first, but after proving stable, they all plummeted at once. Hooked chains rained upon Last Thesi, passing through the tall outer walls and buildings, reducing everything they touched to rubble. Chains plunged down deep into the ocean, only stopping when they reached the bottom with such force that it caused the planet to quake.

Kyoku spun around, dumbfounded by the chaos that surrounded him, with no chance to escape. He had no idea what to do, not until he spied something peculiar westward: chains rising from the ocean. He watched with bated breath, curious what would emerge along with them. What they pulled up caused a tidal wave that was luckily far enough away that it didn't reach him at the shore. The hooks that rose from the water carried a chunk of landmass.

The chains pulled it slowly, up towards the biggest tear in the sky. Kyoku felt the tide at his feet. He had been so enamored that he had paced forward to try to see what was happening. "Don't tell me he found Rekco already? He must have! But then—" Kyoku gazed around at the other chains, still stuck in the ruins of Last Thesi, "... am I next?" He was breathing hard, caught in the position he feared worst, on the verge of losing his freedom for good, on the verge of the end of the world he so tried to protect.

His frantic mind searched for a solution, stopping on a single memory, one haphazardly tucked in the depths of his conscience. He frowned at it, then turned a sad expression to Cathy in his right hand. "I'm sorry, Cathy. It's the only way."

Kyoku closed his eyes. When he reopened them, he was freefalling far above the ocean. He warped a second time, placing his hand and foot on one of the chains carrying the clump of earth into the sky so he could get a good look at it. He warped a final time, appearing on the landmass that was damp and cold, reeking of saltwater.

Steps away from him, Kyoku saw Rekco, laid out on his back, a gnarly wound across his chest and shoulder. Kyoku ran up and kneeled beside him. "Still breathing, huh? It seems the Reaper got to you just in time, I suppose." Rekco's eyes moved. He looked utterly drained, on the brink of death. "I can't believe you defeated that monster. I'm sorry you won't get a chance to tell me about it."

"I thought you were gone already," Rekco said weakly. It was a miracle he could speak at all. The Reaper's chains were teeming with magic, so it wasn't impossible that they were keeping him alive.

"I missed my chance," Kyoku responded, his expression both sour and pained. "Now I'm stuck facing the end of the world with you."

Rekco stared up at the chains pulling him towards the enigmatic tear in the sky with terror in his heart. "What can we do?"

Kyoku frowned. "*You've* already done enough. Now it's my turn." He gazed up at where Rekco was looking, partially lost in his own thoughts. "It's said that the first of the Ten, the Swordsman, once fought death itself to a standstill." He forced a weak smile, hoping Rekco was too far gone to see through it. "Thinking of that kind of gives me hope that this will work."

Rekco's rheumy eyes shimmered. He seemed to no longer have the strength to speak.

Kyoku bent down and placed the black orb, Cathy's soul, in Rekco's hand and closed it tight around it. "I'm sorry I won't be able to help return her—she may very well never return at all now, and I'm sorry to leave you with that burden. Unfortunately, there's no other way." He looked into Rekco's eyes, tears streaming down the dirt caked onto his face. He could see the words Rekco was unable to say. "What will I do? I'll fight—for as long as I can. If I cannot escape my destiny, then the least I can do is prolong it—and in that, prolong yours as well. Now, please, watch over Cathy and what's left of this world, and—live a long and peaceful life."

Rekco gave a weak nod. Kyoku bowed his head and turned away. He needed to summon all the courage and strength he had and more. A crimson glow enveloped his body that made him feel lighter than air; in fact, he was. Kyoku drifted off the land mass and into the sky above, soaring towards the ominous opening in the sky.

This is not quite the destiny I had hoped for, but nor is it the destiny I had been given. For that I am grateful. It gives me peace of mind to know that I am still in control of my own decisions and that I can do some good with the last of this life. Maybe when I return—things will be different.

Kyoku closed his eyes and envisioned an alternate timeline where he'd never been born with a piece of

Dalu's soul fettered to his own, where he was able to lead a normal life into his adolescence and return to his family—wherever they are. He saw a flash of himself, Rekco, and Cathy, all playing and laughing and smiling; in the woods, on the beach, in the grass beneath the golden sun. On that wonderful thought, Kyoku shot into the sky like a missile, and all his vision went red.

*

Far away in the plains of Last Thesi, a convoy of survivors made their way to the edge of the Forgotten Woods. They had wagons full of supplies, bags full of food for the trip, and seeds to grow their futures. They were tired and ornery, but fear and the will to live motivated them to continue. Many of them turned back to face the city in disbelief when a pillar of light exploded into the sky and lit the world as though it were day.

At the back of the group, Mikayla stood with a few elderly and aloof stragglers. She, too, gazed up at the heavenly ray. She still wondered where Cathy, Rekco, and Kyoku had gone, and tried to keep hope that they would find their way to meet with her. The yellow and blue beam burst and rained light all over the land like fireworks from heaven. All the people around her had their eyes glued to the skies, making sounds of surprise, almost gleefully, sounds that quickly turned to terror when the sky opened, and gigantic chains crashed into Last Thesi.

People screamed and panicked, while others began to pray to the gods, who seemed deaf to their plight. Many of them were in such a state of shock and froze on the spot, not uttering a word or sound. The pandemonium was at its peak, until a voice came from the front of the convoy to snap them back to reality.

"C'mon! We have to keep on moving! There's no turning back, remember? That city could all fall to ruin any moment! We need to make sure we're as far from it as possible when it does!" Zeke's boisterous voice boomed as though it were amplified by a megaphone.

Mikayla was absentmindedly clutching the medallion around her neck when Zeke's voice freed her of the stupor she was in. "Aye!" She affirmed, returning to her senses and responsibility alike. "No more rubbernecking! Everyone! Move!"

Dim Smithy, the scholar, came walking down from the front a moment later, checking to make sure everyone was prepared to enter the woods. His voice was not quite as loud or commanding, so he often had to stop to make sure he was heard. "It's almost time to go in. Make sure you put your torches out and huddle up with someone who has a flashlight. Everyone should have a simplified map with directions drawn on it, so nobody should get lost. If for some reason you do, just give a holler and someone will come find you, okay?" Once he reached the back of the line, he stepped to Mikayla. "Hey, Mikayla. Are you ready?"

"As ready as I can be," she said, feigning a smile.

"Good. We're counting on you to keep an eye on the back here to make sure nobody gets separated from the rest of the group. Do you have your light at the ready, and is it in working order?"

"Yeah," Mikayla tapped her hand against the flashlight hanging from her belt. The thought that Cathy might not have made it out of Last Thesi in time made her feel sick. She knew that Zeke and Dim entrusted her with such an important task to help distract her from her hesitancy in regard to leaving the city without having found Cathy first. The extra responsibility kept her from running off on her own to search the ruins of Last Thesi. She turned away from Dim and looked again at what remained of the city; the wall to the Research District had fallen, split into pieces by two chains crashing into it. Her eyes were full of longing.

Mikayla felt Dim's hand on her shoulder. It was as shaky as her composure was, which was reassuring in a sort of way. "Try not to worry. I'm sure Cathy, Koku, and Rekco will turn up. I'm sure they'd do everything in their power to make it out of there *together*."

Mikayla kept her gaze on the city, watching as it crumbled before her eyes. "I hope so."

Just then, a crimson star thrust itself unto the sky and exploded, staining the sky above Last Thesi blood-red. Red sparks filled the heavens and all the chains that hung from them began to burst into ash and fade to nothing before any of the debris could reach the ground. A large black mass could be seen free falling down the bloody sky. Its rapid pace grew slower the closer it got to impact. Mikayla's body tensed up, thinking it would hit the ground like a meteor and blow them all away.

Before it hit, Dim pulled her away and he, along with all the stragglers at the back of the convoy ran into the Forgotten Woods with haste.

*

Deep blue, constricting, and pulsing with magic were the walls within the seventh chamber of the Hall of Fate. The interiors of each room could be changed to meet the will of the tenant, though this room in particular was furnished with nothing at all. The Swordsman sat on the floor with his back up against the wall, facing the open door. Beside him was a woman, sitting upon a footstool. She had long, silver hair, parted down the middle that shone like Hou did in the light. The only sound between them was the soft whooshing of magical wind she was directing into the wound in his side.

The Swordsman kept his eyes closed, thinking of the last time he saw a star-lit sky and how he missed those purple and blue hues; the kinds of colors unseen at the center of the universe. The sound of tiny, frantic footsteps entering the room returned his awareness to the waking world. It was Dr. Gavin. He was huffing and panting, a thick layer of sweat on his protuberant, blue brow. His cheeks were a shade redder than usual.

"Swordsman! I require your assistance right away!" Dr. Gavin clamored as he pattered closer.

"For what? Don't you see that I am still injured?"

"It's that thorn in my side, Rekco Curse—since he began to do battle with Oglis, I have yet to hear back from her. To make matters worse, the Reaper of Worlds has gone silent as well! He went to secure Rekco and Oglis— but was lost within a magical storm! The storm has surrounded the world and the dock around it, acting as a barrier. Anyone that's tried to get near it has been reduced to ash! I need you to cut it down with that sword of yours!"

"*Really?*" The Swordsman said with a faint smirk.

"Yes! In fact, I command it! You must be healed enough by now!" Dr. Gavin made to shoo away the woman medic, but his path was barred by Hou, extending from the Swordsman's hand. "You *dare* disobey?!" he said, his eyes bulging.

"On what authority do you command me?" The Swordsman's eyes were narrowed and full of focus.

"As Keeper of the Hall, it is my duty to take command of the Ten in the event of Oglis' absence!" Dr. Gavin's face was growing redder, making his head look like a fat plum.

The Swordsman stood up, using the disparity between their statures as intimidation. "I, unfortunately, cannot heed your command. It appears that you did not receive the news."

"What news? From who?"

"From Dalu himself," the Swordsman said, making Dr. Gavin reel and tremble at the same time. "I have been relocated to the Archives of Time, along with all the rest of the Ten. It is said that a precious artifact had been stolen from there recently. Dalu wants us to make sure nothing else is taken."

"T—that's—that's—pr—"

"That's all there is to it. Now, leave me. I will depart once my healing is complete." The Swordsman sat once more and set Hou down by his left side. He glared at Dr. Gavin, whose mouth was agape with disbelief. The stumpy doctor scoffed loudly and left in a distraught haste.

Once Dr. Gavin was gone, the Swordsman turned to the woman sitting quietly beside him. She kept her head down, with eyes closed, her focused state akin to slumber. "Thank you for your service. I must take my leave now."

The women's eyes opened slowly, revealing electrifyingly yellow pupils. She smiled a weak, somber sort of smile. "You're very welcome. May I ask why you wished me to spend so much time healing a wound that was no longer there?"

The Swordsman pushed up his glasses by the bridge of his pointed nose and smirked. "I wish not to rain on the small victories of those struggling to shy away from their fate."

"I see," the woman said, still smiling. Her tired eyes gazed at him in an incredibly discerning way, as though seeing something he was not showing. He stared into her piercing eyes, allowing them to see all that they could.

The Swordsman gave the peculiar woman a thorough look over. She was wearing the sort of garb an engineer would; a weathered grey leather tunic forged from stardust, making it resistant to most magics, and matching slacks durable enough to withstand the edge of most metals, yet she donned a green cloth around her arm, signifying her as a healer. "What is your name?" he asked, curious by her.

"Elliane. Why do you ask?"

"No reason beyond knowing who to seek next time I am in need of mending."

"Anytime." Elliane cut off the stream of magic from her hands and shook the stiffness from her fingers. "May I ask you a favor, Swordsman?"

"Hum. Speak it and I will determine if it is a fair exchange for your service."

Elliane glanced around to confirm that there was nobody else nearby. "You have traveled the cosmos, seen the worlds, met their Overseers, and will continue to do so, I'm sure. I ask that—if you see my son out there, could you come back and tell me how he is?"

The Swordsman's eyes became sharp as daggers. He knew that the engineers were not prohibited from having relationships and bearing children, but they were to report such children to their superiors. At which point they would be separated from their parents and sent off to the Pollux, where they would be primed to become workers in the Core. "A son, you say? What is his name?"

Elliane smiled to herself as if reminiscing about the last time she had seen him. "Kyoku. Kyoku Pso'ma."

The Swordsman remained stone-faced upon hearing the name, though his mind contemplated all sorts of things. "I will tell you if I ever run into him." He stood up, taking Hou in his hand, and started towards the door. "Send my regards to Endu."

Elliane's ears perked up. She picked herself up off the floor and tilted her head. "You know of him?"

"The engineers may be stationed well below the Hall of Fate, but word still travels here on occasion. Endu Pso'ma, the head of engineering; the man who developed the schematics for the Waylynx II, the battleship made to combat the Fleeting Requiem."

"Aha," Elliane chuckled softly. "I am honored to know that you know about us engineers. Endu will be pleased to hear it as well."

The Swordsman gave a nod and started towards the door. "Until we meet again, Elliane Pso'ma."

*

There was a crackling sound within the darkness. It was far too distorted to distinguish, but it seemed unending, like a chaotic flame spreading over all the world. Rekco wondered if this was what death was like for the Ten, curious to know what life would be like when he wakes. His mind did not seem to know fear, despite being trapped in this dark place, unable to move or speak.

After a while, a thin line appeared, a horizon far beyond where he could see. The tiniest bit of light shone through it; white at first, then turning orange and purple and red, all weaved together. The line became thicker, as did the light. Rekco's eyes opened fully. He was on his back, the ground rumbling and bumping beneath him, the sound of a babbling brook could be heard faintly, though out of sight.

The wheel of the cart carrying him struck a rock and made him bounce. He groaned in agony. His whole body felt like it was bruised, inside and out. Even his brain and the magic coursing through him felt exhausted. Oddly enough, Rekco couldn't sense any Ather in the air. His being seemed to crave it desperately, feeling as though it were on the brink of starvation.

He wondered where he was, where he was going, and how much time had passed. With great strain, Rekco guided his eyes to see if there was anything near him to be seen. To his surprise, there was a woman sitting upright in the cart by his feet. It took his weary mind a moment to process who she was. It was the younger of the two women reporters, Mindy.

She was looking right at him, yet her eyes did not react at all to him locking eyes with her. Her legs were bent backwards, twisted and broken, and both of her arms were in slings. *Is she alive?* Rekco thought. He tried to speak, but all that came was a painful groan, making him regret having tried.

Mindy stirred at the sound. Her eyes did not move to find him, nor did any of the rest of her. "He's awake!" she cried out without any expression on her face.

Just then, the cart came to a halt and Rekco heard a clamor of voices about it; indiscernible murmurs at first, but one voice rose above them all, drawing nearer with each word. "Rekco! Thank goodness! You really *are* awake!" It was Dim Smithy. He stumbled into view after pushing and shoving his way through the crowd.

"You better make sure he *stays* awake! Sara's story depends on it!" Mindy snapped from across the wagon.

Dim had tears streaming down his face. Rekco wondered why he was so concerned after the terrible falling-out they had, having not spoken to one another since then; though, he was happy to see a friendly face. Instinctively, his eyes looked beyond his long-lost friend, off to the sky. Rekco had no idea where they were. The sky was burnt by the rising sun, and what little he could see of his surroundings showed the peaks of mountain tops in the vast distance, which looked no different than a painting to his unfocused eyes.

"I'm—so glad I got to see you again. I—really wanted to apologize to you—for everything I said to you before,"

Dim said, his voice breaking. Rekco raised an eyebrow at him; it was all he could do in his current state. "When the central Runic Tower fell, it—knocked out most of the High District. In fact, it fell *right on* the abandoned Retallor Tower. If—If you hadn't put a stop to the mayor's plan to lock it down with the people he chose to save inside—I, and my whole family would have been in there, not to mention the countless others. I know my family died in the halvening you may, or may not have, caused, but I didn't—and without me to act as a map and guide, this convoy might not have made it through the Forgotten Woods."

"How *did* we get through the Forgotten Woods, anyways?" Mindy interrupted, sounding suspicious. "I thought there were supposed to be *monsters*."

"There were, and they were *awful!*" Dim assured, wiping the snot and tears onto his sleeve. "That's where Zeke really pulled through—or rather, his *secret weapon* did."

"Did they really fight them all?" Mindy asked.

"Actually, there was no fighting at all, surprisingly enough. Zeke brought this scrawny guy carrying a rolled up carpet with us. The guy never told me his name, but he had messy black hair and a scar on his upper lip. He had this big, bowed sword in a black sheath that glowed with dazzling, shifting colors in the dark. When we encountered the talking trees with their gnarled branches for arms and scary faces, the guy showed them the sheathed sword. They seemed mesmerized by how it glowed—and then, they just—let us pass. All these overgrown flowers with thorn-filled mouths just stood idly, watching us all pass through the woods. It was still plenty scary, though!"

Mindy scoffed. "Likely story! I'd have to *see* it to believe it."

Dim's face scrunched up, then he turned to Rekco with a refreshed expression. "Anyways, Rekco, I'm sorry. If everything hadn't happened the way it had, I might not be here talking with you today, and all the people around you might have gotten crushed by whatever smashed up Last Thesi. We're lucky for Zeke too, of course. After the tower fell, he sent a call out to everyone he could to evacuate all of Last Thesi and put his relocation plan into motion with haste. A lot of people came—some didn't, and some are still—well ... missing."

Dim hung his head low for a moment. "I'll let you get back to resting. The medics are a bit baffled by your situation, to be honest. They can't tell if you'll make it or not. Though, in reality, they don't even know how you're still alive at all. Some workers that were still packing up wagons in the farmland say you hit the beach like a meteor. Luckily, nobody was on the shore at the time. They rushed to see what it was, and found you; not bent, broken, or smashed to bits. Fully intact and alive, albeit unconscious, though that was probably the least of your worries at the time. You'll have to tell me all about what happened to you when you recover—"

"And me too!" Mindy shouted as though they couldn't hear her as it was. "A scoop like this could be just what humanity needs—"

"*Anyways,*" Dim began, casually checking the bandages that covered Rekco nearly head to toe. Dim pinched his eyebrows together and pointed at him. "Say, what's that you've got there? In your hand." Dim tugged at Rekco's hand, but it was bound to the orb, as though by a magical force, and wouldn't budge. "It looks like a glass orb. I've never seen black glass like that before. How on earth did *that* survive the fall too?"

Dim bent Rekco's elbow slightly to show him what it was. Rekco didn't need him to; he already knew what it was, and it pained him to even think about it. He couldn't think of how to ever explain it to him, or to anyone, for that matter. And to be quite honest, he didn't ever want to tell anyone that the object he was holding was Cathy, reduced to her soul, and that he would likely never be able to bring her back. That thought hurt him far worse than any of his injuries.

"By the way, Rekco. Cathy never made her way to us. She's been missing for a while now, actually. A rude little boy named Ikeh has been asking me where she is since before we crossed the woods. I was really hoping she was with you, but it seems like that wasn't the case. A lot of this plan's success is attributed to her hard work. It's unfortunate that she isn't here to revel in it." Dim glanced at the sun rising over the red mountains to the east, looking thoughtful. "Maybe she'll still turn up. I haven't given up hope yet. Mikayla and Zeke haven't either, I reckon. We'll all wait for her." He turned back to face Rekco, whose eyes were full of tears, streaming hot down his bruised cheeks. "You will too, won't you?"

Rekco squeezed the glass bauble in his hand with the little remaining strength he had before he fell unconscious from the exhaustion, only to be met with dark dreams filled with just as many tears.

Epilogue

Despite all that was lost—all the death, destruction, and heartbreak, the world was saved, and humanity would live on.

And thus, the story of Last Thesi, its people, the apocalypse, and the Eminent, came to a close—but the universe is vast, and if the prophecies ring true, the Fleeting Requiem seeks to lay waste to it all.

While the survivors of the apocalypse began anew, trying to mend their scarred lives and prosper, in hopes that future generations would not have to suffer so, something far grimmer than their fates brewed on the other side of the universe.

After reports of Oglis' death were all but confirmed and the murmurs of the Ten's departure to the Archives of Time spread all throughout the Core, Melonine was given an important task. She was relieved of her desk duties and sent off to traverse the five worlds stationed across the universe. Her sacred duty was to inform the Overseers of the events regarding both the Ten and the Reaper of Worlds, and the chaos that might ensue in their absence. Throughout her quest, she was to meet with Tsu, the Mortal, Egin and Ura, the Painters, Shamooga, the Survivor, and Alabesh, the Insatiable—though one of them was unreachable, as World One remained sealed by a crimson magical barrier. Finally, after meeting with the others, Melonine met with Zerus, the Worldmaker himself.

Zerus' home was unlike any of the other Overseers, for he did not reign over a singular world, nor did he live beneath the glass of a snow bauble. Despite that, the Worldmaker's abode was little more than a flat platform of brick and stone floating idle at the edge of the universe. The ruined-looking courtyard appeared as ancient as time itself, its floor full over pitfalls and cracks in the crumbling, sandy brick. At its back was a veil of blackness, devoid of life and untouched by time, so premature in its development that it could not be breached.

Melonine fluttered down to the ruins as gentle as a dandelion from the far reaches of space, frozen in time. When her pristine white shoe touched upon it, the protective bubble which she used to travel the cosmos burst. There was nobody in sight—no man, that is. Zerus kept a host of elementals as both company and guards to his research. A being made up of icicles stood guard at the edge of the courtyard, adjacent to the brilliantly colored cosmos before it.

She gave it a quick glance, acknowledging that it was alive. The elemental stirred in response, making a crystalline sound akin to music. It let her pass without any trouble. She strode through the decrepit courtyard, careful not to step anywhere that the ground appeared brittle. A bauble of living magma awaited her, floating above an archway leading to a somewhat indoor chamber where Zerus did much of his work; the trap was contrived to rain hellfire upon anyone who deemed to trespass—luckily for Melonine, she was not an unwelcome guest. The liquid bubbled, speaking words she could not discern, then let her pass.

The room beyond the archway was vast, yet cramped. It was full of tables and shelves adorned with scientific and magical equipment she was unfamiliar with, as well as the many ingredients used to create worlds: magicked glass, stone, and essences of the universe and life itself, preserved within phials. The wall to the right of the entrance of the room was knocked down, which made it feel far less suffocating.

Melonine hadn't a moment to glance at any of the trinkets upon the tables before a voice called to her from across the room.

"Why, hello there, Ms. Nine. You're finally here," the voice of an old man said.

Melonine spun around to find Zerus standing in the shadows in the corner of the room, like a predator lying in wait. He stepped forward, the light from the cosmos and the eternally burning lanterns that adorned the walls of his abode revealing his face. It had been some time since she had last seen the Worldmaker face to face. He appeared as decrepit as ever; his hands were bony, fingers furled and withered, with no hair remaining upon his egg-shaped head, and a face so gaunt, that it looked like a leather bag loosely holding a melon.

All of Zerus' visible orifices were caked over by a thick, yellow crust; even his eyes were sealed shut by the dried pus. Despite his fragile appearance, Zerus was a formidable wizard, second to none, in fact. The wicked staff he used as a walking cane was taller than he, its color shifting beneath the light. It was rumored that Zerus could unleash spells that could cross the entirety of the universe, should it be that he ever needed to.

Melonine gave him a sideways glance, unlike anything her sisters would ever express before a superior. "*Finally*, you say? Did Dalu tell you to expect me? He did no such service for the other Overseers I visited."

Zerus shook his rickety head along with his whole body, his shabby and tattered, brown robes dancing along the floor as he did so. "No, but I expected you all the same." He stamped the bottom of his twisted, crystalline staff against the floor and a large telescope appeared, pointing out at the unmoving cosmos through the fallen wall. "I've *seen* you along your quest to meet with each of the Overseers. I knew my turn would come eventually, though, I had hoped sooner. I am far too busy for such trivial distractions."

Melonine nodded. "Of course. I will keep it brief then, though my reason for coming here is everything but trivial. Some increasingly troubling events have occurred during Oglis' most recent mission to subdue one of the Ten." Zerus raised a wispy eyebrow, his eyes otherwise remaining closed. "Not only has an artifact been stolen from the Archives of Time, but Oglis has gone silent. It is assume she has been killed while combating the Eminent."

"What became of her bounty then? Was the Reaper sent to finish the job?"

"Yes, as is the protocol regarding such ordeals. Unfortunately, the Reaper, too, has gone silent. It appears that his attempt to enter World One was thwarted by the Overflow."

Zerus grimaced as he tugged at his long, white beard. "So *that's* what caused that unsightly red storm."

"Yes. The red storm in question has engulfed World One entirely, making it inaccessible. So, as it currently stands, the Ten is without a leader and the universe is without the Reaper of Worlds."

"Allowing any world jumping vagrant or traitorous engineer defector free reign to do as they please, then?"

"So it seems," Melonine said in a stiff tone.

"Is that all then? Be off with you if so." Zerus prodded at her feet with his gnarled staff, forcing her back towards the exit of his research chamber.

"I was not sent only to inform you, sir Zerus," she began hastily while being corralled backwards. "I was hoping to get input from all of the Overseers about what can be done. I especially was hoping to get the opinion of someone as adept in magics as yourself."

Zerus stopped still for a moment. "What, to regain access to World One and reclaim Oglis' bounties? What a waste of time and effort that would be! That storm will cease on its own once the one who created it runs out of magical reserves—*and dies*. Such a thing could not go on forever, you know. But that should be the least of your worries right now," the old wizard spat, jabbing again at Melonine's feet with his staff.

Melonine became frazzled by Zerus' haste. Instead of quietly leaving him be, she kicked out at his staff, pinning it to the ground with her shoe. "What are you talking about? What could be more important than everything I just told you?"

The next moment, Zerus was gone, staff and all, causing Melonine to lose balance. He reappeared inches before her face, looming over her with a furrowed brow and frown that bore his bottom row of rotten teeth. His sunken eyes were wide open, pure white and covered with throbbing veins. "Do you know what it is I do in this room, and have done for millennia, Ms. Nine?"

Melonine took her eyes off his disgusting face and glanced about the room. "Creating new worlds to replace those that gutter out when their time comes? That is your job, is it not?"

Zerus' face twisted madly; his frown warped into a scowl and his brow became wrinkled with rage. "NO!" his godlike voice boomed, making Melonine wince as she covered her ears. He disappeared again, reappearing a second later beside a table littered with shards of glass and stone. A single glass globe sat at the center of the clutter. Zerus pointed the tip of his staff at it, making the empty globe light up, revealing its contents. Black and white liquid swirled beneath the glass in a chaotic fashion, unable to mix together, yet unable to separate.

Melonine raised her eyebrows in shock. She had seen such a thing before, though on a far greater scale. She turned away from the globe and glanced out the torn down wall at the universe. In the distance, a mass of black and white churned endlessly. She turned back to Zerus' globe. "It's—just like—"

"The Sturm, yes. My prime task may be to create new worlds, but I can create them far faster than they burn out.

In the meantime, I have been tasked with researching this light and dark phenomena we call the Sturm."

"What of it? I have never heard of anyone being all that concerned with it. Though it seems to pine desperately to enter the Core, it has never been able to do so since the dawn of time."

"The dawn of time," Zerus said with a reminiscent snicker. His tone became ornery and venomous. "What would you know of that, *doll?*" His staff lit up and sent a pulse of magic into the little globe before him. Fire, ice, wind, and lightning, all barreled into the swirl of light and darkness, each dissipating faster than they were conjured, lost within the roiling liquid. "Light—and darkness—two forces that little is known about—forces immune to all forms of magic. They cannot be destroyed, nor created. Even my most powerful destructive magics ..." Zerus said as red magic trickled from his fingertips into the globe, the same kind the engineers in the Core used to create and destroy. It, too, guttered out just as the elements had. " ... cannot undo them."

Melonine looked at the infallible energies with concerned eyes. She did her best to keep her heart out of her mind's matters and responded as logically as he could. "Despite that, the Sturm does not appear hostile. It has never attacked any of our ships that have passed through it while leaving or entering the Core—"

"Not yet," Zerus interjected, his expression grim. He tapped his staff against the ground, summoning the telescope to his side. "The Sturm has begun to act unusual as of late. Before, it seemed to contest with itself outside of the Core irrationally—but now, well, why don't you see for yourself?" He directed Melonine's attention to the telescope.

She glanced at it with hesitation before kneeling to peer through it. It was aimed directly at the Sturm, at the point of interest the Worldmaker spoke of. "What is that?" Melonine gasped as she stared through the magnifying lens. It looked like the elongated, warping shadow of a titan moving about, barely visible within the chaotic storm of light and darkness.

"*That*—I have recently dubbed as one of the 'Lords of the Sturm.' It is a concentrated form composed of either pure light or pure darkness. Their movements and mannerisms are far more nuanced than their brethren, almost mirroring that of you or I."

"*One of?* Do you mean to say there are *more* of them?" Melonine shuddered involuntarily at the thought.

"That's correct. I have seen more than one at a time, as if interacting with one another as people would."

"But—what does it mean?"

"It means that the Sturm may be evolving—that our worst fears may come to pass, that an indestructible force may be developing free thought, and with that—the ability to plan—and *dream*."

Melonine understood all too well how powerful free thought could be. She stood up from the telescope, perplexed and worried all at once. "Do you have any idea when or why this behavior began?"

Zerus' glazed eyes pulsed with a red glow, and he furrowed his brow in concentration, searching the confines of his ancient mind for an answer. "Yes, I do. I know *precisely* when it began, which makes it all the more concerning." Melonine gave him a sideways glance, imploring him to continue. "Some time ago, a certain kind of soul traversed through the Sturm via ship—it was one of the Ten. I cannot say for certain if such a thing has ever happened before, but I will say that the Sturm reacted to its presence in a dire way."

Melonine's purple eyes grew wide. "You don't mean—"

"Correct. The Overflow—the very same person who has obstructed entry to World One with his duel with death itself." Zerus paced towards Melonine, drawing closer and closer, uncomfortably so. She inched back as much as she could, until her heel was at the edge of the platform overlooking the cosmos. "Do you know what calamities could ensue should the Lords of the Sturm discover the Overflow's capabilities and purpose?"

Melonine didn't need to think twice to come to the same terrifying realization that Zerus was implying. "They could turn their attention away from the impenetrable Core and set their sights on Kyoku, in hopes that they could seize his power and elicit the creation of a new universe—"

"At the cost of our own." Zerus said, his face contorted with rage. His dour expression faded in an instant, turning to one of fear and remorse before he turned away from Melonine and slunk in the opposite direction. He paced about his research room as he spoke, "After all of our preparations to forestall the coming of the Fleeting Requiem, it seems that such plans must be put on hold while we deal with this new universal threat."

"What would you have me do?" Melonine asked, eagerly seeking a solution from the great Worldmaker.

Zerus whipped around, having adopted a cruel, godlike expression to match his title. "What could *you* do?" he said scornfully with a mocking tone. "You'll have to do what a doll does best, I suppose: take orders! I'll have you send word of the coming calamity to all of the Overseers, then return to the Core to spread the word amongst your sisters and anyone else who'll listen. It's all that can be done, all whilst hoping the warnings reach Dalu before it's too late."

Melonine pinched her eyebrows together, saying, "Dalu? Are you not in direct contact with him? Your role as Worldmaker is integral to the universe. There must be some way for you to—"

"Quiet, doll!" Zerus snarled, his white eyes pulsing in their sunken sockets. "It is true that my work is important—more so, my research. I was instructed to seek Ms. One, Two, or Three should I make any important discoveries. Imagine my disappointment when *Nine* was the one I found skulking in my domain."

Melonine's face got hot at the mention of her superior sisters, Melone, Melwo, and Melree—Dalu's favorites—the only ones who knew how to reach him. She had only ever seen Melone once; the way her golden hair shone was unlike anything Melonine had seen in the physical world. The thought of it alone reminded her of the failure she was seen as, forsaken by her creator and shackled to her desk in the endless ballroom within the Core. She felt important to be entrusted with Zerus' task to bear the ominous news, despite how bitterly he bestowed it upon her. "I will do as you say, Master Zerus. I'll scour the universe if I have to, in search of my sisters to assure the information reaches Dalu!"

"Good, good," the loose skin of Zerus' face contorted to form a toothless smile. "Go on then, at once! The fate of the universe itself rests within the knowledge I've bequeathed to you."

Melonine turned and left Zerus' study at his word. Her heart was racing by the time she arrived at the landing guarded by powerful elemental beings. She gazed out at the cosmos; its colors and designs were beautifully splattered upon the black reaches of space, filled with flecks of unborn stars—ones that may never become anything at all should time not return to them.

Melonine pushed off with her elevated heel and a spherical barrier enveloped her. She soared ever upward, away from Zerus' domain, and back towards the Core that was hidden behind the swirling mass of torment. The Sturm writhed, emitting an endless supply of bitter anguish mixed with a contagious sense of vengeance that was as righteous as it was evil. It was like a curious, beating heart—one Melonine wished she had the means to understand, so that Zerus' fearful predictions could be averted.

As she drew closer to the unruly Sturm, Melonine's eyes were drawn to the right, where off at the distant corner of the universe was a crimson cloud. It shrouded the landing to World One. The cloud, too, exuded emotions—though the ones it did were far more somber. The red, glowing storm showed no sign of weakening, not anytime soon, at least. She gazed at it with eyes full of longing, knowing what lay within.

"Kyoku," she began thoughtfully, "I'm sure ... that we'll meet again someday."

What will become of the universe when *The Sturm Awakens*?

The story of the Fleeting Requiem will continue …

Thanks for reading!
Follow me on social media for updates regarding future books and projects!

https://linktr.ee/marvinnorth

Or scan the QR code below.

Made in the USA
Columbia, SC
10 February 2024